PENGUIN BOOKS

FRENCH KISSING

Catherine Sanderson is a thirty-six-year-old Brit who was bitten by the
French bug while still at school and has never looked back. Her first book,
Petite Anglaise, a memoir, was published to fantastic acclaim in 2008. Her
website of the same name is one of the best-loved British personal blogs.
She lives in Belleville, Paris, with her French husband and her daughter.

French Kissing

CATHERINE SANDERSON

PENGUIN BOOKS

PENGUIN BOOKS

Published by the Penguin Group
Penguin Books Ltd, 80 Strand, London WC2R ORL, England
Penguin Group (USA) Inc., 375 Hudson Street, New York, New York 10014, USA
Penguin Group (Canada), 90 Eglinton Avenue East, Suite 700, Toronto, Ontario, Canada M4P 2Y3
(a division of Pearson Penguin Canada Inc.)
Penguin Ireland, 25 St Stephen's Green, Dublin 2, Ireland (a division of Penguin Books Ltd)
Penguin Group (Australia), 250 Camberwell Road, Camberwell, Victoria 3124,
Australia (a division of Pearson Australia Group Pty Ltd)
Penguin Books India Pvt Ltd, 11 Community Centre, Panchsheel Park,
New Delhi – 110 017, India
Penguin Group (NZ), 67 Apollo Drive, Rosedale, North Shore 0632, New Zealand
(a division of Pearson New Zealand Ltd)
Penguin Books (South Africa) (Pty) Ltd, 24 Sturdee Avenue, Rosebank,
Johannesburg 2196, South Africa

Penguin Books Ltd, Registered Offices: 80 Strand, London WC2R ORL, England

www.penguin.com

First published 2009

1

Copyright © Catherine Sanderson, 2009
All rights reserved

The moral right of the author has been asserted

Typeset by Macmillan Publishing Solutions www.macmillansolutions.com

Printed in England by Clays Ltd, St Ives plc

ISBN 978-0-141-03124-8

www.greenpenguin.co.uk

for M, the online date
who became my husband

I

If a fortune teller had predicted I'd not only find myself a single mum, but would contemplate joining a French online dating site before the year was out, I would have joked that her crystal ball must be in need of a service.

I'd been living in Paris for a decade, in a state I'd describe, with hindsight, as unmarried complacency, although at the time I mistook it for unmarried bliss. Then, six months ago, the unimaginable came to pass: I left my French partner, Nico and moved out with our four-year-old daughter, Lila. His actions left me no other choice.

And so here I was, hunched over my purring laptop, watching intently as the Rendez-vous homepage loaded, text first, pictures slowly filling out from top to bottom. I wasn't sure which was hardest to overcome: my lingering scepticism about seeking out some sort of connection online of all places, or my trepidation at the idea of sprucing myself up and putting Sally Marshall back on the market. But something had to be done to plug the gaping hole where my social life should have been. In the daytime I had work to distract me, or Lila for company. But the evenings were barren, and I'd spent far too many of them lately curled up on my sofa with the remote control and a box of tissues.

The Rendez-vous website was an exercise in tasteful minimalism. It had an off-white background, against which the text and borders were picked out in muted shades of purple and green, colours which market research had, no doubt, deemed gender neutral. Having specified at the point of entry that I was *une femme* who wished to meet *un homme*, I was amused to see a handful of likely, and less likely, male candidates being paraded across the bottom of the screen as bait. Below the logo of interlocking, pixellated hearts in the top right-hand corner was the infamous Rendez-vous slogan: '*l'amour en un clic!*' Those words – 'love is only a click away' – emblazoned across billboards in métro stations all over Paris, had taunted me for weeks. Until, on this lazy Sunday morning, I'd caved in and made the first click.

The form I'd begun to complete with my personal details was already causing me problems, however. There was precious little room for manoeuvre: a series of tick boxes and drop-down menus seemed intent on bossing me around and putting words into my mouth. Sighing, I removed my hands from the keyboard for a moment and let myself sag back into the sofa. Did I really want to do this? Was I ready?

Lila – whose name I pronounced the French way, *Lee*-lah – was munching a slice of apple by my side, her mouth open as she ate, her hazel eyes superglued to the flickering television screen. The top of her head almost reached my left shoulder and, flaring my nostrils, I caught a faint whiff of the strawberry-scented conditioner I'd combed through her curls the night before. The slender legs which protruded from her pink nightdress were bruised and scabbed, as usual. The summer holidays had given way to *la rentrée* only a couple of weeks ago but, judging by the state of her knees, anyone would think four-year-olds engaged in playground warfare. 'Remind me to clip your terrible claws later,' I murmured, as my gaze scrolled down to her feet and I registered the length of her toenails. 'Otherwise you'll end up looking like Max from *Where the Wild Things Are* . . .'

'Shhh, Mummy! I watching my mermaid DVD,' Lila complained in her accentless English, her eyes coming unstuck from the cartoon for long enough to shoot me a look of pure reproach. On the television screen, Ursula, the wicked octopus witch, was trying to persuade the Little Mermaid to part with her voice in exchange for a shapely pair of human legs so she might step onshore and begin wooing her landlocked prince. I braced myself: having sat through the DVD countless times, I knew the witch was about to launch into a song about 'poor unfortunate souls', and the irony was not lost on me. Surely there could be no more fitting backing track to my surfing for a soul mate on the internet's answer to a lonely-hearts column? I leaned forward again, nevertheless, and laid my hands reluctantly across the keys. I might as well at least go through the motions. There could be no harm in looking to see which of these 'poor unfortunate souls' would be deemed suitable company for me. Even if I doubted many people really found *l'amour* via Rendez-vous, I'd settle for a few interesting nights out to start with, or maybe even a fling.

With a determined click – less satisfying on the trackpad of my laptop than it might have been using a proper mouse – I ticked the box next to '*célibataire*'. Here was a fine example of the kind of word my A-level French teacher, Mr Granger, would have referred to as a 'false friend', since it bore a misleading resemblance to 'celibate' in the English language. Not that I wouldn't have been able to tick such a box if Rendez-vous had thought to provide one, mind you. But *célibataire* in French simply means 'single'.

'Jamais mariée' was my next selection. How relieved I was now that Nico and I had never made it as far as the altar. Moving out and carving up Lila's time had been heart-wrenching enough, without becoming mired in the quicksand of an acrimonious divorce. The other options, I noted in passing, were 'separated', 'divorced', 'widowed' and 'married'. I wondered how many people owned up to the latter. My gut feeling was that most would favour the discreet, none-of-your-businesslike *'je le garde pour moi'* instead.

In the *'date de naissance'* field, I selected first '20', then 'July' and had to scroll an alarmingly long way down *'année'* (which began, horror of horrors, with 1989) before I alighted on the year of my birth: '1975'. From this, Rendez-vous calculated my age without mishap: thirty-two years old.

'Enfants?' shouldn't have been difficult to answer – even I didn't need to use my fingers to count up to one – but I hesitated all the same. Here was my first real dilemma. Should I leave the 'children' box blank, or lay my cards on the table from the outset? Any man with two brain cells to rub together was bound to assume leaving such an important field *'non renseigné'* was tantamount to an admission of parenthood. But the problem with choosing 'one' was that it might well lead hundreds of prospective dates to

exclude my profile, filtering me out without so much as a cursory glance at my photo or description.

Lila, her sense of timing unnerving, chose that very moment to grasp my left wrist with her right hand, coating me with sticky apple residue. 'The witch is a bit scary,' she whispered, her annoyance at my interruption already forgotten. 'But she'll be gone in a minute. I just hold your hand until she goes away. Okay?'

I planted a kiss on my daughter's head, ashamed of the treacherous thoughts running through my mind. It wasn't that I considered being a single mother some sort of guilty secret. Nor did I believe any man worth knowing – in the long term – would be deterred by it. But I was pretty sure I wasn't ready for 'long-term' just yet. And putting a number in that box would label me as a mother in a place where I wanted to be seen, first and foremost, as a single woman, like any other. Was it so wrong to want to keep things separate? To want to be liked for Sally Marshall in the beginning, long before I allowed my daughter to become part of any equation?

Lila's grip on my hand relaxed. The Little Mermaid was setting her course for the shore, hell bent on seducing her prince and blithely unaware of how difficult this would be without the voice the wicked witch had taken from her in exchange for human legs. In some ways we were in the same boat, she and I. The playing field was anything but level; the odds were stacked against us.

'The thing is,' I said to Kate, my oldest friend in Paris and owner of the language school which employed me to teach business English, 'I have no idea how to play it – if "play" is even the right word. But dating is supposed to be sort of like a game, isn't it?' I pushed the remains of my salad around my plate. I'd polished off the most interesting bits – the diced Emmental cheese, the cubes of fatty bacon the French call *lardons*, the undercooked poached egg which had been perched in the middle when it arrived, with a typical Gallic disregard for salmonella – and now I was left with nothing but a huge mountain of lacklustre *salade frisée*, smothered in French dressing.

Setting down her knife and fork and smoothing imaginary creases from her black suit, Kate considered my words for a moment, her expression thoughtful. 'I suppose if you do say you're a mother, then you're liable to attract the single-dads brigade and spend your first dates swapping stories about raising children instead of flirting and making small talk,' she ventured. 'But then again, deceiving people doesn't seem like a very healthy place to start either, does it? Any man you meet will have to find out you're a mother sooner or later. And let's face it, Sal, you wouldn't take kindly to seeing a man a few times before finding out he had children, would you? It's almost as shady as someone hiding the fact that they're married . . .'

Kate had spent the first half hour of our lunch – a ritual we did our best to observe every other Monday – acquainting me with a disturbing story about a friend who'd caught her husband doing precisely that: surfing Rendez-vous to meet unattached females for a string of one-night stands. If Kate was to be believed, this kind of behaviour was depressingly commonplace. For many men, online dating had become a modern, low-cost alternative to keeping a mistress waiting in the wings. Kate's cautionary tale was designed, I suspected, if not to put me off the idea altogether, then at least to ensure I kept my wits about me and wore my cynicism on my sleeve. She had a point: I may have bandied about words like 'light-hearted' and 'fling' in the course of our conversation, but that didn't mean I wanted to be someone's side order, married or otherwise. Not after everything I'd been through with Nico.

'You're probably right,' I admitted grudgingly. 'I doubt I'd last five minutes in conversation without mentioning Lila, anyway, let's face it.'

'So you're really going to do this?' Kate seemed to be hoping I'd shelve the idea. 'If you *must*, you will take precautions, I hope, Sal?'

'Of course,' I insisted. 'I'm not using my real name. I'll Google people beforehand, meet them in a public place . . .' The truth was, after spending most of Sunday agonizing over whether to answer 'one' or 'none' to the children question, I hadn't even submitted my profile yet, let alone set up any dates. It had taken me over half an hour to come up with my pseudonym, the nonetheless unimaginative 'Belleville_girl'.

'It all sounds like such terribly hard work to me.' Kate wrinkled her delicate nose in distaste. Turning to catch the waiter's eye, she gave the universal sign language for 'I'd like the bill, please'. 'Got to dash off early today, I'm afraid,' she apologized, her eyes flickering momentarily down towards her lap. 'James called in sick this morning, so I'm doing his two o'clock at Monceau.'

I grinned as I fumbled in the leather satchel I carried on teaching days, looking for my purse. 'You do realize, don't you, that when you're deliberately vague about work, you sound more like a high-class hooker on her way to turn tricks in a hotel than an English teacher?'

'But of course . . .' Kate's blue eyes glinted with mischief and, for a second, I caught a glimpse of the twenty-two-year-old I'd befriended the summer we'd both worked as waitresses at El Paso, a seedy Tex Mex bar in rue de Lappe, near Bastille, which had long since closed down. But when the waiter appeared at her elbow, Kate's expression became businesslike once more and, before I could protest, she'd slotted her credit card into the hand-held machine and paid for us both. 'Oh, and before I forget' – Kate was already rising to her feet, allowing the waiter to help her into her black trench coat – 'I'm having a little work gathering at my place on Saturday, a sort of *fête de la rentrée*, inviting a few friends, clients and teachers, but no Nico. You could bring Lila if you can't get a babysitter, and put her to bed with my boys. And there's one person in particular coming' – she paused for dramatic effect – 'who I'd really like you to meet.'

'Who*m* I'd really like you to meet,' I corrected, mock-pedantically, as I slung my satchel on to my shoulder. 'Lila's with Nico all weekend, so I'll definitely be there . . . But this mystery person: is it a he or a she?'

'You'll have to wait and see,' said Kate airily, her expression giving nothing away. Most definitely male, I decided. Matchmaking wasn't Kate's style, but maybe my mention of internet dating had spurred her into pre-emptive action?

We parted at the corner of rue Cambon, by the Paris branch of W. H. Smith, and I paused to watch Kate hurry across the road and disappear down the steps into Concorde métro station, several heads turning as she passed by leaving a pungent trail of Chanel Allure in her wake.

In the decade she'd lived in the City of Light, Kate had acquired the outward appearance of a chic *Parisienne*: her strawberry-blonde hair pulled back into a chignon, her clothes well cut, her nails manicured and painted a deep shade of red. I envied Kate her poise and that svelte figure of hers – quite how she managed to look so consistently amazing when she had two boys under the age of six and her own business to run never ceased to perplex me – but I wasn't fond of her husband, Yves. Not that I saw him very often: he had a high-powered job in private equity which entailed frequent business trips and fourteen-hour days in the office. But when our paths did cross, Yves had always struck me as a cold fish, devoid of anything approaching a sense of humour. His bank balance was doubtless awe-inspiring, and he was handsome, if a little predatory looking. But I sincerely hoped Yves had hidden depths or, at the very least, an uncommon amount of talent in the bedroom. Anything was preferable to the idea that my elegant, witty friend might have sold herself short.

Catching sight of my own reflection in the window of a boutique selling vulgar-looking designer clothes aimed at tourists with more money than fashion sense, I was convinced no one would imagine I was anything but British. My wavy light-brown hair was tucked haphazardly behind my ears, my fingernails shied away from close encounters with an emery board and my 'English rose' complexion was so pale it was almost translucent.

I was wearing a patterned wrap dress that day, chosen for the forgiving way it draped around my hips and concealed my tummy, which wasn't too round but had never fully regained its pre-Lila muscle tone. I'd always been what women's magazines charitably describe as pear-shaped: anything I ate seemed to take a one-way ticket to my bottom and thighs. In honour of my lunch date with Kate I was wearing my smartest footwear – a pair of brown knee-high boots – and I'd brought along the only tailored jacket I possessed, which I threw on for a few minutes before each lesson. Seeing Kate always inspired me to make a bit more of an effort with my appearance, but whenever I wore smart clothes I wound up feeling self-conscious. I'd spent half my morning furtively tugging the neckline of my dress upwards. Maybe I was being paranoid, but it seemed to me that my pupils – two male analysts who worked for an investment bank near Place Vendôme – had kept on darting glances somewhere south of my face as we talked.

I had a good half-hour to kill before my appointment with Delphine Andrieu, a statuesque clothes-horse a couple of years older than me who happened to be one of the most highly paid personal assistants in the capital. Her boss, Bertrand Rivoire, head of a vast luxury-goods empire, boasted a half-page entry in the *Bottin Mondain* – the French *Who's Who* – and hovered perpetually in the upper reaches of France's version of the Rich List. When Yves and Nico had first learned of my involvement with his secretary at Kate's last New Year party, their ears had pricked up at once. In awe-filled tones they'd pressed me for titbits of information about how his Lordship's office was decorated, even going so far as to enquire as to which brand of stationery he favoured. I'd laughed, rather unkindly, and asked Yves whether he thought some of the great man's business acumen might rub off on him if he wrote with the same fountain pen.

The memory was a barbed one: Nico had upbraided me in the taxi home afterwards. My English sarcasm wasn't funny, he'd said, just rude and unnecessarily cruel. It was ironic, when I thought about it. One of the things he'd loved about me, ten years earlier, had slowly morphed into one of his pet hates.

Delphine's office at Rivoire headquarters was on the top floor of a flawless sandstone building sandwiched between two high-fashion boutiques on avenue Montaigne, only three or four stops away by métro. If I'd followed Kate's lead and taken public transport, I'd have been there by now but, with time to spare, I felt like taking advantage of the pale September sunshine instead. The stretch of the Champs-Elysées running from Concorde to the Grand Palais was the most pleasant: bordered by greenery on both sides, lined with majestic trees and devoid of any buildings which could be converted into MacDonald's or down-market chain stores. Okay, it wasn't exactly fields, as the name suggested – the lawns were like golfing greens and the roar of traffic thundering along in both directions left me in no doubt I was in the centre of the city. But I enjoyed strid-ing along with the breeze buffeting my hair and with wide open space all around me. It was the perfect antidote to all those evenings I spent cooped up indoors while Lila slept.

My telephone throbbed in my jacket pocket – I always set it to vibrate on weekdays, out of courtesy to my pupils – and I whipped it out to inspect the caller ID without adjusting my pace. 'Nico,' it read. The name still lived on in my head and in my mobile phone, even if, since our separation in March, I'd reverted to calling him Nicolas whenever we spoke. It was a demotion of sorts: a fitting way to underscore the fact that everything between us had changed.

'Sally? *Je te dérange pas là?*' Nico was calling from his office and I could hear other voices in the background: female voices. Maybe one of them belonged to Albane, the *stagiaire* he'd been seeing since about five minutes after we parted. I'd never seen his young trainee in the flesh but in the picture I carried in my mind a forked tail protruded from the bottom of her pencil skirt.

'Nicolas. No, I'm not busy. You caught me between lessons.' I spoke evenly, in keeping with the civility pact we'd struck in the interests of Lila's wellbeing. We'd always conducted our conversations this way: he addressed me in French, I replied in English. Neither of us liked being at a disadvantage and this method evened up the balance of power between us. 'What's up?' I continued. 'Please don't tell me there's a problem with next weekend?'

'Sophie called earlier,' Nico replied, ignoring my question, 'and she asked for your number. Do you mind if I pass it on? I thought I'd better call you straight away, before I forgot . . .' Sophie was Lila's aunt, and my ex-not-quite-sister-in-law. Three years younger than Nico, she had the same dark hair and Mediterranean colouring. She also had a son, Lucas, who was only a year older than Lila. I liked Sophie – her presence had been one of the few redeeming features at Canet family gatherings – but

I hadn't seen her since before the break-up, and things were bound to be awkward. What, I had to wonder, had prompted her to contact me now?

'Sophie . . . Right . . .' I hoped the growl of traffic in the background masked the reticence in my voice. 'Well, yes, by all means, give her my mobile number. It's best if she calls me in the evening some time.'

'Good. I'll see you this weekend, then. I'll come for Lila on Saturday morning, around ten. Friday's going to be a late finish at work.'

'Weekends are *supposed* to start on Fridays,' I said, bristling, convinced the Sophie question had been a pretext to deliver this, rather less palatable news. 'But if that's the best you can do, I'll explain the situation to Lila.' My tone made it quite clear I thought his best was far from good enough.

I was nearing the Grand Palais as I slipped the phone back into my pocket, conscious of a familiar tightness in my chest. I didn't believe the work excuse, not for a moment, and suspected I was being played for a fool.

If I were to call Nico's bluff on Friday night by phoning him at the office, I was willing to bet he'd be nowhere to be found.

2

My footfalls echoed as I crossed the vast lobby of Rivoire headquarters to the reception desk where two young women in pristine navy-blue uniforms, their dark hair pulled back into sleek ponytails, were conversing in low voices. The security guard manning the nearby turnstiles looked thoroughly uncomfortable. It was as though he suspected he was the subject of the girls' gossip but, try as he might, couldn't quite make out what they were saying.

Although I'd been coming here every other Monday for the best part of a year, I'd rarely encountered the same *hôtesse d'accueil* twice. My guess was that an agency somewhere in Paris specialized in supplying these flawlessly groomed and fully interchangeable receptionist clones. As I drew closer, it became clear that Receptionist 1, who was buffing her fingernails under cover of a tall vase of white lilies, wasn't planning to acknowledge my presence. Instead, Receptionist 2 inclined her head and uttered a haughty '*Bonjour, Madame*'.

'*Bonjour. Je viens pour le cours d'anglais de* Delphine Andrieu.' I fished in my satchel for the embossed ID card bearing an unusually flattering photo of a rather younger Sally – I'd persuaded Kate to re-use it every time she issued new cards – below the name of Kate's language school: 'Tailor-Made'. Kate, whose maiden name was Taylor, had dreamed up the name, as well as the French subtitle, '*Cours d'Anglais sur mesure'*, at the end of a long, vodka-fuelled brainstorming session to which I'd been invited five years earlier. Once she'd jumped through all the bureaucratic hoops which make France the last place on earth where anyone in their right mind would choose to set up a small business, she'd poached me from the Berlitz language school and I'd become her first full-time employee.

As the name suggested, Tailor-Made's main selling point was that our lessons never followed a 'one size fits all' approach. After an in-depth interview with each pupil to establish their level and the type of spoken and written English they needed for work, we devised personalized lesson programmes. With Delphine, for example, my main task had been to work on drastically improving her pronunciation. Her overall level wasn't half bad and, somewhere along the line, she had carefully memorized her ultra-polite 'you're welcome's and a whole host of other set phrases. But, to Delphine's eternal chagrin, her strong accent sabotaged her efforts, making her difficult to comprehend over the phone.

Once through the turnstile I summoned the lift, tapping the heel of my boot against the marble floor while I waited, enjoying the pleasing sound it made. The doors slid open to reveal a mercifully empty mirrored capsule. I touched my index finger to the sensor beside the number 8, recalling how awestruck I'd been on my first day when one of Rivoire's bodyguards had scanned my fingerprint into the security system. Only a privileged few had access to the inner sanctum of the eighth floor, and it was surreal to think that I, of all people, numbered among them.

When I arrived at my destination, however, Delphine was nowhere to be seen. That was odd. One of the receptionists must have called ahead to announce my arrival, and I was usually greeted, if not by Delphine herself, then at the very least by one of her anxious-looking understudies. I took a seat on the cream leather sofa opposite the lift doors and resolved to wait until someone materialized, pretending to look over the day's lesson plan. I'd been cautioned to approach Delphine's office, which interconnected with Rivoire's, under no circumstances. The mere sight of an unfamiliar face drove '*Monsieur*' to distraction, or so I was told, and I had no desire to be held responsible for provoking one of his legendary rages.

I'd often thought how much I'd hate to work in a position like Delphine's. Her surroundings might be luxurious – an original Picasso hung in the meeting room where our lessons were held – but there was something stifling about the atmosphere. Conversations in the corridors were conducted in hushed tones and often I sensed a palpable undercurrent of panic, which made the hairs on the back of my neck stand on end. My head bent over my notebook now, I failed to hear Delphine approach: the deep pile of the beige carpet muffled her footfalls.

'Good *h*afternoon, Sally. Sorry about ze delay . . .' I rose to my feet, and Delphine stretched out a long-fingered hand to shake mine. She wore a slim-fitting trouser suit and shoes with vertiginous heels. Delphine would have towered over me even in her stockinged feet. I had to crane my neck to make eye contact and admire her freshly highlighted blonde bob.

As I followed her into the meeting room, my eyes were irresistibly drawn, as always, to the panoramic view it afforded across the rooftops of the neighbouring buildings. I pulled out a chair and set down my work satchel and notebook on the smoked-glass tabletop. 'Did you get a chance to draft the emails we discussed last time?' I enquired, slipping into the BBC English accent I affected during lessons, without raising my eyes from the lesson plan. 'I thought we could maybe start by checking those over?' But when I glanced up, I saw Delphine standing immobile, her back pressed to the closed door, her eyelids shut. For the first time I noticed how chalky-pale she looked under the layers of make-up; how blood-shot her eyes were. 'Are you okay?' I dropped my businesslike teaching voice and used the tone I'd adopt when talking to a friend. Rounding the table, I took a hesitant step towards her. 'Delphine? What on earth's the matter?'

'*Je suis tellement épuisée.*' Delphine's voice was little more than a whisper. Slipping back into her native French was against the rules, but I didn't have the heart to reprimand her. 'I was up half the night,' she continued in her mother tongue. 'Suzanne, my daughter, is sick. And there was an art auction in New York, so I was bidding on the telephone for paintings *Monsieur* wanted all evening and trying to look after her at the same time . . . Then at 3 a.m., *Madame* called to scream at me because she was leaving her charity gala and couldn't see her driver anywhere. Even though it was her usual driver, and she has his number programmed into her telephone, because I put it there myself . . .' Delphine crossed the room and sagged into a chair. 'Sometimes,' she said, putting her hands on the table to still their shaking, 'I dream about walking out of this office and never coming back.'

'Is Suzanne better now?' I seized on the safest subject. 'Who's looking after her today?' Kate had always cautioned me against joining in employer-bashing sessions. It wasn't rare for pupils to use their English lessons as a place to vent, but when they did, it was wise to do no more than listen. I'd answered Delphine in French, a line I'd never hitherto crossed. But I was still reeling from the unexpectedness of it all. Delphine was one pupil whose soft centre I never thought I'd see.

'My babysitter's with her,' Delphine mumbled, her cheeks colouring. I sympathized. There was nothing I hated more than being separated from Lila when she was ill; nothing that made me feel guiltier for choosing to be a working mum. I'd only had to get external help once – when Lila caught chickenpox at the age of two and needed to be quarantined for a whole week – but I'd hated every minute of it. 'I'm on my own, you see,' Delphine added, a hint of defensiveness creeping into her voice. 'Her father, well, he's never really been in the picture.'

'My daughter's father would never have volunteered to stay home if she was sick, even when he *was* around,' I said, my wry tone eliciting a lukewarm smile from Delphine. 'And he's not living with us any more, either,' I confided. 'So, you see, I do know what it's like . . .'

It was the first time either of us had strayed from the script of my painstakingly planned lessons on to more personal territory, and we lapsed into an uncomfortable silence, unsure where to go from there. Delphine regained her composure before I did. I watched as she slipped on her perfect personal-assistant mask, straightening her back and squaring her shoulders. Taking my cue from her, I switched back into teaching mode, nudging the conversation into English.

'Shall we start with a listening comprehension, today, for a change?' I suggested, thinking the exercise would give us both some breathing space. Delphine nodded, and I took out my hand-held digital audio player and set it on the table between us.

When Delphine accompanied me back to the lift an hour and a half later – where I was mortified to catch sight of the lingering imprint of my bottom, plainly visible on the leather sofa – she let her guard down once more, for a few seconds. 'Would you like to have lunch with me some time when *Monsieur* is away on business?' she asked me, her eyes mutely imploring me to accept her invitation. 'If you could come an hour before my lesson, the chef would cook us something nice. I'm not permitted to leave the office, you see . . .'

'I'd love to!' I was relieved that Delphine didn't seem to have misgivings about confiding in me. It wasn't unheard of for a client to call Kate and request a change of teacher after confusing an English lesson with a therapy session and feeling uncomfortable about it later. But Delphine flashed me an unmistakably genuine smile before she disappeared in the direction of her office. She seemed to harbour no regrets.

As the mirrored cabin plummeted downwards, I realized I now envied this princess in her thickly carpeted ivory tower even less than I had before. How on earth did she cope with all the stress and responsibility of her job alone, with no one but her young daughter to turn to? For a *parent isolé*, the parenting wasn't always the hardest part, in my opinion. After all, millions of women in relationships do the bulk of the childrearing work with minimal help from their partners. The isolation – the 'lone' in 'lone parenting' – was another matter. When the going got tough, who could Delphine lean on?

My three-thirty lesson with Marc de Pourtalès – Rivoire's human resources director – on the third floor of the same building, was much less eventful. He asked if I wouldn't mind casting an eye over a PowerPoint presentation he was preparing for the board of directors, a task which easily filled half our session together. His English was flawless, as usual, and I could find little to criticize, aside from the fact that he manoeuvred his chair a little too close to mine for comfort and appeared to have rounded off his lunch with a particularly ripe goat's cheese.

Now I was hurrying back to the Champs-Elysées to catch the métro, my teaching day over, and it was time to snap back into the role of mother for a few hours before Lila's bedtime. I was looking forward to turning my attention back to my partially completed Rendez-vous profile once she was tucked up in bed. Kate's reticence and Delphine's loneliness had made me doubly determined to take the plunge.

The *ligne* 1 – represented on métro maps as a horizontal yellow line slicing Paris neatly in two just north of the river Seine – was jam-packed, as always. On the train, I brushed past a herd of Japanese tourists clutching the day's purchases from Louis Vuitton to the section where two carriages fused together. The floor, walls and ceiling were made of overlapping metal plates, built to slide over one another, allowing the train to bend and flex as the tracks curved to the left or right. It took a certain amount of practice to stand here without toppling over, especially when the driver jabbed at the brakes, but at least there was room to breathe in this unpopular spot. Stowing my satchel between my feet, I fished out my copy of *Libération*, the left-leaning newspaper I bought every morning, and hooked my arm through the nearest metal hand rail to stabilize myself.

Nestling between *Météo-Jeux* (sudoku, chess, weather maps) and *Culture* (devoted to Vanessa Paradis' latest album) was my favourite part of the newspaper: the small ads. The job vacancies and apartments to let held little interest for me. It was the personals in the *Entre Nous* section I found fascinating and, in particular, those filed under the heading '*Transports amoureux*'. That day, there was only one, but it was a classic example of the genre. Puzzling over how best to translate these ads into English was a favourite pastime of mine, and one I often used to help me get my brain into gear in the mornings.

'Monday 5 September, RER B between Luxembourg and Gare du Nord, 11.30 a.m.,' I translated. 'We contemplated one another in silence. You: long black hair, melancholy eyes. Me: captivated. Dare I hope to see you again?'

Cupid seemed rather partial to French public transport. Almost every day *Libération* published tales of eyes meeting fleetingly in the métro, tentative smiles exchanged across crowded buses, trains or even aeroplanes. The messages were heavy with regret – 'I wish I'd dared speak to you'; 'If only we'd exchanged numbers' – but they were also filled with a childlike hope. Realistically, the odds of a declaration reaching its intended were slim: the sender might as well have placed a handwritten message in a bottle and dropped it into the River Seine. And supposing it did? If Cupid had let only one arrow fly, the whole enterprise would still be futile.

The ads were invariably couched in poetic French, which was the reason I found translating them into English such an interesting challenge. And while I was no hopeless romantic – I was far too cynical for that – every time I scanned *Transports amoureux*, it was fun to entertain the surreal idea that one day, while I'd been busy compiling a mental shopping list, staring through the man opposite with unseeing eyes, he might have been composing rhyming couplets about me in his head.

When the métro pulled into Châtelet station – the point on the map where the highest number of coloured lines converge – the majority of my fellow travellers spilled out on to the platform. Following the flow of people along a series of concrete staircases and white-tiled corridors, including one so long that it contained an airport-style travelator, I arrived at my *correspondence, ligne* 11, colour-coded a deep chocolate-brown. I'd made the journey so many times that my feet instinctively knew the way, and I could have managed it blindfolded. Reaching the platform, I continued to its furthest end and collapsed into an empty seat in the last carriage of the waiting train. Belleville was only six stops away, along tunnels which twisted and turned far more than the stylized *Plan du Métro* let on. Ten minutes later, I was through the exit barriers and riding an escalator up to street level. Belleville_girl was home.

You'd be hard pushed to find any picture postcards of Bas-Belleville on sale in Paris, and no area contrasted more with the Champs-Elysées I'd just left behind. On one side of rue de Belleville, where the pavement was widest, unsightly blocks of flats built in the sixties and seventies towered overhead. On the opposite *trottoir*, the facades of many of the older buildings were veined with cracks and crying out for a fresh coat of paint. Abandoned newspapers rustled underfoot, broken fruit and veg crates surrounded the overflowing municipal bins, and an assortment of empty beer cans and wine bottles testified to the favourite pastime of the neighbourhood's tramps. The pavements were always choked with people, whatever the time of day, and I had to duck and weave to overtake slow-moving pensioners hauling rickety shopping trolleys and a glut of African women with pushchairs. As I hurried by I heard snatches of conversations in Arabic, French and Mandarin, along with other languages I was unable to identify. This was the reason some people referred to the neighbourhood as Babel-ville.

Leaving the main road behind for the relative calm of newly cobbled rue de Tourtille, I reached Lila's school, where a steady stream of children – variously accompanied by mothers, fathers, older siblings or babysitters – were already spilling out of the front porch. A glance at my watch revealed it was 17.36. When Lila had started school, aged three, I'd worked part-time so that I could collect her from school an hour earlier and stay at home with her on Wednesdays. This year, however, I'd had, with a heavy heart, to extend my teaching day and sign Lila up for both the after-school *garderie* and the *Centre de Loisirs*, the playscheme held there on Wednesdays. I had no choice: living alone was so much more expensive, and my teaching salary plus Nico's monthly maintenance payment didn't exactly pave the way for a life of luxury.

Scurrying past the African lady who guarded the front entrance impassive as a sphinx, I muttered the obligatory '*Bonjour, Madame*' under my breath. In the *préau* – the school hall where the children's activities were supervised by the staff who took over after the teaching day was over – I caught sight of Lila at once and made a beeline for the long, low table where she sat next to a Chinese girl with intricately braided hair. A blue crayon in her hand, Lila was bent over one of her mermaid masterpieces, concentration furrowing her brow.

'Wow, haven't you been busy!' I exclaimed, bending to plant a kiss on her forehead, delighting, as I always did, in the startling softness of her skin against my lips.

'I been drawing lots and lots of tiny *écailles* on the mermaid's tail, Mummy,' Lila said, puffed up with pride, holding her picture aloft for closer inspection.

'Oh yes, what pretty scales she has!' I cooed, dutifully admiring my daughter's handiwork. 'Would you like to finish your picture off at home, Lila? How about I put it in my bag, to keep it safe, and you can help me find the peg where you hung up your coat?' Lila nodded, and I noticed, with a pang, the dark smudges underneath her eyes. The extra hour at school was tiring her out.

It took ten minutes, that evening, to retrace my steps to the bakery on the corner of rue de Tourtille for a *demi-baguette*, then walk the couple of hundred yards uphill to our front door, along another quiet one-way street, rue Jouy-Rouve. Accepting the hunk of warm bread I proffered without a word of thanks, Lila refused to grasp my outstretched hand or fall into step with me. Tiredness always made her uncooperative and she dawdled as far behind me as she dared, dragging her free hand along the windowpane of every shop we passed until her palm was a filthy shade of grey. When I paused in front of the heavy double doors which led to our building and began tapping in the five-digit entry code, she launched into one of my least favourite subjects.

'When am I going to stay at Daddy's house? Is it tomorrow?'

'No, not tomorrow,' I replied, as the door clicked and I pushed it open. 'I think Daddy's coming to fetch you on Saturday morning, which is after five more sleeps . . .' I held up five fingers, wiggling them cheerfully. Would she remember that, last time she'd asked me the same question, that very morning, prior to Nico's call, I'd held up only four?

'But five sleeps is a really long time, Mummy,' she protested, lingering on the word 'really' for dramatic emphasis. 'Why do I have to wait so long?'

'Daddy would love to see you sooner, but he has to work very late in his office,' I replied evenly, drawing on reserves of diplomacy I had no idea I possessed. Please don't let this turn into yet another 'Why don't we live with Daddy any more?' discussion, I prayed. I'd lost count of the number of times I'd had to repeat calmly and patiently that, although Mummy and Daddy were still friends, living together didn't make us happy any more; that it was no one's fault, just something which happened to grown-ups sometimes.

Every time we covered that well-trodden ground, an alternative answer – unfit for four-year-old ears – echoed inside my head. 'We don't live together any more, Lila,' the voice said bitterly, 'because Daddy fucked his secretary.'

3

The following Saturday, ten o'clock came and went with no word from Nico. After dialling his mobile number, I handed the phone to Lila and crossed the living room into the open-plan kitchen, where I filled the kettle and set it to boil, deliberately keeping my distance. Anything I said would be interpreted as a rebuke. Lila's voice, on the other hand, would convey only her eagerness to see her daddy.

But the rapturous '*Papa!*' I was expecting to hear never came. Instead, after a hesitant '*Allô*', Lila held the phone away from her ear. 'There's a lady talking,' she said in a stage whisper. 'Mummy did get the number wrong.' Dropping the handset on to the sofa in disgust, she returned to the elaborate dolls' tea party she was hosting on her bedroom rug.

A wrong number was impossible: Nico's mobile was programmed into my speed dial. Cheeks flushed with sudden righteous anger, I lunged across the room and grabbed the phone. '*Je suis* Sally, *la maman de* Lila,' I said frostily. '*Nicolas n'est pas là?*' At first I heard nothing but the hiss of dead air and assumed whoever it was had taken fright and hung up. But after a moment there was a resigned sigh, and a French woman – or a girl, by the sounds of it – reluctantly introduced herself.

'*C'est* Albane *à l'appareil.* Nico's in the bathroom. I'm sorry, I shouldn't have . . . I didn't mean to . . .' There was a second excruciating silence, which I was momentarily too stunned to fill, followed by a muffled altercation – her voice and Nico's – which was accompanied by an unwelcome vision of Nico standing in front of her, a towel around his midriff, his muscular shoulders covered in droplets, his wet hair stuck to the nape of his neck.

'Sally!' Nico said jovially. Having recovered possession of the phone, he'd decided to pretend nothing was amiss. '*Donne-moi dix minutes.* I had a late night at the office and I'm afraid I overslept . . .'

'I see you even brought some "work" home,' I replied tartly. 'How conscientious of you.' Before he had a chance to reply, or to comment on my sarcasm, I jabbed the 'end call' button with my index finger. Unbelievable, I thought, crumpling on to the sofa. Albane, the trainee from his office, was there, at his place, right now! And as if that wasn't a bitter enough pill to swallow, she'd referred to him as 'Nico', with an easy familiarity that made me ache. Now that I'd heard her voice, my mental image of Albane was suddenly less two-dimensional. I pictured a twenty-something with glossy hair and bee-stung lips, her stomach toned and taut, devoid of stretch marks.

I'd first heard Albane's name almost two years earlier. We were out to dinner with Yves and Kate, and Nico had told us about the new trainee his law firm had recruited for his department, fresh from university. She was eight years younger than me; not much older than I'd been when I first laid eyes on Nico at El Paso. The adjective Nico had used when describing Albane to Yves – '*pneumatique*', presumably in the *Brave New World* sense of the word, rather than her being, literally, inflatable – had

27

caused my hackles to rise. 'I don't think that's the sort of feedback she'll be needing on her evaluation form,' I'd protested, provoking a snigger from Yves, and an amused eye-roll from Kate.

I was almost certain nothing had happened between Nico and Albane until after I walked out on him. She was his consolation prize after I left, when Nico's secretary tired of him and applied for a post with another law firm, in search of a new relationship to put in jeopardy. I couldn't be sure of the timing, though. I hadn't suspected Nico of regularly wining, dining and bedding his secretary over a twelve-month period either, had I? Not until the evidence was staring me in the face.

'The lady on the telephone was a friend of Daddy's, called Albane,' I said, popping my head around Lila's door. 'But Daddy will be here soon, poppet. Just like he promised.'

'Would you like a cup of tea, Mummy?' said Lila, gesturing for me to join her dolls' tea party and showing no sign of having heard or processed what I'd said. I nodded, taking a seat beside her on the floor and holding out my hand for a cup and saucer. Once Lila had mimed pouring tea from the china teapot I'd played with as a child, added two lumps of white Lego sugar and watched as I pretended to take the first sip, I decided to risk a question.

'Have you ever met this lady called Albane?' I asked, hesitantly. 'Actually, she's more of a girl than a lady. About the same age as Blandine, the girl who comes to babysit for you sometimes . . .'

Lila shook her head. 'I think Daddy talks to her on the telephone sometimes,' she replied, 'but I did never meet her before.' Her face lit up as though an appealing thought had occurred to her. 'Will she be there when I go today, Mummy? Will she play with me, just like Blandine?'

I realized I had no idea whether Albane would be sticking around or not and resolved to ask Nico. 'I tell you what,' I replied, 'shall we get your coat and shoes on, and your bag packed? We can ask Daddy about that when he gets here.'

Despite the fact that his apartment – the home we used to share – was only a five-minute walk away, Nico didn't arrive until a full twenty minutes later. When the *sonnette* trilled I opened the door, unsmiling, and stepped aside to let Lila pass, clutching her weekend bag in one hand and the least bedraggled of her Little Mermaid dolls in the other. Nico hoisted her up into his arms for a hug. Knuckles white around the door handle, I didn't trust myself to speak at first.

'Still as sarcastic as ever, I see,' Nico murmured in French over Lila's shoulder. My parting shot over the phone seemed to have hit home. He didn't preface his remark with a '*Bonjour*', nor a 'Sorry I'm late'. Nico had always been unflinchingly direct. It had been one of the qualities I'd admired in him when we first met.

'Will *she* be spending the weekend with you and Lila?' I'd found my tongue, but not the ability to utter Albane's name.

'Albane just left actually, so no, she won't,' he replied. 'It's nothing serious, this thing with her,' he added. 'As I've told you before. Not that it's really any of your business.' I nodded and relaxed my grip on the doorknob, the blood returning to my knuckles.

'I'll see you both at six on Sunday, then, shall I?' I said, stepping forward to plant a goodbye kiss on Lila's cheek and effectively bringing my and Nico's conversation to an end. It was a movement which brought me too close to Nico for comfort; close enough to catch the scent of his old-fashioned Vetiver aftershave.

'*Dimanche à dix-huit heures*,' he repeated, setting Lila back on the floor and grasping her hand. I watched their receding backs until the curve of the stairwell took them out of my line of vision, then nudged the front door closed, resting my forehead against the peephole, my head in turmoil.

Whenever I saw Nico, I found myself caught up in a tangle of conflicting emotions. Bitterness and anger were mingled with sadness and disappointment. There was a numbness, a void, where fonder feelings had once been, before his actions had caused them to shrivel up and disappear. I felt their absence keenly; I minded the gap. It reminded me of running my tongue obsessively over the space left by a lost milk tooth as a child, trying to touch what was not there.

Sometimes I was conscious of a spark of residual physical attraction, triggered by something seemingly insignificant: his laugh, his aftershave. Or was it simply nostalgia for the comforting familiarity of this person I'd spent a third of my life with? What I did know was that all the negative feelings jostling to gain the upper hand whenever I saw him were tempered by the simple fact that he was, and always would be, my daughter's father.

Lila did seem to have been dipped in Nico's gene pool, not mine, despite all those months I'd carried her around in my belly. They had the same dark-brown hair and hazel eyes, and Lila even had a matching dimple in the middle of her chin. 'Lila, *c'est* Nicolas *tout craché*,' his mother Catherine never tired of saying. It had amused me, the first time I'd heard her say it, that the French have a similar phrase for 'the spitting image'. The resemblance undeniably worked in Nico's favour now. It was difficult to hate the man who shared my daughter's face.

The ringing telephone startled me from my reverie and I peeled my forehead away from the front door, following the sound to locate the handset. It lay on the sofa, where I'd flung it down earlier. Kate was calling: a welcome interruption.

'Hi, Kate,' I said, trying to sound brighter and more upbeat than I felt. 'How are things?'

'Busy but good,' she said briskly. I could hear the sound of a knife against a chopping board in the background, and suspected Kate was multitasking, her phone cradled between her ear and shoulder while she got a head start on preparing lunch. 'I'm ringing to check you're still on for tonight,' she continued. 'Did Nico take Lila this weekend, like you planned?'

'Yes. They've just left.' I bit my lip, debating whether to recount the events of that morning, but rejected the impulse. For all I knew, Yves could be in the room with Kate, and I didn't want to risk him overhearing. He was in the habit of meeting Nico for lunch from time to time, their offices only a few blocks apart. 'I don't suppose you're ready to tell me who this person is that you want me to meet?' I asked in a wheedling tone, instead. 'You were being awfully mysterious about it the other day.'

'You'll just have to wait until tonight,' Kate replied, her voice filled with amusement.

'Want me to come over a bit earlier and help you get set up?' I offered, fully expecting a rebuttal. Knowing Kate, much as she loved cooking, she'd have enlisted the help of a *traiteur* for the evening's refreshments, and it would simply be a matter of chilling champagne and laying out canapés while her live-in nanny readied her two boys for bed.

'No need for that,' she said, as I'd predicted. 'Just slip into something sexy and bring yourself over around eight.'

Setting the phone back into its cradle on the kitchen workbench, I spent the next hour or two in a whirlwind of domestic activity, a strategy to keep thoughts of Nico and Albane at bay. I threw our bedding into the washing machine, gathered up the tea set scattered across Lila's rug and vacuumed every centimetre of the wood floors, cursing when a treacherously transparent piece of Lego rattled up the tube.

The apartment I'd moved into when I left Nico was cosy, but pitifully small compared to where we used to live. The main room – which the front door opened directly on to – served as living room, dining room and open-plan kitchen rolled into one. Two doors, set into the wall furthest from the kitchen, led through to the bedrooms: mine big enough to contain a wardrobe and double bed but little else; Lila's, which doubled as her playroom, a little larger. To the right of the front door, by the kitchen, there was a tiny, windowless bathroom with a miniature bathtub, basin and toilet.

All in all we had forty square metres of living space, according to the lease, although I'd struggled to account for them all when I'd taken a tape measure to the place myself, the day the estate agent handed over the keys. Nico's parents had taken Lila for the Easter holidays and, when she'd returned, it had been to our new home. I'd done my utmost to make our fresh start a positive one, investing in cheerful, space-saving furniture and painting Lila's room in shades of lilac, her namesake colour. With the practicalities of the move out of the way, I'd been free to focus my energies on the hardest part of all, dealing with the emotional fallout: answering Lila's pitiful questions, which ripped my heart to shreds; cradling her in my arms in the middle of the night when she awoke and sobbed for her daddy.

Once I'd finished my chores, I made myself a cup of tea and settled into the corner of the sofa, my laptop warming the tops of my thighs through the thin fabric of my oldest pair of jeans, which still bore traces of lilac paint around the ankles. It was time to begin my lesson planning for the coming week. Tedious it might be, but if I ended up overdoing the champagne at Kate's, work wouldn't be an option tomorrow.

In my inbox was a message from Rendez-vous. It wasn't an admirer making the first move, but an automatically generated message advising me that my profile photograph had been approved, at long last. My first attempt, a blurred, sepia-toned shot taken with my mobile phone on Monday evening, had not found favour with the site's moderators, who'd rejected it forty-eight hours later. A frantic search through my computer hard drive had yielded only endless photographs of Nico and Lila and, at my wits' end, I'd resorted to scanning in the colour photo from my 'Tailor-Made' access badge and submitting that instead. It was a little outdated, true, but, judging by the photos of the men whose profiles I'd browsed through so far, this kind of cheating was par for the course. Either that or I'd have to start by asking some of the miraculously wrinkle-free forty-five-year-olds if they wouldn't mind letting me in on their anti-ageing secrets.

Following the link within the email to Belleville_girl's completed profile – which, I was informed, had now gone 'live' – I re-read the text I'd submitted as my *annonce* the previous evening. It made me cringe, but not to the extent I'd feared. Translated into English, it read something like this:

> Ten years in Paris, yet still English through and through.
> I like: living in Belleville, playing with my daughter (4),
> the company of good friends, reading '*Transports amoureux*'
> on the métro, the smell of baking bread, people who
> make me laugh . . .

Would anyone look at my profile, read those two short sentences and think, 'Now there's a woman I'd like to meet'? And if they did, what were the chances – given what Kate had told me – that they would make contact for the right reasons? I felt sure the odds of finding someone special were almost as slim as those of a stranger falling for me in a crowded métro carriage. But it didn't matter: I'd decided I didn't mind if some men had less than honourable intentions. Nico hadn't wasted any time finding a bit of light entertainment, so why should I play by a different set of rules?

Seven o'clock found me dithering in front of the wardrobe in my underwear, agonizing over what to wear to Kate's party. My clothes were crammed in, owing to the lack of space, and it was hard to find anything, or even remember what, among the things I owned, might be remotely suitable. Going out had been far simpler in my twenties. When I was slimmer and fresh-faced, looking good had required only a pair of smart jeans, a dressy top, tousled hair and a touch of mascara. So much more work was involved now. My post-partum curves were better served by dresses, which, in turn, cried out for tights and feminine footwear. As for my face, I'd had to abandon the 'less is more' approach: cracks needed papering over; fine lines camouflaging. The challenge was to achieve this without going overboard with the liquid foundation and winding up looking about as natural as a geisha.

After lengthy deliberations, I settled on a scoop-necked navy jumper dress, coupled with a pair of thin tights and my brown knee-high boots. I transferred a few essential items – my Navigo métro pass, my purse and my keys – from my work satchel into a small brown clutch bag. The weather was mild and I threw on a beige mac I'd bought at H&M a couple of years earlier, leaving it unbuttoned. As I walked downhill towards Belleville métro, the cleavage I'd left on show drew appreciative stares from male passers-by.

It was a little before eight, and night hadn't yet fallen, although the backlit signs – most of which were written in both French and Mandarin – above the shop fronts I passed were already switched on, making their primary colours more vivid. The Chinese restaurants were teeming with diners, and the supermarkets were still open, although men in white overalls were busy packing away the fruit and vegetable stands in readiness for closing time. Plunging down into the métro, I selected *ligne* 2, colour-coded dark blue, which would take me all the way to Monceau, the stop nearest to Kate's. The journey began underground, but soon the train emerged into the outdoors again, climbing a steep slope to continue along a metal viaduct which elevated us far above road level, although I could still hear beeping horns and see cars milling around below. The *métro aérien*, as it was called, continued its overground course across Place de Stalingrad and along the centre of boulevard de la Chapelle, moving east now and skirting the bottom of the eighteenth arrondissement. It plunged underground again at Anvers, robbing me of a view of the Moulin Rouge and the tacky sex shops of Pigalle, and remained underground until I arrived at my destination, five minutes later.

Kate's neighbourhood couldn't have been more different from my own, I thought, as I climbed the litter-free steps and emerged by the Monceau park railings. The boulevard de Courcelles was lined with expensive-looking cars, and the damp pavements bore witness to a recent hosing down by a municipal cleaning truck. The majestic sandstone apartment blocks overlooking the park – one of which housed Kate's own apartment – were well maintained and, craning my neck upwards, I caught sight of an enormous crystal chandelier through a second-floor window.

In a way, Kate's choice of neighbourhood mirrored her personal style: elegant and refined, without a single hair out of place. Come to think of it, perhaps Belleville summed me up too: a little ramshackle and chaotic on the surface but, if you were willing to overlook a few faults and stray off the beaten track into the lesser-known cobbled side streets, it was still possible to find the *belle* in Belleville.

The *digicode* outside Kate's building was made of brass, which was an augur of the luxurious shape of things to come. Before the letterboxes, two mirrors in arched gilt frames were set into the facing walls on my left and right. The effect, when you stood and gazed into either one, was of an infinite number of reflected selves framed in mirrors stretching into the distance, each one a little smaller than the last. Lila, who was a huge fan of her own reflection, loved dawdling in the hallway whenever we paid Kate and her boys a visit. Beyond the mirrors and letterboxes was an intercom and, once I'd been buzzed through, I had the choice between a wide red-carpeted stairway and an old fashioned lift with a metal gate. At this time of night the building's *concierge* would be off-duty, but I still could have sworn I saw the curtain behind the glass front door leading to her quarters twitch as I passed.

I took the lift to the fifth floor, then pressed the buzzer to the right of the double doors in the centre of the landing and waited, fiddling nervously with my hair. It was my first lone outing to a gathering of this size, and standing here brought home to me how accustomed I'd grown over the years to drawing the lion's share of my self-confidence from Nico's presence by my side. I'd been blissfully unaware of this at the time, taking it for granted. But now, without him, I felt naked and exposed; bashful and shy.

Yves answered the door, his eyes flickering over my *décolleté*, his '*Bonjour*, Sally' devoid of any real warmth. He'd always had an unpleasant habit of pronouncing my name as though it were the French word '*sâli*' – the past participle of the verb to dirty, to sully – and this never failed to rub me up the wrong way, which was doubtless his intention. Yves wore chinos and a polo shirt with a pair of expensive-looking beige shoes with clownlike, elongated toes. I bet he wears that kind of thing to work on 'casual Friday', I thought to myself, suppressing a smirk. Smart casual was not a look I was very fond of, on men. A well-tailored suit, fine. A pair of worn jeans, all well and good. But this no-man's land in the middle, where the aim seemed to be to dress as though you were on your way to the golf club, was so easy to get wrong – especially for Frenchmen, who all too often tucked their shirts inside their trousers.

Yves disappeared inside the spare room with my mac and handbag and I dithered by the front door, debating for a moment whether or not to wait for his return. In the end, I opted for making my entrance alone. It might be daunting, but I was less likely to be introduced to Yves' tedious banker friends that way.

Kate's living room was large enough to contain my entire apartment. It was high-ceilinged, with a marble fireplace at either end. Four tall windows overlooked Parc Monceau, the park Kate's boys crossed every morning with their nanny on their way to their expensive bilingual school. The Roche Bobois furniture had been evacuated or pushed back against the magnolia-painted woodwork in honour of the party and, judging by the lingering odour of beeswax, the cleaning lady had buffed up the oak floorboards that afternoon. Most of the twenty or so guests already present – Tailor-Made teachers, Yves' banker set and a smattering of VIPs Kate wanted to impress – lingered by the tables set up in front of each fireplace, champagne *flûtes* at one end of the room, canapés at the other, to encourage mingling.

I spotted Kate straight away, in her perfect LBD and glittering diamond earrings, and flashed her a wide smile. I refrained from approaching her as she was deep in conversation with a portly man I didn't recognize, no doubt a high-ranking businessman from one of the firms we worked with. I made a beeline for one end of the drinks table instead, where I'd spied Ryan, a fellow teacher I used to see a lot of before Lila came along. He was chatting to a tall, dark-haired girl I'd never seen before.

'Ooh, I was hoping I'd run into you here, Sally darling,' Ryan exclaimed, interrupting his conversation to plant two enthusiastic kisses on my cheeks, then pouring me a glass of champagne. 'I haven't seen you in faaar too long!' Taking a step back, he looked me up and down. 'Officially foxy,' he pronounced, his hands drawing quotation marks around the word 'officially' to underscore his verdict. 'In fact, were I of the straight persuasion,' he continued, 'I'd definitely have designs on you this evening . . .'

Ryan was not, as he so charmingly put it, 'of the straight persuasion'. His appearance didn't give much away – he wasn't one for clingy T-shirts or edgy haircuts – but his mannerisms were deliciously camp. I had no idea whether he'd guessed how nervous I was tonight, but intentionally or not, he'd done an amazing job of putting me at my ease.

'You're looking very well, yourself,' I replied, taking a sip of champagne, which was crisp and spiky, just how I liked it. 'Rather trim, in fact. Have you been working out?'

It was true. He did look good. His hair was cropped shorter than I'd ever seen it before and the weight loss I'd referred to was most noticeable in his face. He'd made an effort with his clothes too. Jeans were pretty much his uniform, but he'd worn a smart purple shirt and discarded his usual trainers in favour of smart shoes.

'Good gracious no, I'd never make it out of the men's changing rooms,' Ryan said with a fiendish grin, 'but I have been sticking to my new diet plan. It's an invention of mine I like to call "No Solids till December", which is why I'll be spending the evening at this end of the room only . . .' The dark-haired girl by his side giggled. 'Oh dear, here I am, forgetting my manners,' Ryan apologized. 'Sally, let me introduce you to Kate's newest recruit, Anna. Anna, meet Sally, Kate's *oldest* recruit. We were busy deconstructing *The Wizard of Oz* before you arrived. You're no stranger to my Judy Garland obsession, of course, Sally. And imagine! Anna grew up in Kansas . . .'

'Nice to meet you, Anna,' I said, registering her properly for the first time and liking what I saw. Anna had accentuated her feline green eyes with a bold stroke of black eyeliner, and her dark hair was cropped short and wispy – the kind of Hepburn-style haircut I'd always dreamed of, but never dared try. She looked about my age, stood about a head taller, and wore a black tunic dress with calf-length boots not unlike my own. The notable difference was that she had worn them with a pair of electric-blue tights. Anna, I deduced, was no shrinking violet.

'So I guess you must have been working for Kate for, like, five years?' said Anna, raising a neatly plucked eyebrow. 'You and Ryan are both Paris veterans, compared to me. I moved here a year ago. My husband got a job with UNESCO and I've been going batshit crazy with boredom ever since, while I tried to figure out how to get a work permit . . .'

'Is your husband here?' I was already scanning the room, wondering how Anna's mate would look.

'Uh, well, he and I are kind of separated,' Anna said with a grimace. 'Or rather, I left him. A few more glasses of champagne and I'm sure I'll wind up giving you the low-down on how and why . . .' I was about to comment on how subtle Anna's accent was, when Kate caught my eye and the penny suddenly dropped. Anna was the mystery person Kate had so wanted me to meet. She'd been matchmaking all right, but not quite in the way I'd expected.

'I suspect,' I said, taking the empty champagne glass from Anna's hand and pouring her a refill, 'that you and I are about to find out we have way more in common than a contract with Tailor-Made . . .' I held up my glass, waiting until Ryan and Anna did the same, Ryan's eyes glinting in anticipation, because there was nothing he loved more than a good bitching session. 'I'd like to propose a toast,' I continued, looking Anna straight in the eye. 'Here's to new beginnings.'

4

Anna and I hit it off, just as Kate must have suspected we would. I began by dusting off some of my favourite expat anecdotes, comparing them with Anna's more recent experiences, and we talked at length about what we loved and hated most about our adoptive city.

'I can't believe that you gave birth to your daughter in a French hospital,' Anna exclaimed. 'If that isn't going native, I don't know what is!' And as the champagne progressively loosened our tongues, we moved on to far more interesting territory, namely how we were coming to terms with being thrust, kicking and screaming, back into the single life.

'I never thought I'd have to go through the whole tedious process of auditioning men again,' Anna said, her voice laced with bitterness. 'That part of my life was supposed to be so over. I've spent years listening to my single friends moaning about how all the good men are already taken, and feeling smug because I figured I'd never have to live by *The Rules* or read *He's Just Not That Into You*. I have no time for all that "Thou shalt not return his call until the fourth day" bullshit . . .'

'You mean there are rules?' I feigned astonishment. I'd never opened a self-help book in my life, but could imagine all too easily the kind of advice dispensed within. 'Last time I was in the market for a boyfriend – ten long years ago – I just invited him to a party I was going to after work,' I explained. 'Things seemed to happen kind of organically in those days . . . There were no strategies or magic formulas.'

When I confessed I'd signed up with Rendez-vous, Anna admitted she'd toyed with the idea herself. The main sticking point – the reason she'd never had the guts to go through with it – was her rudimentary grasp of French. There were a few expats online – I'd spent an evening playing with language and nationality filters and found a couple of hundred men of all ages hailing from Australia, the US and England – but the majority of Rendez-vous members were, of course, French. 'I'd love to meet a Frenchman, in theory,' Anna said in a wistful voice, 'but he'd have to be bilingual, otherwise I'd require the services of a full-time interpreter . . .'

'Full-time could be problematic,' Ryan smirked. He'd been uncharacteristically quiet since I'd begun talking to Anna and I'd noticed his eyes flickering repeatedly in the direction of one of Yves' banker friends on the other side of the room, admiring the scenery.

'Sure could,' Anna agreed. 'I mean, I pride myself on keeping an open mind, but I'm pretty sure threesomes are *not* my thing . . .'

I'd been right about Anna's age: she was thirty-one, a year younger than me. She and Tom had tied the knot only eighteen months earlier. The way she told it, marriage had been a pragmatic decision prompted more by Tom's imminent transfer to Paris than by a genuine desire to be united in the eyes of church or state. Now, faced with figuring out how best to get a divorce in a foreign country whose legal system she couldn't begin to comprehend, she had her misgivings. She and Tom might not have got around to starting a family, but things were complicated all the same. A tangled web of joint credit-card debts needed paying off back home in the States, and they hadn't yet figured out how to divide up a number of expensive wedding gifts.

I was about to cut to the chase and quiz Anna about what had prompted her to leave Tom when Kate appeared at my elbow and steered me purposefully across the room to meet another of her recent recruits. Tessa was a softly spoken woman with mousy brown hair and a grey wool twin-set. Her age remained a mystery – any figure between thirty and forty seemed plausible – but I was willing to bet she lived alone; there was an aura of spinster about her. 'Tessa would love to pick your brains about prep work,' Kate said, shooting me a look which managed to convey both a sincere apology and an entreaty to take Tessa off her hands. I found myself fielding Tessa's volley of earnest questions, shooting jealous looks at Ryan and Anna over Tessa's shoulder all the while. They'd taken up residence next to the food table now – despite Ryan's dietary resolution – but I suspected this had less to do with cosying up to the *petit fours salés* than it did with a desire to move closer to the attractive banker he'd been eyeballing. From time to time Anna threw back her head and laughed. I would have given anything, right then, to be privy to their jokes rather than talking shop with tedious Tessa.

When Tessa excused herself to visit the bathroom, I seized my chance to escape. Scanning the room with a frown, I spied Ryan, who had made his move and was now deep in conversation with his quarry, but Anna was nowhere to be seen. Shooting a quizzical glance at Ryan as I passed, I slipped into the hallway, where I was relieved to see Anna chatting to Kate. As I approached, Yves emerged from the spare room with a coat the same shade of blue as Anna's tights.

'Oh, are you leaving already, Anna?' I interjected, dismayed. 'That's a shame! I was hoping we'd have more time to chat . . .'

'My brother and his wife are in town,' Anna explained, slipping her arms into the coat, which Yves held gallantly out for her, 'and I kind of promised I'd meet them after dinner. Wanna meet for coffee tomorrow, instead? I often head down to the canal and sit in Chez Prune with a newspaper on Sundays. Their all-day brunch isn't bad . . .'

'Sounds good,' I said. 'Chez Prune isn't far from where I live.' I was surprised and pleased that Anna was familiar with one of my favourite haunts. In my experience, far too many expats never strayed from the *beaux quartiers*, unaware that such a thing as a canal existed within the city limits unless they happened to have seen *Amélie Poulain*. We decided to meet around two, and grabbing a pen and paper from Kate's hall table, I scribbled down first Anna's phone number, then mine, and tore the page in two, handing her a strip.

'I thought you two would get on,' said Kate with a wide smile once Anna had left. 'I think I missed my vocation. Forget the language school, I should have set up a dating agency . . .'

'*Effectivement*,' said Yves, who was listening in. 'Who needs Rendez-vous with you around, darling?' He turned on his heel and disappeared into the living room.

'I know what you're thinking,' Kate said hastily, seeing the colour slowly draining from my face, 'and, before you ask, I didn't tell him anything about our discussion the other day.' She frowned for a moment, then shrugged. 'It must have been a coincidence. There's no way he actually *knows* . . .'

'Maybe it's time for another drink,' I suggested, trying to banish from my mind the image of Yves and Nico with their heads bent over my dating profile, sniggering unkindly. Kate had a point. Online dating didn't strike me as Nico's cup of tea, and Yves had no business whatsoever visiting a site like Rendez-vous. She'd mentioned matchmaking, and Yves had named the best-known dating site in France, that was all. There was no reason to be paranoid.

'You deserve a refill, after Tessa-sitting for me for all that time.' Kate linked her arm through mine. 'Come on, Sal! The night is young, and I have another case of Veuve Cliquot on ice in the bathtub . . .'

I rose at one on Sunday, showered and pulled on jeans, a simple, long-sleeved Lycra top and flat ballerina pumps. Hurrying out for my lunch 'date' with Anna, I was filled with optimism. After going out last night, seeing Ryan again and meeting Anna, a possible kindred spirit, it felt as though my social life was on the mend. If only I could begin making plans to meet a few Rendez-vous dates too. But there wasn't much danger of that at the moment: my inbox remained stubbornly empty.

Crossing the courtyard, where the only sound was a bird chirping in the bushes, I pressed the door-release button and then stepped out into the hubbub of the street. I might occasionally bemoan the grubbiness of my neighbourhood but, on most days, I couldn't imagine living anywhere else. Kate could keep her chic apartment in the bourgeois *dix-septième*, her park where every blade of grass seemed to stand to attention, her local shops so pristine they reminded me of Main Street at Disneyland Paris. I'd often joked that if I lived at Kate's I'd feel obliged to don my Sunday best and full make-up just to fetch a baguette from the *boulangerie*. In Belleville, on the other hand, there was no need for keeping up appearances. I could slouch along the street in my oldest jeans, my hair uncombed, and blend happily into the cosmopolitan crowds.

As I neared the bottom of the hill, where the pavement was cluttered with unlicensed Chinese-food stalls, I had to adjust my pace to navigate around the slow-moving Sunday shoppers. The Chinese community was out in force with their wheelie carts, housewives fingering the fruit and vegetables laid out on trestle tables in front of the supermarket, most of which I'd struggle to name in either English or French. Next I passed the Chinese bakery – the 'princess-cake shop' as Lila called it – with its window display of distinctly un-French-looking cakes: sponge sandwiches frosted with white icing and decorated with hundreds and thousands, or twee piped flowers in pastel shades.

Crossing rue Dénoyez, where a group of graffiti artists were hard at work on a huge wall mural, my eyes flickered over the outdoor tables in front of Aux Folies. The bar was one of the few bastions of Frenchness remaining on this stretch of rue de Belleville, although, in truth, the owners were Algerian. The former Folies Belleville cabaret next door, where Piaf once sang, was now an ED discount supermarket, staffed by the slowest checkout staff in the world, and not a trace of its former glory remained. On the *terrasse* of the Folies, an assortment of grungy-looking twenty- and thirtysomethings were drinking espressos and pulling needily on their cigarettes.

When I'd first moved into the neighbourhood with Nico, we'd remarked upon how the Chinese shunned the Folies, their menfolk patronizing a Chinese-owned *Café-Tabac* a few doors up instead, congregating indoors to play Rapido Lotto. Similarly, the Tunisian Jewish population favoured the couscous restaurants along the boulevard de Belleville, and the *Camerounais* and *Sénégalais* hung around in groups in rue des Couronnes or fried corn cobs in upturned oil drums in rue Bisson. Ethnically diverse the area might be, but the only place where the different populations converged was in the neighbourhood's schools, such as Lila's *maternelle*.

Quickening my pace, mindful that it was almost two o'clock, I crossed over the boulevard, past Le Président, the largest and flashiest of the Chinese restaurants, and continued my downhill trek along rue du Faubourg du Temple, passing an endless stream of bargain clothes shops and snack bars. There was nothing picturesque about this stretch of road, and my mind wandered as I strode along. What were Lila and her father doing now? Were they in the park, my daughter pedalling furiously on her bicycle while Nico trailed, hands in pockets, some distance behind? Or was she parked in front of the TV watching cartoons while he sat in his favourite leather armchair, laptop on his knee, reviewing documents from work?

One of the hardest things about moving out had been adjusting to spending alternate weekends without Lila. However much I might have craved the occasional day off to indulge in a lie-in or a shopping trip when Nico and I were still together, the pendulum had suddenly swung too far the other way. It was hard to feel elated about my new-found 'freedom'. I hadn't asked for it, it had been thrust upon me, and forty-eight hours without my daughter felt like an eternity, at first. Kate was forever urging me to take myself off to the cinema, to visit new exhibitions in the city's museums, or to indulge myself in the *grands magasins* but, over the past few months, I'd fallen into the habit of sleeping late instead in a bid to shorten my childless Saturdays and Sundays. More often than not, I stayed at home, spending hour upon mind-numbing hour in front of the television in my pyjamas, longing for Sunday evening to arrive, when Lila would be returned to me. Pulling on clothes and facing the world had seemed to require levels of strength, motivation and enthusiasm I simply hadn't possessed. But having a sense of purpose today – a place to go, a new friend to meet – I felt as though I was turning a corner. My toast the previous night – to new beginnings – echoed in my ears.

At the next junction, the Canal Saint Martin was visible to my right but disappeared under the middle of the road to my left, continuing its course towards Bastille inside a hidden underground tunnel. I faced down a car at the pedestrian crossing, forcing the driver to stop when he manifestly had no intention of doing so, then followed the pavement running parallel to the opposite side of the canal. A crowd had gathered on a bridge to watch the hypnotic sight of the water level dropping to allow a barge to navigate the lock. Beyond it, the waterway widened, no longer hemmed in by fences, and the cobbled towpath was punctuated with park benches. It was a popular spot for a stroll or a picnic, and the Parisians were out in force today, soaking up the last few rays of the Indian summer.

As I took the zebra crossing which delivered me directly on to Chez Prune's *terrasse*, I scanned the outdoor tables clustered on either side of the front door. My hunch was that on such a fine day Anna would have elected to sit outside and, sure enough, I soon spotted a woman with her head bent over the *Herald Tribune*, a giveaway electric-blue coat flung over the crimson wicker chair by her side. My shadow fell over her newspaper as I approached, and Anna looked up and smiled.

'Hey, you made it!' she said, hastily transferring her coat to the back of her own chair and motioning for me to sit. She was fresh-faced this afternoon, her hair pulled back with a black Alice band, but she still wore mascara and two bold strokes of black eyeliner. 'I wished I could have stayed longer last night,' she added. 'My guests were so beat after walking around Paris all day that they only stayed out for a nightcap. I was tempted to come back afterward, but I didn't have the energy to hop on another métro . . .'

'Well, if it makes you feel any better, you didn't miss an awful lot,' I reassured her. 'The party pretty much wound down after you left . . .' I tried and failed to catch the waiter's eye as he rocketed by, ferrying a full tray of soiled cups and glasses back indoors. 'I mean, it's always fun to spend time with Ryan,' I added. 'And Kate's my oldest friend in Paris. But she was busy playing hostess and smooching her VIP clients all night and, as you saw, Ryan had set his sights on that banker.'

I made a mental note to text Ryan later and ask if his night had been a success. Once upon a time, he and I were very close, meeting up at least once a week for dinner or drinks. Ryan's flamboyant side was all for show, really, and when you got to know him better, he could be a great listener and a very perceptive, caring friend. I'd often regretted the fact that we'd drifted apart after Lila was born and was determined, now, to do everything in my power to make him a regular fixture in my life once more.

The waiter ground to a halt in front of our table, ready to acknowledge our presence. 'Were you planning on eating?' I asked Anna, eyeing the menu dubiously. 'Because although you mentioned brunch, I think maybe I'll just get a *café crème*. All that champagne last night . . . I don't know if I could stomach a meal.'

As we waited for our coffees to arrive, we talked about our favourite spots in the neighbourhood and swapped stories about our respective Tailor-Made pupils. Occasionally Anna would seize on my English turns of phrase. 'You English are so quaint with your "shan't"s and your "daren't"s,' she said. 'Talk about two countries divided by a common language.'

'I could say the same about all your bizarre "gotten"s and "someplace else"s,' I retorted, pouring the contents of a paper tube of white sugar into the cup the waiter placed in front of me and stirring vigorously. I hesitated for a moment. It hadn't seemed polite to dive straight in and ask my new friend about why she'd left her husband, not without some sort of cue. But with the way things had clicked into place between us from the start, Anna already felt less like a new acquaintance than an old friend. Curiosity was getting the better of me, and I found I could hold fire no longer. 'So . . .' I began tentatively, 'I was wondering how you came to leave Tom. I think perhaps you were about to tell me last night, just before I got kidnapped by Kate . . .'

'Okay,' said Anna, wiping milky bubbles from her top lip with the back of her forefinger, 'I tell you what, I'll show you my scars if you'll show me yours.' She paused for a moment, staring into the distance with unfocused eyes as though she were gathering her strength, and I began to wish I'd held my tongue for a little while longer. Our banter had been fun, and now I'd spoilt the mood, transposing our afternoon into a minor key.

'It happened two months ago,' she said slowly. 'I was home alone, reading through an English essay for a French friend of mine, to help pass the time. I'd been going insane, you know, with nothing to do but explore Paris on my own or go to French lessons while Tom was out at work. I even found myself playing the Stepford Wife – which is *so* not like me – preparing elaborate dinners for when Tom got home, shuffling our furniture around the apartment to try out new configurations, that kind of thing . . . Anyway, it was this gorgeous hot July day, and I got stir crazy and decided to take a break to buy groceries from my favourite street market in rue Cler, near the UNESCO building where Tom worked.' Anna took another sip of her coffee and set her cup carefully down on its saucer. Her movements were controlled and deliberate, but I could sense her inner turmoil nonetheless, like molten lava bubbling unseen beneath the surface crust. 'I was buying organic apples when I saw them,' she continued, a tremor in her voice. 'Tom and Annik, a Dutch woman I'd seen at one of his work functions. They were strolling along, hand in hand, and his head was bent close to hers so that he could whisper something into her ear. I shadowed them for a while, keeping a safe distance like a detective in a movie, until they stopped at a café for lunch. They were so wrapped up in one another that neither of them noticed me standing across the street, staring. I knew from the way he was looking at her – the way he couldn't keep his hands off her shoulder, her forearm – that he'd fallen for this woman. And that they were already intimate . . .'

Anna had confronted Tom that very evening and all was as she'd suspected. She described Tom's reaction so well that I could picture the scene unfolding. He'd gone sickly pale when she told him what she'd seen, and had made no attempt to deny anything, heading straight over to the drinks cabinet to pour himself a large glass of Bourbon. When he spoke he'd sounded distraught and sincerely sorry. Mortified that Anna had wound up finding out, he hated himself for not having come clean sooner, although he assured her that, for what it was worth, his affair hadn't been going on long. He swore blind that he'd been waiting in vain for the 'right moment', nearly choking on the meals she prepared for him, wrestling with the guilt of having uprooted Anna's life so she could follow him to Paris, only to leave her high and dry a few months down the line. He kept repeating, 'I hadn't planned for this,' over and over, as though somehow the fact that none of it had been intentional absolved him from any responsibility.

What Tom hadn't been, Anna noted wryly, was filled with remorse. She'd been replaced in his affections, and there seemed to be no question in his mind of him giving up this other woman or trying to save their marriage. Anaesthetized by shock, or perhaps resigned to the fact that any protests would be futile in the face of what was ostensibly a *fait accompli*, Anna hadn't screamed or shouted. She'd left the room instead, packed a suitcase and walked out of the front door, never to return.

When I asked Anna if she'd considered taking flight, in the most literal sense, by hailing a taxi to the airport and returning home to the States there and then, she pursed her lips and shook her head. 'At first I stayed on a friend's sofa, because the idea of going back, with my tail between my legs, and admitting to everyone who'd come to our wedding party that it had all been for nothing was too awful,' she confessed. 'I wasn't ready to face anyone.' But then a couple of opportunities had fallen into her lap in rapid succession. A friend of a friend who was leaving the city convinced his landlord to let her take on the lease to his studio apartment near République; the same day she'd happened upon the Tailor-Made website and made contact with Kate. 'It felt like a sign,' she said, shrugging her shoulders as though to indicate that superstition was not ordinarily her thing. 'And, you know, even if my first year in Paris wasn't all that, this city kind of has a way of sneaking its way under your skin, doesn't it?'

'Tell me about it,' I said. I knew that feeling only too well. 'You're looking at someone who came here for three months and ended up staying ten years.'

5

By the time we'd drained the dregs of our coffee, the sun had taken refuge behind a sprawling mass of white cloud, and I began to shiver, wishing I'd thought to bring a jacket. Anna seemed to have told as much of her story as she was able, for today. I'd made sympathetic noises in all the right places, but I'd said little. If there was one thing I'd learned from my own break-up with Nico, it was that meaningless platitudes and mixed metaphors about fishes in the sea and relationships running out of steam afforded more comfort to the speaker – who felt the need to fill uncomfortable silences – than they did to their target audience.

'Do you fancy a walk along the canal?' I fumbled in my jeans pocket for some coins to scatter on the table. 'I've still got another couple of hours before I have to think about getting back to pick up Lila, but I'm getting a bit chilly sitting still . . .'

'So long as you're happy walking and talking,' Anna concurred, gathering up her coat and newspaper, 'because I'm going to hold you to your side of the bargain, now, Sally. Fair's fair.'

Setting our course north, in the direction of La Villette, we joined the hordes on the cobbled towpath, walking at a leisurely pace. Clusters of people were gathered here and there with the remains of their lunch, seated on the benches or the raised concrete kerb which divided the pavement from the canal, their feet dangling nonchalantly over the khaki-green water. The opposite bank was busier still, on account of a bar owner with an eye for an opportunity who'd had the brainwave of serving takeaway beer in plastic glasses. The sun had been good for business today: empty beakers littered the cobbles, and a few even bobbed on the surface of the water.

Before I launched into my story, I back-pedalled a few years to set the scene. 'Nico and I were never that interested in getting married,' I began. 'We always thought having a child together was the biggest commitment of all. We met ten years ago, in a bar near Bastille. The same bar where I first met Kate, in fact, while we were both working there as waitresses, the summer after I graduated. I hadn't planned to stay in France, but meeting Nico changed all that . . . We moved in together at the end of that summer and I took a TEFL diploma and got a job with Berlitz. Lila came along six years later, and when I left Nico, back in March, she was almost four.'

'What were your career plans before that?' Anna asked. 'I mean, what did you have to give up in order to stay?'

'I wanted to teach history to teenagers,' I explained, 'so it wasn't such a huge leap to reconcile myself to teaching English as a foreign language instead. How about you? I don't think you told me what you did before, back in the States?'

'I worked in a friend's bookstore mostly,' Anna said, with a dismissive gesture of her hand. 'I majored in American Literature and I started a PhD, but it kind of ended up falling by the wayside. So following Tom didn't mean turning my back on a glittering career.'

As we drew level with another lock, the pavement narrowed, forcing us to walk in single file for a hundred metres or so. Acutely conscious of the fact that the next instalment of my story wasn't going to show me in the most favourable of lights, I seized the excuse to stall for a couple of minutes. But once we were clear of the lock and back on the wide cobbled towpath opposite Jardin Villemin, there was no escape. Taking my courage in both hands, I soldiered on.

'Nico left his work computer at home one day when I was off work sick,' I explained, my eyes fixed on the cobbles underfoot. 'It was switched on, logged in, the works. I don't know what got into me, and I'm not proud of it, but I couldn't resist snooping. It wasn't as if I suspected him of any wrongdoing, and I wasn't searching for anything in particular. We were happy enough. Or at least I thought so. If anything, I was curious about his work life. He'd been spending a lot of time at the office, but he never really talked about it much at home . . .'

I remembered the scene I described next so vividly. Seated in his favourite armchair, I'd lifted Nico's MacBook on to my knee and watched the screen flicker to life. The MSN Messenger icon was bobbing up and down at the bottom of his screen and my mouse hovered over it, my finger poised to click. I had no inkling then that the way I saw my relationship with Nico was about to change irrevocably.

In the Messenger program, I'd seen the names of his colleagues. Some I'd recognized, such as his secretary, Mathilde, or his trainee, Albane. Others I hadn't, no doubt because they were listed under nicknames I'd never heard before. Nico had once talked me through where to find the conversation archive, years ago, when he was away on business and needed to retrieve a phone number from an exchange with his boss. I had no idea what perverse impulse prompted me to go trawling through his message history on that fateful day. It was as though there were a devil perched on my shoulder, urging me on.

I glanced across at Anna, searching her face for signs of disapproval, but her expression was unreadable. 'The first conversation I read was innocent enough,' I explained. 'It was a two-line exchange with his trainee, asking her to fetch some files for him.' Albane had been the only work colleague of his I'd ever felt insecure about, and I remembered smiling to myself, as I scrolled through yet more harmless snippets of dialogue, reassured that I'd never had anything real to worry about on that score. 'Then I read a conversation between Nico and his secretary, Mathilde,' I continued, blushing as I recalled the sexually explicit nature of *that* exchange, the words forever scorched on to my brain. 'At first I thought it must be a mistake. You know, she'd got her wires crossed, she thought she was talking to her boyfriend and accidentally chatted up Nico – because it was intimate, the stuff she was saying to him. Sexual and kind of possessive. Proprietary, almost.'

'I imagine you didn't stop reading there?' Anna prompted gently. 'I know *I* wouldn't have.' I nodded, grateful to her for saying that. Of course I hadn't stopped reading there. I'd thrown up my breakfast in the bathroom and sobbed out loud until I was hoarse. Then I'd returned to Nico's armchair and read every single message in his archive. That was when I realized I hadn't stumbled upon evidence of a virtual, unconsummated flirtation. No. Nico had been carrying on with Mathilde for months. He'd pretended to work late, but instead he'd been sneaking off to hotels, or taking taxis back to her place, and weaved an intricate web of lies to cover his tracks. There were pictures too. Pictures she'd sent him of herself posing in expensive underwear he'd bought her on Valentine's Day; pictures where she wore no underwear at all.

It was an act of pure masochism, staring through eyes blurred by tears at every single photo, reading every last word of their online conversations. I wished I hadn't, afterwards. Certain words and phrases in the French language had been durably tainted by their association, in my mind, with Nico and Mathilde's affair. Only the other day, when Lila had asked for one of the lollipops in the jar by the till at our local *boulangerie*, I'd seen the brand name 'Chupa Chups' and blanched.

'*Mon chéri*, you look stressed today,' Mathilde had written to Nico one morning. 'Can I be of assistance in any way?' When Nico had prompted her to elaborate on how she proposed to help, she'd simply responded, '*Chupa*.' It didn't take a genius to work out what she'd been insinuating.

'I'm so glad I've never had that level of detail to torture myself with,' Anna said, her expression thoughtful. 'Once you've read something like that, I bet it stays with you for ever.'

It was only when I heard the distant screech of the *métro aérien* crossing place de Stalingrad that I realized how oblivious I'd been to our surroundings as I talked. We'd come a long way, and across the next junction was the final stretch of the Canal Saint-Martin before it changed its name to the Canal de l'Ourcq. Walking along the towpath, we passed a fire station and drew level with the Point Ephémère. A grungy bar, concert venue, art gallery and restaurant rolled into one, it was housed inside a hangar-like building which must have been some sort of warehouse in the days when the canal still carried freight. I'd been inside, once before, with Nico, although he hadn't liked it much, as his tastes, these days, were more in line with Kate's than mine. I excused myself as we reached the entrance, muttering something about needing to use the ladies. In truth, I craved a couple of minutes by myself. Re-living that sickening moment of discovery for Anna's benefit had shaken me up far more than I'd expected.

When I emerged, cheeks damp from the icy water I'd splashed on my face in a bid to snap myself out of the sombre mood which had overtaken me, I found Anna standing on the edge of the towpath, her back towards me. On the opposite bank, a horde of homeless people had pitched tents, creating a semi-permanent encampment in the shadow of the bridge. A year earlier, a charity had distributed tents as a publicity stunt to raise awareness of the plight of the *sans abri* among Parisians. Unfortunately, they had almost become part of the scenery now, stripped of their initial power to shock. If only I could say the same about Nico and Mathilde's MSN exchanges. Familiar they might be, but thinking about them still brought bile to the back of my throat.

'I'm guessing that when you confronted him, he went batshit crazy about how you'd violated his privacy?' Anna speculated, shooting me a reassuring smile over her shoulder and picking up the conversation where we'd left off.

'Oh yes.' I gave a hollow laugh. 'The way he saw it, *I*'d behaved as badly as *he* had, if not worse. It was almost as though our sins cancelled one another out on some sort of moral balance sheet. Do you know, he even had the gall to tell me I didn't have the right to reproach him for something I should never have known about? He said I'd betrayed *his* trust. As far as he was concerned, I was the villain of the piece.'

Anna gave a long, low whistle. 'Aren't men incredible sometimes? Jeez. So . . . Is Nico with this Mathilde now?'

I shook my head. 'From what I gather she met someone else around that time,' I explained, 'and it was already over. Or so Nico claimed. He gave me this speech about how Mathilde had meant nothing to him, how he still loved me, how men's needs are different . . . And, frankly, I didn't want to know. As far as I was concerned, he'd broken us, beyond repair. So I moved out with Lila, as soon as I could find a place, and soon afterwards he hopped into bed with the trainee from work. I don't think Albane means that much to him, but he doesn't seem to know how to be alone . . .'

It was the first time I'd told the story from start to finish in such detail, and the experience had been exhausting. Kate had heard it all in real time, of course, as had my mother, albeit over the phone, and other people, such as Ryan, had made do with the broad brushstrokes. If today's gruelling unburdening had taught me anything, it was that I wouldn't be giving a repeat performance in a hurry. I felt so washed out that I longed to crawl back under my duvet and close my eyes.

'Well, you were right when you said you thought we'd have a lot in common at the party.' Anna flashed me a wry smile. 'What a pair we make. The Wronged Women's Club.'

Anna and I parted ways outside the McDonald's on the corner of avenue Secrétan soon afterwards. We hugged, a touch woodenly, as new acquaintances do, and promised to call one another soon and make plans to meet again. Lost in my thoughts, I meandered past the shuttered fronts of the shops, only deciding to take the bus home when it wheezed to a halt at the stop a few paces ahead of me. I dragged my bag across the sensor on autopilot, negotiated the glut of pushchairs in the middle of the bus and collapsed gratefully into a free seat near the back.

As the bus rumbled along avenue Simon Bolivar, my brain seemed intent on replaying extracts from the evening I'd confronted Nico with the evidence of his infidelity, as though now that I'd opened Pandora's box, the lid stubbornly refused to close. 'It's ironic, isn't it,' I'd shouted, pain spurring me to new heights of sarcasm, 'that the word "cuckold" doesn't even have a female equivalent? It's almost as though a man cheating on his girlfriend is such a given that no special word is required . . . Well, I'm sorry, Nico, but my definition of "girlfriend", or "partner", or "mother of your child" never included the assumption that I'd tolerate repeated acts of infidelity. We're over, as far as I'm concerned. I hope she was damn well worth it . . .'

'Mummy, why you shouting at Daddy?' Lila had cried from her bedroom, awoken by our raised voices. I'd stepped around Nico, giving him the widest possible berth – the idea of brushing against him made me nauseous – and rushed to her bedside, finding her curled into a tight ball, her face wet with tears, her hands pressed to her ears. I'd pulled back the covers and slid into bed beside her. Matching the rhythm of my breathing to hers, I'd drawn an instinctive animal comfort from the scent of her skin, the tickle of her curls against my nose. I'd fallen asleep in Lila's bed, fully clothed, never hearing the front door slam behind Nico. To this day I had no idea where he'd spent that night.

I'd called in sick the following morning, dropped Lila off at school and spent the day combing through the classifieds and making phone call after phone call, devoting every iota of energy I possessed to the search for a new place to live so that I wouldn't have any space in my head to devote to Nico and Mathilde. As for Nico, he'd come home late every evening after that. He slept on the sofa, taking care to rise and tidy away the bedclothes every morning before I roused Lila so that he wouldn't have to answer any difficult questions. In her presence we both did our utmost to remain civil; when she slept, we skirted gingerly around one another and rarely spoke.

Only once, on the night I announced I'd signed a lease and would be settling in over the Easter holidays, did Nico try to persuade me that leaving wasn't necessary. 'It doesn't have to be this way,' he'd protested. 'We could try again, for Lila's sake.' But for me this was a classic case of too little, too late. Nico's heart didn't seem to be in it, and mine had gone AWOL.

I left the bus at the stop a few metres from Nico's building, punched in his familiar door code and took the lift to the sixth floor. In the wake of all the memories I'd stirred up this afternoon, my need for Lila had become overwhelmingly physical. I longed to clutch her to me, to draw comfort from her unconditional love.

'*Je veux pas partir avec Maman!* I want to stay here with you, *Papa*,' Lila cried as Nico opened the front door. I flinched as though I'd been struck: this was the opposite of the rapturous welcome I'd been hoping for. I knew, from experience, that no sooner were we down the stairs and out into the street, Lila's tears would miraculously evaporate and she'd chatter away, nineteen to the dozen, as though the tearful scene had already been erased from her mind. But she often put on this little performance when I came to collect her, and the injustice of it never failed to sting. Here was I, doing the lion's share of the parenting and being thoroughly taken for granted, while Nico, who waltzed into Lila's life on alternate weekends, was revered like some sort of demi-god.

As Nico dropped to his knees and tried to coax Lila into her coat, I remained in the doorway. I hadn't crossed the threshold into our old apartment since I'd collected the last of my belongings, six months earlier. My eyes were drawn to a brown tortoiseshell hair clip which lay on the hall table, next to the telephone. A single strand of dark hair was caught fast between its teeth. Long and straight, it dangled insolently over the edge of the table, the first tangible proof I'd seen of Albane's occasional presence in Nico's home. At the sight of it, something inside me snapped. 'For God's sake, hurry up, Nico,' I barked. 'Don't you dare humour Lila. This is all just a silly act for your benefit.'

'We had a lovely weekend, thank you,' said Nico pointedly, straightening up and handing me Lila's weekend bag.

Lila stepped meekly forward. Something in the tone of my voice had got through to her. 'If this is still about that phone call on Saturday,' Nico frowned, 'I told you . . .'

'Give *Papa* a cuddle and kiss. We're going,' I interrupted, ignoring Nico and addressing Lila instead. 'And don't even think about pulling that Friday-night working-late scam on me again,' I added, shooting Nico an angry glance over my shoulder as we left. 'I wasn't born yesterday, you know.'

As I stomped down the stairs hand in hand with Lila, I savoured the combination of confusion and guilt I'd seen in Nico's face. Let him think this was about me feeling jealous of Albane, if he wanted. My only desire, just then, was to put as much distance between us as possible.

No sooner had the words 'online' and 'dating' popped out of my mouth, than I wished I could swallow them back down again. But it was too late: they'd hurtled along the fibre-optic network, under the English Channel, and they were already bouncing off my mother's right eardrum. I heard her sharp intake of breath and knew any minute now she'd launch into one of her infamous monologues, regurgitating every online-dating disaster story she'd ever read in the pages of the *Daily Mail*. Why on earth hadn't I held my tongue? Hadn't my weekend been challenging enough?

'Sally, is this really what you want?' Mum replied, her tone making it clear she was convinced the only correct answer to her rhetorical question was 'no'. 'I mean, the *internet* is no place for someone like you to go looking for a nice man.' It had struck me before that, in my mother's mouth, 'internet' sounded like an unspeakably dirty word.

To Mum, cyberspace was a dark, dangerous place filled with all manner of terrible things beginning with the letter 'P' – such as paedophiles and porn. 'And those *singles* sites,' she continued, 'aren't they really for people wanting something casual? Surely, for someone in your position, Sally, they –'

I cut her off in full flow: something about the way Mum had emphasized the word 'single' had made me see red. 'Correct me if I'm wrong here, Mum,' I snapped, 'but aren't I single too? Or are you trying to say that I'm not a normal single woman and it's inappropriate for me to try and behave like one?'

'I think you need to be extra careful, that's all,' Mum said defensively. 'You're *not* like those other singles, you're a single *mother*, and you need to put Lila's interests first.'

'I haven't taken a vow of celibacy, Mum,' I riposted furiously, 'and I happen to think I have every right to go out and meet a few men. What is it that *you* think I should be doing instead? Should I sit on my sofa crying over spilt milk and wait for a knight in shining armour to gallop on through my living room?'

'There's no need to get so cross, Sally,' Mum replied in a low, chastened voice. 'I've obviously called at a bad time.' I could picture Dad sitting in the living room, pretending he wasn't listening in through the serving hatch. While Mum had always made her feelings about my break-up abundantly clear, it was hard to know what Dad made of it all. He tended to let Mum do most of the talking, rolling his eyes at me discreetly if he thought Mum had gone too far.

'You know what, Mum, it *is* a bad time . . . I'm tired . . . Let's speak later in the week.'

When I'd pressed 'end call', I headed straight for the kettle, as if a cup of tea could cure all my ills. Mum's use of her pet phrase about 'putting Lila's interests first' had really sent my blood rocketing up to boiling point. She'd never come straight out and said so, but I knew my choosing to leave Nico was a prime example, in her book, of me *not* putting Lila's interests first. She'd been horrified at the idea of her own granddaughter coming from a 'broken home'.

In Mum's ideal world, I'd return to live with Nico one day, however unhappy it made me.

6

Over the next, uneventful, couple of weeks, the highlights mostly involved Anna.

The Thursday after we met, she came over to my place after work to share some takeaway, disappointed to find Lila already asleep when she arrived, as she was dying to meet her. As though there were some sort of tacit understanding between us, we kept steering the conversation away from Nico and Tom that evening. I think we'd both sensed that the 'Wronged Women's Club', to use the phrase Anna had coined, could all too easily turn into something negative; a forum for us to dwell on our grievances with our respective exes. I don't think either of us wanted our budding friendship to be limited to a series of embittered ex-bashing sessions.

The following weekend, Lila and I met Anna for brunch at Breakfast in America in the Marais, a favourite lunch spot of Lila's. The queue was mercifully short, and the three of us were soon wedged into a booth, hands on the Formica table, poring over our menus. Lila, who could be shy with other children but always seemed to take meeting new adults well within her stride, had conducted a concerted charm offensive from the moment she laid eyes on Anna. 'You talk like the Little Mermaid,' she said, picking up on Anna's American accent straight away. Anna frowned, less familiar with the Disney cartoon than I was.

'The Little Mermaid – she says "priddy" instead of "pretty",' Lila clarified. 'Mummy says she doesn't speak English, she speaks 'Merican!'

It took me a while to put my finger on why I felt abnormally self-conscious over lunch, but as I removed Lila's errant fingers from our self-service toaster for the tenth time, it suddenly hit me. I couldn't remember the last time I'd made a new adult friend who wasn't a parent. In Anna's presence, I was suddenly hyper-aware of the 'mother' persona I adopted around Lila, using a different voice when I addressed her and beginning far too many of my sentences with the word 'don't'. When I confessed this to Anna, she shook her head in disbelief. 'Whatever will you do when you meet a guy?' she said, her lips twitching with suppressed laughter. 'I mean, he'll have to meet Lila sometime and you'll have to find a way to lose that king-sized chip on your shoulder.'

Lila looked at both of us as though we'd taken leave of our senses. 'Mummy hasn't got any *frites* on her shoulder,' she said, provoking giggles all round. 'Anna's talking nonsense!'

As far as meeting guys was concerned, to say I'd got off to a slow start on Rendez-vous would have been something of an understatement. Clicking on '*Qui a parcouru mon profil?*', it seemed the only men who had given me the virtual once-over were either fresh-faced and barely legal, or situated so far at the other end of the spectrum they were nudging retirement. My most ardent elderly admirer, *papinou*, whose profile shot resembled the famous photograph of Albert Einstein with his white hair standing on end, seemed to want to be anything but a surrogate grandpa. Every day for a week he'd sent me a 'flash' – the

Rendez-vous equivalent of a wink, or perhaps a wolf whistle. The first time the notification message popped up, I'd burst out laughing. The French often misappropriated my mother tongue – the English language was seen to confer instant 'cool' – and I imagined the aim had been to evoke the idea of a '*coup de foudre*', a lightning flash, the most commonly used metaphor, in French, for love at first sight. But, to me, 'flash' conjured up only a deeply unattractive mental image of a lecherous old man wearing a mackintosh but little else and leaping out from behind a bush to show me his wares.

The tide began to turn when I uploaded a new profile photo. Kate had whipped out a camera towards the end of her party and somehow she'd managed to catch me unawares, grinning at one of Ryan's jokes, and the result, which she'd sent me by email, was the most flattering shot I'd seen of myself in a long time, and one that blew my serious-faced Tailor-Made ID shot out of the water. Once I'd added the new photo to my Rendez-vous page, my inbox began, slowly but surely, to fill up. The time had come to sift through my messages and sort the wheat from the chaff. And, perhaps, if someone inspired me enough, to take things to the next level.

I planned to devote my energies to this task one week-night after work, once I'd dispensed with Lila's evening ritual of bath, tooth brushing and bedtime stories and wolfed down my own dinner. Perched on a stool at the kitchen counter, I was reflecting on how ironic it was that I went to such lengths to feed Lila balanced meals, covering all the major food groups and bribing her to finish off her vegetables, and yet, as soon as I was alone, I'd tuck into a plate of buttered pasta. It was easy to develop such bad habits with no witnesses around to catch me in the act, red-cheeked, fork suspended in mid-air. My next interaction with the talking bathroom scales wasn't going to be much fun.

I was chasing a piece of pasta around the slippery plate when my mobile began to jiggle about on the countertop. 'Ryan!' I said, swallowing the last mouthful without chewing, surprised to hear his voice. 'To what do I owe this unexpected honour?'

'I'm in your neck of the woods,' Ryan half-yelled, a rumble of traffic and beeping horns almost drowning out his words. I'd realized in one of my lessons the previous week that the French language doesn't have a word for 'road rage'. The theory I'd advanced to account for this was that France's horn-happy motorists are assumed to be impatient and short-tempered by default. 'I thought I might pop in to see you, if you fancy some company,' he suggested. This was a most unusual but very welcome development. Outside of working hours, Ryan seldom left his beloved Marais.

'Fantastic timing! I was about to uncork a bottle of red . . .' I replied, taking the corkscrew out of the cutlery drawer with my free hand and reaching towards my wine rack to make my white lie come true. 'So, yes, by all means, come over. There's something you may be able to help me with, actually.'

Ryan tapped at the door ten minutes later, mindful of my instruction not to ring the bell, for fear of waking Lila. Dressed in jeans and a tweed jacket, he was brandishing a flimsy pale-blue carrier bag, the kind used by most of the city's corner shops. Through the translucent plastic I could make out another bottle of wine, a thoughtful last-minute purchase.

'Nice place you've got here,' he said, stepping inside and surveying the room. 'Compact and bijou, as they say, but you've made good use of the space.'

'God bless Ikea,' I said dryly, as I rounded the kitchen counter, a glass in each hand.

'I'm very partial to all things Swedish, as well you know,' Ryan said, his eyes twinkling. He was referring to Klaus, his sometime lover from Stockholm and the only boy-friend of Ryan's I'd ever met. They had split up at least three years earlier and, as far as I knew, Ryan had been single ever since.

'You also seemed to be rather partial to that banker at Kate's party the other week,' I said, arching an eyebrow. 'Did anything come of that? Was he even gay?'

'Your gaydar is terrible, isn't it?' said Ryan, grinning. 'Of course Eric is gay. Otherwise I'd never have bothered . . .'

'Is that why you were in my neighbourhood?' I asked him, fishing for more information. 'Does this Eric live nearby?'

'Well, you're lukewarm actually,' Ryan admitted. 'He doesn't live around here, but I was seeing him off from Gare du Nord . . . He had some meeting in London, and we had a drink before he caught the last Eurostar.'

'Good for you,' I said forcefully, taking a seat by his side on the sofa. 'It's about bloody time you met someone nice.' Ryan was blushing, I noticed. He'd got it bad. 'I was hoping,' I said, gesturing in the direction of my laptop, that you might be able to help me find some man candy of my own. I've had all these bites on Rendez-vous, and I need to decide if anyone deserves a reply . . . Fancy lending me a hand?'

'Deal,' Ryan replied, rubbing his hands together in anticipation. 'But only if we can do a bit of window shopping first. I know you've got the straight filter on, but a man can dream . . .'

Pulling the Rendez-vous page up on my browser, I navigated to 'Who's online now?' This generated a huge mosaic of faces without a shred of accompanying information – online man-hunting at its most superficial. It soon became apparent, though, that our tastes didn't overlap much. The men who caught my eye were all between thirty and forty, with a full head of hair and a five o'clock shadow. Ryan, on the other hand, seemed to prefer his men fresh-faced and clean-shaven, and appeared to have a soft spot for those men who were wearing a suit on their profile photo. We were unanimous, however, when it came to the subject of 'chin caterpillars'. An alarmingly high proportion of the men on Rendez-vous had a single strip of facial hair running from the centre of their bottom lip down to their chin. And as Ryan said with a shudder, 'That is *soooo* not a good look.'

'Right,' I said, setting down my glass and clicking decisively on the link leading to my inbox. 'Enough frivolity. Time for the serious stuff. Tell me what you think of this lot . . .'

An hour later, the first bottle of wine stood empty and Ryan reached for the corkscrew and bottle number two before I could protest. Four suitors had been disqualified on the grounds of their pseudonyms alone: exit 4Your-Pleasure, KissFactory, Anaconda and *Amour_à_3*. Nine others we'd consigned, without remorse, to the virtual dustbin, given they were between five and ten years outside my target range of thirty to forty. A further five we sidelined because, for one reason or another, I couldn't stand their choice of profile photo. What on earth possessed *Romain_du_*Marais to use a badly cropped picture in which a slice of ex-girlfriend's cheek was distinguishable, pressed against his? And did the thirty-eight-year-old man who'd posted a holiday snap of himself in his early twenties really think he could get away with it?

There were three emails from men whose profile bore no photograph at all. 'The thing about not posting a photo, regardless of whatever plausible-sounding excuses they make about not wanting to be recognized by people from the office,' said Ryan, his tone sceptical, 'is that one assumes they're either lying about being single or they're singularly unattractive.'

'I suppose I could request a photo,' I ventured uncertainly. 'There was one I quite liked the sound of – the graphic designer who lives near Père Lachaise . . .'

Ryan shook his head vigorously. 'Supposing he sends you a photo and it turns out he's the Elephant Man's cousin? Is it worth having to tie yourself in knots, wondering how to let him down gently?'

Only three of my original twenty-four suitors now remained. Ryan, who had enjoyed the elimination process immensely, appeared to be channelling a favourite TV-talent-show judge known for his ruthless approach. 'Okay,' he pronounced, 'here's my verdict. This first one is lame, lame, lame . . . It looks to me like he's copied and pasted the same email and sent it to twenty different women.'

'Plus it's full of spelling mistakes,' I added. 'And you know how much that kind of thing grates on me.' Ryan was already opening the next email and, from the look on his face, the prognosis wasn't good.

'Now, maybe I'm being too cynical here,' he said, cocking his head to one side, 'but I'd say this specimen has noticed your profession and is hoping for a few free English lessons . . .' I sighed. I'd entertained the same suspicion myself. And if the level of Goldorak's written English in the email he'd sent me was anything to go by, a date conducted in my mother tongue would sap my very will to live.

'Which leaves only one,' I said gloomily, emptying the remainder of the wine into our glasses. 'Number twenty-four. So, go on, tell me, what's wrong with him?' To my surprise, however, when I glanced back at Ryan, he was staring spellbound at the enlarged version of a rather attractive profile photo and didn't seem to have anything negative to say.

I leaned in closer for a better look. Number twenty-four – or Montreuil36, as he called himself – had piercing blue eyes, a square chin and a healthy head of thick dark hair, which was beginning to recede at his temples. Pictured sitting in a garden chair, one leg crossed over the other, a half-read book dangled from his left hand, and he gazed, not into the lens, but at something or someone else we couldn't see. 'Mmmm,' I murmured appreciatively. 'There *is* something likeable about him.'

'Of course, his address-plus-age pseudonym isn't very imaginative,' Ryan said, as though it was his duty to point out the negatives, 'but I'm all for erring on the side of boring after seeing monstrosities like *Homme_pour_toi* earlier.'

I was inclined to agree. Montreuil, a town on the other side of the *périphérique* ring road which divides those with a Paris postcode from those without, wasn't dissimilar to Belleville. Aside from where the guy lived, however, there wasn't a whole lot else to go on. Most of the fields in his profile had been left blank, or *'non renseigné'*, and his email merely stated that he liked the look of my profile and thought we should 'connect'. 'Quite the man of mystery, isn't he?' Ryan said thoughtfully, clicking from field to field but finding no further information. 'Worth investigating further though, I'd say . . .'

Heaving the laptop off the table and on to my knee, I clicked on 'reply'. I'd got as far as *'Cher* Montreuil36' when a pop-up window appeared with a loud *ping* that almost made me jump out of my skin, announcing that Montreuil36 wanted to invite me to chat. Whipping my fingertips off the keyboard as though I'd been burned, I looked askance at Ryan, unsure what to do. I'd have much preferred to compose an email at my leisure: chatting was so direct, and only marginally less painful than having to flirt with a complete stranger on the phone. And what Ryan didn't know – because I'd spared him the gory details – was that the very concept of 'instant messaging' was forever associated in my mind with Nico's tawdry exchanges with Mathilde.

'Come on, Sally, it would be rude not to,' Ryan said firmly, leaving me with no choice. My stomach fluttering with nerves, I took a deep breath, clicked on 'accept invitation' and reluctantly took the plunge.

I realized as I began to type that I was more than a little tipsy, but my suitor – real name Florent – didn't appear to notice anything amiss and even complimented me on my

French. Once we'd made our introductions, I began to take him to task about the paucity of information available on his profile, emboldened by the wine circulating in my bloodstream.

'You don't give an awful lot away,' I said playfully. 'Does that mean your closets are full of skeletons?'

Florent countered that he'd left the blanks on purpose. 'You can tell a lot about a woman by the questions she chooses to ask,' he explained. 'You have three questions. What would you like to know?'

'He's a clever one,' Ryan said approvingly, as I wrinkled my brow, wondering how best to proceed.

'Question one,' I typed, 'is why Rendez-vous?'

'Because good things don't always come to those who passively wait,' came his reply. I smiled, remembering having said something similar to my mother on the phone the other day. In spite of myself, I was starting to enjoy this.

'What do you do for a living?' was my next question. I argued, in brackets, that I knew this was a boring and conventional question. But there was no escaping it: how a person spends most of their waking life does tend to define them.

'I work for a film production company,' Florent replied. He didn't specify in what capacity, but I didn't want to use up my third question finding out. I liked the idea of meeting someone who worked in film, though.

'Final question,' I said aloud, drumming my fingers against the keys as I pondered and accidentally typing a long line of 'f's, which I hastily deleted.

'How about "What have you learned about me from questions one and two"?' Ryan volunteered.

'Ooh yes! I like that. I like that a lot.' I translated Ryan's suggestion into French and pressed the 'enter' key with a flourish.

'How about I tell you over a drink?' came Florent's rapid-fire reply.

I gave Ryan a jubilant look and he winked and gave me a thumbs-up. Maybe I'd been wrong about Rendez-vous. Not only had I found an intelligent life form out there, but an intelligent life form who was attractive, worked in an interesting field *and* wanted to meet me.

'I think, my dear, that this evening has been what I'd call an unqualified success,' Ryan said, looking pleased with himself. 'Do let me know if you require my filtering services in the future. It's been most enjoyable.'

7

'Lila, honey, we really have to get a move on,' I yelled through the open bedroom door, knocking back the remains of my coffee with a grimace. My head throbbed, as I'd known it would. I hadn't been able to stomach any breakfast. The previous night's wine glasses leered at me from the coffee table but there was no time for tidying up. I'd managed to hit 'off' instead of 'snooze' when the alarm clock sounded that morning, and Lila and I were now running disastrously late.

French infant schools impose a strict drop-off window in the mornings. At Lila's *maternelle*, doors opened at 8.20 a.m. and woe betide any straggler who rang the intercom to gain entry after they were closed and locked at eight-thirty. It had only happened to us once – Lila had tripped and landed in some runny green pigeon mess one morning and we'd had to dash home to change her trousers – but I still smarted at the memory of the reprimands that little episode had earned me from the headmistress, and her gatekeeper had shot me baleful looks for several days afterwards.

Luckily for me, Lila seemed to be in a cooperative mood. She'd already pulled on the clothes I'd hastily picked out and slung over the end of her bed and, when I hurried through into the living room, she was executing the complicated manoeuvre she'd learned at school to put on her coat unaided. Laying it on the parquet, lining side up and hood towards her toes, she crouched down low to hook her hands inside the sleeves. When she got to her feet and raised both arms in the air, the coat flipped over her head and settled on her back, as if by magic. The only thing Lila couldn't manage without my help was the zip. Dropping to my knees and fastening it right up to her chin, I took the opportunity to plant a kiss on her porcelain cheek, as cool as mine was feverish. 'Mummy,' Lila said, screwing up her nose in distaste and taking a step backwards, 'your mouth smells of not nice, today!'

'Charming,' I muttered, snatching up my satchel, praying there might be a stray pellet of chewing gum somewhere in its depths. 'Come on, Madam. I haven't got time to brush my teeth. We've got to dash . . .'

My watch read 8.32 when Lila and I scuttled across the threshold of the school, but the wall clock in the entrance hall appeared to be slow, so I escaped my second scolding of the term by the skin of my teeth. Darting across the empty *préau*, we hurried upstairs to the first floor, where the classrooms were located. Sandrine, Lila's teacher, a wiry fortysomething who seemed to run on inexhaustible reserves of nervous energy, was lying in wait in the classroom doorway. Something about her stance – which reminded me of a coiled spring – told me she was about to pounce. Sure enough, no sooner had I hung Lila's coat on its labelled peg than she accosted me. I sighed. So much for making a quick getaway.

'Madame Canet? *Ça vous irait de nous rejoindre pour la sortie, jeudi?*' I frowned, irritated at being addressed with Nico's name, as though I were his wife. As for the school trip,

I had an inkling I'd read something about it on one of the printed handouts Lila brought home, but I couldn't for the life of me remember where the children were going. At any rate, helping out was an impossibility. Thursdays were one of my most hectic days.

'*Je suis navrée*,' I apologized, '*mais c'est vraiment pas possible Je travaille toute la journée . . . Et, en fait . . .*' I was about to remind Lila's teacher of my correct surname, but my sentence died on my lips. Sandrine had already turned away, setting her sights on a dishevelled-looking father and son who'd somehow managed to arrive even later than Lila and me.

'*You're* not called Canet, are you, Mummy?' said Lila indignantly. '*La maîtresse* did get it wrong! Daddy and me are Canet, but you're a *Marshall*.'

'Never mind, sweet pea.' I planted a kiss on Lila's forehead and shooed her inside the classroom. 'I'll talk to Sandrine about it some other time. You have a lovely day at school, won't you? I'll see you tonight . . .'

Nonetheless, I was fuming as I half walked, half jogged down to the bottom of rue de Belleville and veered left into the newspaper kiosk to grab my copy of *Libé*. Being called 'Mrs Canet' was tantamount to a slap in the face. Hadn't I made a point of taking Sandrine to one side at the beginning of the school year and apprising her of the fact that Nico and I were separated? And while I could forgive her for not having memorized my unfamiliar, English surname – after all, she had twenty-five children in her class – using Nico's by default was a clumsy mistake to make. Less than half the babies born in France these days have married parents and, even when they do, many married women choose to retain their maiden names. Wasn't it more prudent, under the circumstances, for teachers like Sandrine to simply call every mother '*Madame*', rather than to risk causing offence?

As I hurtled down the concrete steps into the bowels of Belleville station, my watch read 8.49. I was going to need unusually clement métro conditions to get me to my first appointment on time. Thankfully, as I reached the platform, a train was pulling into the station. Darting inside, I perched on one of the fold-down *strapontin* seats by the doorway and opened my newspaper. The day had got off to a shaky start but, with any luck, there would be a new *Transports amoureux* for me to translate. Anything to prevent me from checking my watch every thirty seconds as the train clanked and rattled its way through the tunnels.

'*Métro ligne 8, Ledru-Rollin/Madeleine, mardi 15 septembre vers 19h00,*' I read. '*Regards échangés et connivence immédiate. Vous: cheveux blonds et rire exquis. Moi: veste en cuir et cœur conquis.*'

The French sounded so graceful and concise, but I knew from experience that, once I transposed the words into English, any poetry would be lost. My best effort went something like this: 'Glances exchanged, immediate complicity. You: blonde hair, exquisite laugh. Me: leather jacket and conquered heart.' I'd managed to convey the meaning accurately enough, but, just as I'd thought, the result not only no longer rhymed but read more like a stilted telegram than a love poem.

I'd once had a discussion with Kate – who naturally knew of my fondness for the *Transports amoureux* – about the kind of man we thought might pen such a message.

'Definitely not Yves,' she'd said with a smile and a shrug. 'He's much more at home with numbers in spreadsheets than he is with words . . .'

'Nico can only write in long-winded legal jargon,' I'd retorted. 'So that rules him out too.' We'd come to the conclusion that, of all the men we knew, we couldn't imagine any of them in the role of métro Romeo. Kate's theory was that all the ads were sent in by the same person, a single sensitive soul who rode the métro and fantasized about strangers all day long.

When I'd pooh-poohed that idea, pointing out that the targets were of both sexes, even if the majority did seem to be written by men, she'd raised an eyebrow. 'I know you've led a sheltered life, Sal,' she joked. 'But have you never heard the expression "swings both ways"?'

The memory of that discussion made me smile, momentarily, but lacked the force to sweep aside my hangover and the black clouds which had been gathering ever since I'd opened my eyes that morning. To add insult to injury, Tuesday was my least favourite teaching day. In a stuffy, windowless room, which was little more than a cupboard, I taught three ninety-minute lessons one after the other. The client – a French recruitment consultancy – was in dire need of an office makeover. The rooms where they met with clients were presentable enough, but the day I'd first stepped behind the scenes, I'd been shocked by how cramped their offices were. My teaching room was separated from the photocopying room by only a thin, plasterboard partition and, as a result, lessons were set to the regular, mechanical sound of sheaves of paper being sucked through the copier, punctuated by the occasional frustrated opening and slamming of drawers whenever some unlucky soul fell foul of a paper jam.

My empty stomach began its persistent grumbling at eleven, but I was out of luck: my lunch break wasn't scheduled for another two and a half hours. Meanwhile, I kept catching myself staring blankly at the whiteboard in the corner of the room with its half-erased scribblings – the images forming upside down on my retina never quite making it as far as my fogged-up brain – and I had to haul myself forcibly back to the task in hand. I'd have to avoid wine on weeknights in future. I wasn't sure which was to blame, slipping the wrong side of thirty or becoming a mother, but my body didn't seem able to recover from a few glasses of red the way it used to.

As for Florent, I'd studiously avoided thinking about him all morning, knowing full well that it wasn't a good idea to dwell on how our exchange had come to an unexpectedly sticky end when I was feeling so fragile. When my third student bent her head over a reading comprehension about the town of Florence, however, I found I could hold the memory at bay no longer.

To Florent's 'How about I tell you over a drink?' I'd replied with a flippant 'Why not?' It was only then that the practical implications of what I was doing began to hit home. This coming weekend I'd be with Lila. My next free evening, as things currently stood, wouldn't be for another ten days. There was a girl I occasionally called in to babysit, but I had no idea if and when she'd be free. And, even if she could help me out, was I willing to pay eight euros an hour for the privilege of going on a – more or less blind – date?

'Saturday night?' Florent suggested. I looked at Ryan and groaned.

'I'd love to,' I typed, 'but there's the small matter of finding a babysitter . . .'

There was an ominously long pause. 'Ah, okay . . . I see,' Florent replied. 'I hadn't realized you had a child.'

'So much for saying he liked the look of my profile,' I wailed, curling my hands into fists. 'He never even bothered to read it.' I was busy casting around for a suitably sarcastic retort when I realized, with a sickening jolt, that Florent was no longer online. He'd fled the chat room, without so much as a word of farewell. 'Well,' I said flatly, slumping back into the sofa, 'it would seem you've just witnessed my very first online rejection.'

'Look at it this way, sweetie,' Ryan said gently, slipping an arm around my shoulders and giving my arm a consolatory squeeze. 'Better to work out he's a loser today than to waste precious time meeting the guy . . . Don't worry, not everyone out there will be like Florent, Sally.'

'They'd better not be,' I said darkly. 'Otherwise I'm going to regret the day I signed up for a twelve-month membership . . .'

I'd learned two things about Rendez-vous that night. The first was that there was no guarantee prospective suitors would have even bothered to read the profile I'd so painstakingly created. The second was that normal rules of etiquette didn't seem to apply in the virtual-dating arena. Not only had Florent changed his mind about wanting to meet me, mid-conversation, but he'd felt he owed me no explanation. Out of common courtesy, couldn't he have at least said 'Thanks but no thanks', or 'Goodbye and good luck' instead of vanishing into thin air?

What I found most depressing, though, was that my initial fears about joining Rendez-vous hadn't been so wide of the mark. Some people really would dismiss me outright as dating material when they noticed I was a mother. Bracing myself for this eventuality hadn't made it any easier to stomach. I'd held my tears in check until Ryan left, but as soon as the door had closed behind him, I'd taken the tissue box to bed and held a pity party for one.

When the morning's interminable lessons came to an end at last, I bought a Pomme de Pain sandwich to take away and began tucking into it on the platform of St Augustin métro station, en route to the management consultancy where my two afternoon lessons would take place. Fellow travellers gave me disapproving glances as I dabbed at the corner of my mouth with my serviette, removing the excess mayonnaise which was seeping out of my baguette. Despite the arrival of an army of gleaming vending machines on underground platforms a few years earlier, I hardly ever spotted French people eating on the move. It seemed to be an activity they frowned upon. But my time-table was so tight I often had no alternative but to weather their withering stares and munch heroically on. I could hardly go hungry.

I was fiddling with the controls for the air conditioning, trying to coax the temperature of my teaching room a lit-tle higher, when Robert Cazenove breezed in for his two o'clock lesson. Tall and broad-shouldered, Robert was wearing a slim-fitting grey suit I'd admired before, and a salmon-pink shirt. Robert oozed self-confidence – he was a product of one of the Parisian *grandes écoles*, which groom their students to join the ranks of France's elite – but, to my constant frustration, his level of spoken English never seemed to improve. I could repeat until I was blue in the face that he should never reply to 'How's your team?' with 'They're very fine' or 'How's your new assistant doing?' with 'She's going well', but it never seemed to make a blind bit of difference.

If Robert noticed I was a little out of sorts and more short-tempered than usual, he certainly didn't show it. He remained as calm and unruffled as ever, and I was grateful for that. I was feeling so brittle today that even a solicitous glance might have cracked my thin veneer.

When his lesson time was up and he stood to leave, I caught myself staring at the band of pale skin on the ring finger of Robert's left hand. I wasn't sure I'd ever noticed his wedding ring when it was there – I couldn't have said, for example, whether it was gold or platinum – but its absence, today, was striking. Ever since I'd left Nico it was as though I'd been tuned into a new frequency, hyper-aware of the evidence of other people's break-ups and divorces all around me.

Once he'd left I crossed the room to the sideboard, where a metal Thermos of filter coffee stood on a tray alongside three bone china cups and saucers decorated with the company logo. Uncapping the flask, I'd begun wrestling with the screw-top inside when my mobile began to vibrate in the depths of my satchel. If the caller was Nico, I resolved not to pick up. But it was Kate, and she only ever called during teaching hours if it was an emergency.

'Kate?' I tried to keep my voice brisk and professional. 'My two o'clock has left, and my three-thirty, Barbara, isn't here yet. What's up?'

'Sal, listen, Barbara cancelled this week's lesson – she's out of town on business – and I'm afraid I completely forgot to warn you. I'm so sorry.' Kate sounded flustered and contrite. She knew how much I needed every centime of my teaching income. Last-minute cancellations meant docked wages, and docked wages meant I'd be faced with a '*fin de mois difficile*', when next month's salary came up short. 'Yves is away,' Kate added, 'and I'm preparing a couple of pitches to new clients. It's no excuse, I know, but Barbara completely slipped my mind . . .'

This was most unlike Kate. She timetabled our lessons with military precision and it was the first time in five years that she'd forgotten to warn me about a no-show in advance. But there was no sense in making her feel worse than she did already. 'Not to worry, Kate,' I replied. 'To be honest, I've been feeling a bit under the weather today anyway, and it'll do me good to get home early.' Cradling my phone between my ear and my right shoulder, I began sliding my folders and textbooks into my satchel, eager to make my exit.

'Nothing serious, I hope?' Kate's voice betrayed only friendly concern for my health, but I knew her well enough to know her mind would be racing ahead, debating how best to cover the rest of the week's shifts if I called in sick.

'Nothing a good night's sleep won't sort out,' I re-assured her, unwilling to admit that I was simply hungover and feeling sorry for myself. There was a pause, and I could have sworn I heard an unfamiliar baritone voice in the background. 'Oh, goodness. Are you out at a pitch meeting now?' I said, wondering if she'd interrupted something important to speak to me. 'You should have told me. I'll leave you to it . . .'

'No, no, nothing like that,' Kate said quickly. 'I'm elbow deep in Tailor-Made admin at home, as usual, and I've got the radio on in the background to keep me company. But you're probably right; I ought to get back to work . . .'

As the lift hurtled downwards, I savoured my imminent freedom. It had been a trying day but, perverse as it might sound, it had done me the power of good to be reminded just then that even Kate wasn't perfect all the time.

8

I was sifting through a box of cereal – picking out a few extra chocolate-coated flakes to make their wholewheat counterparts more palatable to Lila – when the phone rang on Saturday morning. Lila, who was standing by my side, her hand darting out from time to time to intercept a particularly large chocolate flake before it hit her cereal bowl, got there first. 'It's *Tante* Sophie,' she said, passing me the handset. 'She wants to talk to you, Mummy.'

Several weeks had passed since Nico had mentioned Sophie would be getting in touch and, although I'd been apprehensive about her impending call at first, when she didn't manifest herself, our exchange had slipped my mind. 'Sophie?' I leaned forward to rest my elbows on the countertop. '*Ça va?*' I said cautiously. '*Ça fait super longtemps!*'

'As I said to Nico, I didn't want to lose sight of you,' Sophie replied. She'd spent a couple of years living in London with an English boyfriend when she was in her twenties and had an impeccable English accent, although the occasional French turn of phrase – like 'lose sight of' instead of 'lose touch with' in this instance – gave the game away. 'I thought maybe we could go in the park with the children one day,' she continued. 'That big playground at La Villette, perhaps. I would drive, and pick you up.'

'I'm sure Lila would love to see Lucas.' I tried to picture Sophie and me trying to make small talk while our children raced yelping around the playground. Usually I hated trying to catch up with fellow parents in that kind of context. I was incapable of conducting anything resembling a conversation while simultaneously trying to keep an eye on Lila, head spinning with the collective shrieks of a hundred children. Kate and I had set aside 'grown-up time' for our fortnightly lunches for that very reason, after a number of frustrating playdates at the Parc Monceau, peppered with unfinished sentences. In this instance, however, I suspected our children might be a welcome distraction. I'd only ever seen Sophie at Canet family gatherings in the past, never for a tête-à-tête.

'I could pick you up in an hour,' Sophie suggested, catching me off my guard, 'that is, if you're not doing anything special today?' I had to hand it to her – she was crafty, obtaining my agreement in principle and then presenting me with a *fait accompli*, like that. I didn't have sufficient wits about me to invent an alibi at nine in the morning, and a glance out of the window revealed pale-grey October skies, but no sign of rain.

'Okay, we'll see you then,' I replied, trying not to sound as though I'd been backed into a corner.

'Marvellous,' said Sophie. 'I'm looking forward to it.'

A little over an hour later, Sophie, teeth white against the remnants of her deep summer tan, sprang out of her black Clio and raced over to give Lila a fierce hug and me a peck on both cheeks. After breakfast, I'd dressed both myself and Lila in haste and we'd raced down to the corner *boulangerie* for provisions. The least I could do if Sophie was ferrying us back and forth was provide some sort of late-morning snack. On our way back, just as we'd reached our front door, I'd heard the enthusiastic tooting of a horn. 'Look!' Lila exclaimed. 'There she is: my *Tata* Sophie!'

Once Lila was strapped in next to Lucas in the back, she flashed her cousin a delighted smile. I might not have seen Sophie since Christmas, but Lila saw plenty of Lucas when she spent school holidays with her grandparents. Stowing my bag of provisions by my feet, I pulled the passenger door closed rather more enthusiastically than I'd intended, rocking the whole car. Inside, it was as immaculate as I remembered but, despite the air-freshener 'tree' hanging from the mirror, I could still discern a background odour of stale cigarettes. It had always amazed me that Dr Sophie, *médecin généraliste*, had never managed to kick the habit. She'd weaned herself off her Lucky Strikes with the help of nicotine patches while pregnant with Lucas but, as soon as he was born, she was back on the balcony of her apartment in the twelfth arrondissement, overlooking the cour Saint Emillion, puffing away. I reckoned she was terrified of putting on weight if she gave up, and she was certainly slim now. Covertly comparing my jean-clad thigh to hers was a depressing exercise.

Once I'd enquired after Sophie's husband Jean-Luc – also a doctor – and the doctor's surgery they'd set up together, I swivelled in my seat and began chatting to Lucas, leaving her free to concentrate all her attention on the road. There was no doubt Lucas took after his mother, with his glossy dark hair and hazel eyes, and the resemblance between Lila and her only cousin had always been striking. Sophie must have briefed Lucas beforehand, because he didn't seem the slightest bit puzzled that Lila and I no longer lived in the same street as before. Nor did he ask why *Tonton* Nico wasn't accompanying us to the park.

I'd always found that, with children Lila and Lucas's age, it was easy enough to win them over by showing an interest in their toys or playing alongside them, but abstract questions such as 'Do you enjoy school?' or 'What have you been up to recently?' tended to elicit one-syllable responses or blank looks. Ask Lila what she'd had for lunch at school on any given day and most of the time she could be relied upon to execute a perfect Gallic shrug. Her memory didn't seem to be fully functional yet, even if, perversely, a *gros mot* she'd heard six months earlier could be retrieved within seconds. In the absence of props, my conversation with Lucas soon ran dry. There was a silence, and I turned back to gaze out of my window, putting a hand up to fiddle self-consciously with my hair.

'You are still working with this friend – how is she called? – Kate?' Sophie enquired as we cruised along rue Manin, parallel to the Buttes Chaumont park railings. I saw a flash of white as we passed the main gates opposite the town hall. A white stretch-limousine was parked in the lay-by – one of two that were a permanent feature around Belleville – and a dozen-strong Chinese wedding party was picking its way across the lawn to take up a position in front of the artificial lake, photographer in tow.

'Yes, that's right. Same old same old,' I replied. 'I'm working a few extra hours, so Lila takes her *goûter* at school. Our new routine seems to work well enough . . .' I let my sentence tail off, but my meaning – I was managing fine *without Nico* – was abundantly clear. Sophie shot me a sidelong glance, which I found hard to decipher. I sensed she wanted to say something, but was biting her tongue, mindful of the children.

At the end of avenue Jean Jaurès nearest the *périphérique*, Sophie pulled up level with the yellow 'M' of Porte de Pantin métro and dropped the three of us off, speeding away to look for a place to park. We started walking – Lila on my right, Lucas on my left – in the direction of the Jardin des Dunes et des Vents. Sliced neatly in two by the Canal de l'Ourcq, Parc de la Villette was a vast space containing a science museum, a 360-degree cinema in a dome, a concert venue and countless other attractions. I was unfamiliar with huge swathes of the park, but the main children's play area, towards which we headed, I knew well enough. I had to keep walking with the Grande Halle to my right – a glass and metal building which once housed the city's largest abattoir – and I couldn't go wrong.

By the time Sophie joined us, I was sitting cross-legged on a bench watching the children spin round and round in an oversized hamster wheel, praying Lila's breakfast cereal wasn't about to make an unscheduled comeback. Watching Lila and Lucas together, as similar as siblings, was a bittersweet experience. I'd always imagined Nico and I would give Lila a baby brother or sister, and we'd even discussed it a few months before we separated. The chances of that had all but evaporated. One day Lila might have a half-brother or -sister, at best.

'I had a job getting them into the under-fives enclosure,' I said, as Sophie perched on the bench beside me, patting her pockets for her matches and lighting up a cigarette. 'Lucas was rather taken with those bouncy castle "dunes" at the other side, but I said we'd come here first and he could ask you if he's allowed later.'

'Too many *grands* over there,' Sophie said, shaking her head. She took a deep drag from her cigarette. 'Nico misses you, you know,' she said, catching me off my guard for the second time that day. 'What he did was wrong, but I wish you didn't have to throw away the baby with the water from the bath.'

'With the bathwater,' I murmured automatically, eyes locked on Lila, who had managed to disembark from the hamster wheel and had now set her sights on the neighbouring climbing frame. I shifted my position, so I could keep her within my line of vision while we talked. 'Sophie,' I said gently, 'it's good to see you, and I'm glad you got in touch, but there's no point in us having this conversation . . .' I paused, selecting my words with care. 'One "indiscretion" – as you French call it – I might have been able to cope with. Who knows? But the thing with Mathilde went on for ages. Almost a year. If Nicolas could deceive me for so long, that was a symptom that something had gone very wrong with our relationship.' I picked absent-mindedly at the loose threads around the ankles of my frayed jeans as I talked, my eyes still following Lila's movements.

'I don't agree,' Sophie said earnestly. 'I don't think it has to mean there was something wrong between you and him. People have affairs – Mitterrand even had his parallel family – but I honestly don't think Nico loved you any less.'

'Well, even if that were true, maybe he's made it impossible for *me* to love *him*,' I replied evenly. 'Listen, Sophie, maybe I seem naïve and idealistic to you, but I've made my decision, and I'm sticking by it.' I rested my feet on the bench, wrapping my arms around my shins and resting my chin on my knee. 'And, let's not forget,' I added, taking sanctuary in sarcasm, 'the man you claim is missing me so much is now busy bedding his *stagiaire*.'

Sophie fell silent for a moment, frowning as she stubbed out her cigarette on the side of the bench and let it fall to the floor. 'You mean this Albane girl?' she said with a sigh. 'You know, I feel only pity for her. I think Nico is having – how we say – "hygienic" sex. If Albane thinks it is more than that, she is veiling her face.'

I remembered happening across the phrase '*sexe hygiénique*' once before, flicking through a copy of *Psychologies* magazine in a dentist's waiting room. Another 'false friend', '*hygiénique*' had little to do with cleanliness in this context. It referred to a sex act divorced from any emotional context; sex as pure physical release. But Nico had been sleeping with Albane on and off for months now, and I was loath to believe their relationship hadn't developed into something more than the regular scratching of an itch. 'Whatever it is, I don't want him back,' I said evenly, 'so it's a moot point.' I was pretty sure Sophie wouldn't know what a 'moot point' was, but I didn't have chance to clarify, because Lila and Lucas chose that moment to come bounding over. They were hungry, and Lila had evidently had a flashback to our pit stop at the baker's that morning.

'Mummy, are the *pains aux raisins* in your bag for now, or for later?' she asked in a sly voice.

'For now, my love, if you're hungry.' I offered the open bag first to the children, then to Sophie, who, although she looked tempted for a moment, held herself in check. I was grateful for this respite from our conversation – forcibly cut short while the children munched in silence – because I suspected I knew what Sophie would ask next, once Lila and Lucas had drifted out of earshot. What about me? Was I seeing anyone? Whatever I replied, I felt sure Nico would be informed of my response before the day was out.

Taking a *viennoiserie* from the bag to buy myself some extra time, I resolved to remain coy. I would make no mention of joining Rendez-vous to Sophie. Not under any circumstances.

'It would be a terrible idea for me to have a one-on-one with Tom's sister,' said Anna, rolling her eyes, when I'd finished recounting the choicest morsels of my conversation with Sophie.

'Don't get me wrong, I like Sophie a lot,' I explained. 'But breaking up with Nico was bad enough, and having to justify why I left him to members of his family feels a little beyond the call of duty . . .'

Anna and I were at a party in an apartment in the Marais, sipping surprisingly good margaritas from clear plastic goblets. An American couple, vague acquaintances of Anna's, were hosting their annual burrito and margarita party and she'd managed to persuade me to come, despite my reservations about tagging along where I wasn't invited. The irony – that my babysitter was available and I would have been free to go on a date with Florent, had he not been so Mummy-phobic – had not been lost on me.

Our hosts' apartment was similar to the one I used to share with Nico; the apartment where he still lived now.

The living room had once been formed of two separate square rooms: the interrupted pattern on the parquet floor gave that away. A wrought-iron balcony ran the full length of the street side of the building and, as the evening was mild for mid-October, the double doors leading outside had been left ajar. Next door to the living room was the poky space in which we now stood: a typically Parisian apology for a kitchen. There wasn't room to swing a kitten, and it was difficult to imagine anyone doing much more than brewing coffee in such a cramped space.

'I suppose I should be grateful that Sophie was upfront with me,' I replied. 'I mean, she didn't even try to conceal her agenda . . . If it was *her* agenda.' I'd spent much of that afternoon wondering whether Nico had sent his sister on some sort of fact-finding mission. It didn't seem like something he would do, but how well did I really know him? I was about to solicit Anna for her opinion, but her gaze had strayed towards the door. The latest arrival, a lone man in a corduroy jacket and small, wire-rimmed glasses had wandered into the kitchen in search of a drink. He'd found the punch bowl of margaritas, and now cursed under his breath as a thick slice of lime plopped from the ladle into his plastic goblet, spattering droplets across his white shirt.

Anna and I had been meeting up regularly, but this was the first time since we'd met at Kate's that we'd been to a social gathering together. Ever since we'd arrived, I'd found myself torn between what I instinctively wanted to do, which was to bend Anna's ear, and what I felt I *should* be doing: making more of an effort to mingle and meet new people, men in particular.

Not that we'd been taking refuge in the kitchen all evening. We'd made polite conversation with our hosts: Paul, a portly, red-faced journalist who worked for the *Herald Tribune* and looked like he enjoyed the good things in life, to the detriment of his health, and his wife, Philippa, an ageing hippy dressed in a long, flowing dress and a chunky jade necklace. We'd also been introduced to a shy French couple, Sylvie and Jean-Luc, from the apartment next door, who had probably been invited out of courtesy and seemed rather ill at ease. Then there was Miles, a photographer friend of Paul's with a weather-worn face who'd spent much of his career working in war zones. Everyone seemed nice enough, but I'd spent the last couple of hours on the edge of other people's conversations, listening in, nodding and smiling, and never finding much to contribute. Looking around me, I was depressed to note there wasn't a single man in the room who sparked my interest. So when Anna suggested we head into the kitchen for refills, I'd jumped at the chance to take a breather and have a proper conversation with my friend.

When the man in the corduroy jacket had finished dabbing ineffectually at the margarita stains on his shirt, he latched on to Anna, introducing himself as Guy, which in French was pronounced '*ghee*', like the Indian butter. Anna began fielding the usual stock questions about what she did for a living and how long she'd been in Paris, all in her unashamedly broken French, while I sipped my drink, willing Guy to leave us in peace. But when he was joined a few minutes later by another, more attractive, new arrival whom he introduced as his friend Fabien, things took a turn for the better. Fabien, who must have thought he'd be trespassing on Guy's territory if he struck up a conversation with Anna, turned towards me instead.

Tall and slim, with unkempt dark hair and green eyes, Fabien was dressed in skinny jeans and a once-black shirt which had faded to slate grey. He told me he worked for a buzz marketing agency, and as I wasn't positive I knew what this entailed, I nodded and smiled, making a mental note to Google the term later. But Fabien was soon complimenting me on the fluency of my French and I began to relax and enjoy myself. I noticed little details as we talked: the neatness of his short fingernails, the way his eyebrows almost joined together in the middle, his old-school Casio digital watch. It was puzzling: here was a genuine-seeming, rather handsome man who hung attentively on my every word. So what was wrong with me? I wondered. Why wasn't my pulse racing? Why wasn't I feeling the stirrings of physical attraction? Was some vital part of me numb, or had it ceased to function?

Fabien suggested a trip to the balcony so he could roll a cigarette, and I acquiesced, shooting Anna a questioning glance as we slipped away. I was unable to determine whether she was enjoying herself or finding Guy heavy going, as she simply gave me an enigmatic smile and continued her conversation. Once outside, Fabien set down his drink and began rolling a joint on a small metal table. When he lit up and offered me a drag, I declined. 'I've got to keep my wits about me,' I said, not wanting him to think I disapproved. 'I'll have to face the babysitter soon, and I'll be up early in the morning . . .'

'You've got a little one?' Fabien sounded surprised, but not deterred.

'Yes, I have a daughter. Lila. She's four.' I took a sip of my margarita. 'I left her dad earlier this year.' I felt my shoulders tense as I braced myself for the volley of tricky questions I thought must surely follow.

'My brother's got a three-year-old son,' Fabien replied, proving my instincts wrong. 'It's a wonderful age.' He smiled for a second, then took a long drag on his joint. 'I wish I saw more of him,' he added, his voice wistful. 'He changes so fast. But my brother and his wife live in Antibes, and I don't get down there as often as I should . . .'

Our forearms resting on the railings, Fabien and I took root on the balcony, staring out over the high stone wall opposite into the gardens of the Picasso museum. I forgot to wonder how Anna was getting on back inside, caught up in the easy ebb and flow of our conversation. We'd veered on to the subject of being single in Paris – I'd invented a fictional friend who'd signed up to Rendez-vous, interested to see what Fabien thought of online dating – when Anna appeared at my elbow. 'What time did you say your babysitter needed you home?' She glanced at her watch. 'Because it's after one, and I thought . . .'

'After one? Oh shit! How on earth . . .? She's going to be furious!' I turned back to Fabien, switching back into French. 'It was lovely to meet you, but I'm sorry, I'm going to have to dash off . . .' Backing off the balcony and into the living room, I retrieved my bag and coat from the cupboard in the hallway and clattered down the stairs, hoping Anna would explain the reason for my sudden, panicked departure to our hosts.

When I arrived at street level, I glanced up. Fabien was still at the second-floor window, staring out across the park, tendrils of smoke rising from another joint in his hand. There was a figure by his side, and it wasn't until she threw her head back and let out a distinctive peal of laughter that I realized who it was. Then I saw Anna reach across and take hold of Fabien's joint. As she put it to her lips, I felt a sudden surge of jealousy.

This is how it's always going to be, I thought to myself, waving frantically to flag down an approaching taxi. I'm a single woman, like Anna, but I don't have anywhere near the same freedom. I'll have to get used to leaving parties before they get going. I'll have to resign myself to missing opportunities left, right and centre. This is the reality of the life I signed up for when I left Nico and decided to go it alone with Lila.

Admittedly, there had been no irresistible pull of attraction between Fabien and me, but supposing things had been different? By the time he left the party, several hours later, his memory of chatting to me would be hazy to non-existent. Some other girl would have superimposed herself on his mind and left with his phone number or, worse still, on his arm.

Opening the taxi door and sliding reluctantly on to the back seat, I realized I'd have to steel myself for the eventuality that one day, 'some other girl' might mean Anna.

9

After the party I returned to Rendez-vous with a renewed sense of purpose. If I threw my energies into meeting men for one-on-one dates as opposed to at parties, I reasoned, there would be a lesser likelihood of someone I liked being poached the moment my back was turned. Anna had left neither with Fabien, nor his phone number – or so she told me – but that, I decided, was beside the point. I hadn't enjoyed feeling as though we were in competition for the slim pickings available that night, and suspected it was only a matter of time before we ended up pursuing the same man, our friendship curdling as a result.

But hunting alone on Rendez-vous by no means eliminated the threat of competition. I couldn't see the thousands of *Parisiennes* I was pitting myself against, but it was as though they hovered tauntingly just outside the periphery of my vision. I'd developed a sixth sense for when a man was trying to charm several girls simultaneously on Rendez-vous chat, for example. Lengthening gaps between a man's responses were a dead giveaway, because, let's face it, no one has to mull over their answer to a straightforward question such as 'Which neighbourhood do you live in?' Occasionally, someone I'd been chatting to for several minutes would clam up, without warning, as though they'd been struck dumb. 'Did a better option present itself,' I typed crossly, when a science-fiction fiend called neuromancer lost his tongue for the second time in the space of a single conversation, 'or should I dial 15 for emergency services?'

Fortunately, not everyone had such a gaping void where their manners should have been. There were those who took the trouble to provide an alibi when their attention wandered. '5 min – *téléphone*,' I came to recognize as shorthand for 'Someone foxier has signed in, I'll come back to you if she's not interested.' 'Have to sign out now – my flatmate has walked in,' I translated as 'the girlfriend/ wife's home.' I dropped anyone who used that last line on me like a hot potato. It was all too easy to picture Nico chatting to Mathilde on MSN from home and typing something similar when I walked into the room.

After sifting through that first batch of emails with Ryan's help, then a second, equally dispiriting batch on my own, I decided the demure, passive approach – waiting for emails from ill-suited suitors to thud on to my virtual doormat – wasn't paying dividends. Instead, I bit the bullet and took matters into my own hands, sending a 'flash' here, an email there. And much as I disliked the idea of exploring multiple avenues simultaneously, I soon came to realize keeping several plates spinning was the only sensible thing to do.

Rendez-vous came with no guarantees. I could invest an hour of my precious time chatting with *beau_ténébreux*, only to find he'd dropped off the face of the earth the next day. Had he met someone he liked, or let his subscription lapse? I'd probably never know. Similarly, there was nothing to prevent *clair2lune* from standing me up, or sending an apologetic text message minutes before we were due to meet, calling everything off. Online dating reminded me of the HBO crime series I'd spent so many hours watching. Every available lead had to be examined, and many trails would, no doubt, go cold. But one day my perseverance would pay off. That was the way these things worked.

A lazy Saturday morning in late October found me surfing Rendez-vous in my pyjamas, as raindrops pitter-pattered against the living-room window. I'd stuck half a dozen Post-it notes around the edges of the screen: *penses-bêtes*, each one bearing a pseudonym, along with a few salient, memory-jogging details so I could remember who was who among the handful of members I was currently targeting. Nico's mother, Catherine, would be collecting Lila that afternoon to take her to their house in Chantilly for the first half of the ten-day Toussaint school holiday, and my mission was to pepper the coming Lila-free week with after-work rendezvous.

Lila, who had been engrossed in the construction of an elaborate pink and white Lego castle since breakfast time, hopped up on to the sofa to nestle in the crook of my arm, curious to see what was monopolizing my attention. When the screen darkened for a moment, shifting down a gear into power-save mode, her hand shot out, quick as lightning, to stroke the mouse pad and restore the brightness. I chuckled. Ryan had once told me his cat Clyde did exactly the same thing.

'Is it a shop, Mummy?' Lila asked, staring at the Rendezvous homepage. 'Like the Ooshop, where you buy things for our dinner?' I smiled and shook my head. I could appreciate why Rendez-vous reminded her of the online supermarket: the fonts were identical, the colour schemes similar. The only real difference: in place of pack shots of cereal there were headshots of men.

'No, darling, it's not a shop.' I was reluctant to elaborate further, anxious to minimize the chances of her repeating something compromising to Nico. 'It's a place where Mummy can talk to people with her computer.' If only things were that simple. If only I could select a man, pop him into my virtual shopping basket, then press 'Proceed to checkout'. Mind you, some sort of 'Try before you buy' or 'Satisfaction or your money back' guarantee would be necessary. You couldn't trust Rendez-vous packaging to be entirely accurate about its contents, as I'd already learned to my cost.

My first proper date had taken place the previous weekend. After a few lengthy chat conversations with an English accountant, pseudonym *Rosbif*, I'd decided that, if I was going to meet someone in the flesh, at last, he'd be good for a trial run. Chatting in my mother tongue had made the first moves refreshingly easy, lulling me into a false sense of security, perhaps. There had been none of the agonizing over genders and verb conjugations which tended to slow me down when typing my retorts in French. Nor did I have to wince at his horrendous grammar or wait an eternity for him to riposte, as I often did with those Frenchmen who insisted on practising their faltering English. So when *Rosbif* – real name Marcus – suggested meeting for a Saturday-afternoon drink in an English bar in the Marais, I accepted. I had fond memories of Stolly's, his suggested venue, off rue Saint Antoine. I'd spent many a night there with Kate back in our El Paso days.

Alighting from the métro at Hôtel de Ville, I caught sight of my nervous reflection in the windows of the shops I passed as I walked briskly towards my destination. I'd kept things simple: jeans, trainers, a favourite T-shirt with a bow detail on the neckline, a lightweight coat. It was Saturday afternoon and I wanted to look casual, as though I'd taken a break from a shopping trip to meet Marcus for an hour. My heart drummed in my chest nonetheless, and my breaths came short and shallow. This was a big deal. I'd been a member of Rendez-vous for a little over a month now, and Marcus – although I hadn't told him as much – was about to be my first offline contact.

It was only when I pushed open the door and stepped inside the bar that I realized somewhere so small – and so quiet during the day – wasn't going to be the most discreet place to pop my blind-date cherry. It was daunting enough, the prospect of having to make small talk with a complete stranger, let alone having to do so with half the bar listening in.

Marcus, who'd been pictured looking tanned and rugged against an Alpine background on his profile, had put on some weight since the photo was taken, and his natural skin tone was as pale as my own. He'd arrived at the bar before me and commandeered one of the few tables to the left of the entrance – a blessing, as I couldn't imagine perching side by side on one of the high bar stools lining the other walls. Before him sat a half-empty pint of stout and a copy of the *Guardian*, which was folded and unread. He glanced over as I crossed the threshold and flashed me a welcoming smile. Faced with the reality of him, my first impression was that he looked a little too English for my liking.

Comparing every man I met to Nico would get me nowhere, I knew that, but breaking the habit of the last decade was easier said than done. The thing that had always set Nico apart from all the other men I'd been out with was that he'd seemed exotic. He was a foreign, alien territory I'd set out to conquer; a person whose thought patterns would never cease to astonish me, so different were they to my own. Marcus, on the other hand, looked almost familiar, as though he were a composite of half a dozen people I'd studied with at university. There was nothing exotic about him, or at least nothing immediately obvious.

'You must be Sally,' Marcus said, standing for a moment and shaking my slightly clammy hand. His plummy, public-school voice sounded too high-pitched for his frame, and I realized that, when we'd chatted online, I'd imagined it sounding deeper and more virile. 'What'll you have to drink?' Marcus gestured towards the tiny bar behind me. I caught sight of a poster on the exposed stone wall behind him advertising the in-house brew – 'cheap blonde' – and decided half a lager would do just fine. Then I slid into the seat opposite Marcus, wondering whether the disappointment I'd felt when I'd first laid eyes on him had been writ large across my face.

'Don't you wish you could buy the proper version of the *Guardian* in Paris, instead of this pithy little export edition?' I said, casting around for something to say and taking my cue from his prop. 'I always feel a bit short-changed when I buy it.'

'Oh, I'm not all that bothered, to be honest . . .' Marcus's tone was dismissive. 'I only tend to read the sports pages . . .' If things coasted downhill from thereon in, it wasn't solely because Marcus's social life seemed mostly to consist of propping up the bars of various English pubs while he watched the football or the rugby on their widescreen TVs, with the occasional pub quiz or curry night with 'the lads' from his firm thrown in. It was also because his level of French, as he admitted without apparent embarrassment, was poor, even though he was taking weekly lessons. There wasn't much incentive to improve, he explained, because the official language of his office was English.

As for meeting women, he'd been out with a few 'French birds' – as he so charmingly put it – but qualified them as 'excessively high maintenance'. 'My last girlfriend, Diane, a secretary from work, was a full-time job in herself,' he complained. He took a long sip of his stout and I wondered whether to point out the creamy moustache it had left on his top lip, before deciding against it. 'I couldn't go anywhere on my own without her sulking,' he elaborated. 'What a nightmare that was! I swore off French birds after that. I unticked the "French" nationality box on Rendez-vous.'

I flinched at his last two words and looked around, wondering whether anyone in the bar had overheard, uncomfortable with the idea of people knowing how and where we'd met. But the handful of customers appeared to be either engrossed in their own conversations or reading their newspapers. I'd have to stop being so paranoid.

Although I'd been quick to judge Marcus, when I'd first arrived in Paris, ten years earlier, I'd lived much as he seemed to now. Kate and I had been regular fixtures at a number of well-known Anglo-haunts: the Lizard Lounge, the Auld Alliance, even the Frog and Rosbif pub. When Marcus asked me what had brought me to Paris in the first place, I launched into the well-worn story of how I'd become friendly with a French girl called Elodie, an ERASMUS exchange student, in my final year at Manchester university. She planned to be away all summer, on holiday with her family, and was looking for a summer tenant for the tiny maid's room she rented in the Latin Quarter. When I split up with Gavin, my boyfriend of three years, days before our finals, our plans to go travelling together for a few months had bitten the dust. I couldn't face going alone, but the idea of moving back in with Mum and Dad for the summer depressed me, so I begged Elodie to rent her garret to me. My French was pretty ropey back then – I'd studied it to A-Level, then dropped languages in favour of history – but it was good enough to get by in a waitressing job. Once the summer season was over, I'd return to England to study for a PGCE. I planned to teach history in a secondary school.

I glossed over meeting Nico – saying only that I'd met a Frenchman and decided to stay on when the summer came to an end – but falling for Nico and falling for Paris were two things I found difficult to distinguish between, so tightly were they bound together. As I began to spend more and more time in Nico's company, I'd deserted my English haunts, moving on to pastures French. Kate met Yves not long afterwards, and her life had followed a similar trajectory.

The changes had been subtle at first. Back in England, I'd eaten all meat well done but, with Nico's guidance, I was soon ordering my steaks *à point*, then *saignant*. I graduated from Emmental and Comté cheese to Roquefort,

Camembert and St Marcellin, although I still had a problem with anything that looked too mouldy and alive, as though it might crawl off the plate if left unattended. My French had improved to the point where I was often mistaken for a native. Ten years later, I was no *Parisienne*, but I'd come a long way – far enough to find the prospect of taking a step backwards, by getting involved with someone like Marcus, unattractive. For an Englishman to appeal to me now, I realized, he'd have to be a committed Francophile, not someone who, by his own admission, wasn't even interested in scratching the surface.

When I'd drained the bitter dregs of my rather flat lager, I decided to make my excuses and leave. 'I'm afraid I have to get across town to meet a friend,' I apologized, glancing at my watch. 'I'm sorry. I should have set aside more time. I'm new at all this . . .'

'Don't worry, I get it. I can tell the sparks aren't flying today, if you can forgive me for being blunt,' said Marcus, surprising me by showing he was far more perceptive than I'd have given him credit for. 'But if you wanted to tag along and meet the lads sometime, for a pub quiz or a drink . . . They're a nice crowd.'

'The thing is,' I said carefully, 'being a mother and all, I have so few nights free . . . I'm not really in the market for new *friends*.' I certainly didn't sign up so I could be co-opted into an Anglo pub-quiz team, or cast in the role of honorary bird on some lads' nights out.

'Fair enough.' Marcus stood up, rolling his newspaper into a cylinder and stuffing it into his jacket pocket. 'But I should probably mention that I'm also available for no-strings sex,' he added, his expression deadpan. I gave a nervous laugh, temporarily lost for words. The answer was no – I had no desire whatsoever to see the pale, freckled torso which surely lay under Marcus's rugby shirt – but I couldn't work out for the life of me whether he was making a joke or a serious proposition. I decided to consider it the former and thanked him mock-graciously for his 'kind offer'. Seconds later, I beat a hasty retreat.

'I'd definitely rather be alone than with someone like Marcus,' I mumbled to myself, shuddering at the memory. After tutting over his misleading profile picture one last time, I deleted Marcus from my Rendez-vous 'favourites'. Lila, who'd tired of watching me 'manshopping', had returned to her Lego castle and didn't even look up. 'Back to the drawing board,' I said with a sigh. 'I have to be able to do better than this . . .'

Catherine rang the doorbell at two on the dot, as punctual as always. When she'd finished hugging, kissing and coo-ing over her granddaughter, she pulled herself upright, one hand clutching the kitchen counter to steady herself, and turned her attention to me. After the briefest of hesi-tations, she deposited a resounding kiss on both my cheeks. I took this as a sign: Catherine was determined to behave as though nothing had changed between us.

Surveying the living room, she gave an almost imper-ceptible nod of approval. Last time she'd seen it, back in April, the parquet was covered with plastic sheeting and I'd greeted her wearing my oldest jeans, a paint-splattered bandana shielding my hair. Catherine was dressed as she was now, in a pencil skirt and cashmere twin-set, her brown bob glossy, fresh from a *brushing* at her local branch of Jacques Dessange.

Her appraisal of my apartment complete, she turned back to me, addressing me in French, as always. I happened to know her English wasn't half bad but, like Nico, she preferred to address me in French, so as not to put herself at a disadvantage. '*Vous avez bonne mine, en tout cas,*' she remarked, looking me up and down with narrowed eyes.

I'd often meant to ask Nico whether the French equivalent of 'You're looking well' was intended as a backhanded compliment. In Yorkshire, coming from my mother or one of her friends, it passed as a not-so-secret code for 'You've put on weight.' But today the second half of Catherine's sentence fascinated me even more. What did she mean by 'in any case'? Was she unpleasantly surprised that my new life as a single mum seemed to agree with me? Maybe I was being oversensitive, but I felt certain there must be a mild rebuke lurking in there somewhere.

'Can I get you a coffee?' I said, knowing full well that Catherine, whose capsule espresso machine was her pride and joy, would consider my lowly Carte Noire filter coffee little better than dishwater, but offering for the sake of form. I didn't expect Catherine would want to stay and chat. Seeing her without Nico was even more surreal than seeing Sophie had been.

'*Merci* Sally, *je ne dirais pas non,*' Catherine replied, to my amazement, lowering herself gingerly into the sofa. 'My back's playing up today,' she explained. 'I find Philippe's new car even more uncomfortable than the last. I wish he would let me test the seats for comfort before he buys them . . .' Philippe, Nico's father, seemed to be forever trading in and upgrading his cars and was often to be found with his nose inside the *Argus de l'Automobile*. After parking at Nico's, he'd taken a métro down to Hôtel de Ville to spend an hour or two in the basement of the BHV department store. Ever since he'd retired from his job as a tax inspector a couple of years earlier, Philippe had become almost as obsessed with home improvements as he was with cars, and no trip to Paris was now complete without a pilgrimage to BHV's cavernous '*rayon bricolage*'.

Spooning coffee grounds into the conical paper filter, I made a mental note to casually move the open laptop, which lay on the sofa, centimetres from Catherine, at the very first opportunity. There were some things my ex-almost-mother-in-law didn't need to know about me, and the fact that I'd joined Rendez-vous was top of that list.

'Are you meeting Philippe *chez* Nicolas?' I enquired, pointedly using Nico's full name, my back to Catherine as I hunted for the sugar bowl in the crockery cupboard. Mission accomplished, I set two miniature coffee cups and saucers on a small tray, added hastily polished tea-spoons, then rounded the kitchen counter and tidied away the laptop. The coffee machine was doing a great deal of hissing and bubbling but, so far, there wasn't much to show for its labours. 'Lila's suitcase is all packed . . .' I gestured towards the garish pink Hello Kitty suitcase which stood by the coffee table. Packing for the week's holiday with her grandparents had been a fastidious chore. Sorting through Lila's clothes, I'd carefully checked for stains which hadn't washed out, frayed hems or missing buttons, before giving everything a quick once-over with the iron. Folding her T-shirts and laying them carefully in the suitcase,

I'd chastised myself inwardly. Why was I still pulling out all the stops to impress Catherine? Why crave her Chanel No. 5-scented approval now, when I would never officially be a part of the Canet family? I supposed it was a question of pride: I didn't want to give Catherine any excuse to think I wasn't managing fine on my own.

Nico's mother had always been terrifyingly meticulous. She could afford to be: a cleaning lady looked after her house, ironing her bedlinen and waxing her floors, leaving her free to obsess about the finer details, like plumping the sofa cushions just so, or laying the table with the kind of precision you'd expect in a Michelin-starred restaurant. The first time I'd dined at the Canet house, on the outskirts of Chantilly, I'd been assigned my own cloth napkin, complete with silver napkin ring. Six months later, when we made our second visit, I'd discovered my name engraved upon it. It was a gesture I'd found both touching and unnerving, because of the permanence it implied. Had my name now been removed, I wondered, leaving a blank canvas for my successor? Or was the napkin ring languishing in the back of a drawer, in case I came to my senses, as Sophie seemed to think I should?

I'd been right about one thing: Catherine hardly touched her coffee when I set it down in front of her. Staying for a drink had indeed been nothing but a pretext for a 'little chat'. Luckily, after rapturously greeting her beloved *mamie*, Lila had returned to the episode of *Charlotte aux Fraises* she'd been watching before Catherine arrived, sitting cross-legged on the floor – a little close to the screen for my liking – and adopting her habitual trance-like TV-watching expression. 'I wouldn't normally allow Lila to watch television when there's a guest in the house,' I said, helping myself to sugar and settling into the sofa by Catherine's side, 'but if there's something you want to talk to me about, I can leave it on for a while, if you like?'

'I did want to ask how you think *la petite puce* is coping with all the changes, Sally,' Catherine confirmed in a low voice. 'I've asked Nicolas a few times, but he never says a great deal to me . . .' She twisted her thick gold wedding band as she spoke and, for the first time, I noticed her once-elegant hands were showing signs of the onset of arthritis, the joints beginning to stand out like knots on a tree trunk.

Taking my cue from Catherine, I decided to avoid using Lila's name, to minimize the chances of her listening in on our conversation. 'When we first moved in here, she cried for her *papa* every night at bedtime,' I admitted. 'And for a while I was at my wits' end.' For weeks, I'd remained by Lila's bed until the sobbing subsided and her breathing became slow and regular, silently cursing Nico as tears slid down my own cheeks. The mornings were no better: Lila would come padding into my room at daybreak, making hopefully for Nico's side of the bed, her face crumpling when she saw that *Papa* had failed to materialize in the night. 'But things have improved a lot since the *rentrée*,' I continued, anxious to show Catherine that we'd turned the corner. 'She's used to the new routine, and she looks forward to the weekends where she has her *papa* to herself . . .'

'I had a conversation with Sophie the other day.' Catherine was still fiddling with her wedding band, not quite able to look me in the eye. 'About that distasteful business with his secretary, and about that young girl he's seeing now . . . I'm so disappointed, frankly. I always thought that, one day, Nicolas would phone to tell me he'd proposed to you, or to announce there was another baby on the way. The whole thing in March came as such a shock. Everything seems to have disintegrated so quickly . . .'

'To be fair, Catherine,' I said evenly, 'I didn't see any of this "distasteful business" – as you call it – coming either . . . Not until the evidence was staring me in the face.'

'Philippe had a mistress once – or once that I know of,' Catherine said suddenly, almost causing me to capsize my cup and saucer in shock. Nico had never alluded to anything like this, and I was willing to bet he'd been kept in the dark. 'My generation,' Catherine continued with a sad smile, 'was brought up to turn a blind eye to that kind of thing. We were supposed to accept it as part and parcel of married life, and simply carry on . . .'

'I could never have done that, Catherine,' I interjected, convinced I knew where the conversation was leading. If Catherine and Sophie were singing from the same song sheet, a plea to reconsider my decision would follow. 'It's not as if this was one isolated occurrence. I don't know whether it's a generation thing, or because I'm English, but I couldn't have carried on. Knowing what I knew, I couldn't trust him any more . . .'

'Oh, I wasn't implying you should have done as I did,' Catherine insisted, 'only that I know things have changed. I didn't feel I had any other choice back then: I'd never worked, and I couldn't conceive of living on my own. I never even confronted Philippe with what I knew, but it took me years to trust him again; years to stop looking over my shoulder. Even if I'm happy enough now, I'm not sure I'd wish that life on anyone.'

Reeling from the shock of Catherine's admission, I fell silent for a moment. I needed time to digest everything she had said. It was so unexpected, that this proud, private woman, so attached to keeping up appearances, had decided to show me her Achilles heel. She'd never let me glimpse the merest hint of vulnerability behind her cashmere armour in the past, and taking me into her confidence now wasn't a decision she could have taken lightly – not least because it meant discarding the blind loyalty she'd always shown towards her children, and Nico in particular.

'This Albane girl, have you met her?' Catherine continued, before our emotionally charged silence could become too deafening.

An image of the tortoiseshell *barrette* I'd seen on Nico's hall table swam to the forefront of my mind, but I shook my head. 'I've heard *about* her, and heard her voice on the phone . . .'

'Sometimes I wish I could still put Nicolas across my knee and give him a good *fessée*,' Catherine said, clenching her fist in her lap. It was the word '*fessée*' that wrenched Lila's attention away from Strawberry Shortcake and brought my surreal discussion with Catherine to a premature end. Lila turned to face us, eyes wide, as though to proclaim her innocence.

'Who's getting a *fessée*? Not me, *Mamie*? I haven't done any *bêtises*!'

'Nobody's getting spanked, Lila,' I reassured her, scooping her into my arms for a forceful hug and shooting Catherine an amused look over my shoulder. 'Now, why don't you go and fetch me your coat and shoes. It's time for you to go on your holidays.'

Before she left, Catherine pressed an envelope into my hand. 'Philippe and I missed your birthday in July,' she said by way of explanation, 'but I wanted you to have something. Don't go buying things for Lila, mind. Promise me you'll treat yourself instead. Buy yourself something *frivole . . .*'

Alone in my living room but for the lingering scent of Chanel No. 5, I tore open the envelope. My trembling hand withdrew four crisp fifty-euro notes.

10

A couple of days later, I was performing my habitual balancing act between two métro carriages on the *ligne* 1, this time on my way to Rivoire headquarters to take Delphine Andrieu up on her lunch offer, when the day's *Transports amoureux* almost caused me to laugh out loud.

'*À Delphine, charmante « passante » du TGV* Paris–Marseille *le samedi* 24/10,' it read. '*Pardonnez ma maladresse. Faites-moi signe sur mon portable. J'aimerais vous revoir.*'

I was intrigued. '*Maladresse*' could be rendered into English in several different ways, but none were positive. The author could be apologizing for clumsiness in the most literal sense, having trampled on her foot or dropped his holdall on her head when removing it from the overhead racks. My preferred translation was 'tactlessness': in conversation with her he'd committed a terrible gaffe, causing offence. Had he made an indecent proposal? Would the Delphine in question now read his apology, decide to forgive him and call the number provided, or would their paths never cross again?

'I don't suppose you happened to take a TGV to Marseille last Saturday?' I asked Delphine as she led me towards our usual meeting room, twenty minutes later, addressing her in French to show that we were off-duty until our lesson officially began, after lunch. Stepping inside, I noted that the table had been enveloped in a crisp white tablecloth and set with polished silverware. Two gilt-edged plates covered with gleaming silver domes stood ready on the sideboard. At Rivoire headquarters, nothing was done by halves.

'I wish I had,' Delphine replied, in French, with a mildly puzzled frown, 'but no, I was working from home that day. Not even weekends are sacred in this job.' She caught sight of my newspaper, which I'd laid on the table to one side of my plate, still open on the classifieds page. '*Ah, les Transports amoureux!* I used to read *Libé* all the time before I worked here, but *Monsieur* can't stand the sight of it. He's got shares in *Le Figaro*, you know. So unless any of the other papers prints a character assassination of one of his rivals, they're all newspaper *non grata* around here . . .'

Her boss might be out of town, but Delphine looked as chic as ever, dressed in a fitted skirt and jacket, gossamer-thin tights and high heels. As she ferried the covered plates from the sideboard to the table, one by one, I noticed the huge Technicolor bruise on her right shin, visible through her tights. 'I did that this morning,' she said, intercepting my stare and giving her calf a quick rub before taking a seat opposite mine. '*Monsieur* called me from his private jet. I ran into his office to read his share prices off the Reuters screen on his desk – he hates waiting, and you never know when that aeroplane phone will cut out – and I slammed into the corner of his coffee table. I've done it a thousand times. I keep spare pairs of tights in my desk drawer as a precaution . . .'

'What would he have done if you'd kept him waiting too long?' I asked, genuinely curious. 'Would he hang up on you?' Delphine nodded. Once again I thought to myself that I wouldn't do her job for all the money in the world. My four-year-old Lila sounded more reasonable than Monsieur Rivoire.

Delphine lifted the silver dome off her plate, and I followed her lead, unveiling a beautifully presented fillet of sea bass, baked in its skin, the scales golden and crispy. The fish was perched atop a mound of fragrant saffron rice and garnished with cooked cherry tomatoes. I picked up the cutlery – a fish knife and fork, naturally – and laid my napkin across my lap. Nico's mother would be in her element in such refined surroundings, but I felt ill at ease. The tomatoes, in particular, looked treacherous, and I prayed I wouldn't manage to squirt juice across the pristine tablecloth when I tried to skewer them with my fork.

Not only would I have to mind my manners, but I was under strict orders to watch my words too. When I'd called Kate to let her know I'd be meeting Delphine for lunch instead of honouring our usual fortnightly arrangement, she'd been audibly lukewarm. 'Let her do most of the talking,' she'd advised. 'Rivoire's definitely one client I can't afford to rub up the wrong way.'

'I'll be careful,' I'd promised. 'And I'll treat you to a full post mortem tonight.' I was looking forward to the coming evening. It was Lila's third night away, and when Ryan had invited Kate, Anna and me for a housewarming dinner in his new apartment, I'd been delighted to be able to accept on the spur of the moment, without recourse to a babysitter, for once.

Delphine seemed quite happy to lead the conversation. She was far more talkative than usual, on account of being permitted to speak in her native tongue. She started by quizzing me about Lila – how old she was, where she went to school, whether she looked like me – then asked if I minded explaining how I came to be separated from her father. In between mouthfuls of my lunch – which was delicious but disappointingly tepid – I served up a condensed and rather sanitized version of the events I'd recounted to Anna. 'I found out my partner had been having an affair,' I explained, rejecting the urge to shovel up my rice with the fish knife and transferring it to the back of my fork instead, 'and I didn't feel able to turn a blind eye to what he'd done, or to forgive him. So I decided to leave . . .'

'Did you know the other woman?' Delphine set down her knife and fork and dabbed the corner of her mouth delicately with her napkin, her eyes never leaving mine.

'I knew *of* her, but we'd never met,' I replied, shaking my head.

'It's ten times worse when you do,' Delphine confided, her voice bitter. 'My ex cheated on me with one of my oldest friends. So I ended up losing them both.'

'Nico's affair was with his secretary,' I clarified, regretting my words as soon as they'd escaped from my mouth. The last thing I wanted was for Delphine to think I was implying that all secretaries set out to seduce their bosses. The only way to dig myself out of the hole, I decided, was to elaborate. 'When I found out, it had been going on for some time,' I added, with a sigh. 'Mathilde was older than me; in her early forties. It's ironic really: I'd always thought she had such an innocent-sounding name. I had this mental image of her as a *vieille fille*, you know, a prim little spinster in high-necked blouses, but that couldn't have been further from the truth.' I grimaced. 'She turned out to be a wolf in sheep's clothing . . . Or rather a wolf in Aubade lingerie.'

'If I had a hundred euros for every time one of the senior executives has propositioned me,' Delphine said sardonically, 'then I'd be a *very* rich woman.' She noted my shocked expression with evident amusement. 'It goes with the territory,' she said, candidly. 'I'm a single mother, and I work such ridiculous hours that I have little or no hope of meeting a man of my own. So I'm seen as fair game for a bit of extra-marital fun . . . But more importantly' – she paused for dramatic effect – 'I'm Rivoire's assistant. Landing me as a mistress would be considered hitting the jackpot, around here. But it would be less about sex than about *les confidences sur l'oreiller*, if you see what I mean. Either way, being someone's "other woman" doesn't interest me.'

There was a lot more to Delphine than initially met the eye but, nonetheless, fielding indecent proposals from men who wanted to pump her for pillow talk about her boss couldn't be much fun. 'So, do you ever find the time to meet men outside of work?' I asked her, curious to see whether Delphine had any sort of love life. 'Have you ever tried a dating site, say, like Rendez-vous?'

'I signed up once, a couple of years ago,' Delphine admitted, 'without using a photo. And I saw so many married men I recognized on there that it made me think twice.'

'I joined recently,' I confessed, 'but I do have reservations about it, and so far I've only been on one very bad date . . .'

'I'm sure it *is* possible to meet decent men that way, if you filter very carefully,' Delphine replied, her doubtful expression contradicting her words somewhat, 'but Rivoire made me sign something last year to say I wouldn't join any networking sites at all. He's paranoid about security. Always worried about people getting to him via me . . .'

'Isn't that a bit extreme, policing your personal life?' I said, incensed on her behalf. 'I mean, isn't it hard enough for single mums to meet people as it is?'

'You don't have to feel sorry for me, Sally,' Delphine said with a knowing smile. 'I knew when I took this job that I was selling my soul to Rivoire, and I went into it with my eyes wide open. He wanted me *because* I'm a single mother. I've got no husband to complain when I stay late, or hit the roof when I have to take work calls in the middle of the night. Rivoire pays well, and I'm saving like a squirrel. But I don't intend to remain at his beck and call for ever. Financial security is all very well, but I'm fed up with my daughter seeing more of her babysitters than she does of me.'

By the time I'd polished off the raspberry *sabayon* and coffee that one of Delphine's minions carried in soon afterwards on an intricately engraved silver tray, my pupil had succeeded in overturning every preconceived idea I'd held about her since we'd first met. This was no damsel in distress, imprisoned in her ivory tower, I realized. She was a level-headed, ambitious career woman who had managed to turn her personal circumstances into something which gave her an edge over her rivals.

I'd never want to emulate Delphine, but I was in no doubt that she deserved my grudging respect.

'I can't believe you've moved to rue des Mauvais Garçons, bad boy,' I remarked as I settled on to Ryan's leather sofa, a gin and tonic in my hand, causing Anna, seated to my right, to snigger. It was almost eight, but Kate hadn't arrived yet. She'd phoned to let us know she'd been held up with work and would join us later, which was annoying, because I itched to fill her in on my lunch with Delphine.

'I looked at a place on rue des Vertus, but it just wasn't *me*,' Ryan retorted, popping a plate of savoury *petits fours* on the table with a flourish and taking a seat in the armchair opposite. 'Now, ladies, I'm afraid these are only nibbles I got at my local Picard and defrosted,' he said apologetically. 'I didn't have time to don my apron and start baking in your honour, much as I'd have loved to . . .'

Ryan's new place was very cosy and had a similar layout to my own, except that he had only one, much larger, bedroom. Anna and I had been treated to a guided tour, causing his skittish tortoiseshell cat, Clyde, to flee from room to room, finally taking refuge underneath Ryan's double bed.

'So, how are things with Eric?' I enquired, darting a mischievous look at Anna, as Ryan adopted his usual coy expression. 'Are we allowed to refer to him as your boyfriend? Or would that be a little premature?'

'Ladies, I wish I knew,' he said, shrugging his shoulders. 'The thing is, he travels a lot with his job, and he's going to be oversecing some project in Eastern Europe for a while. So it looks like we'll have to put everything on hold . . . I suppose the real test will be whether I can behave myself in the meantime.'

When the conversation turned to my lunch with Delphine, neither Ryan nor Anna seemed surprised by what I told them and I began to wonder aloud whether I wasn't embarrassingly naïve. 'What I'd like to know,' Ryan mused, 'is whether sleeping with Rivoire is part of Delphine's package. It often is, you know. I mean, not contractually, so to speak, more by tacit understanding.' I shuddered. I'd passed Rivoire in the corridor only once, but I'd seen his photograph in *Libération* often enough. He was well preserved for a sixty-year-old, but his face had a pinched, ruthless look, and he wasn't my cup of tea.

'Have either of you guys ever had pupils come on to you at work?' Anna's question didn't sound neutral and, when I turned to look at her, her gaze fled mine. 'It's just that I had a bit of a situation the other day in one of those basement meeting rooms at the insurance company at La Défense,' she continued, telltale spots of red appearing on her cheeks. 'And I couldn't stop thinking about how *anything* could happen down there. The door was closed, there are no windows . . .'

'What kind of a situation?' I said, setting down my drink on the glass coffee table more violently than I'd intended. 'Did someone try to paw you?'

'Oh. Nothing serious,' said Anna, flustered now and possibly wishing she'd never spoken up. 'It was all verbal, nothing physical. I was following a lesson plan from that financial English book, the one about liquid metaphors – you know, cash flows, being awash with funds, that sort of thing – and the guy I was teaching made some pretty gross *double entendres* about bodily fluids . . .'

'Ew! That's not on, is it?' I appealed to Ryan, who nodded vehemently in agreement. 'You might want to think about asking Kate to give that pupil to someone else,' I suggested. 'She can pair him with a male teacher if you don't want to face him again . . . Don't worry, she's used to that sort of thing. It's never happened to me, but there have been quite a few cases over the years of people making unwelcome passes at their teachers. Haven't there, Ryan?'

'Passes both unwelcome, and welcome,' said Ryan, smiling a sly smile. 'Not to make light of your ordeal, Anna, but I once had a very pleasant experience with a male pupil in a stationery cupboard.' He put a finger to his lips. 'Don't forget you're under oath not to tell Kate, Sally,' he said in a stage whisper. 'I don't think the boss lady would approve.'

'Don't worry, Ryan,' I replied, giving Anna a sidelong glance, glad that Ryan had found a way to lighten the mood and make her smile. 'Your stationery-cupboard secrets are safe with me.'

'I actually happened across one of my pupils on the Gaydar France website the other week,' Ryan continued. 'If I remember correctly, he was looking for "*un plan cul immédiat*", although I didn't care to investigate further . . .'

'Good God! That's a bit direct! They don't have options like that in the drop-down menus on Rendez-vous,' I exclaimed, genuinely shocked. Anna was looking confused and I cast around for a translation. 'It basically means "a no-strings fuck, as soon as possible",' I explained, blushing as I did so. Somehow, using such language in French was easier. '*Un plan cul*' sounded so much less vulgar to me than its English translation.

We were still plying Ryan with questions about Gaydar, where nude profile photos were de rigueur and even close-up anatomical shots were not unheard of, when the doorbell rang, announcing Kate's arrival. 'You're just in time to hear about the Tailor-Made pupil Ryan found online in his birthday suit,' I said, pouring Kate a gin and tonic once she and Ryan had completed the thirty-second apartment tour.

Kate smiled and rolled her eyes, but she looked weary and a little dishevelled. Her usually sleek hair hung loose and her clothes looked as though they'd been thrown on in haste. It's not like Kate to let those impossibly high standards of hers slip, I thought to myself, although I refrained from commenting on her appearance, as I knew I always felt ten times worse when someone pointed out I was looking tired or under the weather. Instead I gave her a recap of the highlights of our conversation so far, including my lunch with Delphine and Anna's close encounter, while Ryan offered her the plate of appetizers and graciously gave up his armchair, sitting cross-legged on the floor by her side.

'I told Anna that amorous advances from pupils were nothing unusual,' I said, giving Kate a wink. 'You should tell her about that big-shot businessman you taught, Kate. You know, the one who used to book the centre table in posh restaurants so he could invite you out and parade you around in full view of his friends, hoping everyone would assume you were his mistress . . .'

Kate had a handful of CEOs whose teaching she delegated to no one. Apart from replacing us when we were out sick, these were the only sessions she'd kept on, once her language school was up and running and the lion's share of her time was devoted to admin. Her anecdotes from these lessons had often been a source of amusement when we met for our fortnightly lunches. But tonight, for some reason, she seemed unwilling to play along. 'Oh, he was pretty tame and harmless, really,' she said with an exaggerated shrug. 'But, Anna, I totally understand if you need me to shuffle some teachers around. I don't pay any of you enough to put up with sleaze.'

Kate loosened up over the course of the evening, but she still seemed uncharacteristically quiet, to me. If it had been only the two of us, I would have had no qualms about asking her what was wrong, but I didn't want to put her on the spot in front of Ryan and Anna, and when, a few minutes after midnight, she reached for her phone and called a taxi, I knew I'd missed my chance. 'Does anyone else want a cab?' she asked, holding the phone away from her ear while the holding symphony played.

'You're walking home, right?' I said to Anna, who nodded and glanced at her watch. 'Well, in that case,' I replied, 'I'm good thanks, Kate. I think I'll walk Anna to République and catch a métro from there.'

As Anna and I meandered along rue des Archives, the gin and tonics we'd put away insulating us from the biting cold of the November night, I pointed out the Cox Bar, confessing I'd walked past it for almost a decade before the phonetic reality of the name of the infamous men-only establishment had hit home. 'I read somewhere there are private cubicles in the basement, like in a swingers club,' Anna said with a smile. 'I don't know if it's urban legend, or actually true. Not that I've ever been to a swingers club . . .'

'If you do ever fancy trying one, all you'd have to do is join Rendez-vous,' I retorted. 'I've got invitations to places like that coming out of my ears.' It was true: my inbox had been swamped lately with men trying to persuade me to accompany them to various *clubs échangistes*. I'd been outraged at first, but curiosity had got the better of me one day and I'd checked out a couple of the most famous clubs' websites. It hadn't taken me long to work out it was not only cheaper for a man to gain entry if he had a woman on his arm but, in some clubs, house rules stipulated that lone men weren't admitted at all. Once I'd realized that, seeing men trawling Rendez-vous for plus ones made a seedy kind of sense.

'Tempted?' Anna raised a questioning eyebrow.

'Oh God. Not at all,' I replied. 'I mean, maybe I'm a prude, but I'm not sure I can imagine going to a place like that with my *partner*, let alone some stranger I'd met on the internet.' We walked on in silence for a moment, pausing at the junction where rue des Archives met rue Rambuteau to let a motorbike speed by, then plunging on into the next section of the street, where the pavements narrowed and restaurants gave way to shuttered shops. Anna had rammed her hands deep into her coat pockets and walked with her head bowed; she appeared to be deep in thought.

'Talking of partners,' she said at last, her eyes still downcast, 'I agreed to have lunch with Tom last Sunday. He's moved in with that Dutch woman. And now he wants to file for divorce.'

'Oh Anna, I'm so sorry . . . That must have been awful . . . The finality of it, I mean.' Anna nodded. She'd slowed her pace and, as we passed under a streetlight, her eyes gleamed, as though filled with tears. 'You do know,' I added, 'that if you are ever feeling rotten, you're always welcome to come over? I mean, apart from weeks like this one – school holidays – you can pretty much always count on me being home with Lila . . . And if you don't have the energy for that, you can always call . . .'

'Yeah, I thought about calling, but I just needed to be alone for a while,' Anna confessed. 'I'll be okay, Sally. I mean, I was expecting this to happen, sooner or later. But it's really daunting having to organize all this shit in French. I have no clue where I'm supposed to start . . .'

'I could ask Nico, if you like?' I offered, feeling guilty that I'd been so busy wondering what was going on with Kate all evening that I'd been less than attentive to Anna. 'I can see if he's heard about any good English-speaking lawyers on the grapevine. You never know, he might be able to help.'

'That would be great,' said Anna. 'If you really don't mind.' She shook her head. 'I keep wondering how I managed to get myself into this situation, you know. This is so not how I expected my life to turn out . . .'

We parted ways – graduating from our usual gauche air kisses to a proper hug – by the wrought-iron railings enclosing the Square du Temple, a few hundred metres short of Place de la République. Resuming my journey, my breath forming white clouds in front of my face, Anna's words echoed in my ears: 'This is so not how I expected my life to turn out,' she'd said. I knew *that* feeling, all right.

I I

Once work was over on Tuesday I caught a métro to Hôtel de Ville, my destination a paved cul de sac in the Marais, not far from Ryan's. After Catherine and Lila left on Sunday, I'd decided to brush aside my disappointment with Marcus and get back in the Rendez-vous saddle. It wasn't often I had a whole week of child-free evenings to look forward to, and I rather owed it to myself to make the most of my temporary freedom. Following a short exchange of emails, I'd agreed to meet a French guy who went by the name of Fred37 for a drink at the Café du Trésor. He taught maths at a nearby lycée, he'd complimented me on my French, and his black and white profile photo was really quite promising.

In person, Fred was pleasant-looking but not nearly as attractive as his photo had misled me to believe. His skin was pitted and rough-looking and his nose looked as though it had been broken and badly reset when I saw it in profile, something which hadn't been apparent on his full-face picture. Dressed in black trousers and a biscuit-coloured polo-neck jumper, he recognized me as soon as I walked into the sparsely populated bar, springing to his feet and offering to help me out of my heavy winter coat.

After we'd said our '*bonsoirs*', I resorted to commenting on my surroundings to break the ice, just as I had with Marcus, only this time the conversation was in French. 'Wow,' I said, looking around me in astonishment, 'this place has had a makeover since I was last here! In the old days there were old vinyl twelve-inches decorating the walls, and I think there used to be a DJ booth at the back . . . It had so much more character than it does now.'

'I can't say I remember any of that,' Frédéric replied, looking around at the white-painted walls and red-orange upholstered seats as though he was struggling to imagine what I described. 'But then, according to your profile, you've been living in Paris for far longer than I have, "Belleville girl". In fact, you probably qualify as an honorary *Parisienne* by now . . .'

I ordered a beer, and as I sipped it, Frédéric asked me the usual questions about how I'd come to live in Paris, and I began trotting out my stock answers, telling him pretty much the same story I'd told Marcus. One question surprised me though, as it was something no one else had ever thought to ask. 'When you came to be alone,' Frédéric asked me, his pale-grey eyes never leaving mine, his expression serious, 'didn't you ever consider leaving Paris with your daughter and making a fresh start back in England?'

'Um, no. I don't suppose I did,' I said slowly. 'I've spent my whole adult life in France, and I don't think I'd have a clue where to start if I were to return to England today, which town to live in, what to do for a job . . . And, of course, apart from anything else, I can't contemplate separating Lila from her father. That wouldn't be fair on either of them. So I suppose I've always seen my future in Paris . . .'

When I asked Frédéric whereabouts in Paris he lived, he dropped his bombshell: at the not-so-tender age of thirty-seven, he was living with his mother in Melun, a town half an hour away by train. 'I realize that sounds bad,' he said cagily, 'but let me explain . . . I used to live in Paris with my girlfriend, you see, and when she left, about a year ago, it was a difficult time . . . I was signed off work for a couple of months, money was tight and I had to let our place go because it was too big for just me . . . Anyway, things are much better now and I'm hoping to move into my own place again soon. I'm not some sort of "Tanguy". It was just a temporary glitch . . .'

I smiled at his reference to Tanguy, a well-known French comedy about an ageing single guy whose parents have to resort to increasingly desperate measures to encourage their son to fly the family nest. But, in truth, alarm bells were jangling. I appreciated Frédéric's honesty – I wasn't sure that if I'd had some sort of breakdown I'd have admitted it on a first date – but he was obviously fragile, and the way he'd laid his cards on the table from the outset suggested to me that he was looking for something serious. Still on the mend myself, I knew I wasn't strong enough to shoulder someone else's problems. I already had someone to take care of, and that someone was Lila.

Excusing myself to go to the toilet a few minutes later, I stood with my back against the tiled wall and decided I couldn't face getting a second drink with Frédéric. There wasn't the faintest whisper of attraction, and the silences were already lengthening between us as we fumbled for things to say. I made a great show, as I crossed the room to return to our table, of frowning at an imaginary text message on my mobile phone. 'I'm so sorry,' I said, unhooking my coat, scarf and satchel from the back of my chair, 'but something's come up and I'm going to have to call it a night.' Frédéric looked crestfallen for a moment, then swiftly pulled himself together and adopted a more neutral expression. He was as easy to read as Lila, I thought to myself: every emotion passed across his face in real time.

'Well, perhaps we could meet again, some other evening?' he suggested, drawing my attention to the flaw in my getaway ruse.

'Um, yes . . . Let's do that. I'll email you to let you know when I'm free . . .' I was aware I was nodding a little too vigorously, and I was far from sure that Frédéric had been fooled by my charade as I stepped outside, leaving him seated at his table, nursing his half-full pint of lager.

Was there any kind way to extricate myself gracefully from a bad-date situation? I wondered as I retraced my steps along rue du Trésor, winding my scarf around my neck and pulling on my leather gloves. I felt sure it was preferable to cut a rendezvous short, rather than stringing someone along, allowing him to buy me several drinks over the course of the evening and getting his hopes up, only to spurn his advances when the time came to leave the bar.

Nonetheless, the stunt I'd just pulled wasn't a million miles away from the vanishing acts I'd witnessed on Rendez-vous chat, and I remembered how I'd fumed when someone I'd been talking to had suddenly signed out, giving a flimsy excuse or, indeed, no excuse at all. Would I prefer a date to nip a rendezvous in the bud if he found himself regretting his decision to meet me? I supposed it was a question of perspective: one person's cowardly was another person's exercise in damage limitation.

My gut feeling was that prolonging the agony was senseless: when I met someone new, I could often tell within seconds if I wanted to get to know them better. And if I didn't, my free evenings were too scarce a commodity to be frittered away in the wrong company.

When I paused at the end of the street and glanced at my watch, I found it was only quarter past seven. I couldn't face catching a métro home, just yet. The idea of a post-date post mortem was appealing, but Ryan's phone went straight to voicemail, and I thought I remembered Anna mentioning something about going to the cinema. I didn't feel like calling anyone else and decided to take a stroll through the Marais on my own, instead. Heading north along rue du Faubourg du Temple, I turned into rue des Rosiers on a whim.

When I'd first moved in with Nico, our Sunday pilgrimage to this neighbourhood had been a non-negotiable part of our weekend routine. First we'd queue for takeaway falafel, served inside tinfoil-wrapped pitta bread and overflowing with colourful salad garnishes, topped with chunks of deep-fried aubergine. Once we'd eaten those, seated on a park bench in the Square Langlois, we'd head to one of the nearby kosher bakeries to round off our Sunday lunch with cheesecake and coffee. Passing 'L'As du Falafel', I hesitated for a moment, sorely tempted to take my taste buds on a trip down memory lane. But it was freezing cold, and the idea of eating takeaway food alone in the street at night time wasn't half as appealing as it would have been with an accomplice. With a heavy heart and a rumbling stomach, I continued on my way, taking a right turn in the direction of Hôtel de Ville and a métro home. So much for revelling in my freedom. At this rate I'd be ensconced on my sofa before the clock struck eight.

True to my prediction, shortly after eight I kicked off my shoes, set a plastic bag containing takeaway noodles, a napkin and chopsticks down on the coffee table and cast around for the remote control. At first I couldn't find it; it was hidden behind the screen of my open laptop. Stroking my finger across the track pad caused it to wake from its slumber, and I felt another stab of guilt as I saw Frédéric's email confirming our date in the foreground. I was about to close the window by clicking on the cross at the top right-hand corner of the screen – the 'tiny kiss', as Lila called it – when a pop-up window appeared, stopping me in my tracks.

'Manu_*solo veut vous inviter au chat*,' the message read.

'Does he indeed?' I said, out loud. 'Well, it's about time. I "flashed" him at least three days ago . . .'

Manu was a thirty-three-year-old single dad whose profile I'd come across quite by chance on the 'Who's online now?' page. I wasn't quite sure how he'd managed to get his ill-lit, black and white profile photo past the site's moderators, given that much of his face was in shadow. But his *annonce* blurb had appealed to me because, in some ways, his life seemed to mirror my own. 'In my bathroom cabinet, you'll find condoms,' he'd written, 'but also infant cough medicine and Spiderman plasters. My walk-in wardrobe doubles as my seven-year-old son's bedroom when he visits. I live a dual existence – bachelor one day, *Papa* the next – and while it's not always easy, I'm not unhappy with the cards life has dealt me so far . . .' Scanning his words for the second time, I was struck by how much more confident and together he sounded than poor, damaged Frédéric.

'*J'aime ton profil*,' Manu typed as soon as the chat window loomed into view. Apparently he wasn't one to stand on ceremony: there wasn't a '*bonsoir*' or a '*ça va?*' in sight. '*Dis-moi*,' he continued before I'd had a chance to make any reply, '*t'as un truc de prévu demain soir?*' As a matter of fact, I had no plans for Wednesday evening, or indeed for the rest of the week.

'*Pas encore*,' I replied hesitantly. 'What did you have in mind?'

'Café des Phares, Place de la Bastille, *à* 21h00,' Manu shot back. And with that, before I could accept or decline, he promptly signed out.

There was something compelling about being commanded to be in a certain place at a certain time by a man who didn't appear willing to take no for an answer. His behaviour could be interpreted as arrogance, of course, and both his flippant manner and the mention of the condoms in his bathroom cabinet in the very first line of his profile gave me reason to believe Manu was looking for something casual, if not purely sexual. But hadn't I told myself, in the beginning, when I signed up to Rendez-vous, that the odd casual encounter might do me good? Maybe an evening with Manu would turn out to be exactly what the doctor ordered.

My mind wandered off teaching topics and returned to my impending date at regular intervals the next day at work, and home time couldn't come fast enough. I'd felt nervous before meeting Marcus or Frédéric, but nothing akin to the breathless anticipation I now felt when I imagined meeting Manu. This *frisson* of excitement was something new. My whole body tingled with anticipation.

Once I got home from work, with a couple of hours stretching out before me, I took a number of unprecedented steps as I readied myself for my date. Too unsettled to eat, I took a long, hot shower instead, washed and blow-dried my hair and picked out one of my sexiest sets of matching underwear. I pulled on a favourite black knitted dress which clung to my curves, and swapped my work satchel for a smart black handbag. 'To hell with being sensible, Sally,' I said sternly to my reflection as I applied make-up and sprayed perfume on my neck and wrists. 'What's the worst thing that can happen? If he's another Marcus or Frédéric, there's nothing to stop you bailing out early. And if he's not, then who knows . . .?'

I pulled *Libération* out of my bag as the métro carried me in the direction of Bastille but found myself unable to concentrate on the words which danced on the page in front of my eyes. After skimming over a back-page interview, I took a second look at the day's *Transports amoureux*. There were three, but two were long-running repeats, leaving only one which had been published for the first time that morning. It was short and sweet, and contained an Edith Piaf lyric from the famous song in which she likens her lover to a merry-go-round who makes her head spin. '*TGV* Paris–Angoulême, *le 3 novembre*,' it read. '*Nous avons bu un café ensemble et tu m'as fais tourner la tête. Je veux te revoir.*'

Kate and I had often grabbed a bite to eat at the Café des Phares before our shifts at El Paso. They'd served a mean Croque Monsieur with lashings of béchamel and, back then, toasted sandwiches were one of our low-budget staples. An unexpected, but not unwelcome, side-effect of signing up for Rendez-vous was the number of former haunts I was now revisiting for the first time in almost a decade. First Stolly's, then the Trésor, and now here. In my mind's eye, as the métro pulled into the station and I stood with one hand on the spring-loaded door-release handle, I could see Kate and me sipping beers on the *terrasse* of the Café des Phares as we waited for our food to arrive one mild summer evening; younger, more carefree versions of our current selves. In my memory, a shadow fell across our table. It was Nico, commandeering an empty chair from the next table and joining us for a drink.

What rotten timing: Nico had no business popping into my head minutes before a date. Almost everywhere I'd been in Paris in the last ten years had an image of the two of us superimposed upon it, and reminders of him, of us, shadowed me relentlessly wherever I went. The only way to chase them away, I suspected, and exorcise his ghost would be to fall for someone else. Then I could manufacture a whole new set of memories to take their place.

Climbing the steps up to ground level, I was blasted by one of those icy winds which howl along the underground tunnels, even when there isn't the slightest breeze to be found outdoors. I'd chosen the exit nearest the Café des Phares, opposite the Opéra Bastille, even if my view of the opera house was partially obscured by the column — complete with gold-leaf-covered winged cherub — which dominated the centre of the traffic island. Cars careened around the unmarked, multi-lane roundabout, weaving and zigzagging around one another without once using their indicators. How their drivers remained unscathed as they rocketed around place de la Bastille or, worse still, executed a lap around the place de la Concorde, had always been a mystery to me.

A red and white awning covered the wide expanse of *terrasse* in front of the café and hemmed it in on both sides, creating a sort of outdoor room under a tent. As I approached, I scanned the wicker chairs and round tables, one by one, searching in vain for Manu. The fact that all the chairs in front of French cafés face outwards makes them perfect for watching the world and his dog stroll by, but I'd always found taking centre stage before a sea of out-turned faces to be an unnerving experience, and my confidence ebbed away with every passing second. I was about to slink off in the direction of the nearest free seat, forcing my date to come looking for me instead, when I felt a light touch on my arm and heard an unfamiliar voice say, 'Belleville girl?'

When I span round to face the owner of the voice, I was simultaneously flustered and relieved. The all-important first impression was a good one. Manu looked better 'in real' – as Lila was fond of saying, translating '*en vrai*' a touch too literally – than his brooding profile photo had led me to believe. Effeminate pronounced cheekbones were offset by a shock of unkempt black hair and a thick layer of stubble on his cheeks and chin. He radiated self-assurance, as I'd suspected he would, and didn't appear to be phased in the slightest by the fact that half the people assembled on the *terrasse* were watching the first few seconds of our encounter with undisguised interest.

'Hi. Yes. My name's Sally,' I mumbled shyly in French, desperate to flee the spotlight and sit down.

'I'm Manu, as you know. Short for Emmanuel,' he replied, guiding me towards a table under the awning, below one of the battalion of outdoor heaters. When a waiter appeared, summoned by a confident gesture of Manu's, he ordered a vodka tonic and I opted for the same, hoping a strong drink would steady my nerves.

'Warm enough?' he enquired, once the waiter had withdrawn, 'because we can move indoors if you prefer?' He'd kept his black overcoat buttoned, and I followed his lead, thinking what a shame it was that he wouldn't get to see my slinky dress underneath.

'Oh, I'm fine for now.' I squinted up at the enthusiastic blue flame belching out of the heater above our heads. 'But ask me again later . . . In my experience, the heat from those things tends to gently roast your head but never quite thaws your feet.' Manu smiled, and slowly I began to relax. 'It's always amazed me,' I continued, using my surroundings as a conversational crutch once again, 'this bizarre practice of heating the outdoors. I mean, it's hardly ecologically sound, is it?'

Manu pulled a packet of Marlboro lights from the inside pocket of his coat and laid it on the table. 'You're right,' he concurred. 'But how else are bar owners supposed to survive the smoking ban?' I took his point, even if I was sceptical about putting smokers' comfort and bar profits ahead of the survival of the planet.

At first, I reasoned that Manu was so attractive that he was out of my league, although if he was disappointed with how I looked in the flesh, he did nothing to show it. He also turned out to be surprisingly easy to talk to, and our conversation grew more animated with every repeat round of vodka tonics he ordered. He talked at length about his son, Paul, and I reciprocated with a few of my favourite Lila anecdotes, feeling jubilant every time I managed to make him laugh. I avoided the subject of Nico, aware that it was dangerous ground to cover while I was well on the way to becoming tipsy, but Manu, on the other hand, didn't hold back from talking about his son's mother. His tone of voice became dismissive and flippant when he described how she'd tired of the anti-social hours he kept as a session musician and left him when Paul was only two years old. But despite the alcohol fogging up my brain, I wasn't fooled: I sensed the presence of deep wounds which had yet to heal.

'I can't blame her, I suppose,' he said reflectively, staring into the bottom of his glass. 'I was never easy to live with, and she's better off these days, without me. She married a dentist with a nice steady income, in the end. He gives her and Paul – and his new little sister – everything they need . . .'

When our conversation veered on to the subject of Rendez-vous, Manu made no bones about how he'd used the site with a single aim in mind: to organize a series of no-strings, one-off dates. It was my turn to stare fixedly at the glass in my hand, wondering whether I was supposed to read this as an admission that, for him, the outcome of our date had been a foregone conclusion from the start. If I was honest with myself, I'd been entertaining the idea ever since I'd decided to meet him. And now that he was here in front of me, charming and good-looking – even if, for some reason, his presence didn't send shivers down my spine – I couldn't help speculating that, if he was as promiscuous as he claimed, he might well be rather good in bed. With four or five vodka tonics swilling about my empty stomach, I was beginning to feel uncharacteristically self-confident. Why not nudge things in that direction, I decided, and see what developed?

'My feet are turning into blocks of ice,' I said with an exaggerated shiver, joking that frostbite was rather a high price to pay for spending time with a man, however charming. Manu took the bait, singing the praises of the central heating in his nearby flat and, the next thing I knew, he'd escorted my swaying form along boulevard Richard Lenoir to his apartment building and I was seated on his living-room floor, warming my stocking-clad feet against the radiator.

Manu's place was modestly furnished. There was a beige sofa which had seen better days and a pine coffee table, pitted, scarred and patterned with the overlapping rings left by a multitude of wine glasses and coffee cups. A weeping fig was slowly losing its leaves in the corner furthest away from the radiator, its roots no doubt in dire need of a larger pot. The focal point, however, was the collection of half a dozen electric guitars propped against the walls, next to an amplifier and a spaghetti-like tangle of gold-tipped leads.

'Aren't you going to serenade me with some music?' I slurred, pulling myself to my feet and steadying myself against the wall. Manu, who had emerged from his kitchen bearing a glass of water, looked at me in amusement.

'No, Sally, I'm going to fetch you a pillow and a blanket,' he replied, shaking his head. 'You can sleep here on the sofa. You've missed the last métro, and I'm not sure it would be wise for you to take a taxi in this state . . .'

'Not wise?' I said indignantly, taking a step forward. 'What do you mean? I'm fine . . .' But I wasn't fine. The carpeted floor was pitching and rolling like a boat on stormy seas and, after taking the glass Manu held out to me, I lowered myself on to the sofa and closed my eyes for a moment.

When I opened them again, it was to see Manu depositing a pile of bedclothes on the floor by my feet. 'You're not even planning to take advantage of me?' I said plaintively, squinting up at him from behind a lock of hair which had fallen across my face. My voice sounded younger and more petulant than I'd intended, as though the alcohol had stripped fifteen years off my age. 'I thought one-night stands were your thing? Why did you bring me back here if your intentions were honourable?'

'You're a lovely girl, Sally,' Manu said firmly, 'but also a very drunk one.' He dimmed the lights and pulled down the living-room blind with a decisive noise that sounded like a full stop. 'And, surprising as this may sound, I enjoyed meeting you tonight and I don't want to mess you around.'

An explanation for Manu's unlikely chivalry flickered across my vodka-addled brain. 'Is this because I'm a mother?' I asked him slowly. 'Please don't feel you have to handle me with kid gloves. Maybe I *want* you to mess me around. Ever think of that?'

'Sally, get some sleep.' Manu paused at the door to what I supposed must be his bedroom and flipped off the living-room light to signal that our discussion was at an end. 'We'll talk in the morning when you're feeling better. I promise.' The last thing I heard before I passed out was the sound of the coins from his pockets clattering to the floor as he took off his jeans.

I came to, fully clothed on the sofa, at 5.50 a.m. It took me a moment to work out where I was, and I groaned out loud as the mortifying end to my evening – my pitiful entreaty and Manu's polite but firm rejection – came back to me in a flash. When I realized it was Thursday, and that I had a full day of teaching ahead of me, I groaned again. What on earth had possessed me to let myself get into such a state? I'd jeopardized everything.

The door leading from the living room to the bedroom was ajar, and through it I could hear the rumble of gentle snoring. I realized I had no desire to face Manu when he awoke and, besides, I needed time to get home, shower away the alcohol seeping through my pores, pull myself together and dress for work. Without leaving so much as a note, I took one last look at the guitars lined up around the living-room walls, then slipped out into the hallway and pulled his door softly closed behind me. At the bottom of the stairs, it took me a while, in my disorientated state, to locate the button which would release the front-door lock and set me free, but eventually I found it; it was masquerading as a light switch. Out in the street, the sting of the cold November air against my cheeks had an immediate sobering effect.

As I trudged back towards place de la Bastille to catch a métro, I cut across one end of what would soon be the Thursday-morning fruit and vegetable market on boulevard Richard Lenoir, attracting some knowing stares from the stallholders setting up their trestle tables and unpacking their wares. Thank goodness my mother can't see me now, I thought to myself. Or worse still, Nico. Or Lila's *maîtresse*. No doubt all would agree that a mother my age had no business performing an early-morning walk of shame, dressed in yesterday evening's clothes and make-up.

Manu_solo sent me a follow-up email message later that day, and it confirmed that my gut instincts had been correct. 'I'm sorry about last night, Sally,' it read. 'I hadn't studied your profile carefully enough and had no idea you were a single parent, like me, until we began talking. As I think I told you, I use Rendez-vous to find attractive women I don't give a damn about, sleep with them once, then move on. I didn't feel I could do that with you, even if you claim that's what you wanted. You asked me whether that was because you are a mother, and I honestly don't know. All I do know is that I'm not relationship material. So I think it's probably best if we don't meet again.'

That night I took the Rendez-vous homepage off my bookmarks list, abandoning any nebulous plans I'd had to fill the remainder of Lila's school holidays with fresh dates. It had brought me nothing but disappointment so far, and I wasn't sure when, if ever, I'd be able to face signing back in for more.

12

It was the Monday evening after my disastrous date with Manu – two days before Lila was due home – and I was starting to feel my daughter's absence keenly. Instead of revelling in the extra time I had to get ready every morning, I missed padding into Lila's bedroom to coax her awake and claim my morning cuddle. I missed hearing about her surreal dreams of unicorns and mermaids while I sipped my coffee, or hurried along the street to school. Our little routines structured my days and, without them, I was bereft. Balancing a bowl of salad on my knee as I watched the *Journal de 20 heures*, I was acutely conscious of the fact that the door to Lila's room stood wide open, revealing her empty bed.

I'd never much cared for home-grown French television, and even the handful of British and American series I followed religiously lost much of their appeal when dubbed into French. Favourite actors were saddled with unlikely voices, and award-winning dialogue lost its bite in translation. Pretty much the only French programme I made an exception for was the evening news, and that was less about keeping abreast of current affairs and more about admiring how amazingly well put together newsreader Claire Chazal always looked.

Chazal was in her early fifties, but the French paparazzi regularly snapped her sunbathing topless on the beach with a succession of lovers, each one younger than the last. Not only did she have a body I'd have killed for, but the publication of these candid shots never seemed to undermine her serious reputation one iota. Kate and I had often remarked upon how you had to hand it to the French: they didn't seem to judge public figures in the same way the Brits were wont to do, firmly believing a person's private life had no relevance whatsoever to how they performed their job. Chazal could date an eighteen-year-old boy if she pleased, as far as the French were concerned, as long as she continued to read the day's headlines with the same measured professionalism.

When the news was over and my bowl empty, I flicked listlessly through the other channels, spurning a reality-TV show called '*Île de la Tentation*' in which a group of couples was deposited on tropical 'Temptation Island' and then separated, the girls staying in a hotel filled with eligible bachelors, the boys let loose in the midst of a dozen nubile bachelorettes, with predictable results. The title of a talk show airing on France2 caught my attention. Written in white against a blue background, the day's subject burned a hole in my retinas: '*Qui va vouloir de moi et de mes enfants?*'

'Good grief!' I cried out in exasperation, sorely tempted to throw something at the TV screen. '"Who's going to want to take on me and my kids?" What kind of a title is that?'

My eyes drawn to the screen in spite of myself, I watched spellbound as series of short films aired showing various *parents isolés* – all female – talking about the difficulties they'd encountered while looking for a new partner. Interspersed with these were live discussions choreographed by a rubber-faced male presenter who was canvassing members of the studio audience for their reactions. A twenty-year-old brunette bemoaned the fact that all the boys she met turned on their heel when she explained she was a stay-at-home mum with a six-month-old baby. She was shown dressed up to the nines in a nightclub, fielding approaches from a series of men whose interest evaporated soon after she apprised them of her situation.

'Sweetie, I don't think it's the fact you have a child that's turning these men off,' an older woman in the audience piped up, echoing my own thoughts. 'The way you chat men up reminds me of a job interview! I'm not convinced going on the defensive and interrogating every man you meet about whether he has any problem with dating a single mother is the best way to break the ice . . .'

'But what else am I supposed to do?' retorted the brunette, the camera zooming in to show tears glistening in her eyes. 'Being a mother is my occupation right now. I'm not going to lie about it. The guys will have to find out sooner or later . . .'

Her dilemma reminded me of the day I'd filled in my Rendez-vous profile. Watching her made me realize how lucky I was that Lila was old enough to be at school and that I hadn't contemplated giving up my job altogether when she was born. I'd given it some thought but, even if we could have scraped by on Nico's salary alone, I'd been unwilling to sacrifice my independence. How glad I was that I'd clung to my livelihood now.

After a commercial break filled with ads for infant ready-meals and washing powder, the programme resumed with footage of various men giving their opinions on the subject. 'I dated a *divorcée* once,' said a man in his forties who was trying to hide his advancing baldness with a none-too-subtle comb-over. 'I really liked her, but I wasn't equal to the task of taking on her children too and I ended up breaking things off . . .'

'I wouldn't rule out dating a mother in theory,' explained a pimpled shop assistant, the name tag pinned above his shirt pocket blurred so that his workplace couldn't be identified, 'but it would mean a lot of responsibility very soon in a new relationship. Ideally, I'd want to enjoy life as a couple, *before* bringing any child into the equation.'

The last man interviewed was a handsome thirty-five-year-old who reminded me a little of Manu. 'The way I see it, there's no such thing as a casual fling with a single mother,' he said reasonably, pictured in front of his computer, the scrambled Rendez-vous logo on screen clearly recognizable to an initiate like myself. 'She's not someone you're going to feel comfortable trifling with,' he continued. 'And even if she's not looking for a replacement father for her child, she's going to need someone she can lean on for support. I'm young and I'm looking for a good time. I want a girl I can go clubbing with, not someone who's ankle-deep in nappies . . .'

I couldn't bear to hear any more and, switching off the television set in disgust, I took my empty salad bowl over to the kitchen sink, the rattling of my knife and fork against the Pyrex rim alerting me to the fact that my hands were shaking. I wanted to call a friend and rip the show to shreds. I wanted someone to reassure me that the opinions those men had aired had been an unrepresentative sample, chosen for their shock value. I wanted someone to tell me with absolute certainty that I wasn't destined to remain forever alone with my child. But who could I call? Ryan and Anna would trot out platitudes, but they wouldn't really understand. Neither would Kate, secure in her rock-solid relationship with Yves, and I couldn't even be sure that my own mother would provide a sympathetic ear.

I kicked myself for not thinking to ask Delphine for her mobile number. It was at times like this that I longed to speak to someone who was in the same boat, someone who would be able to empathize with the terror that an inane TV show had struck into my heart.

At first glance, I thought the next morning's *Transports amoureux* had been written by a man who had fallen for a mother he'd seen on a train. '8 *novembre*, 18h10, *TGV* Paris–Bellegarde,' it read. '*Une maman remarquable, son petit blond mignon, vivant, charmant, aux lunettes bleues toutes rondes et chaussettes à rayures.*' My spirits soared as I translated the first sentence. 'A remarkable mother, her cute little blond boy, lively, charming, with little round blue glasses and stripy socks.' Here was welcome proof that *Qui va vouloir de moi et de mes enfants?* hadn't been telling the whole story: some men considered parenthood a turn-on. But when I scanned the next and final sentence – '*Ils me manquent . . .*' – my heart sank like a stone. If the author was missing them, it suggested he'd known the mother and child all along. It was, I realized, most likely a message from a father who had hijacked the *Transports amoureux* section to send a note to his wife, away with their child for the school holidays.

The métro was passing through Concorde station, half-way to the recruitment consultants and their cupboard-like meeting room, when I heard my phone vibrating in the bottom of my bag. 'Nicolas? Is Lila okay?' The signal was patchy, and Nico's voice was almost inaudible over the soundtrack of screeching brakes as the driver halted – mid-tunnel – for a red light.

'*Oui, oui . . . Tout va bien*. My mother's returning Lila tomorrow evening, as planned,' Nico replied. 'I was wondering whether you'd be free to have dinner with me after work? We pass Lila back and forth without ever having a real opportunity to discuss anything . . . And while she's away, we're both free. At least, I am . . . Are you?'

'I, um, didn't have any firm plans for tonight, no . . .' I was mystified. Nico and I hadn't spent any time alone once since I moved out: Lila had always been close by. I wasn't sure how I felt about a prolonged tête-à-tête. There must be a reason for him summoning me to dinner like this. What on earth could it be?

By the time I found myself sitting opposite Nico at his chosen venue, Le Chapeau Melon, a tiny table d'hôte restaurant on rue Rébeval, halfway between my place and his, I'd had a whole day to turn every possible scenario over in my mind. Nico's motives could be purely practical, I supposed. Perhaps he wanted to change the frequency of Lila's visits, or the amount of child-support money he paid me each month, although I couldn't see why he would need to invite me to a restaurant – and quite a pricey one at that – for that type of discussion. My gut feeling was that he wanted to make some sort of announcement. Was it something about his job? Something about Albane? I couldn't for the life of me work it out.

When I'd called Anna at lunchtime and told her about Nico's invitation, her first reaction had been envy. 'I've been wanting to eat there for a while,' she'd said wistfully. 'It's had some great press, but I showed up a couple of times and got turned away.' This new information left me wondering how spur-of-the-moment Nico's gesture had really been. From what Anna had said, he would have had to reserve a table well in advance.

I must have walked past Chapeau Melon's green-painted shop front, with its display of bottles in the windows either side of the door, more than a dozen times without realizing that it wasn't a wine shop. Inside, the walls were lined with wooden shelving and more bottles of wine, and there were only a handful of wooden tables, a group of them pushed together to welcome a large party who had not yet arrived. Seated at a tiny table for two, Nico, who was dressed in one of his most expensive work suits, got to his feet when I entered. At first I thought he was going to greet me with a kiss on both cheeks – something we hadn't done since we separated – but then he hesitated, evidently thought better of the idea, murmured an awkward '*bonsoir*', and sat down again. As I hung my coat on a nearby wall hook, I saw from the corner of my eye that he had backed away slightly from the table, no doubt wanting to give my knees the widest possible berth. I smiled to myself at the memory of my exchange with his sister. How misguided Sophie had been to think that Nico would ever attempt some sort of reconciliation. When I'd wondered about his motives for meeting tonight, that was one possibility that hadn't even crossed my mind.

When the waiter appeared from a room at the back, he seemed to assume we were an item, and made a show of lighting a candle in a small glass and placing it between us. It was a reasonable enough assumption, I supposed. The friction between us was palpable, but we could all too easily have been a couple in the throes of a domestic argument. He then proceeded to walk us through the evening's menu – a fixed four-course meal – and began extolling the virtues of the *vins naturels* on the shelves around us, persuading us to try a little-known wine from the Jura as an aperitif. When he disappeared to fetch the bottle, I was unable to bear the suspense any longer. 'It's a lovely choice of restaurant, this,' I began cautiously, not wanting to sound ungrateful. 'I have to admit, though, I've been wondering why you invited me. Was there something in particular you wanted to talk to me about?'

'Well, yes, there were a few things actually . . .' Nico ran his right hand through his hair, a tic he'd inherited from his father, Philippe; something I'd seen him do a thousand times. For a moment I felt confused. It was surreal, sitting here like strangers, when I'd known Nico intimately for so long. 'The first reason was Lila actually,' he explained. 'She's been asking a lot of difficult questions lately . . .'

'Difficult questions?' I said, frowning. 'Questions about us, you mean?'

Nico nodded. 'Let me see. "Did you do something to make Mummy not love you any more?" is a recurring one. At the weekend, when I went over to visit her in Chantilly, she asked me if you'd moved out because I'd *"fait une grosse bêtise"*. Then she asked what would happen if she did something naughty, and I suppose the implication was that she was worried you'd walk out on her, if she did . . .'

I fell silent as the waiter returned and asked Nico to taste the wine, filling my glass, then his, once Nico had nodded to indicate his approval. Hearing Lila's words, even second hand, had cut me to the quick, and I needed a few seconds to collect my thoughts. I should have been more careful when I'd discussed the new status quo with Catherine while Lila was within earshot, I realized. She had obviously been far less engrossed in her cartoon than she'd been letting on.

It was heartbreaking to imagine Lila wondering, even for a second, whether I might be capable of abandoning her. I wished I could hold her tightly in my arms, there and then, shower her with kisses and leave her in no doubt as to the unconditional nature of my love. But I also felt an overwhelming sense of injustice. Nico had wronged me but, somehow, because I'd done the leaving, it felt as though he was laying the blame for the damage our separation had wrought squarely at my door.

'I don't know where she got an idea like that from,' I said finally, unwilling to hint at the discussion I'd had with Catherine and determined to cling to the moral high ground. 'All I've ever said to Lila is that Mummy and Daddy stopped loving each other and decided we'd be happier living in separate apartments. I never implied you might have done anything bad, or that my moving out was some sort of punishment.'

'I'm not accusing you of anything,' Nico countered with a frown. 'I'm just saying Lila's capable of coming to twisted conclusions like these all by herself. And so I wondered whether it might be a good idea to organize a few sessions with a *pédopsychiatre* . . . Sophie and Jean-Luc know someone who specializes in counselling kids when their parents get divorced.'

'You think Lila needs therapy?' I set down my glass, shaking my head in disbelief. 'That's ludicrous! I strongly disagree. She's not throwing tantrums or misbehaving at school or showing any worrying signs of distress . . . Asking you a few questions is healthy, it doesn't warrant some kind of external intervention! God, Nico, you can be so French sometimes!'

Kate and I had often marvelled at how many of the French adults we knew had spent time in therapy or psychoanalysis. It almost seemed to be the norm, whereas in England, when I'd succumbed to a bout of depression at university, I remembered seeing my local GP and being told to buck up my ideas and take up some regular exercise.

'It was only an idea I wanted to run past you,' Nico said sharply. 'There's no need to get aggressive or start French-bashing.'

The waiter chose this moment to appear with our entrées – half a dozen pieces of raw, marinated salmon with some sort of sesame crust – and we put our conversation on hold while we thanked him and exclaimed over how good everything looked, for the sake of form. 'I'm sorry,' I said in a small voice, once the waiter had moved away again. 'I do appreciate the fact that you're concerned. And I think we should probably discuss how things are going more often, so we can put our heads together and think about how to answer Lila's questions.

But I really don't think therapy is necessary,' I continued, as diplomatically as I could. 'I'd like to hold that option in reserve for now, and only use it if she starts showing signs of actual distress.'

'But what would those signs of distress be?' Nico looked sceptical. 'I mean, she often has nightmares when she sleeps over at my place, for example. Does she have them when she's with you?'

'Oh, I bet if you asked Kate and Yves, or Sophie, they'd tell you their kids all went through the monsters-under-the-bed stage when they were four or five,' I said with a smile, seeing an opportunity to lighten up the conversation and seizing it, gratefully. 'She doesn't have too many at my house, I must admit. Her dreams are usually populated with princesses and unicorns, judging by what she tells me when she wakes up in the morning . . .'

While we'd been deep in conversation, the restaurant had filled to capacity and the jovial group occupying the largest table was dominating the room, making me feel less conspicuous, less like Nico and I were on display. I put a piece of salmon in my mouth and savoured it for a moment, enjoying the feeling of the different textures. The tension in the air since I had first arrived, which had spiked at the mention of child psychiatrists, was now slowly beginning to dissipate. Regardless of what had happened between us, I had a feeling we'd always get a kick out of talking about Lila and playing the role of the proud parents. It stood to reason: sometimes when our daughter said something perceptive or did something funny I'd had to stifle the impulse to give Nico an impromptu call to tell him all about it.

I found myself studying Nico's face as we ate, sizing him up with as objective an eye as I could manage and wondering idly what my first impressions would have been if he was a Rendez-vous date I'd only just met. I'd always loved the dimple in his chin, and the fine lines that fanned out from his eyes whenever he laughed or smiled. Looking closely now, if I wasn't very much mistaken, his wrinkles seemed to have deepened and he looked older than his thirty-four years. But he was still, beyond a doubt, far more attractive than any of the men I'd met so far via Rendez-vous, and realizing this made me feel a twinge of wistfulness.

Feeling distressed that the man I'd loved had betrayed my trust and soiled my memories of our relationship was a familiar feeling, but today I found myself recalling something Sophie had said that day we took the children to the park. 'Better the devil you know,' she'd said, gesturing at the men all around us, the devils we didn't yet know. 'My Jean-Luc has his faults,' she'd added, without throwing any light on what they might be, 'but, at the end of the day, you have to tell yourself that no man is perfect.'

'You look good tonight,' Nico said, his eyes flickering across my face and down towards my *décolleté*. I was wearing the wrap dress I'd worn to work that morning, and I'd applied a little make-up before I left home, not so much for Nico's benefit as to give me a thin layer of matt-finish confidence. 'I saw a nice picture of you recently, too,' he added. 'I think it must have been taken at that work party of Kate's . . .'

'Oh? How come you saw that?' Yves and Nico were in the habit of meeting in bars near the Champs Elysées, where they both worked, but it was hard to imagine them looking over photos of Kate's party together. Nico lowered his eyes and fiddled with his serviette for a moment, looking like he wished he'd held his tongue and, just as he opened his mouth to speak, I realized with a heart-stopping jolt that the photo in question was my profile picture on Rendez-vous.

'A colleague of mine got this email,' he said quickly, embarrassment colouring his cheeks. 'A Rendez-vous mailing-list thing: "Ten new members you might like to meet." Anyway' – he glanced up at me, as if to gauge my reaction – 'he recognized you and forwarded the message on to me. I didn't look at your profile, but it was a shock seeing the mother of my child on there for anyone to see . . .'

The truce we'd been enjoying for the past few minutes was over in an instant and I stared at him, feeling waves of anger wash over me. What right did Nico have to sound so possessive? What right did he have to criticize me – the 'mother of his child' – for putting myself out there and trying to rebuild my life?

'Don't you think that's a bit rich, coming from the man who brought his *stagiaire* home the second my belongings were out of the door?' I retorted, sarcastically, laying my hands on the table and seeing the crescent moons where I'd dug my fingernails into my palms. 'You obviously didn't mind what your colleagues thought about that. Talk about double standards . . .'

'I'm only saying I don't like the idea of you bringing a succession of different online dates home!' Nico's eyes flashed: my reference to Albane had hit home. 'I'm concerned about the effect it might have on our daughter . . .'

'Oh, for God's sake,' I said, exasperated, raising my voice now, not caring whether anyone else could hear me. 'Do you think I'd ever invite anyone over when Lila was with me? The last thing I want is her padding into my bedroom one morning and finding a stranger in my bed. How could you imagine I'd do such a thing?' Pushing back my chair, I rose to my feet, ignoring Nico's entreaty for me to remain seated. 'You have no right to police my love life, my sex life, or whatever it is that I may be looking for on that site,' I said, throwing down my serviette and casting around for my coat. 'I may be a mother, but mothers have needs too, you know. And as for you, you forfeited the right to comment on my private life the day you started fucking Mathilde.'

As I came to the end of my monologue, the waiter arrived with the main course, a braised lamb shank. 'I'm sorry, but I'm feeling unwell and I won't be staying,' I mumbled, taking down my coat and hanging it over my arm.

Giving Nico one last defiant glare, I turned and stormed out of the restaurant, my head held high. It had been a mistake, accepting his invitation, and I wouldn't make the same mistake twice.

13

Once the Toussaint holidays were over, the next few weeks scurried by in a blur of routine. When I woke Lila in the mornings, the sky outside her window was dark, and in the evenings when we trudged home from school the street lamps were already lit. I reverted to old habits: hibernating in front of the flickering television screen. I'd sworn off Rendez-vous for a while, although my profile remained online and the monthly payments still left my bank account, regular as clockwork. I met with Anna and Ryan for lunch on weekdays when our teaching timetables permitted and we'd enjoyed a long boozy brunch on my last child-free weekend. As for Kate, she'd cried off two of our fortnightly lunches in a row, citing last-minute work emergencies each time.

When there was no sign of Danièle, the paralegal I taught every Wednesday at three, I leafed through my notepad and found a blank page, intending to use the down time to work on my Christmas-shopping list, instead. There were three weekends before Christmas, true enough, but braving the crowded shops with a four-year-old in tow was not my definition of fun, so it was high time I got myself organized.

I'd need presents for Mum and Dad, with whom Lila and I would be staying for a few days either side of Christmas, and several things for Lila, of course. Kate had been on my list for years, and she and I had got into the habit of buying gifts for our respective children. I was less sure what to do about the Canet family. Traditionally I'd always been in charge of finding something for Catherine and Philippe, even if the tag claimed the gift came from 'Sally, Nico & Lila'. Similarly, 'Lila' had always bought something for Lucas, and Sophie always reciprocated. Adding these names to the bottom of my list, I frowned at the page. I would send Nico's parents a couple of nice bottles of wine as a token of my gratitude for all the time they spent looking after Lila during school holidays, I decided. Quite apart from the unexpected confidences she'd shared with me, hadn't Catherine made a point of remembering my birthday on her last visit?

The one name conspicuously absent from this year's list was Nico's. I flirted with the idea of buying him something tagged 'from Lila', but rejected the impulse before I'd had time to finish the third stroke of the letter 'N'. Deep down, I knew, if I did so, my motives would be murky at best, Machiavellian at worst. I'd coaxed Lila into crafting a home-made Father's Day card back in June, and Nico had been touched when she'd pressed the envelope into his hands. It was his visible discomfiture when he'd realized he'd let Mother's Day slip by unacknowledged that had given me the greatest pleasure, though, and I'd resolved never to stoop so low again. Gift-giving should never descend into a shaming game.

I was still agonizing over what on earth to buy for Mum and Dad when Danièle made her tardy entrance. 'Sorry I am late, Sally,' she gasped in English, her face flushed and her breathing laboured, as though she'd been running. 'My department had a little Christmas celebration lunch today,' she explained, pulling out the chair opposite mine and flopping into it. 'We lost all notion of the time . . . And yes, I know, we are only December 5th today,' she added, reading my mind, 'but one of the girls is going on her *congé maternité* tomorrow and we wanted her to join with us.'

I had a soft spot for Danièle. Short and a little on the round side, her cropped hair was dyed the aubergine shade of brown favoured by many French brunettes in their late forties as they fought back the advance of their first grey hairs. She wore small, dark-rimmed glasses that would have looked severe on anyone else, but on Danièle, who was rarely to be seen without a smile, they somehow ended up looking jaunty.

Danièle's command of English was surprisingly good and she'd been upfront with me from the start: she hadn't signed up for my lessons out of any real need to improve her language skills. 'Some time far from my desk is important for my sanity,' she'd told me good-humouredly at the beginning of her first session. 'The firm pays for language tuition and I choose English every single year because I enjoy it . . .' To say that she didn't take herself too seriously would have been an understatement.

But today, as our lesson unfolded, I realized Danièle wasn't just her usual good-humoured self, she was really rather tipsy. Her responses were slurred and, when I handed her a photocopied sheet to use for a reading exercise, instead of poring over the text, she began to use it to fan herself. 'This room is too hot, no?' she said, stumbling to her feet and lunging for the thermostat on the far wall, without waiting for my reply. As she crossed the room, she snagged one of her heels in the piece of loose carpet which had been used to conceal the wires snaking from the nearby video projector and, unable to check her forward momentum, she stepped clean out of her right shoe. 'I do not fool you, do I?' she said, putting a hand out to grip the sideboard to steady herself, giggling like a teenager. 'I had a few glasses of champagne with lunch, and they climbed straight to my head. I have no idea how I will work this afternoon.'

'Why don't you sit down, and I'll turn down the heating and fetch a carafe of water,' I suggested, my mouth twitching with mirth as I closed my textbook. 'I don't see any reason why we can't spend the rest of the lesson "practising your conversation skills".' I drew airborne quotation marks around the last four words with my fingers – a gesture I'd picked up from Ryan – to make it clear we'd be going through the motions. In Danièle's current state, there was no sense in trying anything ambitious. So, once I'd served her a large glass of water, I asked about her plans for the festive season.

'My son and his wife will come to dinner on Christmas Eve,' she replied, after draining her glass in a single, thirsty gulp. 'They're expecting their first baby, you know,' she added, beaming. 'I'm going to be a grandmother next year.'

'Congratulations! That's fantastic news!' I couldn't remember how it had come up in conversation but, on more than one occasion, Danièle had told me how impatient she was for her son to start a family. Her enthusiasm today was infectious and I was genuinely thrilled for her.

'And you, Sally? Where will *you* spend the holidays?' Danièle leaned forward in her chair and eyed me speculatively. 'Will you take your daughter to see your parents, in

England, or will you stay with your French *beaux-parents*, instead?' She seemed to be taking an excessively personal interest in my reply, and I suspected she was projecting ahead, wondering which set of grandparents her son and his wife would favour at this all-important time of year.

'Well,' I said slowly, 'Lila and I are going to stay in England for a few days over Christmas, and then she'll go with her father to see his family for the second half of the school holidays. No doubt we'll do things the opposite way round next year . . .'

For a second Danièle looked baffled. 'You are separated?' she said, when understanding dawned at last. I nodded in confirmation, and she gave a tiny grimace, no doubt hoping such a fate would never befall her unborn grandchild.

'It will be our first Christmas apart,' I explained, keeping the focus of our conversation on Christmas, as opposed to my failed relationship with Nico. However much I liked Danièle, I wasn't comfortable straying into territory too personal – such as why we'd chosen to separate – during lesson time. 'I'm kind of finding my way,' I added with a sigh. 'I was in the middle of deciding whether I should still buy Christmas gifts for the French side of the family when you walked through the door.'

'And what did you decide?' Danièle looked at me intently. Our subject matter seemed to have had a sobering effect on her. She was no longer slurring her words.

'Well, they're still Lila's grandparents, so I'm keeping them on my list,' I replied. 'The only difference will be that this time the gift will be from me only.' Danièle nodded, seemingly satisfied with my decision.

'I hope that something like this never happens to my son's couple,' she said, touching her palm to the wooden table superstitiously as she did so. 'But if one day it does, I hope my *belle-fille* will be as sensible as you. I really do.'

Deep in thought as I crossed the foyer of Danièle's law firm, I didn't see the tense figure waiting for me – just to the right of the sliding doors, where the sensor couldn't detect her presence – until I was almost close enough to reach out and touch her arm. 'Kate? What on earth are you doing here?' I said, slamming on my internal brakes and executing an exaggerated double take. 'Did I miss your call? I had no idea you were coming to meet me . . .'

Kate shook her head. She looked a mess. Not tired and dishevelled, like she'd been at Ryan's housewarming dinner a few weeks ago. No, there was more to it than that: it was as though every muscle in her body had been pulled taut with tension. I was so accustomed to envying my friend her confidence, her polish, that it came as a shock to see her this way, her eyes bloodshot, her jaw clenched. Her forced smile of greeting, as she murmured my name and kissed the air next to my cheeks, mechanically keeping up appearances, seemed to cost her a great deal of effort. It was plain to see that something was horribly wrong.

When I gestured in the direction of the café across the road, Kate gave a terse nod. I'd never set foot in the place before – on Wednesdays I finished at four and had got into the habit of using the free hour before I had to pick up Lila to run a few errands, as Kate well knew – but with its burgundy awnings and marble-effect *brasserie* tables, it had a reassuring air of anonymous, generic efficiency. Heads bowed to protect ourselves from the icy drizzle which had begun to fall while I was with Danièle, we narrowly missed being mowed down by a courier on a motorbike who had decided to cut across a corner of the pavement to save himself the bother of stopping at the traffic lights. '*Connard!*' I shouted, shaking a fist at his retreating leather-clad back. Kate shook her head and said nothing.

We chose a table in a corner, as far away as possible from the only other customers, four businessmen who were lingering over coffee and *digestifs* after what must have been an unashamedly long lunch. We'd only had time to remove our coats when an elderly career waiter in a white shirt and black apron appeared, right on cue. With a slight inclination of his head and a rising intonation on the word '*Mesdames?*' he managed both to greet us and to enquire about what we'd like to order, all in two economical syllables.

'*Un café pour moi, s'il vous plaît,*' I replied without even glancing at the menu, '*et un grand verre d'eau.*' Kate ordered a pot of mint tea. Her hands shook as she set her handbag on an adjacent chair and I noticed that, for the first time in years, she wasn't wearing her trademark carmine nail polish.

'I've done something awful,' Kate said in a low voice, 'and you're probably going to find yourself hating me when I tell you what it is.' Her eyes met mine for the briefest of instants before darting away, evasively.

'I can't imagine anything you could possibly do that would make me hate you,' I said, mystified. 'Is it work-related?' It must be, if whatever Kate had done was set to affect me in some way. Was she thinking of selling Tailor-Made? Or moving away? Had Yves accepted a job abroad? None of those scenarios seemed likely. As far as I knew, Tailor-Made's turnover was healthy, and Yves had invested a significant sum in the business using his last Christmas bonus. And after a brief stint at the head office of his bank in New York, back in the days when he was a lowly analyst, Kate's husband had never shown any sign of wanting to uproot his family.

Our waiter appeared before Kate could answer, setting down first her teapot, then my coffee and water. Glad of something to occupy her hands, she began agitating the teabag in the hot water with her teaspoon, cursing when the string spiralled around the stem like bindweed, impossible to dislodge. 'I've been unfaithful to Yves,' she said suddenly, setting down her spoon with a clatter and looking straight at me with watery eyes. 'And I'm pretty sure he suspects something . . . Now I know that after everything you went through with Nico, you're the last person I should be burdening with this,' she added, her voice beginning to waver, 'but I didn't know who else to tell.' She dug deep in her handbag for a packet of tissues, dangerously close to tears. 'I've fucked up, Sally,' she said pitifully. 'So badly. And I'm terrified I'm going to lose him.'

'Been unfaithful? With who? Why? Kate, I . . . I don't understand.' I stared at my friend, aghast, feeling as though the floor had been pulled out from under me. Over the past few months I'd got so used to – indeed, so comfortable with – playing the role of the wronged woman whose partner had strayed that it fitted me like a second skin. Kate had been so supportive throughout all that. She'd even made a point of introducing me to Anna. But now here was my best friend in the world telling me she'd behaved no better than Nico . . . Maybe Kate had indeed chosen the wrong shoulder to cry on – because my first instinct, despite the feelings of antipathy Yves had always aroused in me, was to think myself into his shoes. These were unexpected emotions: I was sorry for Yves, and furious with Kate. In the space of a few sentences, Kate had managed to turn my world on its head.

'*Who* it was is kind of beside the point,' said Kate, with a dismissive gesture. 'Although you did say something rather close to the bone a few weeks ago, at Ryan's house-warming.' I stared at her, my eyes narrowed. The missing pieces of a jigsaw I hadn't even known I was assembling were now clicking into place. The unfamiliar male voice I'd heard in the background that day Kate had phoned me, flustered, about my cancelled lesson; the missed lunches; her reluctance to talk about her flirtatious VIP client in front of Anna and Ryan. It was obvious: Kate had succumbed to the charms of one of her VIPs. She must have been gadding about with him while the rest of us were at work.

'I can guess what you're thinking, Sal.' Kate tensed her hands around her teacup, but did not raise it to her lips. 'You need to let me explain, though,' she added. 'There are things – important things – that you don't know about. Things which won't justify what I've done, but that will explain my actions, at least . . .'

'Well, I've got half an hour,' I replied, pivoting my wrist to glance at my watch. I felt sick to my stomach, but what choice did I have but to hear my friend out?

'The first bit you know about,' Kate said quickly. 'The VIP I told you about, François, the one I always referred to as "*le PDG*". He made a few passes at me over the years – inviting me to lunch, asking me to go on a business trip to interpret for him, that kind of thing – and I always side-stepped his invitations as politely as I could. I didn't want to lose his business, as you know. I couldn't afford to offend someone so important . . .'

I kept my eyes riveted on Kate's face. 'So what made you change your mind?' I prompted, as she paused for a moment, gnawing her bottom lip. I scarcely recognized my own voice: it sounded harsh, accusing and cold. Had Nico and Yves conducted a perfect mirror image of this conversation back in March, with Nico describing how he'd fought off his secretary's advances until, one day, for some reason I knew nothing about, he'd found his resolve weakening?

'I lost a baby in April,' Kate said quietly. 'I was four and a half months pregnant. We'd had all the routine scans and blood tests, and my doctor encouraged me to have an amnio, because the chances of Down's Syndrome looked abnormally high. But before we even got the results, before we'd even got as far as discussing whether we'd terminate if the baby tested positive, I lost her.' Tears shone in Kate's eyes now and her voice was desolate. 'I didn't tell anyone about it at the time,' she continued. 'That was how I coped: I kind of pretended none of it had happened. Luckily for me, I wasn't really showing much, and we'd held off telling anyone the news until the tests were completed. But Yves and I went through a really bad patch afterwards. I was angry because he didn't seem to be grieving the way I was. I accused him of never even wanting a third child in the first place . . .'

Tears prickled the backs of my own eyes as I tried to cast my mind back to our lunches in April. Had there been obvious signs of distress: clues that I'd missed, wrapped up as I'd been in my own dramas? I must have sat opposite Kate and gone on and on about Nico and Mathilde, blind to Kate's grief, assuming that she was upset only on my behalf. 'I'm so sorry,' I stammered, putting my hand over hers. 'I wish I'd known . . . I wish you'd told me . . . You must have been to hell and back. But, forgive me: I still don't understand how this relates to François?'

'Well, the physical side of things suffered a lot,' Kate replied, blushing as she always did whenever she evoked sex. 'What happened had driven this huge wedge between us, and Yves worked later, and went on more business trips. He never seemed to touch me any more and I was horribly lonely and sad. My self-confidence hit rock bottom. With the baby gone, I felt like a useless empty vessel. One day in June, when François asked me to join him for dinner, I found myself saying yes.'

Kate spared me the details of what had happened, where or how often, and I was grateful for that. It would have been unbearable, imagining her inventing work appointments as alibis, meeting in hotel rooms, treading the same path Nico had when he'd skulked around in the shadows with Mathilde. She told me only that she'd met with François semi-regularly from June until September and that spending time with this gallant, attentive man had diverted her attention away from her grief. In his presence she'd felt sexy and confident, instead of numb and empty. But these feelings had come at a price: Kate was loosening her grip on Tailor-Made and deceiving Yves and everyone around her, all for a fling which she'd known from the outset would never have any future. In October she'd explained to François that she couldn't see him any more, and he'd been surprisingly sanguine, as though for him, too, the fling had run its course. Kate had terminated his lessons and turned the page. More clear-headed than she'd been in months, she was ready to invest some serious time and effort into resuscitating her relationship with Yves.

'I don't understand,' I said frowning. 'I mean, if it's over and Yves is none the wiser, then why is this all a problem, apart from whatever feelings of guilt you're still carrying around with you? Why are you even telling me about it today?' The long and the short of it was that I'd have preferred not to know. However eloquently Kate had argued her case, whatever the mitigating circumstances, I still felt nauseous at the thought of my friend seeking solace in the arms of this François. She'd opened my mind up to the possibility that Nico had been with Mathilde for some rational reason, to make up for something he felt was lacking at home. In my black and white vision of right and wrong, I'd never allowed for any shades of grey, and I wasn't sure I could handle doing so now.

'Because I'm pretty sure Yves suspects something.' Kate put her elbows on the table and her palms to her forehead. 'This morning, when we were having breakfast,

I suggested getting away for a weekend on our own,' she explained. 'I said I thought we could do with some time alone together, without the kids, with no distractions . . . And, Sal, he turned me down.' She shook her head in disbelief. 'He said he didn't think being alone with me just now was a good idea. If anything, he needed more space. Then he announced that he's been giving some serious thought to accepting a secondment somewhere abroad for a few months . . . I don't want to lose him, Sal. We've had a rough patch, but I can't bear the idea of him leaving. I have no idea what he knows or doesn't know, and I can't decide whether to come clean or to keep my mouth shut. It's all such a mess.'

Our time was up, and once I'd paid for our drinks, hugged Kate tightly and bundled her into a passing taxi, I headed for the métro, my head spinning. On the one hand, I sympathized with Yves. Whether he was in full possession of the facts or not, he'd been wronged, just as I had, and if he chose to leave Kate, I could hardly blame him, could I? After all, I'd turned my back on Nico, adamant that there was nothing to be salvaged from our irreparably damaged relationship.

And yet it tore me apart, seeing Kate in pieces like this. I was still reeling from the news of the pregnancy I'd known nothing about and the heart-rending way it had ended, wishing Kate had confided in me at the time. Maybe if she had, none of this would have happened. I'd have done my best to talk her out of succumbing to François, to convince her the risks far outweighed the benefits, that while she was busy enjoying her trysts she was neglecting the real problems she faced at home.

There was no doubt in my mind that Kate had gone off the rails for a while. I abhorred what she'd done: the idea of her as an adulteress made me feel physically ill. But as I crumpled into a yellow plastic seat and waited for the next train, a part of me was nonetheless rooting for her and Yves to find some way to patch things up and carry on.

If they didn't, Kate would be in an even more extreme version of my own situation, with two children to look after and a business to run. And that wasn't a fate I'd wish on my worst enemy, let alone my best friend.

14

When the call came for parents with young children to board the Christmas Eve Cheap Jet flight to Leeds, I gave a silent prayer of thanks.

Our journey so far had been a nightmare. The taxi I'd reserved had turned up late, condemning Lila and me to a tense fifteen minutes of shivering on the pavement, surrounded by our suitcases, while I called *Taxis Bleus*, one anxious eye on my watch, the other frantically scanning rue de Belleville. When the car deigned to show up and we clambered inside, I leaned forward to question the driver about the state of the traffic, half shouting to make myself heard over the noise of his radio. 'Well, the *périphérique* was all snarled up this morning,' he replied matter-of-factly, causing my blood pressure to scale new heights, 'but the situation now' – he shrugged – 'well, it's anyone's guess . . .' It was only when we cruised down the slip road at Porte de Bagnolet and the electronic signs overhead announced that the ring road was '*fluide*' – a phrase which reminded me of Anna's unfortunate lesson about liquid metaphors – that I began to relax.

We were rocketing past Ikea, five minutes away from Charles de Gaulle airport, when Lila began to complain of a stomach ache. 'The *ceinture* is squishing my breakfast,' she said in a pitiful voice, tugging at her seat belt. 'Mummy, I think I'm going to be sick.'

'We're nearly there, my love,' I reassured her. 'You only have to keep the strap on for another five minutes and then we'll be able to get out.' Rifling through my rucksack, I removed the snacks I'd brought from the plastic bag which isolated them from the various colouring books, pens and card games we'd brought along for the journey, holding it ready just in case. 'If you're a good girl,' I added, wielding a carrot which, in my experience, was far mightier than the sword, 'then after we've checked in our luggage, I'll buy you a *pain au chocolat.*'

My attempted bribery did little to stem the tide of regurgitated cornflakes intent on making an appearance a few seconds later. Lila gave a strangled cough and, in an admirable show of damage limitation, I managed to catch all but a few drops of curdled milk in the transparent bag. Lowering my bounty gingerly to the floor, praying the bag wasn't riddled with holes, I dabbed at Lila's clothes with a tissue. Fortunately, our driver, deafened by his radio and focused on the road, remained blissfully ignorant of what had just come to pass.

Nursing a paper cup of lukewarm tea an hour later, I stared out of the plane window over Lila's shoulder. She'd recovered from her little episode in the car, as quickly as only a four-year-old can, and was now playing her favourite game, telling me which animal each of the clouds filing past the window resembled. It was my turn to feel nauseous now: knots of apprehension had been tightening in my belly ever since the alarm clock had sounded that morning. Our last visit to Mum and Dad's, back in July, hadn't gone well and, in the interim, many of my fortnightly phone calls to Mum had been fraught with tension.

I'd discussed my reticence about the visit with Anna over lunch earlier that week. 'Spare a thought for me when you're slicing into your Christmas turkey,' she'd said enviously. 'I'll be thousands of miles away from my family, no doubt with my nose stuck in a glass of bourbon.' Anna had been invited to a Christmas pot-luck lunch with a group of American friends she'd met through Tom, long before they broke up. Her plans sounded heavenly to me and I told her so, but Anna pursed her lips and shook her head.

'The thing about Christmas,' she explained, 'is that you're *supposed* to fight with your family. That's the whole point. I can cook lunch and get drunk with a gang of expats any time. There's nothing remotely festive about it . . .'

'Well, you're welcome to take Lila to Mum and Dad's,' I joked. 'If we bought you a curly brown wig, I bet my parents wouldn't even notice the difference. These days, I'm just the chaperone. They only have eyes for Lila . . .'

My words came back to haunt me with a vengeance when Lila and I arrived at Leeds Bradford airport. Mum had come inside to wait for us at Arrivals, while Dad executed leisurely laps around the airport's perimeter fence, loath, as always, to pay the parking fee, which he qualified as 'daylight robbery'. As soon as Mum caught sight of us, she let out a delighted cry and crouched down to give Lila a hug. It was only once she'd finished exclaiming over how much her granddaughter had grown and how her pigtails looked that she straightened herself up again and turned to greet me with a forced smile.

Mum, who looked much like me in the photos I'd seen of her in her thirties, had cut her hair progressively shorter as the years passed and opted for blonde highlights when grey began to gain the upper hand over mousy brown. I'd inherited my pale complexion and my pear-shaped figure from Mum's side of the family too. Uncharitable as it was, it had occurred to me more than once that she and Catherine were opposites. Mum came from down-to-earth Yorkshire stock, and when we laid the dinner table, there wasn't a napkin – let alone a napkin ring – in sight.

Dad's estate car pulled up at the pick-up point as we crossed the visitors' car park, and he leapt out of the car to give both 'his girls' a fierce hug. He looked tired, and I knew he was counting the days until he could retire from his middle-management job at an insurance company in Leeds the following summer. Once we'd exchanged a few meaningless pleasantries, he launched into one of his favourite diatribes about the number of speed cameras on his preferred route home from the airport.

That afternoon, listening with one ear to the sounds of Mum and Dad playing Jenga with Lila downstairs, I lounged on one of the twin beds which now occupied my child-hood bedroom, frowning at a copy of the *Radio Times*. My spirits sank further with every passing minute, and it had nothing to do with the fact that there didn't seem to be much on TV apart from pre-historic comedy re-runs and seasonal countdowns. Being home, in this room, cata-pulted me back in time, making me feel like a surly teen-ager again, even if it had been entirely redecorated, and only the framed degree certificate hanging over my bed bore witness to the fact that it had ever been mine.

I'd made countless trips to Yorkshire with Nico over the past years, and having him around had made a huge difference. Mum, in particular, treated me differently when Nico was there, addressing me as an adult equal, and the little things which tended to grate on me after two or three days at home had seemed trivial and harmless in his presence. Pushing the twin beds together every night, we'd poke fun at Mum and Dad's foibles, in French, after we turned out the lights, and there had been lots of muffled sex. There was something about the floral wallpaper, the chintzy bedspread and curtains which, Nico once confessed, made him want to 'desecrate' the room.

But when I'd visited in July, for the first time in years without Nico by my side, I'd felt myself slowly succumbing to the undertow, just as I was now. Whether she realized it or not, Mum had reverted to talking to me as though I was a recalcitrant teenager again, now that she no longer had an outside audience. In response I'd become defensive and resentful, reprising the role of my teenage self to perfection, spending much of my time holed up alone in my bedroom.

As dinnertime approached, I forced myself to go downstairs and lend Mum a hand in the kitchen, while Dad and Lila decorated the Christmas tree together in the living room, a task they'd saved until she arrived. 'How do you want these chopping?' I asked, when I'd finished peeling the carrots. Mum, who was busy stirring Yorkshire-pudding batter, looked up from her bowl with a blank expression, as though she hadn't understood my question. 'I thought maybe we could roast them in the oven with some cumin?' I suggested. 'Or we could sauté them with herbs and garlic? You know, for a change . . .'

'I don't think I've got any cumin,' Mum replied, pronouncing it 'come-in'. 'Besides,' she added, 'I think your father would prefer them steamed, as usual.'

I sighed and began chopping, my shoulders slumped in resignation. I knew I had to tread carefully where the subject of food was concerned, and it had, admittedly, been a long shot. 'Just because you swanned off to live on the Continent,' Mum was fond of saying, 'it doesn't mean we all have to start seasoning everything with garlic and eating half-cooked beef with blood gushing out of it.'

Abandoning my chopping board for a moment, I peeped through the serving hatch to see how the Christmas-tree decorating was progressing. Dad was busy untangling the knotted garland of fairy lights, replacing dead bulbs as he went along, while Lila examined the box of decorations with interest. 'Look, Granddad,' she exclaimed, dangling a bauble on a string from her forefinger. 'It's got lots of *paillettes*, this one. It's really pretty.'

'*Paillettes* means "glitter". Or "sequins",' I explained, intercepting Dad's nonplussed stare. Since Lila had started school, her French vocabulary had broadened noticeably. In conversation with me, she'd begun peppering her English phrases with French words, pausing from time to time to give me the opportunity to supply her with a translation. This was fine at home, but at Mum and Dad's, Lila's bilingual sentences caused problems. I'd returned from a trip to the village newsagent on my previous visit to find all hell breaking loose. Lila was refusing to drink her juice without a '*paille*', growing increasingly frustrated at her inability to make herself understood. While Mum looked on helplessly, Dad leafed through my old Collins Robert dictionary, looking for the relevant entry. But as he hadn't a clue how the word was spelled, his chances of success were slim.

'*Arrête tes caprices*, Lila!' I'd bellowed, throwing down my newspaper in exasperation. 'Grandma and Granddad don't have any straws, and you can drink perfectly well without one!' I often found myself reprimanding Lila in French: the language switch was unexpected, and never failed to stop my daughter in her tracks. But I could see from the expression on Mum and Dad's faces that they didn't appreciate this at all. It made them feel excluded in their own home.

'So,' said Mum, when I'd returned to the kitchen table to resume my chopping, 'you haven't said anything more about this internet dating business of yours. Does that mean you've seen sense and decided to knock it on the head?'

'I put it on hold for a few weeks before Christmas,' I replied, resenting both Mum's tone and her dismissive turn of phrase but doing my utmost to remain calm. 'My first few dates weren't up to much, but the chances are I'll pick up where I left off in the New Year . . .' In truth, I'd given serious thought to removing my profile altogether but, in the end, I hadn't gone through with it. For one thing, my one-year subscription hadn't been cheap. And, that aside, my Rendez-vous anecdotes had provided me with plenty of conversation fodder over the past three months. Anna and Ryan, who'd been privy to the most tragic profile pictures and sleazy chat-up emails, were always clamouring for updates.

'Do you even know what it is you're looking for?' asked Mum, her intonation making it plain she very much doubted I did. She'd set the bowl of batter on the sideboard – letting it rest – and turned to face me now, affecting a bewildered expression.

'I don't think I need to define anything in advance,' I countered, my chopping motion becoming more vigorous as my hackles rose. 'I mean, depending on who I meet, I might want a bit of fun, a few dates, a short fling. There's a lot of middle ground between being alone and being in a relationship, you know, Mum . . .' The root of Mum's problem was, I suspected, that she didn't know: Dad had been her one and only boyfriend. Or so the story went. No wonder she found my 'predicament' – as she called it – so difficult to relate to. It was so far beyond her own experience.

'And what does Lila think about her Mummy having "menfriends"?' Mum asked, her tone still sceptical, gesturing towards the living room with the tea towel she held in her hand.

'Absolutely nothing,' I insisted. 'She hasn't met a single one. I only ever go on dates when Lila's at Nico's, and I wouldn't bring any Tom, Dick or Harry home to mine, regardless of whether she was home or not.' Conscious of Lila and Dad in the next room, I kept my voice low, even though it now trembled with anger. It was galling to hear my mother talking as Nico had, that night at Chapeau Melon. Anyone would think the two of them were in league against me.

'I'm sorry, Sally,' Mum replied, sounding anything but. 'I know this isn't what you want to hear, but I can't help wishing you could put all that business from March behind you and find a way to patch things up with Nico. He's a good man. He's Lila's father. He made a mistake, but hasn't he paid for it by now?' She sighed, her eyes glazing over for a moment. 'Perhaps if the two of you had got married – like Kate and Yves – none of this would ever have happened.'

Her mention of Kate – Mum had always adored immaculate, successful Kate – was the drop of water which caused the vase to overflow, as the French would say. 'Mum, you have no idea what you are talking about,' I yelled, too exasperated to hold myself in check any longer. 'Wonderful Kate – whom you've always insisted on putting on some sort of pedestal – is having all sorts of marital problems. You don't know *her*, and you obviously don't know *me* very well either. And you have no right whatsoever to tell me I ought to have stayed in a relationship with a man who thought nothing of cheating on me with his secretary for months on end.'

Leaving my mother opening and closing her mouth like a goldfish, I stormed out of the kitchen and into the hallway, grabbing my coat from its temporary resting place on the end of the banister and sliding my feet into my boots. Dad appeared at the living-room door, still clutching the fairy lights, his face slack with shock. He might be a man of few words, but his silences spoke volumes.

'I'm sorry about the scene,' I said quietly, buttoning my coat with unsteady fingers and feeling dangerously close to tears, 'but Mum was way out of order . . . It's ironic when I think about it,' I added, shaking my head. 'Nico's own mother thinks leaving him was the right thing to do, but mine stands there reproaching me for not taking him back, and seems to think that, if I choose not to, I should resign myself to never going out with another man for as long as I live . . .'

If Lila hadn't appeared in the doorway, trailing a bushy piece of luxury Marks & Spencer tinsel in her wake and looking at me questioningly, I think Dad would have said something. As it was, he gestured at his granddaughter and shrugged. 'Mummy's going out for a little walk, my love,' I said, touching my hand to Lila's cheek, wondering how much she'd overheard, but thankful I'd refrained from mentioning Nico by name. 'I'll be back soon, sweet pea,' I told her, dropping to my knees to encircle her in my arms and give her a reassuring squeeze. 'You finish decorating the tree with Granddad, while I get some fresh air . . .'

After wandering aimlessly for a while in the deserted village streets, stepping in and out of the amber light cast by the street lamps and watching the ice clouds formed by my warm breath, my feet led me along a cut-through I dimly remembered; a snicket running parallel to a field where horses from a nearby riding school had roamed when I was a child. It bordered the perimeter fences of a bland new housing estate now, and the gravelled surface – I had a sudden memory of falling down and Mum painstakingly extracting pieces of grit from my bloodied knee – had given way to a generous layer of tarmac flecked with white stones. When I emerged from the other end, I found myself in the children's playground next to my old junior school. It was smaller than I remembered, and there wasn't a great deal left to play on, these days. The tall metal slide had been removed, along with its concrete base, no doubt having fallen foul of every safety regulation in the book. All that remained now were a row of swings and a wooden chicken on a giant spring.

It came as no surprise that I had the park to myself: night had begun to fall at four and, in almost every single house I'd passed, I'd seen families huddled around their flickering TV sets. I made a beeline for the nearest swing, stepping gingerly over a used condom and an empty packet of Smoky Bacon crisps. It was a snug fit, and the damp plastic seat felt like a slab of ice against my jeans, but I sat down anyway and pushed off, my legs instinctively remembering the movement needed to gain velocity, even though I hadn't sat on a swing in twenty years or more. As I soared higher the swing creaked ominously, the joints straining under my weight, but I continued, regardless, reasoning that I couldn't weigh more than the average obese teenager. In the end it was the wet seat that let me down. Sliding out from under my bottom on a backswing, it left me with no option but to jab my heels into the ground, the impact jarring my knees. When the seat thwacked me in the lower back, a split second later, I yelped in pain.

Abandoning the swings in disgust, I hobbled over to a wooden-slatted bench a few feet away. It was as damp as the swing, the wood tinged with green mildew, but when my enquiring hand came away clean, I lowered myself on to it. I remembered the last time I'd sat on this very bench as clearly as though it had been only yesterday. I'd been sixteen, going on seventeen, and it was a mild summer evening. For half an hour or more I'd stared at my watch and cursed under my breath as I waited for Richard Carter, an older boy who was seeing my best friend, Paula. He was late, but I had no way of knowing why. No one apart from drug dealers and city businessmen had mobile phones back then.

Paula, who was pretty in a very obvious, bleached-blonde, large-chested way, had already had a string of older boyfriends, whereas I'd only managed to harvest a few isolated, cider-flavoured kisses at friends' house parties. Richard wasn't interested in me: our cloak-and-dagger behaviour was all Paula's doing. I'd been over to see her earlier in the day and she'd begged me to meet Richard and act as her courier. He would give me a package – she wouldn't reveal its contents and I wasn't to look inside – and she'd instructed me to bring it to her house and pass it to her discreetly when the coast was clear. Her parents couldn't stand Richard – he had something of a bad-boy reputation after a local had spotted him spraying graffiti on the village bus shelter – and Paula couldn't set foot outside: she'd been grounded for some misdemeanour.

When Richard showed up, he'd barely given me the time of day, clambering off his bicycle for long enough to thrust a white-paper bag into my hands, then haring off along the snicket. I'd sat on the bench for a few moments afterwards, contemplating my bounty. When I peeped inside, giving in to the same impulse to pry which had got me into trouble with Nico, years later, I'd found a rectangular cardboard packet bearing a name I didn't recognize. Inside was a blister pack containing a single white tablet. In one sharp intake of breath I'd understood: it was the morning-after pill.

The discovery had filled me with self-righteous indignation. My friend – my best friend – hadn't even told me she was no longer a virgin, and not only was she secretly having sex, but she'd been taking stupid risks. If she wasn't careful, she'd end up like Sarah McFadden, the girl from our class who'd dropped out of school a couple of months before GCSE mock exams to have a baby.

I think I probably felt a jab of jealousy too, although I doubt I admitted it to myself at the time. Paula had crossed over to the other side, and I couldn't imagine following in her footsteps any time soon. 'I may not be as popular with the boys as Paula,' I remember saying to myself as I turned the packet over in my hands, 'but I'm nowhere near stupid enough to let this happen to me. There's no way I'll ever end up bringing up a child alone like Sarah McFadden . . .'

I'd been wrong about that, hadn't I? Sixteen years later, here I was, living alone with Lila. As for Paula, I had no idea where she was now. We'd lost touch years ago after I left home for university.

Rising to my feet, conscious of the damp cold that had begun to penetrate my core, I slowly retraced my steps to Mum and Dad's. Along the snicket to the road, in and out of the amber light cast by the street lamps, staring at the silent films playing out behind living-room windows as I passed. Sometimes I spied only one parent, but I felt sure the missing mother or father was only temporarily absent from the tableau, busy in the kitchen, or pouring themselves a glass of sherry, just outside my line of vision.

I was still angry with Mum, but I knew part of the reason I'd been so touchy about the subject of Nico was because I was missing his presence, too. It was our first Christmas in ten years without him, and it still felt like Nico's rightful place should be by our side, nursing a cup of coffee while Lila tore the wrapping paper from her presents on Christmas morning.

I didn't want to be with Nico any more, but I missed him, now and then, out of sheer force of habit. And when I padded up the stairs tonight, I knew that seeing the empty twin bed, no longer pushed up close to mine, would make me ache inside.

15

'Have you heard Kate's party's off?' I couldn't see Ryan's face, but he sounded disconcerted at having the plug pulled on his New Year plans only hours before he reached for the bottle of champagne which was, no doubt, chilling in his fridge. He'd lost no time in phoning me: I'd received Kate's cancellation text only a matter of seconds earlier.

'Yes,' I confirmed. 'I just read her message . . .' I was put out myself, but for a different reason. Kate's text had been apologetic but impersonal and I suspected she'd sent the same three sentences to everyone in her phone's address book. Didn't I – her best friend – deserve a more detailed explanation, given the conversation we'd had before Christmas? 'So terribly sorry,' the message had read, 'but Yves and I won't be able to host our New Year's get-together this evening. Please accept our sincere apologies for the short notice. We hope you all have a great evening! – KY.' When Kate and Yves referred to themselves as KY, it usually made me smile – the running gag being that you couldn't fail to get 'well lubricated' at one of Kate's parties. Today, however, it had given me pause for thought. How bad had things got? Was it the very last time Kate would sign off in this way?

Over Christmas, when I wasn't tiptoeing around Mum and Dad, struggling to preserve the uneasy truce we'd reached after I'd returned, shivering, from my trip to the

190

park, I'd spent a good deal of time fretting about Kate and Yves. I knew they'd spent Christmas with Yves' family in Versailles, keeping up appearances, but I'd had no word from Kate since the day I left Paris. Even the text message I'd sent her on Christmas day – including a photo of Lila posing in a ridiculous reindeer costume Mum had picked up in her local supermarket – hadn't prompted any reply, and her silence was troubling, to say the least. Kate was my best friend, but she was my employer too, and my livelihood depended on the health of her business. I wondered what implications it would have for my job – or Ryan's, or Anna's – if Yves decided to leave and take his capital with him.

'Did you have a plan B for tonight?' I asked Ryan, wishing I was as blissfully unaware of Kate's problems as he appeared to be.

'I do have a couple of invitations I'd held in reserve,' Ryan admitted, 'although I suspect neither will be able to hold a torch to Kate's . . .' He sighed. 'Kate always lays on the most fantastic nibbles,' he added mournfully, 'and seeing in the New Year at her place is such a tradition . . .'

'Well, how about I chaperone you to whichever party you rate as the runner-up?' I suggested, thankful Ryan hadn't tried to draw me into any speculation about the likely cause of the last-minute cancellation. 'Lila's with Nico's family, and I don't fancy seeing in the New Year on my own, so let's salvage something out of this wreckage . . .'

'Sounds like a plan,' Ryan replied, perking up audibly. 'I'll conduct some research into our options and, by the time you get over here for your *apéro* at eight, I'll know for sure where we're heading from here. Now, what about Anna? Will you call her, or shall I?'

'Anna's in London for New Year's,' I reminded him. 'Staying with an American friend of hers, remember?' I felt a tiny stab of jealousy when Ryan pronounced Anna's name. We'd known one another since long before Anna arrived on the scene but, given all the extra spare time single, childless Anna had at her disposal, I suspected she'd been seeing far more of Ryan than I had, lately.

As soon as Ryan had hung up, I dialled Kate's mobile. 'You've reached Kate Taylor,' the even-toned, professional-sounding message said, first in French, then in English. 'I'm afraid I'm not available at the moment, but do leave a message and I'll call back as soon as I can.' There was no ringing tone before the message kicked in, which implied her phone was switched off. It didn't bode well, but short of turning up, unannounced, on Kate's doorstep, there wasn't much I could do but wait until she made contact of her own volition.

The first thing I noticed when Ryan threw open his front door was that he looked inordinately pleased with himself. 'You look like the cat that got the cream,' I remarked, stepping inside and prompting Clyde to dart across the living room to his usual hiding place under Ryan's bed.

Ryan grinned smugly. 'Remember Eric, that banker friend of Yves' I met back in September and started seeing on and off?' I nodded. We'd never actually been introduced, but I'd certainly heard plenty about him. 'Well,' Ryan continued, 'Eric's been on a secondment to Latvia, or Lithuania, or somewhere in one of those former Eastern bloc countries, but he's back in Paris for New Year. And he's invited me – or rather, us – to a fabulous party. Some friend of his has an apartment near Bourse with a roof terrace. I'm told you can see the Eiffel Tower from there, so we'll be able to pop outside to watch the fireworks at midnight . . .'

Ryan's studiously vague-sounding 'Latvia, or Lithuania or . . .' hadn't fooled me for a moment. He'd been pining for Eric ever since he'd gone away and I was sure he'd been monitoring his movements closely. 'It sounds perfect,' I said brightly, thinking to myself that it sounded anything but. I had visions of Ryan and Eric gazing into one another's eyes while I played gooseberry. 'Sally, whatever happens, we'll stick together until well after the clock strikes midnight,' Ryan reassured me, as perceptive as ever. 'I'll be taking my chaperone duties very seriously,' he added. 'You'll need me to fight the men off you with a big stick. That dress of yours is divine . . .'

My black dress – an empire-line design which emphasized my bust and camouflaged my hips – was new: I'd caught a train from Mum and Dad's to Leeds to go shopping a couple of days after Christmas. The January sales wouldn't begin for another couple of weeks in Paris, but in England they were already in full swing and I'd finally got around to spending the belated birthday money Nico's mother had given me back in November.

Reluctant to brave the bitter cold and knowing full well it would be impossible to find a taxi, Ryan and I took the métro to the party. Our carriage was packed with revellers on their way out to parties, bars and nightclubs: everyone could ride public transport for free on New Year's Eve, with selected lines running without interruption from dusk until dawn. 'What is it about Christmas and sequins?'

I said, giving a leggy brunette wearing a gold-sequinned mini-skirt a doubtful look. 'The French are so good at pulling off tasteful and understated for the rest of the year. And then on *Réveillon* night it all goes to pot . . .'

'You have a point.' Ryan surveyed our fellow passengers with narrowed eyes. 'At the last count there were twelve feather boas in this carriage alone. And feather boas, in my book, are permitted in two contexts only: on drag queens and inside your daughter's dressing-up chest.'

Coming to a halt on the pavement in front of the address Eric had provided, our eyes were greeted by an uninspiring block of flats, built in the late eighties, at a guess. But when we stepped out of the lift on to the eighth-floor landing and peered through the open double doors into the huge living area, my jaw dropped. 'I'm not sure the word "apartment" does this justice,' I murmured in Ryan's ear. 'This is more like a penthouse suite . . .'

Inside, all was open plan and fiercely minimalist, and it looked as though an interior designer had been let loose with an unlimited budget. A dozen guests were seated on a vast, horseshoe-shaped cherry-red sofa to our right and the glass coffee table in their midst bore several silver champagne buckets and a tray of elegant-looking *petit fours*. To our left was a long dining table laden with more nibbles: *foie gras*, smoked salmon, and blinis with what at first glance looked like *tapenade* but turned out, on closer inspection, to be caviar. Abstract paintings hung on the white walls and glass sliding doors led on to the infamous roof terrace.

'Ah, *vous êtes venus*!' exclaimed Eric, appearing from a corridor to our left. '*Alors, c'est* Sally, *n'est-ce pas?* I don't believe we've been introduced, but Ryan tells me you are both friends of Yves' lovely wife, Kate?' He kissed first me, then Ryan, on both cheeks. Eric reminded me a little of Yves – something about his confident bearing and his choice of off-duty, smart-casual clothes, perhaps – but the way his eyes softened when he looked at Ryan endeared him to me. 'Let me introduce you both to Laurent,' he said, steering us towards the sofa and gesturing to a man with short bleached-blond hair who looked as though he was channelling Jean-Paul Gaultier. 'Laurent is one of my oldest friends,' he added. 'We went to school together . . .'

Perched on one end of the sofa with Ryan by my side and a glass of champagne in my hand, I was glad my friend seemed to feel as awe-struck by the company we were keeping as I did. Laurent, it transpired, was at the helm of a successful TV production company. With a wink, Eric told me that if I played my cards right, I could find myself jetting off to join the temptresses camp on *Île de la Tentation*. 'Knowing my luck,' I retorted dryly, 'I'd end up on that hideous reality show where single city girls are packed off to seduce lonely farmers. You know, the one in which some clueless bimbo always ends up milking a cow while wearing stilettos?'

Among Laurent's guests were a few people I thought I recognized: up and coming TV presenters, a young actress and a waif-like model with razor-sharp shoulders and protruding ribs who looked as though she really ought to tuck into some of the *foie gras*. 'This is officially a people-watching evening,' Ryan murmured in my ear. I knew what he meant. Eric had been doing the rounds, chatting to the other guests, but we were both far too daunted to mingle.

An hour or so after we arrived, Eric leaned over the back of the sofa and suggested Ryan and I accompany him out on to the roof terrace. Ryan sprang up, glass in hand, delighted to have Eric's undivided attention, and I had no choice but to follow, reluctant to remain indoors alone. Although a row of outdoor patio heaters was belting out heat, Eric gallantly offered to put his jacket around my shoulders, and I gratefully accepted. 'This party is about to get a lot more interesting,' whispered Eric, as the three of us leaned against the railings and gazed out across the city skyline. I frowned. I hadn't the faintest idea what he was talking about. Was some celebrity about to walk through the door?

'I brought this . . .' Eric reached into his trouser pocket and withdrew something, opening his palm to reveal a re-sealable plastic bag containing an opaque crystal. '*Du MDMA*,' he explained. 'Very pure, very clean . . . I propose we pop it into a glass of champagne, let it dissolve and share it between us.'

'I'm up for it if you are,' said Ryan eagerly, shooting me a questioning glance. 'What do you think, Sally? Fancy seeing in the New Year with a silly smile on your face?'

I paused for a moment, pretending to be captivated by the sight of the Eiffel Tower, which had begun to sparkle, as it did on the hour, every hour, after nightfall. In truth, I was agonizing over how to respond. It was a long time since anyone had offered me anything like that, and there was a time when I'd have said yes without a moment's hesitation. I had some very pleasant memories of dropping

196

E's in my early twenties, dancing for hours on end in nightclubs, losing all sense of time, hypnotized by the music and feeling – for a few hours at least – as though everything in my life were seamlessly perfect. But years had passed since anything stronger than alcohol had crossed my lips, and I had Lila to think of now. She was staying in Chantilly for a few days, so I knew I'd have plenty of time to recover before she returned, but that wasn't my main concern. What, said a little voice in my head, if something went wrong?

It was as though a switch had been flipped inside me when I became a mother. I became hyper-conscious of my own mortality from one day to the next. This feeling manifested itself in different ways: I refused to cross the road unless the green man showed, I lost my taste for high-adrenalin fairground rides and I'd fallen prey to vertigo the last time I stepped out on to the windswept viewing deck of the Montparnasse Tower. None of these activities had become any more dangerous overnight, but *I'd* changed; my appetite for risk was significantly lower. As a mother, I had responsibilities which childless people like Ryan and Eric couldn't even begin to comprehend. If keeping my daughter safe was my number-one priority, keeping myself out of harm's way for Lila's sake came a close second.

'It's much safer than Ecstasy in tablet form,' Eric added, sensing my indecision. 'Those pills were like Russian roulette: you were as likely to take horse tranquillizer or laxatives as the real thing. But this is the good stuff. It's really mellow. Honestly, Sally, there's nothing to worry about . . .'

I nodded. My resolve was weakening. The last nine months hadn't been a walk in the park, and it was tempting, the idea of stepping outside of myself for a few hours, seeing my life – my messy, complicated life – bathed in a flattering, soft-focus glow. I felt a tightness in my chest as my body remembered what it felt like to come up, fear and anticipation jostling to gain the upper hand. 'Okay, I'm in,' I replied, still half hoping Ryan would back out at the last minute.

But Eric had already emptied the contents of the bag into his glass of champagne. He raised it towards the light, and three pairs of eyes watched intently as the tiny crystal began to dissolve.

It took me the longest time to identify the noise that woke me from my shallow slumber, punctuated with vivid, surreal dreams, late on New Year's Day. First, I reached on autopilot for my alarm clock and fumbled for the 'off' button, to no avail. Next, my hand closed around the mobile phone which lay on my bedside table, but there was no telltale vibration. It was only when the ringing sound had stopped that my brain found a way to interpret what it was hearing and identified the culprit: my landline. Bleary-eyed, I staggered out into the living room, temporarily blinded by the fading afternoon light. I picked up the handset, staring at it uncomprehendingly for a moment, my dilated pupils making it difficult to bring the display into focus.

'Missed call: Kate,' I deciphered. 'Oh shit,' I groaned to myself. I was in no fit state to have a serious conversation with anyone, but I could hardly ignore Kate. Scrolling through the address book, I selected her number, narrowly missing placing an accidental call to 'Mum & Dad', her closest bedfellows on the alphabetical list. 'Kate?' I said as soon as she picked up, my voice still thick with sleep. 'It's me, Sal. Sorry . . . I was in bed . . . I've been worried about you. Are you okay?'

'No. Really not.' Kate's voice was brittle, her words clipped. 'Can I come over, Sal? I need to get out of here and I've nowhere else to go . . .'

'Of course you can,' I said quickly, 'my door is always open. You know that.'

My efforts to spruce myself up in readiness for Kate's visit were tragi-comic. I began to run a bath, it only clicking ten minutes later, when the hot water had run out, that I'd forgotten to put in the plug. I filled the kettle, returning several times to check on its progress before realizing I hadn't switched it on. These were textbook come-down symptoms: my brain was like a slab of Emmental, riddled with huge, irregular holes, or a half-finished game of Join the Dots in one of Lila's activity books. When Kate rang the doorbell, a little over an hour later, I'd managed only to pull on my dressing gown and pour myself a glass of juice.

Kate looked as though she'd been to hell and back. The whites of her eyes were cross-hatched with red, the skin beneath them so dark, so bruised-looking that, for one nauseating instant, I wondered whether Yves had raised his hand to her. 'I know, I know, I look terrible,' Kate said, registering my shock. 'I haven't had much sleep these past few nights. And let's face it,' she added with a hollow approximation of a laugh, 'it's years since you've seen me without any make-up.'

Kate declined tea, requesting a glass of water instead, saying, quite matter-of-factly, that she felt dehydrated from her weeping marathon. We settled into the sofa and I was struck by how vulnerable she looked, dressed simply in faded jeans and a navy V-necked sweater, her knees supporting her chin, her arms wrapped around her calves. 'So, why did you cancel the party?' I decided it was pointless beating about the bush. 'Did Yves find out?' Kate closed her eyes for a moment, then gave a tiny nod.

'In the end he came right out and asked me when we got back from his parents' place yesterday morning,' she explained. 'I think I intended to deny it, but I couldn't get the words out . . . I just stood there looking guilty. So, quite rightly, he took my silence as an admission of guilt. I didn't give him any details, only swore it was over. And he said he wasn't sure how he felt about me any more.' Kate's voice was flat and devoid of emotion, as though she were in a trance or suffering from shock. 'He's sleeping in the spare room for now,' she added. 'He barely speaks to me, and he leaves the room every time I walk in. I couldn't face going ahead with the party under those circumstances. Now I'm praying he won't decide to leave for good . . .'

As Kate spoke, I was transported back in time to the weeks before I left Nico. Kate didn't know how lucky she was to have an apartment which afforded her and Yves the luxury of being able to retreat to separate bedrooms. Nico had slept on the sofa every night, but we couldn't escape one another, not really. I remembered once waging a heroic battle with my bladder because I couldn't face crossing the living room where Nico lay, blocking my route to the bathroom.

'What do you think the chances are of him staying?' I asked her. 'I mean, I don't think I have any idea what Yves' stance on infidelity is. But if he's anything like Nico,

I'd have thought there was some hope? You know, that he'd be able to find a way to take this all in his stride . . .'

'Ah, you'd be surprised,' said Kate, with a wan smile. 'Nico and Yves may be good friends, but when it comes to certain moral questions, they're poles apart . . . When Yves found out what Nico had been up to with Mathilde, he was disgusted with him. Nico came over one night, soon after it happened, and when he started going on about you looking at his MSN and violating his privacy – getting on his high horse and trying to make it sound as though you'd behaved as badly as he had – Yves was having none of it. He's always taken your side. They're still friends, but there are certain subjects they don't broach any more, because Yves made it quite clear how much he disapproved . . .'

My eyes widened in astonishment upon hearing this unexpected information. First there had been the sympathetic reaction from Nico's mother, and now this. 'I knew you'd find that difficult to get your head around,' Kate said, shaking her head. 'I'm not blind, you know. I know the two of you never really hit it off. But Yves has an enormous amount of respect for you, Sal. I think he just finds your humour a bit intimidating; your sarcasm, in particular.'

'I must admit, I never imagined he'd take my side against Nico,' I said thoughtfully.

'. . . Or that you'd find yourself instinctively taking his side against me?' said Kate, finishing my sentence.

'No,' I insisted. 'Kate, it's so much more complicated than that. It's true that I never expected I'd empathize with him like this, one day. I know how he must feel, looking at you, imagining some other man touching his wife. But then I find myself wanting him to make the decision I couldn't make – to stay with you and the boys, regardless – and that's even stranger. You've turned everything I thought I believed inside out . . .'

Kate looked me in the eye properly for the first time since she'd walked through the door, and I could see from her shocked expression that she'd noticed the abnormal diameter of my pupils. 'Jesus, Sal,' she said sharply, 'what on earth did you get up to last night? You sounded spaced on the phone, but I thought it was a regular hangover . . .'

Reluctantly, I recounted the second half of my evening with Eric and Ryan, although there wasn't much to tell. About an hour after I swilled back my share of the champagne, grimacing at the bitter, chemical aftertaste, I'd turned to Ryan and complained that nothing was happening. 'You say that, Sally,' he said, grinning more widely than usual, 'but, believe me, something's going on. Your irises are missing in action, for a start.'

Perhaps my apprehension had held the drugs at arm's length up until that point, but no sooner had Ryan spoken than my skin began to tingle. The quality of the light shifted, just a little, and tiny waves of contentment rippled through me. We'd moved inside, to escape the cold and set the experience to music, and I'd spent the rest of the evening welded to the sofa. Eric and Ryan, seated by my side, were talking in low voices, but I didn't feel the need for speech or interaction. I was self-sufficient, happily locked inside my own skull. I'd forgotten to watch the fireworks at midnight. In fact, I'd spent much of the evening with my head on Ryan's shoulder and my eyes closed.

'It doesn't sound like much fun to me,' Kate said doubtfully, 'sitting on a sofa all evening and not talking to a soul . . .

I thought that sort of thing was meant to make people all tactile and affectionate, not completely anti-social?'

'I think how that stuff affects you kind of depends on the amount, and on the context you're in at the time,' I said with a sigh. 'But it was a mistake, I realize that now. I mean, at my age, I should know better than to cave in to peer pressure. I suppose I'm still feeling my way, you know? Working out, kind of by trial and error, what I can and can't do compared to my childless single friends . . . Or rather, what I feel comfortable doing.'

Kate nodded, seemingly satisfied with this explanation. 'I must say,' I added, anxious to change the subject, 'I did get the impression that Eric and Ryan had a lovely time. We caught a taxi home together and, while I pretended to be dozing, they were locked together at the lips for so long that I thought one of them would suffocate. I think the experience really cemented things between them . . .'

'Good for Ryan,' Kate said softly. 'Yves always spoke highly of Eric. I think Ryan may be on to something pretty special there . . .'

When Kate left, an hour or so later, I replayed our conversation in my head, digesting everything she'd told me. I groaned out loud when I realized how clumsy I'd been, parading Ryan and Eric's blossoming romance in front of my best friend when her own relationship appeared to be teetering on the brink of disaster.

She'd been gracious enough to wish Ryan well, but goodness only knew how much she'd been hurting on the inside. I needed to work harder at being there for Kate. That would be my first New Year's resolution.

16

When I looked out of my bedroom window on my first day back at work after the holidays, our courtyard was covered with a thin dusting of snow. I hurried through to Lila's room to wake her, and she shrieked with excitement as I drew back her curtains. 'It looks like the icing sugar we putted on the mince pies,' she cried, her breath fogging up the window. 'Will it snow some more later, Mummy? Will I be able to build a snowman?'

The skies were white as we set out for school, half an hour later. The powder had settled on the roofs of the parked cars we passed, on the lids of the green wheelie bins which had spent the night out on the pavements, and even in the grooves of the metal shutters drawn down over the shop windows, although underfoot it had already melted to form a dirty grey sludge. Here and there, frosted Christmas trees lay abandoned by the roadside, looking sorry for themselves. 'Now, don't forget that it's Daddy who's coming to fetch you tonight,' I said, as I slung Lila's overnight bag over the peg outside her classroom door. Nico, who'd been away for a few days over New Year, skiing with friends, wasn't due back at work for another couple of days and had called me the previous evening – to my astonishment – to ask whether he might take Lila for the night. Could it be, I speculated, that he'd made a resolution to spend more time with his daughter in the New Year? If so, I certainly wouldn't look a gift horse in the mouth.

There was no sign of the tramps who usually camped out on the strip of pavement in front of the railings by the métro that morning. Presumably they'd migrated to a more clement location, taking their bottles of *vin de table* and tartan-patterned storage bags of belongings with them. Inside the newspaper kiosk, a single electric heater was fighting a losing battle against the cold. '*Ça caille aujourd'hui, hein?*' remarked the elderly owner, stretching out a gloved hand to take my coins. Once I'd descended into the womb of the métro, however, I was forced to unbutton my heavy coat and loosen my scarf.

Settling into a free seat and opening my newspaper to the classifieds, I found a single New Year's *Transports amoureux* entry. '31/12, St Germain *vers* 21h21,' I read. '4 hands in 4 pockets, 2 smiles. Same time and place on Tuesday?' I smiled at the author's use of '*vers*'. Noting the exact time and then pairing it with the word 'around' struck me as paradoxical, to say the least.

The morning's lessons were pretty uneventful. For the most part, I stuck to the exercises I'd prepared from my textbooks, the only half-hearted attempt I made at improvization falling catastrophically flat. I asked Rémy, a bland investment banker with tortoiseshell glasses, if he'd made any resolutions for the New Year, curious to discover if he had any vices. 'I do not believe in make ze personal resolutions,' he replied, looking at me as though he thought I was barking mad. 'I 'av already enough targets to meet in ze office.'

When I arrived at the top floor of Rivoire headquarters for Delphine's lesson, I winced at my first sighting of this year's designer Christmas tree. Two metres high, it was dressed from top to bottom in brown leather baubles, each bearing the famous monogrammed initials of Rivoire's most exclusive fashion brand.

'*C'est hideux, n'est-ce pas?*' said Delphine with a grin, noting my horrified expression as she strutted along the corridor and planted the obligatory New Year's kisses on my cheeks. I didn't encourage pupils to greet me this way but, at this time of year, all sorts of exceptions had to be made to usual *bise* etiquette. The first time a French person saw any colleague or acquaintance after the holiday season there was a compulsory exchange of kisses, whether the meeting took place on New Year's Day itself, or as much as two weeks later. It was a task to which some of my male pupils applied themselves with evident relish, and I was secretly dreading my lesson with Marc de Pourtalès from Human Resources, hoping that, for once, he'd laid off the goat's cheese at lunch.

'How was your Christmas?' I enquired, nudging the conversation into English as Delphine led the way into our habitual meeting room. 'I'm assuming you managed to take a few days off . . . Did you take your daughter to stay with family?'

'I did.' Delphine smiled warmly. 'It was good, even if Madame Rivoire was phoning me often . . . Even on the twenty for*ce*, while I was 'aving dinner with my family!' I raised an eyebrow, but refrained from commenting on what I thought of her employer and corrected her pronunciation of 'fourth' instead. Delphine pulled out a chair and slid gracefully into it, her expression coy. 'I 'ave some news,' she announced, pausing for dramatic effect. 'I met a very nice man at ze *réveillon* party in my parents' village. A divorced man, who *leaves* in Paris. I have a meeting with 'im tonight . . .'

'That's fantastic news, Delphine!' This time I didn't have the heart to correct her pronunciation, but privately I had my doubts as to whether there was room in Delphine's life for another man, given how large Rivoire already loomed.

When our lesson came to an end, Delphine excused herself for a moment while I packed away my teaching materials. She returned carrying a small bag bearing the monogram I'd seen on the Christmas-tree decorations. 'Zees is for you, Sally,' she said, setting the bag down in front of me with a flourish. 'Don't worry,' she added, sensing my discomfiture, 'I expect no gift from you. But at Christmas I send out so many things – 'andbags for the wife of the President, for Catherine Deneuve, a long list of actresses and celebrities. And *Monsieur* authorizes me to give some small gifts to the people I work with too . . .'

'That's so sweet of you,' I exclaimed, feeling oddly self-conscious as I peered into the bag. It was the first time a pupil had ever presented me with a gift. I withdrew a white box, tied with a wide gold ribbon. Inside, swaddled in several layers of rustling tissue paper, was a beautiful silk scarf. 'Oh, Delphine, it's lovely,' I gasped, catching sight of the label as I caressed the soft fabric. From the scant knowledge I'd gleaned from thumbing through back issues of *Madame Figaro* and *Elle* in doctors' waiting rooms, I suspected a scarf like this one must retail for at least half my monthly wages.

'I choose one without ze monogram,' Delphine explained, smiling widely, pleased with herself. 'And when

I saw 'ow you look at the decorations on our *sapin* earlier, I knew I 'ad made the good choice . . .'

Plummeting towards the first floor for my lesson with Marc de Pourtalès, I slipped my hand inside the bag, eased the box open and stroked the scarf covertly with my fingertips. French women seemed to be born with the knowledge of how to knot a scarf casually around their necks or fasten their hair in a loose chignon, almost as though it were programmed into their DNA. But I was no Frenchwoman, and I knew if I was ever to wear it, I'd have to ask Kate – in her capacity as honorary *Parisienne* – to give me a scarf-tying lesson first. Delphine would be offended if I didn't show up wearing my gift the next time we met.

That evening, without Lila's evening routine to attend to, I felt lost. To make matters worse, Nico had told me he planned to take her to see the children's Christmas-window displays in the department stores on boulevard Haussmann after school, taking advantage of the lull between the school holidays and the January sales. This was something we'd always done together, braving the crowds so that Lila could gaze, wide-eyed, at dancing teddy bears, flying fairies or puppet pigs raiding confectionery stores. Was Albane with them this evening? I wondered. Had she stepped nonchalantly into my shoes? It wasn't long before I found myself opening my computer and keying in the Rendez-vous address in an attempt to distract myself from such thoughts.

AussieRob numbered among the five or six people I'd 'flashed' on a whim the night before, after browsing the profiles of the single men in their thirties who lived within a five-kilometre radius of Belleville and studying their photos. When I navigated to my profile, I was informed that not only had Rob returned the compliment, but he was listed as *'actuellement en ligne!'* I'd never initiated a chat session before but, feeling inexplicably bold, I clicked on the *'inviter au chat'* link next to his profile photo. Rob accepted at once. 'Here goes,' I murmured to myself as I laid my fingers on the keyboard, in the ready position. 'Remember, Sally, you have nothing to lose and everything to gain . . .'

'Good evening,' said Rob. 'I must say, I've never been out with a MILF before . . . But I'm definitely open to the idea . . .'

Frowning, I opened up a new tab on my browser so I could look up the unfamiliar word in an online dictionary. 'Slang acronym: **M**other **I**'d **L**ike to **F**uck,' I read, my cheeks colouring. 'A much-used descriptor on the Internet for pornography sites featuring women between the ages of 30 and 55.'

'Well, I've never been called a MILF before,' I retorted, returning to the chat window. I decided not to own up to the fact that I hadn't even been familiar with the term thirty seconds earlier. 'So tell me,' I continued, 'am I supposed to be flattered or insulted by being pigeonholed into a category of porn?'

'Flattered,' Rob shot back. 'No offence intended whatsoever. I guess it's my clumsy way of saying I think you look cute on your profile photo . . . So, what do you say, fancy meeting for a drink?'

I hesitated for a moment, scanning Rob's profile to remind myself why I'd 'flashed' him in the first place. He'd been in Paris a few years, worked as a graphic designer, lived nearby, in Ménilmontant, and was a year older than me. His profile photo showed him sitting cross-legged on the parapet overlooking the rue de Belleville, the Paris skyline laid out behind him. He had an open, honest-looking face and an attractive smile. So, biting my lip, I decided to give Rob the benefit of the doubt, despite his somewhat sleazy opening gambit. 'Okay,' I responded, after a short pause. 'How about a coffee or an *apéro* in the neighbourhood sometime next weekend?'

'Well, actually, I'm about finished up here for the day,' Rob replied. 'So, if you happen to be free tonight, maybe we don't have to wait that long?' I grinned to myself. The timing was almost too good to be true. How often did I get a chance to be impulsive?

'See you at Lou Pascalou in an hour,' I typed, taking a leaf out of Manu's book and daring to log out without waiting for Rob's reply. As I changed out of my work clothes into jeans and a smart jumper, I felt absurdly pleased with myself. It felt good sliding over into the driving seat and taking the wheel for a change.

An hour later, seated on the wooden banquette that ran the full length of the back wall of the bar, I began to wonder whether my impulse had been so very inspired. There was no sign of Rob whatsoever: the only customers on this wintry Monday evening were the handful of middle-aged, ruddy-faced regulars propping up the bar, a couple of students playing chess with fierce concentration, and a geeky-looking guy with a ponytail, his face partially obscured by the screen of his MacBook. Drinking my kir in measured, self-conscious sips, I pretended to study the artwork decorating the walls. The current month's offerings – all for sale – were a series of childlike collages with inflated price tags. Under cover of the table, I tapped my feet against the floor, trying to get my circulation going after the icy walk over. I'll give him half an hour, I resolved. And if our date falls through, it will have been my own silly fault for signing off without even giving him my mobile number.

But suddenly Rob was wiping his feet on the doormat and making a beeline towards my table. He wore a vintage leather jacket over a polo-necked jumper, and a courier-style bag with a diagonal strap. His face was square-jawed and wholesome-looking, his dark hair was clipped short and his eyes were a striking shade of blue. 'Good choice of bar,' he said approvingly as he pulled out the wooden chair opposite mine, stowing his coat and bag on the empty table beside us. 'Sorry to keep you waiting. I got a work call just as I was about to leave. I would have warned you, but . . .'

'. . . I didn't hang around long enough to tell you how to contact me,' I interrupted with a rueful smile.

'No worries,' Rob said nonchalantly, turning in his chair to catch the waiter's eye. He ordered himself a pastis, a Lou Pascalou speciality, his French impressively fluent and Parisian-sounding. When he asked me if I wanted the same, I grimaced and confessed that aniseed had always been a pet hate of mine.

'You should have put that on your profile,' Rob teased. 'It would have saved me a wasted journey. Not sharing my fondness for pastis is a deal breaker, as far as I'm concerned.' I rolled my eyes at him and, turning to the waiter, ordered myself a mojito instead. This all seems rather promising, I thought to myself. He's only been here five minutes, but he already stands head and shoulders above the other Rendez-vous candidates I've met so far . . .

Despite these auspicious beginnings, I was forced to conclude, a couple of hours later, that Rob wasn't really my type. As we talked, I struggled to put my finger on just what it was that wasn't right. He was fun to be with, there was no doubt about that, with a dry sense of humour and a real talent for mimicking people's voices when he told an anecdote. There was something in his manner though – an excess of self-confidence, verging on arrogance – which cancelled out some of the positives, grating on me more and more as the night wore on. Rob's the sort of person who's entertaining in small doses, I decided as I sipped my third or fourth mojito, or maybe as part of a bigger group, rather than one on one. With careful rationing, he could become a friend. But if I was honest with myself, friend-ship wasn't really what I had in mind.

The simple truth was that, from the moment I'd laid eyes on Rob, he seemed like the perfect candidate for a one-night stand. He was handsome in a ruddy, outdoorsy kind of way, and I guessed that under his clothes lurked a taut, muscular body. With every mojito I poured down my throat, the idea took hold. It had been nine long months since I'd been touched by a man, and hadn't I told my mother at Christmas that I wasn't necessarily out there looking for something serious? So when Rob suggested we go back to his place for a 'nightcap', I acquiesced, knowing full well what I was agreeing to. The alcohol didn't cloud my judgement. It simply gave me the Dutch courage required to contemplate undressing in front of a total stranger.

Rob didn't even wait until we'd reached his apartment – a *trois-pièces* he shared with an absent Australian friend in a Haussmann-style building on nearby rue Etienne Dolet – before he started kissing me. Stepping into the entrance vestibule, he pushed me against the wall by the letterboxes, gathering my hair in his hands and leaning forward to cover my mouth with his. It was undeniably strange, the sensation of another man's tongue against mine. For years I'd known only Nico, and the way he and Rob kissed was poles apart. Rob was more forceful and insistent than Nico, and his breath was laced with aniseed.

When he led me upstairs to the second floor, Rob didn't pause to switch on the lights, offer me another drink or give me a grand tour of his apartment. Instead, we staggered into his bedroom and fell on to his unmade bed, resuming what we'd started in the hallway. The only light was a blue glow emanating from the oversized numbers on his digital alarm clock, and I was grateful for the darkness. I had no desire to stare into Rob's eyes. In fact, I didn't need to see his face. This was about sex, pure and simple; about the satisfaction of a basic physical need.

I woke at dawn the next morning and lay perfectly still; eyes open, taking the measure of my unfamiliar surroundings. In the pale light which was beginning to seep through the slatted shutters outside the window, I could see a bookcase, a drying rack covered in clothes, a desk with a computer connected to two large flat-screens and, on the floor, an unruly heap of abandoned clothes, some of which were mine. Last of all I spotted the knotted condom which Rob had tossed carelessly on to the carpet by my side of the bed. I wrinkled my nose in distaste at the sight of it, but was nonetheless thankful we'd had the presence of mind to take precautions.

The sex had been disappointing. There hadn't been much in the way of foreplay and, in any case, the mojitos I'd knocked back seemed to have numbed all sensation between my legs. Rob had thrusted away for what seemed like an eternity, and I'd faked an orgasm in an attempt to bring the proceedings to a conclusion. Inside, I now felt sore, and an unpleasant smell of latex clung to my skin. But my main preoccupation was the pounding in my temples. I needed to escape and, if possible, to do so without waking Rob. I wanted an aspirin and a soak in a long, hot bath. I wanted to wash every trace of my disappointing one-night stand off my skin.

But shifting slightly in the bed, I inadvertently woke my bedfellow. He yawned and snuggled into my back, pressing his crotch into my bare buttocks. Eyelids clamped shut, I regulated my breathing, intent on feigning sleep. But it was too late. Rob was stiffening by the second, his penis poking into my spine, above my coccyx. Clumsy fingers were reaching between my legs, fumbling painfully around, trying to assess my body's degree of receptiveness. I tensed up, a tiny, pained sound escaping my lips. Rather than interpreting this as a signal of distress and discomfort, Rob apparently chose to hear a moan of pleasure. The exploratory fingers were withdrawn and I heard the unmistakable sound of a condom packet being ripped open, the slap of rubber being unrolled on to flesh. Without further ado, he pushed his way inside and began to make slow, mechanical movements, his hands holding my hips in a vice-like grip.

'You make me so horny,' he mumbled into my neck afterwards, when a second knotted condom had plopped on to the carpet, landing close to the first. I made no reply, my whole body rigid with indignation. This time I hadn't made a sound, but the lack of simulated orgasm didn't seem to have thrown Rob off track at all. I couldn't call what had happened rape: I hadn't said 'no'; in fact, I hadn't protested at all. But I felt anything but horny. I felt used and thoroughly dispensable. As far as Rob was concerned, I might as well have been a blow-up MILF doll.

'I have to get going, or I'm going to be late for work,' I said quietly, pulling myself into a sitting position and reaching for my clothes, my back towards him. Only once I was dressed did I stand and turn to face him, as he squinted in my direction in the half-light. My eyes gleamed with repressed tears, but I knew he couldn't see me clearly: he'd told me he was short-sighted, and I dimly remembered him going to the bathroom to remove his contact lenses the previous night.

'Thanks for a great evening. We should do it again sometime . . .' Rob yawned, making no move to get up, kiss me goodbye or escort me out of his apartment. I knew he wouldn't be in touch. We hadn't exchanged phone numbers, and he'd confessed to me the previous evening that his membership was on the verge of expiring. But I had no desire to cross paths with Rob again and, without a word, I picked up my coat and strode out of his bedroom, his apartment and his life.

Half an hour later, sitting in the hot bath I'd promised myself, my knees drawn up to my chin, I stared blankly at the places where the grout between the ceramic tiles was beginning to turn from white to black. Yesterday evening I'd felt so empowered, so liberated; so in control of my life. Today I felt only numb and empty; cheap and soiled. I'd tried a one-night stand on for size and it had been a terrible fit. Meaningless sex was not for me. I'd rather have no sex at all.

As I turned to leave the bathroom, I caught sight of Lila's pink toothbrush and bubblegum-flavoured tooth-paste in her Little Mermaid mug by the sink. How I yearned to wrap my arms around her and bury my face in her hair; to close my eyes and blot out everything else.

It dawned on me, then, why Rob had seemed so blasé about my being a single mother when we'd chatted, the previous night. He couldn't have cared less, because it was irrelevant to him. He'd seen me as a one-night stand from the moment he'd sent me a 'flash', as disposable as the condom he'd tossed on to the carpet of his rented room.

17

As Anna began to tear off the wrapping paper under the collective gaze of the ten or so guests she'd invited over for birthday drinks in her tiny studio apartment, it occurred to me that my gift was open to some misinterpretation. On a hurried, last-minute visit to my favourite bookshop on rue de Belleville, *Le Genre Urban*, I'd picked up a guide to the sex shows, strip joints and swingers clubs of Paris, entitled *Paris Sexy*. Given the frequent jokes Anna and I made about *clubs échangistes*, and the fact that on a recent night out together we'd seen a film, *Shortbus*, about a swingers club in New York, I knew she'd see the funny side. But it was her other guests I wasn't sure about. They weren't privy to our private jokes.

Ryan, flanked by Eric, who was now back in Paris full-time, was sitting closest to Anna, and he guffawed when he caught sight of the cover. 'I'm not sure that's really your scene, Anna darling,' he exclaimed, 'but if nothing else, it will be good for expanding your French vocabulary into raunchy new territories.'

'You underestimate me, Ryan,' Anna retorted, her eyes dancing with mischief. 'Haven't you ever seen my blog, "Diary of an American Libertine in Paris"?' She shot a rapid glance at one of her guests – Alexandre, a handsome, bearded Frenchman whom she'd met at a recent party thrown by some of her American friends – as though trying to gauge his reaction to her provocative reply. When she'd introduced me to him, her tone had been casual and her body language had given little away. But now I was convinced there was – or was about to be – something between the two of them. First Ryan, now Anna. My single friends were dropping like flies.

For the rest of the evening I was torn between feeling optimistic for Anna, who went on to spend much of her party deep in conversation with Alexandre, and feeling pinpricks of jealousy. Three weeks had passed since my one-night stand with Rob and, with the first anniversary of my split with Nico rapidly approaching, my romantic horizon contained not a single serious prospect.

'They're very cute those two, don't you think?' Ryan commented, cornering me alone after he caught me staring pensively in Anna and Alex's direction.

'He does seem very nice,' I conceded. 'And I suppose the timing couldn't be better. Anna's in the middle of those stressful divorce proceedings, and she could do with someone to lean on . . .'

'Your time will come, Sally,' Ryan said quietly, glancing at Eric, who was pacing in the hallway, his mobile phone glued to his ear. 'Probably when you're least expecting it. That's the way these things usually play out . . .'

'Let's hope Alex has some handsome single friends,' I joked, wishing my envy hadn't been quite so transparent. 'If I'm going to lose my wing woman, the least she can do is set me up . . .'

'Talking of wing women, where on earth is Kate?' Ryan frowned. 'And don't fob me off with some work excuse,' he added, wagging his finger at me mock-threateningly. 'I know something serious is going on. I suspected as much as long ago as New Year's Eve. And Eric let slip the other day that Yves is on a secondment to New York . . .'

'Well, I won't go into the details behind Kate's back,' I said carefully, once I'd checked Eric was still tied up on the phone. 'The New York thing is only temporary, but she and Yves do have some stuff they need to work through. In the meantime, as far as I know, he's flying back every third weekend, and Kate's not exactly on top form.'

What I didn't tell Ryan was that the first time Yves had visited, he'd made a point of taking the kids out for the day to Disneyland Paris without Kate, who had phoned me soon after they left in floods of tears. 'I'd rather you didn't mention anything to Eric,' I added, glancing in his direction. 'I doubt Yves wants his marital problems to become the talk of the Paris office.'

Anna's party was still going strong when I left at half past midnight. Ryan had made himself popular by remembering – just as the party was beginning to run dry – that he'd stowed a full bottle of vodka in Anna's freezer when he arrived. A small knot of people had gathered around the birthday girl, including Alexandre, who hadn't left her side all evening. Leafing through *Paris Sexy*, Anna was reading out random entries in her stilted French. When I ducked into her bedroom and re-entered the living room wearing my coat, she broke off midway through a description of a seedy-sounding mixed sauna. 'Leaving already, Sally?' She looked disappointed. 'Can't we tempt you to have one more drink?'

''Fraid not. I've got a babysitter tonight,' I replied, my voice heavy with regret. Clambering reluctantly into my taxi, I gave my address, stopped at a cash point to withdraw money for the babysitter, and relieved her of her duties. As I pulled on my pyjamas, I felt as despondent as I had after the margaritas party, where I'd left Anna standing on the balcony with Fabien. How I hated having to leave early, like some sort of thirtysomething Cinderella, knowing that everyone else was free to carry on having fun without me.

Anna and Ryan could party as late as they pleased and invite Alexandre or Eric — or anyone else, for that matter — to share their beds, enjoy their own personal dose of *Paris Sexy* and sleep well into Sunday afternoon. As for me, I had an early-morning wake-up call to look forward to, followed by a five-year-old's birthday party.

'Mummy, can you put my hair in two *couettes*?' Lila begged, once she was dressed the next morning, holding out a comb and two hair bobbles. 'I want to look really pretty for Clara's party . . . Zino is going to be there, and he's my *amoureux*.'

'I see,' I said with a wry smile, motioning for my daughter to sit on the sofa in front of me. 'So you've got a boyfriend now as well . . .'

'In the *cour de récréation* the other day,' Lila said, turning to give me a coy smile, 'Zino did kiss my cheek. And one day, when I wasn't wearing tights, he did touch my leg and sayed it was very soft.' At the mention of the leg-touching I almost dropped my comb, imagining a grubby little boy's hand on my daughter's thigh.

'When you weren't wearing tights?' I said sceptically, giving the centre parting I'd created a critical look and deciding that it wasn't straight but would do well enough. 'When on earth was that, Lila? You haven't been to school with bare legs in months.'

'When I was wearing trousers!' said Lila, looking at me as though I were an imbecile. She touched the space between my jeans and my socks, furrowing her brow. 'Here, Mummy. How do you say? On my *talon*? I can't remember the right word . . .'

'Ah,' I said, smiling as understanding dawned. 'He touched your ankle. Your *cheville*. Your *talon* is your heel. I had no idea you had an *amoureux*.'

'Really I've got two *amoureux*,' Lila said, as I struggled to position her second pigtail at approximately the same level as the first. 'There's Zino, but sometimes I hold hands with Raphaël too. And Jules did try to kiss me, but I said "no" because his nose was running.'

A little after two o'clock, I tapped on the front door of the address on Clara's birthday invitation: a seventh-floor apartment in one of the high-rise blocks towering over place Marcel Achard. Once she'd finished giving me the low-down on her love life, Lila had somehow managed to persuade me to dress her in her favourite princess costume, complete with tiara, a get-up which had drawn amused glances from passers-by along the way. As for me, I wore smart jeans, a polo-necked jumper and minimal make-up, and I clutched yet another last-minute purchase from *Le Genre Urbain*: a French translation of the *Gruffalo*.

Lila had been invited to only a handful of birthday parties in the past, as most of her classmates' parents lived in flats as tiny as my own and were unable to accommodate a dozen highly strung four- and five-year-olds. What I did know from my limited experience of such events was that there was an outside chance I'd be invited to stay on for a while, to drink coffee and make small talk with the other parents, rather than dropping Lila off and disappearing. It was an intimidating prospect, as I didn't know anyone by name. When we dashed in and out of school, we only had time to shoot one another hurried smiles and murmur a *'bonjour'* in passing.

'Entrez, entrez!' exclaimed Clara's beaming father as he threw open the door, revealing a hallway filled with abandoned pairs of children's boots and shoes. Judging by the noise level, the majority of Clara's other playmates were already in attendance. *'Les gosses sont par ici.* Clara's aunt is putting on a puppet show in the *salon . . .'* he explained, motioning to Lila – who'd removed her coat and shoes – to join them. Once she'd skipped through the doorway, without so much as a backward glance, Clara's father put out his hand to take my coat. 'We grown-ups are enjoying more adult pleasures in the kitchen. Will you join us for a glass of champagne, *maman de* Lila?'

Clara's parents – Vincent and Cécile – appeared to be roughly my own age and, although their apartment building was ugly on the outside, the interior suggested they had both money and taste in spades. The kitchen, large by Paris standards, was furnished with a range of aluminium, free-standing work surfaces, the industrial feel offset by a number of colourful retro appliances from the sixties and seventies. The orange-plastic juicer and the kitsch, apple-shaped kitchen timer and matching icebox served as helpful talking points for the first few minutes as the dozen or so assembled parents cast around for things to say. Vincent placed a full glass of champagne into my waiting hand only seconds after I joined the semi-familiar throng, and I was relieved when he remained by my side and engaged me in conversation.

'So, I hear you speaking English wiz Lila in ze mornings,' he said, switching into heavily accented but fairly accurate English for a moment, before reverting back into French again. '*Ça fait longtemps que vous vivez en France?*'

I was aware of several pairs of eyes swivelling my way, their owners' interest piqued by Vincent's little bilingual performance. I gave him – and whoever else was listening in – my usual potted history: the summer in Paris which had stretched into a decade when I met the Frenchman, Nico, who was to become Lila's father. Vincent looked as though he was trying to summon up an image of Nico from the furthest reaches of his brain. 'I don't think I've ever bumped into Lila's father at school . . .' he said with a frown. 'What does he look like?'

'Ah, *c'est normal*,' I replied, with what I hoped was a nonchalant shrug. 'Lila's dad doesn't live with us . . . He takes her on alternate weekends instead.' Was it my overactive imagination, or did the ambient temperature in the kitchen cool once I'd shared that particular titbit of information? The women who'd arrived as one half of a couple seemed to edge closer to their respective partners, closing ranks as though faced with a dangerous predator. Would any man who dared speak to me from that point onwards be running the risk of an angular elbow in the ribs? I wondered. Or was I being paranoid?

The doorbell rang again and the only unaccompanied male in the room – whom I recognized as the father of the ankle-groping Zino – sidled over to the spot Vincent vacated when he left to answer the door. He reminded me of his son, his head a mass of unruly dark curls, his matte-coloured skin suggesting Mediterranean origins. '*Mon fils* Zino is always talking about your daughter,' he said, positioning himself a little too close for comfort and causing me to take a step back until my back rested against the fridge door. 'He calls her his *amoureuse*.' He looked me up and down in the sleaziest, most obvious way and I felt myself starting to blush. 'Personally, I don't blame him,' he murmured. 'Good looks seem to run in the family . . .'

I laughed nervously and set down my half-full glass, deciding it was time I made my excuses to Clara's parents and extricated myself from their little kitchen party. I knew for a fact that Zino's father was married – he wore a thick gold wedding band – and the last thing I wanted was to gain an undeservedly evil reputation among the parents of Lila's classmates on account of his rather pitiful efforts at flirtation. Stepping back out into the hallway, I retrieved my coat from Vincent.

'*Merci pour le champagne*,' I said, 'but I'm afraid I've got errands to run . . .' I could imagine all too easily the mutterings in the kitchen once I was out of the door. 'Did you see Zino's father hitting on that single mother? Poor thing, she didn't know where to put herself! I'd hate to be in her situation, wouldn't you? At our age, all the best men are already taken.' Maybe I was making a mountain out of a molehill, but I'd felt so uncomfortable that I resolved to return not a minute before the party ended.

Exiting the tower block, I edged past a group of young teenage boys kicking a football around and shouting the sort of obscenities I dreaded Lila learning in the school playground. I'd always found the vast paved square singularly unappealing. It was devoid of any park benches – presumably to discourage tramps or drug dealers from taking up permanent residence – and the children's playground opening off its west side had been off limits for as long as I could remember, the gates fastened with a chain and a nearby sign claiming the area was 'temporarily closed'. Just as the rose garden in front of the nearby trade-union headquarters was imprisoned behind railings, the few token bushes and balding patches of lawn dotted around the edges of the square had been fenced off too. It was hard to imagine what the urban planners who had dreamed up this little corner of hell had been thinking.

When I left Nico, I'd let a smooth-talking estate agent talk me into viewing a twelfth-floor apartment in the building opposite Clara's parents' place; its identical twin. I'd turned down the extra ten square metres of space it afforded, compared to where we lived now, without undue hesitation. Shoebox living – however spacious the shoe box – was not for me. It was old Belleville that I loved, with its cobbled streets and leafy interior courtyards; the few blocks the developers had never succeeded in getting their hands on.

In the absence of any genuine errands to run, two unexpected hours of freedom now yawned ahead of me. Many of the shops at the bottom of rue de Belleville were open on Sundays, and a host of illegal Chinese street vendors were selling basketfuls of chicken wrapped in banana leaves and plastic pails of blackened, fissured hard-boiled eggs. I toyed with the idea of seeking out some mildew spray to combat the black patches in my bathroom. Alternatively, I could nip down to the kiosk for an English Sunday newspaper – preferably the *Observer* – and curl up with it, either inside Aux Folies, or in the comfort of my own living room. Undecided, I dithered outside a Chinese restaurant for a moment, staring absent-mindedly at the display of crispy duck carcasses suspended in the window.

It was when I'd made up my mind and begun to stride towards the zebra crossing opposite Aux Folies that I saw a sight which caused me to stop dead in my tracks, left foot on the kerb, right foot in the gutter. Nico was on the other side of the road, flanked by a young woman who could only be Albane. Flanked wasn't really the right word: Albane trailed a few steps behind him, her head bowed, and it wasn't clear whether Nico was striding impatiently ahead, or Albane was deliberately hanging back.

Time seemed to stand still for a moment as I stared at them, oblivious to the cars zipping past. Nico wore the winter coat he'd owned for years, a woollen three-quarter-length Yves Saint Laurent he'd splurged on in the January sales one year with his hefty Christmas bonus. Knotted around his neck was a scarf I'd bought him in Topshop. In one hand he carried an umbrella, in the other a folded copy of the weekend edition of *Le Monde*. His brow was furrowed, and he looked straight ahead as he walked, confident that Albane, however mutinous she might be feeling, would follow.

Of course, it was Albane I was interested in. Albane, owner of the breathless, apologetic voice I'd heard on the phone many months ago. Albane, owner of the hair clip I'd once seen lying on Nico's hall table with its single, captive hair. Suddenly, here she was, hands shoved deep into her pockets, eyes lowered, long, straight mahogany hair covering her shoulders, the tips of her ears peeping out from under a purple, crocheted cap. She was young, slim and beautiful, just as I'd imagined. She had the kind of effortlessly unblemished skin I remembered taking for granted in my twenties, and bone structure that would serve her well for years to come.

I don't know how I expected to feel, the first time I saw Nico's girlfriend. I'd never regarded her as evil incarnate, like that Mathilde woman: she was just the woman – or girl – Nico had turned to when I left him alone. Staring at her now, I felt no animosity, no hatred, and no jealousy. I simply felt numb. Numb, and a little sorry for Albane. I remembered how infuriating it was to follow a self-righteous Nico down the street after an argument, cursing his indifferent, retreating back all the while. After a fight, he could seldom be prevailed upon to apologize. He argued like a lawyer, never deigning to admit he'd been at fault in any way. These kinds of scenes had been part of my life for ten years and were part of Albane's weekend routine, now. Confronted with this tableau, I realized I didn't miss them at all.

Nico and Albane melted into the crowds milling about by the entrance to Belleville métro, but I continued staring after them until long after they'd disappeared, the beginnings of a smile playing about my lips. I might not have admirers beating down my door. I might not enjoy unlimited freedom, like Ryan or Anna. But I'd proved to myself, beyond the shadow of a doubt, that in less than a year, I'd come a long way. And today, that was good enough for me.

18

From the moment he kissed my cheek and pulled out my chair, I sensed my date with Jérémy was going to mark a turning point in my Rendez-vous experience. My pulse began to race, my palms were damp and I was giddy with excitement. Chemistry, the elusive ingredient which had been missing from all my previous dates, was finally *au rendezvous*.

Here was someone who not only lived up to the promise of his striking profile photo, but exceeded it. His eyes – the colour of the blue/black ink I'd preferred at school – were large and expressive and fringed with long, thick lashes. His clean-shaven face was remarkably unlined and unblemished, and I marvelled at how smooth, how *touchable* his skin looked. His lips were full, with a pronounced Cupid's bow, and when he kissed my cheek – and not the air, as so many people did – they felt incredibly soft. There was something endearing about how his hair – once jet-black – was flecked with grey, particularly around his ears. His pale-blue sweater accentuated his broad shoulders and his old-school Levi jeans clung to all the right places. In short, Jérémy was delectable, and as I slid into the seat opposite, every fibre of my being strained towards him.

My first thought upon seeing him, and seeing how I reacted to him, was relief. It really was possible for me to feel powerfully attracted to someone who wasn't Nico. The ambivalence I'd felt towards the men I'd met since we'd parted hadn't been down to some vital component inside me being irreparably damaged. I simply hadn't crossed paths with the right person; at least, not until now.

Jérémy was older than anyone I'd been out with before; outside the age range I'd decreed as acceptable when I joined Rendez-vous. His profile listed him as aged forty-two – backed up by his pseudonym, Jem42 – but when we'd exchanged emails, following my 'flash', he'd admitted he'd celebrated his forty-sixth birthday a few weeks earlier. '*Pourquoi mentir?*' I'd asked him, in my third or fourth email. 'Or more to the point: why lie and then come clean afterwards?'

'I only joined a couple of weeks ago, but it didn't take me long to realize all the women I was interested in had keyed in a cut-off age of forty-five,' Jérémy explained by return email. 'So I thought I'd bend the rules a little, to help myself over the first hurdle. It seemed a shame to be disqualified before the race had even started.' His analogy reminded me of my first hesitant steps on Rendez-vous, back in September, when I'd agonized over whether to admit to being a mother. Even now, five months later, I confessed to Jérémy, I wasn't convinced the decision I'd made – to be upfront from the outset – had worked to my advantage.

'I think that's one of the big problems with sites like this, with all their databases and search terms and filters,' Jérémy responded. 'People can end up getting too focused on who they see as their perfect match, in theory. Whereas out here in the real world, the things that make a person attractive are far less logical. You're never going to fall for someone because he or she has ticks in all the right profile boxes.'

I admired Jérémy's sincerity and, when we arranged to meet for a drink at Chez Prune, the canal-side scene of my first coffee and stroll with Anna, I'd felt cautiously optimistic. Leaving Lila with the babysitter, I'd wrapped up warmly and taken a métro to Goncourt, then walked along the *quai*, my cheeks stinging in the biting-cold air. When I pushed open the door to the bar a few minutes later, pausing to scan the tables for lone males and comparing them to my mental image of Jérémy's profile photo, his head was buried in a sheaf of papers. Some intuition – or perhaps the draught from the open door – had caused him to glance up, and we'd recognized one another simultaneously. He'd flashed me a wide, welcoming smile and I'd begun to melt, there and then.

'It was much easier to get a table in here than I thought it would be,' Jérémy remarked, gesturing at the half-empty bar. 'I usually hang out at Le Jemmapes, on the other side of the canal. It's a while since I've been here.' He spoke French with a neutral, educated accent and exuded a calm confidence, as though he was entirely at ease in his own skin.

'It's never been a better time to be a *non-fumeur*,' I retorted, stowing my coat, scarf and gloves on the nearby radiator. 'Which you are, aren't you?' I teased, one eyebrow raised. 'Or did you lie about that on your profile too?'

'Everything else on my profile was the gospel truth, I promise,' Jérémy replied, turning down the corner on the page he'd been reading and stowing his papers – which looked like a script of some sort – in a rucksack on the floor, by his feet.

The other thing which had attracted me to Jérémy's profile had been his occupation. '*Acteur*,' I'd thought to myself. Now that made a glamorous change from the other men I'd met. 'Tell me about how you got into acting,' was my first question, my glass of dry Bordeaux blanc sitting untouched before me. I'd resolved in advance that I wasn't about to jeopardize this date by drinking too much too soon in an attempt to steady my nerves. Ordering my least favourite drink was the strategy I'd devised to ensure I stuck to my plan.

Jérémy's potted history was fascinating. In a former life, he'd been a trader at the French stock exchange, a high-adrenalin job which he'd loved but also found exhausting. He'd retired from that profession at the age of thirty-eight, although he confessed he still played the markets for his own amusement. He'd set aside what he described as 'a nice little nest egg' and after taking an extended holiday – travelling around India, Thailand and China – he'd cast around for something else to do.

'I fell into acting quite by accident,' he explained, pausing to take a sip of his beer. 'A friend of mine was making her first short film and she persuaded me to stand in for an absent cast member at short notice. I only accepted because I owed her a favour.' When he described the experience his eyes lit up and he gestured expressively with his hands. I suspected the feeling had been mutual; the camera loving every contour of his face. 'Afterwards I enrolled in an acting class at the Cours Florent,' Jérémy said, casually naming one of the most famous drama schools in the city. A couple of years later he'd had his lucky break, starring in *Célibataires*, a play about a group of single Parisians. An unexpected success, it had enjoyed a year-long run in a theatre near Pigalle.

Reading between the lines, I suspected it had been a while since Jérémy was involved in anything as successful as *Célibataires*. When I quizzed him about his current projects, he mumbled something about a play he and a friend were rehearsing and hoping to showcase in the summer. But what interested me about Jérémy wasn't whether or not he'd achieved – or ever would achieve – some sort of celebrity status. I found it fascinating that he'd walked away from a stable, mainstream career to throw himself into something completely different. It must have taken guts, and I couldn't imagine any of the men I knew doing something so radical and brave. Perhaps I wasn't being entirely fair: if Nico had set aside his plans to join the partnership in his law firm and decided, say, to take up oil painting, instead, I'd probably have been the first to try and talk him out of it. Jérémy, on the other hand, had never been bound by family ties. This probably went a long way towards explaining why he looked so youthful at the age of forty-six.

When the conversation turned to my own job and circumstances – a progression I didn't welcome, as English teaching was bound to sound dull in comparison – Jérémy surprised me by asking a number of searching questions about the kind of people I taught and the relationships I developed with them. Could it be that this attraction I'm feeling isn't a one-way street? I wondered. Could it be that he's as interested in me as I am in him?

'A good friend of mine, Thomas, who has an English father and a French mother, teaches English too,' Jérémy confessed, a little later. 'And this awful thing happened to him once . . .'

'Tell me about it,' I murmured, putting my elbows on the table and resting my chin on my hands, leaning closer. As he talked, I enjoyed focusing on how his lips moved, or the way he gesticulated with his graceful, long-fingered hands. Jérémy explained that Thomas had been teaching Jeanine – a plain, rather plump girl who worked in the human resources department of an insurance company – for a couple of years. He'd long suspected she had a sort of schoolgirl crush on him, but thought little of it until the day he'd returned to work after his honeymoon, wearing a wedding ring. When Jeanine caught sight of his ring finger, the blood drained from her face and she excused herself, claiming she felt unwell. The following week, Jeanine's lesson was cancelled and Thomas learned, much later, that Jeanine had suffered some sort of nervous breakdown the day after their last lesson. 'I've always thought someone should base a script on that story,' Jérémy said, with a faraway look in his eyes. 'I'd write it myself, if I thought I could. Imagine if Jeanine had kept a diary, for example, and documented a fantasy relationship with Thomas. Some sort of bond that seemed real to her but existed only inside her own head . . .'

'So all those questions before . . . Was that you trying to milk me for ideas for your future script?' I said, affecting an offended expression.

'Not at all!' Jérémy shook his head emphatically. 'I simply felt it was my duty to warn you about the seven or eight male students who are busy fantasizing about you right now.'

A few minutes after midnight, Jérémy caught me glancing surreptitiously at my watch and asked me, mock-petulantly, if he was beginning to bore me. 'Of course not,' I replied with a smile. 'I should be getting back, that's all. The baby-sitter I'm using at the moment can't stay out too late. Her parents are very strict . . .'

'Ah of course,' Jérémy said, almost to himself. 'A babysitter.' It occurred to me that we hadn't touched on the subject of Lila all evening and, for one heart-stopping moment, I wondered whether he'd forgotten I was a mother and was now having second thoughts about meeting me. But when he spoke again, I realized I needn't have worried. 'How about I give you a lift home on my motorbike?' he continued, as charming as ever. 'I'll be able to get you there much quicker than the métro.'

It was a long time since I'd been on a motorbike. Yves had owned one, years ago, and all I remembered was how uncomfortable I'd been when he gave me a lift from Kate's to an appointment near his office one day. The ride itself had been exhilarating, although I did panic when our route took us along an underpass which snaked underneath the river Seine and his bike tilted to one side as he leaned into a sharp corner. But it was the mandatory proximity I'd found most unsettling. I hadn't enjoyed being forced to hold on tight.

Needless to say, I felt no such discomfort seated behind Jérémy. As we rocketed along rue de la Fontaine au Roi I savoured the pressure of my thighs against his, my arms encircling his torso, my head resting against his back. He smelled of leather – he wore a thick, sheepskin-lined jacket – and of a distinctive, spicy aftershave I didn't recognize, mingled with a hint of something sweet, like vanilla. When he pulled up outside my apartment building and killed the engine I was overwhelmed with disappointment. I hadn't wanted our journey to come to an end, just yet.

Swinging my right leg over the seat to regain the pavement, I turned to face Jérémy, fumbling with the fastener of the helmet he'd loaned me, which had been concealed in a secret compartment. '*Laisse-moi faire*,' he said, kicking the stand into place and dismounting, removing his own helmet and gloves and putting gentle hands under my chin to work the strap free. My neck tingled when he grazed it with the backs of his fingers. Setting my helmet aside, he put his hands to my flattened hair, pulling it back from my face and hooking a stray curl behind my right ear with his thumb.

I was clear-headed – I'd stuck to my plan and made two glasses of wine last all evening – so while my next move came as a surprise to both of us, I couldn't blame my sudden bold impulse on the contents of a glass. Looking Jérémy straight in the eye, I put my palms flat against his chest and tilted my face upwards, brushing my lips against his. When his lips parted, I leaned in further, closing my eyes and slipping my tongue inside. All the longing I'd felt, sitting across from him for the past few hours, I poured into that long, exploratory kiss. When I felt his arms sliding around my shoulders and running down my spine, towards the curve of my buttocks, I pressed closer still.

When we surfaced for air, a few heady moments later, I took a step back, overcome with self-consciousness and anxious to see his reaction. 'I . . . I don't know what came over me,' I murmured, peering coyly at him through lowered eyelashes. 'I don't usually grab hold of men I've only just met . . .'

'I'm not complaining,' said Jérémy, with what I could only describe as a nervous smile. 'But you're right, it *was* rather sudden, Sally. We have only just met . . .' I froze. That wasn't the reaction I'd been hoping for. In my ideal version of our script, Jérémy would have pulled me back towards him, put his lips over mine and forcefully silenced me.

'Well, I suppose I'd better go and "liberate" the baby-sitter,' I muttered, reversing towards the front door and raising my hand in a pathetic little wave. 'Call me if you fancy doing this again sometime?' I turned and tapped in my door code, my cheeks smarting, refusing to look over my shoulder. Pushing the door open, I lunged inside and let it swing closed behind me with a satisfying, weighty clunk. What on earth had just happened? How could Jérémy regret sharing that sensual kiss?

The next day Anna called, and Lila and I joined her for a stroll in the Parc de Belleville with her temporary companion, Lotta the Shih-tzu. Anna was dog-sitting as a favour for an absent friend and, despite the unambiguous signage at the park gates depicting the silhouette of a dog with a red diagonal line through its centre, we'd decided to press on regardless. Preferring the hairpin paths cut into the terraced hillside to the flights of stairs Lotta was far too small to negotiate, we meandered upwards. 'If I see a park warden, I'll pick up the darn dog and stow it under my coat,' Anna said with a rebellious shrug. 'Isn't that why pocketbook-sized dogs like this were invented?'

Lila, who had begged to be entrusted with the dog's lead, was in her element. She and her canine companion trotted on ahead and, apart from a couple of elderly killjoys who shook their heads and tutted, their mouths gathered around their false teeth like stitching pulled too tight, most of the passers-by smiled at the sight of a four-year-old shrieking with pleasure as she walked a tiny mop-on-legs.

When I brought Anna up to speed about the events of the previous evening, I was relieved to see that her reaction to Jérémy's behaviour mirrored my own. 'That's seriously weird,' she said, rolling her eyes. 'I mean, the way you tell it, he was giving you all these signals, all night long . . . And so what if you've only known each other five minutes! It was only a kiss, goddammit!'

'Well, it wouldn't be the first time that sort of thing has happened to me,' I said, thinking back to the evening I'd spent on Manu's couch. 'You know,' I said with a sigh, 'I'm starting to think that being a mother is a bit like having a "go slow" sign welded to my forehead. I mean, I thought I'd read the situation correctly; I thought I was going with the flow. Now I feel embarrassed, and downright foolish. But it honestly didn't seem like he was kissing me back to be *polite* . . .'

'Maybe he's one of those old-fashioned guys who likes to take the initiative,' Anna suggested. 'How about next time you go out, you let *him* lead the way?'

'*If* there's a next time,' I said darkly. 'Who knows whether I'll ever hear from him again.' Inside my coat pocket, my hand was clenched around my mobile. With every fibre of my being, I'd been willing Jérémy to call since I rose that morning.

When I quizzed Anna about how things were progressing with Alexandre, it was her turn to sigh. 'I don't know,' she said with a sigh. 'I mean, the sex is lovely. He's attentive, he's kind, we have a lot of laughs, we share a lot of interests . . .' As she listed his attributes, I noticed how unconvinced Anna sounded. It was as though she'd been badly dubbed. Her words were positive, but her tone of voice didn't match.

'So what on earth is the problem?' I was confused. 'He sounds perfect. Where's the "but"?'

Anna shrugged. 'I'm not sure I'm ready to devote all my energies to one person,' she said. 'You know, put all my eggs in one basket . . . I don't know . . . Maybe it's too soon after Tom . . .'

'Are there other baskets you could be stowing your eggs in?' I said, borrowing her metaphor. When Anna nodded, I felt a by-now-familiar twinge of jealousy. There was a pupil she liked, she confessed, who had asked her out to lunch. Then there was an American guy: a newcomer to Paris who'd been put in touch with Anna by a mutual friend. 'It must be something to do with being in the first flush of romance with Alex,' I said, doing everything in my power to keep the envy I felt from tainting my voice. 'You've got that glow, and it makes you irresistible not only to him, but to other people too . . .'

'I dunno,' Anna lamented. 'Just as I was beginning to find this single life enjoyable, then *bam!*, along comes a guy who wants to take me off the market. Much as I like him, I can't help thinking it would have been fun to keep my options open a while longer, you know. To explore other avenues . . .'

'It's what we Brits call "Sod's law",' I said with a smile.

'As in Murphy's law?' said Anna, looking puzzled. 'Jesus, you Brits have some weird expressions.' Absorbed in our conversation, we narrowly missed ploughing into Lila and

Lotta, who had ground to a halt on the path in front of us. Lotta had lowered her whiskered chin to the pavement and splayed out her legs, refusing to budge. She looked less like a dog than a miniature version of one of those fake-sheepskin rugs everyone stops to fondle on their way around Ikea. Lila was kneeling in front of her, one hand on her hips, the lead hanging limply from the other. 'Anna, why won't she walk any more?' she wailed. 'Is there something wrong with her? Is she broken?'

'The pooch is tired,' Anna reassured her, scooping Lotta up into the crook of her arm. 'Don't worry, it's not your fault.'

'I'm tired as well,' said Lila, sidling towards Anna's free arm. 'Please, Anna, can you carry me too?' On a previous, equally memorable, visit to the park, Anna had given Lila a piggyback, a move which had ensured her enduring popularity.

While Anna reasoned with Lila, I slowed my pace and allowed myself to lag behind, daydreaming about the previous evening. Jérémy's unexpected reaction still baffled me, but maybe Anna was right and it was a question of letting him make the next move.

Once the babysitter had left the previous evening, I'd spent an hour or more Googling his name, lingering over the promotional shots I'd unearthed for *Célibataires* the longest. Jérémy was pictured in the centre of the troupe, wearing jeans and showing a nicely toned bare torso, while the woman by his side appeared to be naked apart from a man's shirt. As for his Rendez-vous profile, I'd visited it once, for a couple of seconds, so that I could copy his photo on to my desktop. That way I could stare at it for as long as I liked, as often as I liked, without him being any the wiser.

19

Jérémy remained ominously quiet over the next few days, but that didn't prevent my thoughts from returning to our date with alarming regularity. Whether I was waiting for a métro, watching Lila soak in the bath or tapping my pencil against a table in the gap between two lessons, I kept remembering things. Things that we'd said. The way he had looked. His smell. The feeling of my body against his as we rode home on his motorbike. And, last but not least, that lingering kiss.

After coming up with all manner of elaborate theories to account for his behaviour, I moved on to inventing reasons why he hadn't yet got in touch. Mindful of Anna's words in the park, I was determined not to take matters into my own hands and contact him myself so, in the meantime, I gazed doe-eyed at his photo for a few minutes every evening, willing him to call. On one occasion I wasn't proud of, I even logged on to Rendez-vous and sifted painstakingly through the list of members who'd inspected my profile since the evening we met, searching, in vain, for his pseudonym.

When I wasn't mooning over Jérémy, I had plenty of other things to occupy my mind. It was mid-February, and Lila's school holidays were already upon me. Nico's parents were on holiday in Mauritius – a wedding-anniversary gift from Philippe to Catherine – and Lila was staying with me for the full two weeks and attending the *Centre de Loisirs*.

I'd suggested to Nico that he might like to take a couple of days off and spend some extra time with his daughter, in addition to his usual weekend stint, but he'd made a feeble excuse about his workload, forcing me to conclude that he hadn't turned over a new leaf, after all. Instead, he'd spoken to his sister, who was planning to take Lucas to Disneyland Paris for the day. 'Sophie's quite happy for Lila to tag along too,' he'd told me over the phone. 'I'll pay for the ticket.'

The most unexpected development, however, had come in the form of a phone call from Mum, a week earlier. 'I thought maybe I'd pop over and visit you and Lila while she's off school,' she'd announced, out of the blue, at the end of one of our of late rather stilted fortnightly phone calls. 'I haven't seen your new flat, and I fancy a ride on the Eurostar, now it leaves from Saint Pancras and it connects so well with the trains to and from Yorkshire.'

'What about Dad?' I said, surprised to hear Mum talking in the first person singular. 'Wouldn't he be coming with you?'

'Oh, he's got a lot of work on at the moment,' Mum said airily. 'So I thought I'd come on my own.' Nonplussed, I told her to book whatever suited her best. I could hardly dissuade her from visiting, and I knew Lila would be delighted to spend some time with her grandma. A few days later, she'd called to confirm she'd be visiting for two days in the second half of Lila's holidays.

'When *my* mother comes to stay I can never get the woman to put her feet up,' said Ryan, when I met him for a quick baguette and gossip session after morning lessons had ended on the first Thursday of the school holidays. 'Honestly, there's no parting that woman from her Marigolds. If I turn my back for five minutes, you can be sure she'll be busy scouring the u-bend of the toilet, or she'll have found cobwebs in places I'd never dream of looking . . . But tell me about this date of yours. Anna said something about a guy called Jérôme?'

'You mean Jérémy,' I said, wondering idly when Anna and Ryan had got together behind my back. I filled him in on the details of my date and Jérémy's failure to call, despite what Ryan referred to as 'that kiss', using his trademark airborne quotation marks. 'Someone better must have come along,' I said with a shrug of resignation. 'That's always the danger with Rendez-vous. If my inbox is filling up with unread mail from other men, it stands to reason that Jérémy can't be short of admirers either . . .'

When I set down my sandwich and told Ryan Jérémy's disturbing story about Thomas the English teacher and Jeanine the obsessed pupil, it was difficult not to apply the moral of the story – that you never can tell what's going on inside someone else's head – to my own situation. Supposing Jérémy turned on the charm with all his dates, offering them a lift home on his motorbike; mussing up their hair . . . Maybe I was the one who had endowed his every gesture with far more meaning than he'd intended: I'd been so drawn to him that I'd desperately wanted to believe the feeling was mutual.

So when my phone began to vibrate in my bag – just as I was about to tuck into a strawberry tart – my first thought was that the caller must be Kate or Anna. Catching sight of Jérémy's name, I froze. 'Oh my god, it's him,' I shrieked, shooting Ryan a panicked, rabbit-caught-in-headlights look. I was about to flip open the phone and take his call when Ryan put a dissuasive hand across mine, shaking his head. 'Let it ring a little while longer,' he said authoritatively. 'And then, for goodness' sake, don't let on you know who it is. Programming a guy's name and number into your mobile after your first date isn't what I'd call playing things cool . . .'

After a further four rings I answered with a brisk '*Allô?*', earning a thumbs-up from Ryan. 'Sally? *C'est* Jérémy *à l'appareil.*' His voice sent tiny shivers down my spine. '*Comment ça va?*' he continued, his 'how are you' rhetorical, as he didn't pause to allow me to reply. 'I was wondering whether you'd like to come and see a play with me on Saturday night. You said you never go to the *théâtre* and we must do something to rectify that . . .'

'Mmm,' I said, trying to sound as though I were consulting a busy diary. 'Saturday might work . . . I did have some plans, but they've been cancelled. So, yes, okay. It'll be nice to do something a bit different . . .' Ryan was nodding vigorously now: my tactics met with his approval. But when Jérémy offered to collect me on Saturday at seven – even though the theatre was only a few métro stops away, at Bonne Nouvelle – I was unable to keep the smile out of my voice. '*À samedi alors,*' I said gaily, putting down my phone and fanning myself with my serviette. 'I can't believe he called,' I said, trying to recover my composure. 'I really was beginning to give him up as a lost cause.'

'Learned much, my apprentice has,' said Ryan in a quavering voice. 'Strong with you, the force is. Mind you,' he added, his voice returning to normal, 'I'm subtracting points for sounding so keen at the end. I thought you were about to start clapping your hands like an overexcited four-year-old . . .'

'I'm going on a second date with Jérémy, and I don't care what you say,' I chanted, playground style, putting my hands over my ears. My imitation of a four-year-old, thanks to Lila, was second to none.

Waiting for seven o'clock to come around on Saturday should have been excruciating. I awoke soon after dawn, and my brain refused to let me slide back into sleep, intent on mixing and matching every possible outfit in my wardrobe, then weighing up the pros and cons of dipping into my overdraft to buy something new to wear for my date. Fortunately, I wouldn't have too much time on my hands to devote to worrying about this evening: I'd already made plans to meet up with Kate at midday. Yves was back in the country again for his second visit and he'd informed her he was planning to take the children to visit his parents in Versailles for the day, minus Kate. Since Lila would be with Nico all weekend, I'd volunteered to keep my friend company.

When Kate answered her door, the first thing I noticed was how much weight had dropped off her frame over the past three months. She was wearing a pair of jeans I'd seen many times before, but she'd had to cinch them in with a belt to stop them falling down over her narrow hips and, as a result, the material was all bunched up around the waist. Although the weather was mild – a welcome respite from the frosty, headache-inducing weather we'd been having since early February – Kate had enveloped her shoulders in a pashmina shawl. As she raised her arms to give me a hug, the shawl slipped to one side, and I caught a glimpse of sharply protruding collarbone.

'So, do you fancy going for lunch, or shopping, or for a walk somewhere?' I said brightly, trying to sound as though this were a normal Saturday and Kate and I went on these sorts of outings all the time. Back in the days before our children came along, we'd often met up at weekends. But in recent years, shopping sprees had given way to playdates for our respective children, and even those were few and far between, these days. What a pity, I reflected, that we'd been forced to resurrect such a happy tradition in such dismal circumstances.

I followed Kate along the hallway and leaned against a sideboard, arms folded, while she rummaged inside the coat cupboard, pulling on first a pair of Ugg boots, then a thick woollen coat. The door opposite me was ajar, and through it I could see a narrow sliver of Kate's spare room. The bed sheets were crumpled, and an expensive-looking piece of monogrammed luggage – presumably Yves' – lay open on the floor.

'I think I could do with going to a different part of town,' Kate replied, her eyes following my gaze then snapping back to the coat she was frantically buttoning. 'A change of scenery would be nice . . . The Parc Monceau is driving me slowly mad. All those achingly perfect bourgeois families out for a stroll with their kids in Petit Bateau outfits . . .'

'Well, how about we take the métro down to somewhere on the Left Bank, like Saint Sulpice?' I suggested. I'd been studying the map on the way over, trying to formulate some sort of plan. My hunch – that Kate would need me to be decisive in her place – had been correct. 'I haven't been down there in ages,' I added, 'but there are plenty of places we could grab a bite to eat and, if you're feeling naughty, I wouldn't be averse to wandering in and out of a few shops . . .'

Once we were seated on fold-down *strapontin* seats inside the métro carriage, which was bursting at the seams with Saturday shoppers and only marginally less hectic than during the weekday rush hour, I resisted the impulse to pull *Libé* out of my bag and pore over the day's *Transports amoureux*. Better to steer clear of the subject of love. In fact, it wasn't easy to think of any conversation topic which didn't have the potential to destabilize Kate: I'd resolved to keep my butterflies about tonight's date to myself, and even ordinarily safe subjects like children or work were riddled with potholes. So I was almost thankful when a man with a shabby suit and an Eastern European accent wedged himself inside our carriage at Madeleine and began murdering the theme tune from *Amélie Poulain* with an ageing accordion.

The café I'd been picturing in my mind's eye, with tables spilling out on to the square in front of Saint Sulpice church, turned out not to be such an inspired idea. It was one of those places that seemed enormous when the weather was fine and you could take full advantage of the outdoor seating, but possessed only a tiny indoor space which was soon filled to capacity in winter. Turning off into rue des Canettes, I began to hunt for an alternative lunch venue. 'How about we get some *Flammenküche*,' I suggested, pausing to peer inside a bar which, judging by the huge copper tanks in the window, brewed its own beer as well as serving the Alsatian version of 'pizza', a thin bread crust smothered in crème fraîche and sprinkled with bacon and onions.

'Sounds fine,' Kate replied listlessly. 'Although I don't think I've got much of an appetite...' I hesitated a moment, then pushed open the door, determined not to leave until I'd seen food pass her lips. Kate wasn't going to be allowed to fade away; not on my watch.

When our order arrived, served straight from the oven on a large wooden board, I set it to one side to cool for a moment. I'd tucked into a *Flammenküche* prematurely once before, taking a layer off the roof of my mouth in the process, and wasn't keen to make the same mistake twice. Kate, her beer untouched, didn't even seem to notice we'd been served. Her posture was tense and defensive – elbows crossed on the tabletop, hands on shoulders – and she was gazing unseeing into the middle distance, lost in her thoughts.

'I think Yves is seeing someone else,' she said suddenly, her eyes locking with mine. 'He came home wearing a brand-new suit, and with this trendy, expensive-looking haircut, looking better than he's looked in months.' Kate's voice remained steady, but her pallor and her haunted expression left me in no doubt as to how wretched she was feeling.

'Do you have any *real* reason to suspect he's having an affair, apart from this makeover?' I said, trying to keep things rational. 'Or is this pure speculation on your part?'

Kate shook her head. 'I haven't been snooping, if that's what you mean', she said, her voice filled with resignation. 'And, to be honest, I don't think I could handle seeing actual proof of whatever it is he may have been doing. All I know is, he's definitely making an effort and, given the current state of play, it's unlikely to be for my benefit.'

I cast my mind back to the weeks and months before I'd stumbled upon the evidence of Nico's involvement with Mathilde. If he'd gone to extraordinary sartorial lengths to impress his secretary, I'd been oblivious to them. I didn't *think* he had, but I couldn't be sure. Without realizing it at the time, I'd dropped the ball. Maybe one of the reasons he'd been attracted to her in the first place stemmed from the fact that he and I had been together for so long that we didn't really pay proper attention to each other any more; a sobering thought.

'So what are you going to do?' I picked up my knife, intending to slice into the *Flammenküche* but, a moment later, I set it down again, thinking better of the idea. Who was I fooling? Kate wasn't in the mood for eating, and the turn our conversation had taken had seen off my appetite now, too.

'I don't think there's anything I *can* do,' Kate replied doubtfully, her shoulders sloping in defeat. 'His secondment finishes in three weeks' time and I'm on standby, waiting for him to tell me what happens next. I'm pretty sure I've forfeited the right to play the role of jealous wife, so even though I can't bear the idea of losing him, I'm going to have to sit tight, and pray this New York thing – if it exists – is just a tit-for-tat fling.'

'Well, I'm rooting for you both,' I said softly. 'I really don't want you and Yves to go the way of me and Nico. Even if it would mean we could meet up on Saturdays more often.' It was a feeble attempt at humour, and no sooner had the words left my mouth than I wished I hadn't bothered. The last thing Kate needed to hear was that this isolated weekend without the children could be the first of many. When our waiter made his next lap of the room, I signalled to him to bring over the bill. 'Okay, so maybe eating out wasn't such a good idea' – I gestured towards our untouched food – 'Maybe we should go and look in a few shops instead? A bit of *windowlicking* never did anyone any harm.' Kate managed to summon the ghost of a smile at my literal translation of the French phrase for window shopping – *faire du lèche-vitrine*. 'Let's face it,' I said, recycling an old joke of Ryan's, 'most of the size-zero women shopping in this part of town look as though the weight of their shopping bags might snap their scrawny arms in two. They probably *are* ravenous enough to lick a window-pane.'

We were about to cross the threshold of a boutique called 'Les Petites' on rue du Four when my phone began to ring. Fishing it out of my bag, I frowned, perplexed, at the number displayed on the screen. It looked familiar, yet I couldn't quite place it . . . Then, in a flash, I remembered. My old landline. Since Nico always used his mobile, I must have deleted the entry last time I upgraded my phone.

'*Salut*, Nico, *il y a un problème?* Lila *va bien?*' But the stricken voice which answered didn't belong to Nico. It was Albane, and she sounded anything but okay.

'*Je suis désolée*, Sally. I didn't know what to do. Nico isn't answering his phone and I have a big problem here with Lila . . . She's been sick, very sick. And she is crying for her *maman*.' I slumped against the shop window, my head spinning and my eyes unfocused. 'What can she mean,

Nico isn't picking up his phone?' I muttered out loud. 'He's supposed to be there with Lila. Where the hell has he gone?'

'I'll be with you as soon as I can, Albane,' I said, pulling myself together. Now was not the time for questions or recriminations. 'I'm in Saint Germain, but I'll try and flag down a taxi. In the meantime, try and get Lila to drink some water and tell her Mummy's coming.'

When I turned back to where Kate had been standing seconds earlier, she'd disappeared. I span round, panicking, opening my mouth to call out her name. But then I caught sight of her slight figure by the kerb a few metres away: she was opening the back door of a taxi and beckoning me over. 'I overheard enough to get the gist,' she explained, as I hurried across to join her. 'And I'm coming with you.' She lifted a hand as if to deflect any protests. 'Come on, Sal, hop in. Don't tell me you couldn't do with some moral support around Albane.' Having someone else's crisis to attend to had galvanized Kate into action, and she seemed to have set aside her own worries for a time, distracted by my own. It wasn't what I'd had in mind when I'd arranged to spend time with her today, but the transformation was a welcome one, all the same.

Sensing the urgency in my voice when I barked out Nico's address, our taxi driver did his utmost to get us from A to B in record time, speeding along dedicated bus lanes whenever he could, but rejoining the rest of the traffic whenever a slow-moving bus loomed into sight far ahead. As he weaved in and out, I kept my phone handy, dialling Nico's mobile and stabbing my index finger repeatedly on 'redial'. I was determined to give him a piece of my mind. 'What on earth was he thinking, leaving his girlfriend in charge?' I fumed as I got through to voicemail for the fifteenth time. 'Whatever his reasons might be – although I bet you anything he's gone into work – leaving his phone switched off while he's out is so irresponsible!'

When Albane answered the door, dressed in jeans and one of Nico's T-shirts, her hair pulled back into a pony-tail, I darted inside without even waiting for her to speak, following the sound of Lila's sobs along the corridor to the bathroom. I found my daughter sitting on the floor by the toilet, wrapped in a clean towel. Her curls were soaking wet and plastered to her head. 'Mummy, *j'ai vomi*,' she wailed, as soon as she caught sight of me. Dropping to my knees, I wrapped my arms around her. She was shivering, but her skin was hot to the touch and her breaths came short and shallow. 'It went all over Daddy's bed,' she added, her teeth beginning to chatter. 'And all over me. So Albane did wash me with the shower.'

'It's going to be all right, my love. Mummy's going to take you home,' I said comfortingly, unconsciously reverting to referring to myself in the third person, just as I used to when she was a baby. I could sense someone behind me, and half-turned – still hugging Lila close – to see Kate standing in the doorway. 'If you could look inside the cupboard above the sink,' I instructed, 'on the top shelf, I think you'll find a thermometer . . . And maybe some rehydration salts too.'

'Here you go.' Kate passed me the thermometer, then upended the tooth mug sitting by the sink and filled it with water. 'Good stuff this,' she said darkly, tearing open the sachet of medicine and stirring the contents of the mug with the handle of a toothbrush. 'You ought to try it next time you have a hangover, or a bout of uncontrollable weeping . . .'

While we dressed Lila in clean clothes I didn't spare a thought for Albane who was hovering out of sight, in the corridor. It was only later, when Kate and I had got Lila back home – Kate carrying her weekend bag while I somehow managed to transport all fifteen kilos of Lila home in my arms – that it began to dawn on me how difficult the situation must have been for her. It was bad enough being left to deal with Lila – and Lila's vomit – all alone. But Albane had also had to step aside and look on helplessly while two strangers – one of whom clearly knew her way around Nico's bathroom cabinet far better than she did – relieved her of her temporary responsibilities, with scarcely a word of thanks.

Once Lila had been dosed with the French version of Calpol – similarly pink and strawberry-flavoured – and parked in front of *The Little Mermaid*, her eyes soon began to lose their glassy sheen. Tucking her blanket around her and planting a kiss on her forehead, I picked up the phone. Kate, who was busy filling the kettle to make us a pot of tea, looked up in interest. No doubt she assumed I was trying Nico again, and anticipated fireworks.

'Albane? It's Sally. I'm calling to say thank you, and to apologize if I seemed ungrateful when I saw you earlier.' When Albane began to protest that no apology was necessary I talked over her, determined to deliver my speech in full. 'I wanted to say that you did the right thing, by calling me,' I told her, 'and that I thought you handled everything really well. Nico put you in a difficult situation – it was unfair of him – and I'm so sorry you had to cope with all that.' Unwittingly, Nico had managed to rally his girlfriends past and present to a common cause today, uniting us in our disgust for his irresponsible behaviour.

'That was big of you,' Kate said, miming applause, when I replaced the receiver. 'Any sign of Nico yet?'

'Albane said she'd ask him to call me,' I said, shaking my head, 'but frankly I don't think I should let myself speak to him until I've calmed down. I'm guessing he went into work. Unless he's cheating on her now, too . . .'

'Well, so much for things not being serious between them.' Kate handed me a mug of tea and took a seat on one of the stools by the kitchen counter. Seeing my frown, she faltered for a moment, as though she was having second thoughts about what she'd been going to say. 'While you were seeing to Lila,' she said hesitantly, 'I went to help Albane strip off the dirty bedclothes . . . And I couldn't help noticing one of the open wardrobes seemed to be filled with her clothes.'

She must have been relieved when I didn't bat an eyelid. In actual fact, all Kate's mention of clothes had done was to remind me, with a sinking feeling, of my date with Jérémy. Or, more to the point, that I'd have to contact him and cancel it, now that Lila was back home with me. 'Of course, all this had to happen when I had important plans for the evening,' I groaned, picking up my phone again and scrolling through the address book for Jérémy's number. 'A second date with a guy I really rather like, no less.'

'Hang on a minute,' said Kate, as I found Jérémy's number and my index finger was poised to hit 'call'. I looked up at her quizzically, my finger obediently still. 'I've got a few things to do this afternoon,' she continued, 'but I can be back here in plenty of time for you to go out, and I'd much rather babysit for Lila than pace around my apartment alone. Yves and the kids are staying over in Versailles tonight.'

'That's lovely of you, but how can I go out?' I protested. 'I mean, what sort of a mother goes on a date when her daughter is ill?'

'Oh come on, Sal, she only threw up once,' said Kate sensibly. 'Anyone can see that she's feeling much better already. And you know as well as I do that there's a good chance she'll sleep it off this afternoon and be right as rain by teatime. So there's no point cancelling your date so that you can mope around at home this evening and play the martyr. I'm perfectly capable of handling things here.'

Kate seemed to have thrived on today's little emergency, and I was filled with gratitude at how supportive she'd been. 'I'd be happy to take you up on that,' I said cautiously, 'if you're really sure . . .'

'That's settled then,' Kate said briskly. 'Sally Marshall, you *shall* go to the ball.'

20

Last time I'd been to see a play in French – invited out by Nico's parents to see something by Molière at the Théâtre du Châtelet – I'd vowed never to cross the threshold of a Parisian theatre again. French films I could manage, as long as I was held captive in a darkened cinema with surround sound or, at the very least, curled up on my sofa with the TV volume turned up. But the play had taxed my powers of French concentration beyond their limits. It had lasted a full three hours, and I'd only been able to make out three-quarters of the dialogue, partly because my ears ceased to function for a few seconds every time I yawned. 'I don't think I'll ever be truly bilingual,' I'd remarked to Nico in the taxi home. He'd frowned, protesting that, as far as he was concerned, I already was. 'If I was truly bilingual,' I reasoned, 'I'd have the same concentration span in both languages. I'm sure the actors gave fantastic performances, but I'm afraid I kept losing the thread . . .'

But when Jérémy called to say he was waiting downstairs to take me to the theatre, my heart somersaulted in my chest. 'I've got it bad,' I told Kate bashfully, conscious of how irrational this infatuation with Jérémy was. 'The truth is, I'd happily sit by his side watching paint dry if he asked me to.'

Kate had returned before six, bearing a carrier bag full of clothes plucked from her own wardrobe, 'in case I fancied a change'. I'd fallen for a teal wrap dress in a slinky, silk-mix fabric which draped itself around my curves in the most flattering way. With Lila looking on, Kate had proceeded to do my make-up. 'You're taking your fairy-godmother role seriously tonight,' I'd remarked, looking at the ceiling, as instructed, while she brushed mascara across my top lashes. The end result was far superior to anything I'd have been able to manage on my own. 'Mummy, you look like a princess!' was Lila's breathless verdict, the highest compliment a four-year-old girl can bestow.

Pushing me out of the door, Kate wished me luck and advised me to leave my coat unbuttoned until Jérémy had been treated to a glimpse of my dress. Giving my pyjama-clad daughter one last hug, I raced downstairs, too giddy with impatience to wait for the lift.

'*Dis-donc, tu t'es fait toute belle!*' Jérémy exclaimed as I pushed open the front door and walked over to where he stood leaning against his motorbike. I smiled, basking in the warmth of his compliment, thrilled that our evening had got off to such a good start. Leaning in for a *bise*, I touched my lips lightly to his clean-shaven cheeks and inhaled his scent. He looked – and smelled – every bit as good as I'd remembered, and his presence still made me weak at the knees.

Once I'd finished buttoning my coat, Jérémy handed me his spare helmet. My eyes followed his hands as he fastened his own with a deft, economical movement, then travelled lower, lingering on his buttocks, as he hopped on to his motorbike and kicked out the stand from underneath. When he beckoned me to join him, I swung my leg over and positioned myself close behind him, my arms circling his waist with casual ease. As we roared along rue du

Faubourg du Temple, the neon-lit shop fronts darting by in rapid-fire bursts of colour, I relished the feeling of my breasts pressed into his back, loving how intimate it felt, despite the layers of clothes between us. My other senses were working overtime too: the blood pounding in my ears was deafening, the cold air whipped my skin. It was hard to remember whether Nico had had this effect on me, in the beginning. Had his very presence fine-tuned my senses, making colours more vivid and amplifying sounds?

Halfway around place de la République, a taxi cut across our path and Jérémy slammed on his brakes, the forward momentum bringing all my weight to bear against him. I used this as a pretext to grip his torso even tighter, and didn't release him until, all too soon, we'd pulled up opposite the theatre. Clambering off, I watched spellbound as he chained his motorbike to a lamp post.

'*Tu n'y arrives toujours pas?*' Jérémy sounded exasperated when he turned to see me struggling with my chin strap, just as I had on our first date. Letting my hands drop to my sides, I tilted my face towards him, in an exaggerated display of vulnerability. 'You know, I'm beginning to wonder whether you're playing the damsel in distress on purpose,' he said in a sceptical voice, freeing me with his thumb and forefinger. Once he'd stowed my helmet under the seat, he frowned at his watch. 'We'd better get inside if we want to get decent seats. There are no seat numbers in this theatre; it's *placement libre* . . .'

The play Jérémy had chosen was nothing like the Molière I'd seen at Châtelet. It was contemporary, with only two characters, a man and woman in their thirties called Marc and Madeleine. The first scene showed their emotional reunion in a café, years after they'd gone their separate ways, while the rest of the play consisted of a series of flashbacks. At the height of their friendship, Marc and Madeleine had shared an apartment for a year, somehow never ending up in a relationship, despite the almost palpable chemistry between them. The unexpected twist at the end – which made some members of the fifty- or sixty-strong audience gasp out loud – was the sudden realization that the Marc of the present day, who reached for a hitherto unseen white cane when he stood to leave the café, was now blind. It was then that the title of the play – *Revoir Madeleine* – took on its full, bittersweet mean- ing. The only way for Marc to see Madeleine was to lose himself in the memories locked inside his head.

When the two actors had taken their bow and the lights had flickered on, Jérémy and I remained seated for a few moments, waiting for the people at the end of our row to file out of the auditorium. 'So, what did you think of it?' he said, turning to face me. 'Have I managed to convert you into a regular theatregoer?'

'It's left me feeling rather melancholy,' I replied hesi- tantly. 'All those missed opportunities and regrets . . . There were so many moments in Marc and Madeleine's story where I wanted to give them a good shake and shout at them to wake up to themselves and seize the moment.' It wasn't earth-shatteringly profound, but when Jérémy nodded and smiled, I felt as though my response had met with his approval. With any luck, he'd have grasped the sub-text too. While I fully intended to follow Anna's advice and let Jérémy take the initiative tonight, I hadn't been able to resist nudging him in the right direction.

'Would you like to go for a drink somewhere?' Jérémy asked, as we gathered up our coats and made our way towards the end of our row. I was about to reply in the affirmative when a striking woman with closely cropped brown hair appeared out of nowhere and put a hand on Jérémy's shoulder, leaning close to whisper something in his ear. It took me a few seconds to realize I was looking at the actress who had played Madeleine: she'd been wearing a long, jet-black wig on stage. 'Sally, I'm sorry, would you mind excusing us for a minute?' Jérémy's expression was apologetic, but his voice betrayed his excitement. 'My friend Elsa tells me there's a theatre director here tonight I really ought to corner for a chat. If you like, you can wait for me in the lobby. I won't be long . . .'

A full twenty minutes later, Jérémy found me pacing up and down the pavement not far from his motorbike, hands in pockets, head bowed. Maybe I was being paranoid, but the more I'd replayed Elsa's gesture in my mind, the more I'd managed to convince myself there had been something possessive about it; something which hinted at a past or present intimacy. But Elsa was nowhere in sight now, and Jérémy looked so adorably contrite when he saw me that I decided to forgive him for leaving me, quite literally, out in the cold. 'I'm so sorry, Sally,' he said, placing an apologetic hand on my forearm, 'but that took a lot longer than I thought it would. It was well worth it, though. Jean-Jacques – the guy I was speaking to – suggested I audition on Monday for a new play he's producing . . .'

'Shall we go and talk about it over a drink somewhere warm?' I suggested, punctuating my sentence with a theatrical shiver for good measure.

'Any preference?' Jérémy enquired, handing me what I was beginning to regard as *my* helmet. I pondered this for a moment, and decided that my priority should be putting as much distance between ourselves and the theatre as possible, to minimize the chances of running into Elsa and ending up seated together, discussing the play.

'How about you take me to your favourite bar?' I pretended to sift through my brain, searching for the name, even though I remembered it without any difficulty. 'I think you said it was on the Canal Saint Martin, somewhere on the opposite bank to Chez Prune?'

The early stages of a flirtation could be so dishonest, I decided as we plunged into a series of small side streets to return to République, then continued in the direction of the canal. Emotional dissimulation was the name of the game. Determined not to put a foot wrong with Jérémy, I was aware of how I was tying myself in knots to seem witty and intelligent, but also more laid-back and *facile à vivre* than I actually was. Let's face it, if Nico had kept me waiting like that once we'd been together a while, I'd have had no qualms about cutting him down to size with a few razor-sharp words and a baleful glare. I supposed every man or woman in the grip of a new infatuation was guilty to a greater or lesser extent of this kind of 'false advertising'. But didn't it mean setting the other person up for an inevitable disappointment when you let your true colours shine through, much later?

Our destination, a bar with a yellow awning called 'Le Jemmapes' was smaller than my living room, and the only available seats were two tall bar stools close to the draughty front door. When I shivered again – a genuine reflex this time – Jérémy tried to talk me into ordering a *'grog'*, a hot toddy made with rum and flavoured with lemon and cinnamon. I declined, opting for a less medicinal-sounding glass of wine, nonetheless pleased that he was being so attentive. While we sipped our drinks, little more was required of me than to smile and nod at appropriate junctures while Jérémy, fired up after his encounter with Jean-Jacques, talked at length about his upcoming audition. I was a captive, captivated audience, free to enjoy the way the soft lighting of the bar played over his features. Imagine if he got this part he's auditioning for, I thought to myself. I'd get to see him on stage. Back in my schooldays, I'd gone out with a boy who played lead guitar in a local band, and I remembered how electrifying it had been to see him performing, watching all the other girls' eyes on him, but knowing he was mine, and mine alone.

When Jérémy mentioned, in passing, that Elsa had already been cast in Jean-Jacques' play, a stab of jealousy punctured my little fantasy and I decided it was time to pose a seemingly innocent question and find out, once and for all, what their history was. 'Have you two worked together before?' I enquired, as casually as I could manage. 'Or do you have friends in common?'

'Oh, Elsa and I go back a long way,' Jérémy replied. 'She was shacked up with one of my best friends for years. And although that relationship petered out a while ago, I somehow managed to stay friends with both of them afterwards, without having to choose sides . . .' Setting down his drink, he gave me a searching look, and for a moment I thought he'd seen through my studied nonchalance. 'How are things between you and *your* ex?' he said finally. 'Did things get ugly when you separated?'

'Oh, Nico and I are still adjusting to the new status quo,' I replied carefully, thinking what a good sign it was that Jérémy was showing an interest in the practicalities of my situation. 'It's been almost a year since we separated,' I explained, 'so I suppose it's still early days, but there's very little animosity between us, and I'd like to think we'll be able to remain friends, for Lila's sake.' I cast my mind back to the short but vitriolic exchange I'd had with Nico late that very afternoon, when he'd called to apologize and ask after Lila. Saying there was 'very little animosity' in our relationship was stretching the truth, but I sensed it would be best to keep our petty quarrels under wraps until I knew Jérémy better. I began to tell him a little about Lila instead, testing the water to see whether Jérémy was used to being around children. When I told him about Lila's playground relationships, he chuckled. 'It must be pretty amazing watching a child grow up,' he said with a wistful half-smile. I longed to ask him why he'd never had children himself, but I didn't feel sufficiently bold. Perhaps I was afraid he might say he'd never wanted a family. After all, he was now forty-six years old.

When he'd drained the dregs of his second beer, Jérémy announced – to my dismay – that he'd have to be getting home. 'I know it's the weekend, but I'm going to have to make an early start tomorrow if I want to fit in some preparation for my audition,' he explained, offering to chaperone me as far as Goncourt métro. I nodded mutely, a lump of disappointment forming in my throat. Not only was Jérémy cutting our evening short, but he wasn't even offering me a lift home. Was he really being conscientious about work, or was he having second thoughts and trying to let me down gently?

It hardly seemed worthwhile getting on Jérémy's motorbike to travel such a short distance, especially as the one-way system forced us to ride in the wrong direction until we could cross the canal and return via the opposite *quai*. To my surprise, Jérémy pulled over and parked in front of an apartment building on the corner of rue du Faubourg du Temple and Quai Jemmapes, a few hundred metres short of Goncourt métro, and it wasn't until I happened to glance at the column of interphone buttons by the door and spied his surname – Robin – towards the bottom of the alphabetical list, that I realized we were standing in front of his apartment building.

'So, what's your place like?' I craned my neck to look up at the modern facade. 'Do you have one of those big balconies?' I knew it was obvious I was fishing for an invitation, but I didn't care. The opportunity to see Jérémy in his natural habitat was not something I was willing to pass up.

'My place is on the sixth floor,' said Jérémy, holding out his hand to take the helmet I'd finally mastered removing without assistance. He was silent for a moment, as though inwardly deliberating. 'You can come up for a few minutes if you like,' he offered, taking a key from his pocket and unlocking the front door. 'Although I'm warning you, it's a bit of a tip.'

When I stepped over the threshold, my first impression was not so much that I'd walked into an apartment, but rather a specialist bric-a-brac shop. The long, narrow room leading to the balcony was crammed full of all manner of theatre and film memorabilia: adverts for films and plays were plastered across the walls and bookshelves groaned under the weight of hundreds of biographies of actors.

There were crates filled with what looked like scripts, and a collection of vintage stage lights. The only utilitarian pieces of furniture in the room were a small desk wedged into one corner, which housed a computer – his Rendez-vous control centre, as he jokingly referred to it – and a round metal café table positioned in front of the sliding French doors along with a pair of director's chairs.

'So . . . you collect things,' I said, stating the obvious as I turned to face Jérémy, who stood behind me in the doorway.

'You could say that . . .' Jérémy smiled. 'Feel free to take a look around,' he added, making an expansive gesture with his hands. 'I'm going to make myself a *tisane* . . . Would you like one too?' I wasn't at all fond of herbal teas – which often smelled delicious yet almost always tasted bland and disappointing, in my experience – but I accepted his offer, seizing the chance to prolong my visit. After glancing into the tiny kitchen where Jérémy was heating up water in a pan on the stove, showing a typically French disregard for the invention of the kettle, I returned to his living room to explore further.

First, I studied the handful of framed photographs of Jérémy posing with fellow cast members, noting, with satisfaction, that Elsa was nowhere to be seen. Then, moving towards the window, I noticed a white curtain beyond the bookcase, to my left. Drawing it open a few centimetres, I peered through and discovered a second room running parallel to the first, a bedroom containing a wardrobe, a bed with an orange quilt cover, and an oversized yucca plant. My nostrils caught a faint scent of vanilla, and when I spied the coils of incense on the bedside table, I realized I'd solved that little mystery.

When Jérémy reappeared, bearing two steaming cups of pale-brown herbal tea, I'd closed the curtain again and was standing with my back to him, looking out of the French windows at the rooftops, which were backlit by the orange of the light-polluted sky. 'Have you been here long?' I asked him as I took a mug from him and blew on the unidentified liquid, lowering myself gingerly into one of his rickety, canvas-backed chairs.

'Fifteen years,' he replied. 'When I first moved in I was living with someone . . . And when she left, I decided to keep the place on.' I narrowed my eyes, trying to imagine two people living in such a cramped space. No doubt it had only morphed into this eccentric, cluttered *garçonnière* once his girlfriend or partner was out of the picture. If I were ever to consider moving in with Jérémy, I reasoned, unable to switch off that part of my brain that seemed intent on projecting into the future, then we'd definitely need to find a new place. We'd need two bedrooms, for a start. And, if Jérémy would allow it, I'd push for an awful lot of his film and theatre memorabilia to be stored somewhere out of sight. Quirky and original Jérémy's place might be, but it was too much of a bachelor pad for my liking. 'What are you thinking about?' Jérémy had noticed the faraway look in my eyes.

'Oh, I was thinking about the play,' I lied, chalking up another white lie to the evening's tally.

'He didn't offer you a lift home? And you didn't even get a proper kiss?' Kate was flabbergasted. Curled up beside her on the sofa, I was attempting to chase away the taste of Jérémy's herbal tea with a hot chocolate. 'This Jérémy needs his head examining,' Kate tutted to herself. 'I mean, you looked amazing. What on earth is wrong with the man?'

'I wish I knew,' I said with a shrug. I'd tried to laugh off the disappointing way we'd parted when I'd described it to Kate but, frankly, the memory still stung. After lingering over my tea for as long as possible, I'd conceded I should be getting on my way. Jérémy had walked me to the front door and I'd paused in the doorway, eyeing his full lips, my pulse quickening with hopeful excitement. 'I had a lovely evening,' I said, 'thank you for inviting me out again.'

'Me too,' Jérémy replied, leaning towards me, and I lowered my eyelids and parted my lips, fully expecting him to kiss me on the mouth. Instead, he planted a tiny, sterile kiss on my right cheek, then another on my left. 'I'll call you,' he said softly. 'We'll do this again very soon . . .'

Crestfallen, I'd wished him luck for his audition, then walked reluctantly along the corridor to the lift, where I'd contemplated my face in the mirror. Spurning the métro, I'd trudged home, all the while trying and failing to make sense of what had just happened. If Jérémy wasn't attracted to me, I reasoned, he wouldn't keep promising we'd go out again. So there must be something else at work. Maybe he'd been scarred by a previous relationship and it had left him terrified of involvement? Maybe he was cautious, by nature, and liked to advance in slow motion?

Kate wasn't inclined to look upon Jérémy's motives quite so charitably, probably because she'd never met him, leaving her immune to his considerable charms. 'Sal, much as I hate to say this, there's another possibility you ought to at least entertain,' she said, her eyes filled with concern. 'If he's holding back from getting physical, it may be that he sees you as a friend. Next time you two go out, I think you ought to ask him, straight out.'

'I hope your instincts are wrong, Kate.' I sighed, draining the last of my hot chocolate and setting down my mug. 'Because honestly, I'm about *this* far from falling for him.'

I made a sign with my right hand, leaving only a couple of millimetres between my thumb and forefinger.

21

Lila seemed to have slept off whatever had been ailing her the previous day and had no qualms about waking me bright and early on Sunday. Padding through to the kitchen on autopilot, eyes still half-closed, I poured cereal into her favourite Sleeping Beauty bowl and set it on the table. My next mission was to locate the remote control. With a bit of luck, TiJi – her favourite of the various French cable channels aimed at young children – would allow me to doze for a little while longer on the sofa. Nico had arranged to take Lila at ten and keep her overnight, to compensate for the previous day's debacle, and he would deliver her to Sophie the next day, for her trip to Disneyland with Lucas. But ten o'clock seemed a long way away. Try as I might, I'd never managed to convince Lila of the virtues of weekend lie-ins.

Three hours later we were halfway through our second game of Memory – I was letting Lila win, this time, as our first attempt had ended in tears – when I heard a pinging noise emanating from my laptop. It was a sound I recognized: new mail had arrived on Rendez-vous.

Once we'd finished dissecting my date with Jérémy, I'd treated Kate to a Rendez-vous tour, complete with a post mortem of each of my dates so far, illustrated by a peek at their respective profiles. She'd heard all about English Marcus and live-at-home Frédéric, my two non-starters. She'd winced when I told her about my aborted sleepover at

Manu's and, when I came clean about what had happened with Australian Rob, leaving nothing out, she'd been downright horrified. Last, but not least, I'd shown her Jérémy's profile. 'He's devilishly handsome, I'll give you that,' Kate conceded, clicking on *'aggrandir'* to take a closer look at his photo. 'Good grief!' She pointed towards the figure at the top of the screen which auto-refreshed every few seconds to display the number of members online. Despite the anti-social hour – ten past midnight – it was still in the high five figures. 'I can see why finding a decent guy on here must be like looking for the proverbial needle in the haystack,' she said, aghast. 'Don't take this the wrong way, Sal, but I hope I never have to join . . .' Her phrase hung in the air between us for a few excruciating moments while I flailed around for a suitable reply. A reassuring 'Don't worry, you and Yves will be fine' would be meaningless. In the end, a fervent 'I hope so too' was the best I could muster. Kate left not long afterwards, steeling herself to face her empty apartment. I told her she was welcome to sleep on the sofa if she'd rather not be alone, but I could tell she wanted to be home, in case Yves showed up the next morning.

I realized now that I must have left the browser open on the Rendez-vous homepage after Kate left. So while Lila endeavoured to remember where she'd seen the second pig to match the card she'd turned over, I shuffled across the room to switch it off. Leaving myself logged in to the site for hours on end – even if it was by accident – wasn't a good thing. A flashing icon next to my profile picture would be proclaiming to all and sundry that I was 'online now', and being constantly connected smacked of desperation.

Although there were a number of messages in my Rendez-vous inbox, they were all marked '*non lus*' ('unread'). Since meeting Jérémy, I'd been unable to muster up the enthusiasm to follow up any other leads. I intended to ignore the most recent arrival too, until I caught sight of the title: '*Transports amoureux – édition exceptionnelle!*'

'Mummy, it's YOUR TURN!' bellowed Lila, evidently a little put out that she'd failed to find pig number two. Pulling the life-support cables out of my laptop, I returned with it to the patch of floor where the remaining cards were spread out in higgledy-piggledy rows and, momentarily forgetting that I was supposed to be letting Lila win, turned over two tigers in quick succession.

With one eye on the screen and another on the game in progress, I opened my intriguingly titled email. '*Vu le samedi* 16 *février sur Rendezvous.fr,*' it read. '*Jolie petite anglaise habitant Belleville, comme moi, et partageant mon obsession avec les Transports amoureux. Deux bonnes raisons de se rencontrer?*'

It was undeniably the most original email I'd ever received via Rendez-vous. Not only did its author live in the neighbourhood and share my love of *Transports amoureux*, but he'd described me as a 'pretty' English girl. A glance at his profile revealed that its author – pseudonym: dazedandconfused – was twenty-eight years old, a full four years younger than me and the wrong side of the all important thirty watershed. He listed his interests as photography and reading, and his profession as architect. His photo was odd: instead of smiling or attempting to smoulder at the camera, as most members did, he was frowning at the lens in genuine annoyance.

I dismissed dazedandconfused outright as date material. He was too young for me to take seriously, for one thing, and, besides, I was focusing all my energies on Jérémy. I couldn't resist replying to his email, all the same. A little voice inside was telling me that this neighbour of mine might be an interesting person to get to know, so why not use Rendez-vous to try and make a friend? There couldn't be any harm in that, as long as I was upfront about it from the start.

After toying with the idea of trying to compose a copy-cat *Transports amoureux* ad of my own, I decided I'd rather take a different tack. 'What had the person who took your profile picture done to deserve *that* look?' I typed instead, in French, hastily turning over two cards – a lion and a snake – in between sentences to mollify Lila. 'If you can promise you won't look at *me* like that,' I continued, 'then maybe we could meet for a friendly drink between neighbours . . .' Then, closing the computer, I brought my full attention back to the game in hand, allowing Lila to claim a resounding victory.

A few minutes before ten we set out to walk to Nico's. Lila, who darted out of the lift ahead of me, paused in the empty courtyard to stroke one of the neighbourhood cats, an overweight ginger and white monstrosity which belonged to an elderly lady on the ground floor. 'Lila! Please don't touch that cat,' I snapped, impatiently. 'I've told you a million times! She could be crawling with fleas!' Madame Morin always left her window ajar, enabling the cat to wander in and out as it pleased, but she was hard of hearing and unlikely to have a perfect grasp of English, so I wasn't unduly worried about causing offence if she overheard.

'You're English?' The male voice came from somewhere behind me, and I almost jumped out of my skin, not only surprised that Lila and I had company, but that we had English company. Wheeling round, I saw a man standing in the doorway of the concrete bunker where the communal dustbins were stored. Tall and lean, with closely cropped sandy hair and a sprinkling of freckles, he wore faded jeans and a Depeche Mode T-shirt. At a guess, he was in his early to mid-thirties, like me, and his accent, if I'd placed it correctly, sounded Liverpudlian.

'I am indeed,' I replied with a shy smile. 'I'm Sally, and this is my daughter, Lila. Do you live here too? I don't think I remember seeing you before . . .'

'Name's Pete.' He wiped the palm of his hand — presumably the hand which had been grasping a dustbin bag seconds earlier — on his jeans and came closer, extending it for me to shake. 'And I'm new in the building, yes. I moved into the ground-floor flat next door to our ginger friend here last week.' He gestured towards the cat, and I frowned at Lila, who had stretched out her hand to stroke it as soon as my back was turned. 'My son Ethan comes to stay on Wednesdays and every other weekend,' Pete added, looking at Lila. 'He can't be much older than your little girl, actually. He turned six last month.'

Lila had returned to my side, sheepish at having been caught ginger-handed, so to speak, and she now began tugging at my coat. 'I want to go to Daddy's house now,' she said impatiently. 'Come on, Mummy, we're going to be late.'

'As you can see, I have a similar arrangement with Lila's father.' I gave Pete a knowing look. 'Maybe we could have coffee at mine or yours sometime when Ethan is around,' I suggested. 'I'm sure Lila would love to have a playmate in the building . . .'

'That would be great, yes. I'll keep an eye out for you next time Ethan's over, shall I?' Pete replied. I was conscious of him sizing me up, his eyes scrolling down from my head to my feet, then travelling upwards again. 'I wouldn't mind a playmate in the building myself,' Pete added with a mischievous little smile. And with that, he turned on his heel and returned indoors, although not before he'd given us a cheeky little wave.

As we walked along rue Rébeval, hand in hand, I caught myself humming a song Lila had learned at school and performed for me several times that morning. I'd gone to bed feeling glum after Jérémy's rebuttal, but seeing dazedandconfused's message this morning and meeting Pete on the way out had buoyed my spirits. If they both appreciated my charms, there was no reason why Jérémy wouldn't come around too. And really, when I thought about it, our evening had gone incredibly well. It was only the last thirty seconds that I had a problem with.

Wearing the striped bathrobe Mum and Dad had bought him for his birthday, more years ago than I cared to remember, Nico looked contrite when he answered his front door. '*Ça va mieux, mon amour?*' he said, swinging Lila up into his arms for a hug. Lila nodded and hugged him back. It was lucky for him that four-year-olds have short memories and don't bear adult-sized grudges.

'She hasn't been sick since yesterday,' I explained, wondering whether Albane was lurking somewhere out of sight, listening in. 'I never saw the damage, although I hear she did a pretty good job of baptizing your bed . . .'

'To be honest, neither did I,' confessed Nico. 'By the time I got home from work, the sheets were spinning round in the washing machine. But I'm told it was pretty spectacular.' He had the good grace to look guilty about neglecting his duties, but I bet he was relieved to have missed the worst of it. He'd never been much help when it came to unpleasant tasks like changing nappies or administering medicine, and had always left these things up to me when we lived together. '*Alors, mon coeur*,' he said, setting Lila down on the floor again, 'if you go into your bedroom, you'll find a lovely surprise.' Lila needed no further encouragement and scampered off along the corridor. I didn't approve of Nico buying her forgiveness in quite such an obvious way, but was grateful, nonetheless, to be able to snatch a few seconds to talk to him alone.

'Is Albane here?' I spoke in a hushed tone, gesturing towards the living room.

Nico shook his head. 'She's out. So if you want to tear a few more strips off me, be my guest.'

'I was wondering whether you still expect me to believe Albane isn't living with you?' I concentrated on keeping my voice too low for Lila to overhear, and devoid of sarcasm for once. 'Only Kate was here with me yesterday too, and she tells me your girlfriend's taken over half your wardrobe . . .' I paused before I delivered my punch line. 'Forgive me if I'm wrong, Nico, but that sounds like cohabitation to me.'

'It's very recent,' Nico replied, his voice defensive. 'But you know how it is . . . She was always here, and it didn't seem sensible to keep up two apartments . . .' He let his sentence trail off and gave a shrug that spoke volumes. For Albane's sake, I hoped he was playing things down for my benefit.

'Well, who says romance is dead?' I chuckled. 'But seriously, though . . . If Albane's living here with you, then it stands to reason she's going to spend quite a bit of time with Lila. Didn't you think I had a right to know? If only so I could keep an eye on Lila and make sure she wasn't finding the new situation confusing? I mean, not so long ago you were all for consulting a therapist . . .'

Nico contemplated his feet for a moment. I got the impression he was weighing his words carefully: turning them three times around his mouth, as the French say, before he spoke. 'I didn't want to upset you,' he said at last, lifting his gaze to meet mine. 'You're on your own. I'm not. I was hoping to find a way to tell you things were moving in that direction when we met for dinner at Chapeau Melon, but you ended up walking out on me, remember?'

'Well, I know now,' I said, ignoring his reference to our disastrous outing. 'And from what I've seen of Albane, she seems nice. So let's try and all make this work, shall we, and minimize the upheaval to Lila as much as we can . . .?'

'Ta-DAAA!' Lila reappeared in the hallway, looking immensely pleased with herself. She'd removed her clothes and wriggled into a brand-new Little Mermaid costume, the gift Nico had mentioned earlier. 'Am I pretty with my new tail, Mummy?' She twirled around to show me her new outfit from every angle. The 'tail' was composed of two separate sections which hung down at the front and back, gaps at the sides making it possible to walk around.

'You make a beautiful mermaid, honey.' I dropped to my knees and stole a brief hug as soon as she pirouetted within range. 'Now, you have a nice time at Daddy and

Albane's house,' I said, glancing at Nico over her shoulder. 'And I'll see you tomorrow, after school.'

As I walked home, my right hand missing the subtle pressure of Lila's and closing around the keys in my pocket instead, I tried on a mental image of Lila wedged in between Nico and Albane on the sofa for size. It faded, replaced by a picture of Albane wearing a silk negligee and slipping between the sheets of what used to be my bed. But, try as I might, I didn't seem to be capable of causing myself any actual pain. It was like digging a blade into my skin and finding I couldn't draw blood.

I supposed this must be because I'd had almost a year to get used to the idea of the two of them together and, despite Nico's repeated denials, I'd seen the writing on the wall long ago. If anything, I decided, it was a relief that things were out in the open. I had Lila's timely stomach upset to thank for that. Otherwise, goodness knows when I would have found out.

I was pottering around the apartment, putting off my lesson planning for the coming week until the last possible moment, when it occurred to me to sneak a peek at my Rendez-vous profile to check whether dazedandconfused had made any reply to my email that morning. A cursory glance at my inbox revealed nothing new, but when an 'invitation to chat' window popped up, seconds later, there he was, online.

'*Ça te dirait de prendre un verre aux Folies, ce soir?*' he suggested. 'Unless you have your daughter with you, that is?' I smiled. Without making a big deal of it, he'd shown he was making allowances for the impact motherhood must have on my freedom of movement. It was the first time someone I'd met on Rendez-vous had struck the right balance.

'20 *heures, ça te va?*' I wasn't in the mood for playing hard to get or pretending I'd had important plans which had been cancelled. 'My name's Sally, by the way,' I added, deciding it was time to lure him out from behind his pseudonym. '*Et toi, tu t'appelles comment?*'

'*À toute à l'heure*, Sally ... *Moi, c'est* Matthias,' he replied, leaving me his mobile number in brackets. 'And don't worry, I promise not to give you that look,' he added, signing out before I could riposte.

After signing out myself, I couldn't resist clicking on the jpeg of Jérémy's theatre poster that I'd saved to my desktop and sneaking a peek at his naked torso before I got down to some lesson planning. If he were to call me today, I'd have no qualms about bowing out of my arrangements with Matthias. In my mind, there was no ambiguity about where my priorities lay.

2 2

I was walking down rue de Belleville – dawdling not out of reluctance or nervousness, but to compensate for running early – when I became aware of someone quickening their pace behind me, drawing almost level, then slowing the tempo of their footfalls to match my own. At first I pretended not to notice, keeping my eyes on the pavement ahead. It wasn't unusual for someone to accost me for a light or some spare change on this stretch of road, or even for a complete stranger to try and strike up conversation or invite me for a drink, and the best strategy I knew for warding off unwanted attention was to avoid making eye contact in the first place.

But it was also possible that the person on the periphery of my vision could be someone I knew and, in the end, I allowed curiosity to gain the upper hand. In my preferred scenario, of course, my pursuer was Jérémy. But when I darted a glance over my left shoulder, I locked eyes with my new neighbour Pete, instead. 'Sorry for creeping up on you,' he said with a lopsided smile. 'I thought it was you, but I wanted to make one hundred per cent sure . . .'

'Hello again.' I blushed involuntarily at the memory of the comment Pete had made about playmates, a few hours earlier. Had he seen me crossing the courtyard from his window, I wondered, and thrown on his jacket and shoes in haste so he could follow me out and waylay me in the street?

'I wanted to apologize, for earlier,' Pete continued, confirming my suspicions. 'It occurred to me afterwards that what I said might have made you uncomfortable. I mean, not everyone gets my sense of humour, and I'd hate to think you imagined I was being weird . . .'

'Oh no, not at all,' I reassured him with a smile. 'Don't worry about it. I'm pretty sure I took it in the spirit in which it was intended.' I was secretly rather glad Pete had caught me looking my best. I hadn't gone to the same lengths for Matthias as I might have done for Jérémy, but I'd pulled out the stops halfway. It was a mild evening and my coat was unbuttoned, revealing a black cashmere jumper with a deep V-neck. I'd swapped my trainers for boots with heels that elongated my jean-clad legs. As for my make-up, I'd attempted a toned-down version of the look Kate had created: my eyes were outlined with a hint of grey and my lips wore a sheer coat of pale gloss. All in all, I'd left home feeling pretty good about myself and, judging by the appreciative expression on Pete's face, he thought I scrubbed up rather well.

Keeping up the pretence – if indeed it was a pretence – that he was on his way somewhere too, Pete walked alongside me as I crossed rue Julien Lacroix, then adjusted my trajectory to avoid the overflowing bottle bank in front of place Fréhel, which wasn't so much a square as a tarmacked area where a building had once stood. The '*place*' was best known for its *trompe l'oeil* artwork: the exposed stone wall of an adjacent apartment building was decorated with a lifelike sculpture of a man standing on a platform suspended below a huge black billboard, his workmate taking a break seated on the rooftop above, his legs dangling over the side of the building. '*Il faut se méfier des mots*,' the text on the billboard read, in large white cursive script. The official translation in guidebooks tended to be 'beware of words', although I felt '*se méfier*' was much less categorical than that. 'Be wary' would have been more accurate, as far as I was concerned, but I was nit-picking, as ever.

'It's cool, isn't it, that sign?' Pete gestured upwards. 'It took me years to spot that second figure . . . The one sitting up top.' I noted the implication – that Pete was a long-term Paris resident, like me – with interest. I also had an inkling of what he might be going to say next, and my mind was already racing ahead, plotting how to reply. We were nearing the Folies now, where Matthias was doubtless waiting. And sure enough, Pete popped the question a few seconds later. 'Do you fancy grabbing a drink?' he suggested, his voice casual. 'If you have a bit of free time, that is?'

'I'm afraid I have plans,' I replied, shaking my head regretfully. 'I'm on my way to meet a friend.' I gestured towards Aux Folies, praying that Pete wasn't bound for the same destination. I didn't much fancy trying to make self-conscious small talk with Matthias while Pete's eyes burned holes in the back of my head.

'That's a shame. Well . . . Another time, perhaps . . .' I nodded and smiled, pausing in front of the Folies and pretending to wait for my 'friend' outside, at least until Pete was out of view. Thankfully, he didn't linger. He gave me a little wave instead, and then turned to dart across rue de Belleville in the gap between two cars, without waiting for the pedestrian crossing to give him the all clear. Once he'd disappeared behind one of the white, graffiti-covered traders' vans parked in front of the Chinese restaurant opposite, the coast was clear. It was a pity, really. It would have been refreshing to do something so spontaneous. But I could hardly stand up Matthias at such short notice, could I? And Pete would keep. I knew where to find him.

There was no sign of anyone resembling Matthias at the outdoor tables, so I pushed open the swing door and stepped inside. The room was wider than it was deep, with only two rows of tables running between the glass front of the café and the long zinc bar which spanned most of its width. Pausing inside the door, I scanned the half-dozen tables to my left, beyond the *Sopranos* pinball machine, but drew a blank. When I hopped to the right to avoid the waiter, who swept past me with a full tray of drinks on his way to serve the smokers outside, I detected something soft and yielding under the heel of my right boot and heard a sharp intake of breath. Turning to apologize to the owner of the trampled foot, seated at the table to the right of the front door, I realized my boot had instinctively found my date for the evening.

'*Ah là la, je suis désolée,*' I exclaimed, mortified, as Matthias limped to his feet and leaned over the table to plant a kiss on both my cheeks. Without removing my coat, conscious of the draught from the front door, I pulled out the chair opposite his so I could sit, a position in which, I joked, I would constitute less of a threat. Matthias's lips twitched in response to my attempt at humour, but his watering eyes couldn't lie. I'd really hurt him. What an inauspicious start to the evening.

'Don't worry about it,' he replied in surprisingly competent English. '*Comme on dit,*' he continued, switching back into his mother tongue, 'it will make a great story to bore our grandchildren with one day. You know, instead of the usual "Our eyes met across a crowded bar," we'll be able to say "Our feet touched, with a crunching sound, as boot met bone" . . .'

'Anything has to be better than owning up to meeting on Rendez-vous, don't you think?' I said with a wide smile. Sizing Matthias up as I spoke, I found I was pleasantly surprised by what I saw. He was a lot better looking than his sulky profile photo had led me to believe. His brown hair was cropped short and there were patches of prematurely grey hair around his ears, reminiscent of Jérémy's, which gave him an air of maturity beyond his years. His chin was peppered with a few days' stubble; his eyes were a rich dark chocolate-brown. Dressed in the same casual uniform as everyone else in the Folies – indigo jeans and trainers, with a pale-grey jumper layered over a white T-shirt – he looked very much at home.

If Jérémy hadn't come along first, it's possible Matthias would have piqued my interest. So much depends on timing when you meet new people, I thought to myself. In this case, timing hadn't worked in Matthias's favour: my head was filled to capacity with thoughts of Jérémy. 'I must admit though,' I continued, 'yours was the most original email I've ever received on Rendez-vous. It was so refreshing to hear from someone who had read my *annonce* and bothered to refer to it. It stood head and shoulders above the rest.'

'I'm glad you liked it.' Matthias grinned, showing a set of white, slightly uneven teeth. 'It's surprisingly hard to write a *Transports amoureux* spoof without sounding like the sort of stalker you'd want to place under a restraining order. And as for meeting through Rendez-vous' – he paused for a moment – 'I do know what you mean. I chose my pseudonym – dazedandconfused – because it expressed my total *désarroi* at finding myself signed up on a site like that, and I have to say, I could only bring myself to subscribe for one month. The idea of becoming a long-term member, making monthly payments by direct debit for six months, or even a year . . .' Matthias didn't have to finish his sentence: I was already nodding vigorously in agreement.

'But doesn't that mean you have to date rather, um, intensively to get your money's worth?' I said slyly. 'Signing up for one month is way more expensive, isn't it? They make that option as unattractive as possible, to dissuade people from doing it . . .'

'It was expensive, yes, but so far it's been worth it,' said Matthias enigmatically. Was I supposed to take his ambiguous remark as a compliment, I wondered, or assume he'd been meeting a different girl every night?

'I joined last September,' I confessed, 'but I had my misgivings and it took me a while to work up to actually meeting anyone. So, actually, in five months I've only met five different people. But there was an awful lot of filtering involved in between. I've lost count of the number of emails and flashes I've had to wade through . . .'

Matthias made no comment about this, but I thought I read something like approval in his eyes, as though I'd confirmed some impression he'd had of me before we met. 'I read somewhere that the male-to-female ratio is out of kilter and it's become a real problem,' he said gravely. 'Some girls are getting turned off by all the men bombarding them with messages and leaving the site altogether. Which will make things even worse for the rest . . .'

From the outset, I felt incredibly relaxed in Matthias's company. For the first half-hour at least, he quizzed me about what it was like to be an expat, where I'd learned French, what I enjoyed about teaching and why I'd chosen to live in Belleville. When I mentioned the name of Lila's school, he did a double take. 'One of my best friends has two children at that school!' he exclaimed. 'Lucie and Léo – Lila might know them, actually – I call them my little *nièce* and *neveu*.' He shook his head. '*Comme le monde est petit!*'

'Your friends must have started a family early?' I said, frowning as I performed the mental arithmetic. 'I mean, if they have two kids at *maternelle* and they're twenty-eight, like you . . .'

Matthias looked amused. 'Is that your way of telling me you think I'm a bit too young for you?' he asked, narrowing his eyes. 'Because I happen to think age doesn't count for much once you get beyond a certain point. We're both adults. We both work. Okay, I haven't fathered any children yet' – he tapped his palm against the side of the wooden table, mock-superstitiously – 'but I was in a six-year relationship until a year ago, and I can't say I never gave the subject any thought . . .'

'I was twenty-eight when I had Lila,' I admitted. 'So I suppose I do take your point.' I refrained from adding that, if my life had gone according to plan, Lila should have had a brother or a sister by now. Taking a sip of my beer, I decided it was my turn to quiz Matthias. I learned that he worked for a small firm of architects based nearby, in rue Ramponeau, and his eyes sparkled when he started to tell me about the projects he'd worked on when he was still a student. He'd spent a year in Mali, working for a non-profit organization, where he taught people how to construct buildings using local materials, reviving methods that had long fallen into disuse.

'It was ironic, I suppose,' he conceded, 'that a French guy in his twenties ended up showing Malians how to make traditional dwellings. But the knowledge was dying out. They'd started building to Western specifications. It made no sense at all . . .'

When Matthias excused himself to go to the bathroom, I realized the collage covering our square table was composed of a few dozen cuttings taken from a newspaper, each with African *marabouts* advertising their skills. Every table at Aux Folies was covered in a collage, some papered with posters from the era when the bar had formed part of a music hall next door, others peppered with old photographs or random newspaper clippings. What a coincidence it was, I pointed out to Matthias when he returned to his seat, given the subject of our last conversation, that ours had an African connection. I read one of the adverts aloud in French. A clairvoyant by the name of Monsieur Diakhaby listed his skills as 'Resolution of all problems. Removal of curses. Bringing back loved ones. Increasing the profitability of your business . . .'

'I've got a better one,' Matthias retorted, pointing to a clipping in the centre of the table. 'I found it while I was waiting for you, earlier. Listen to this. "Monsieur Moro: will bring loved ones crawling back on four legs, as obediently as dog follows master."'

When I finally stopped laughing, dabbing at my watering eyes with a tissue, Matthias asked me if I'd like to go for something to eat. 'We could go to Krung Thep, on

Julien Lacroix,' he suggested, 'if you're hungry and you like Thai food . . .'

My last visit to Krung Thep had been with Nico, a few weeks before we separated. Aside from the unfinished meal at Chapeau Melon, I hadn't eaten out in my own neighbourhood in the intervening months, partly because I didn't get out much, but also because I'd been wary of running into Nico and Albane. But after performing a rapid internal inventory of the contents of my fridge, I green-lit Matthias's plan without further hesitation: I felt as relaxed as I would in the company of Kate, Ryan or Anna and drifting to another location to prolong the evening felt like a natural progression.

Rounding the corner of rue Lesage, I remembered the other reason why I hadn't been to this particular Thai restaurant in so long. Without a reservation, it had always been nigh on impossible to get a table, and I'd lost count of the number of times Nico and I had been turned away by the surly waiting staff. The interior, with its raised banquettes – carpeted benches constructed to give diners the impression they were sitting cross-legged on the floor around a series of low tables – was tiny, and there were only two sittings per evening. But when we stepped inside, the forbidding-looking owner nodded at Matthias and waved him straight over to the only two spare seats in the house. 'I called ahead,' Matthias confessed, offering me his hand to steady myself while I clambered over the banquette to wedge myself in behind the table. 'And look,' he said, pointing out a yellowing press-clipping of Queen Elizabeth II in full ceremonial dress, posing stiffly with a group of Thai dignitaries, sandwiched between the tablecloth and its protective glass pane, 'we're in good company.'

'That rather depends on what I think of the monarchy,' I retorted with a smile. 'Don't forget, I do read *Libération* . . .'

We ordered a mountain of crispy Thai spring rolls, followed by a prawn dish served inside half a hollowed pineapple for me and fish wrapped in banana leaves with sticky rice for Matthias. 'It's spicy, which is more than I can say for most Parisian Thai food,' I said appreciatively, draining the dregs of my Thai beer as I finished my main course and signalling to the waitress my urgent need for a carafe of water.

'You should order some fresh mango to put out the fires,' Matthias suggested. 'It's the only decent dessert on the menu.'

'So you come here a lot?' I said, thinking back to how the owner had recognized him and wondering how many other Rendez-vous dates he'd booked a table for, 'just in case'.

'There was a time, a few years ago, when I ate here three or four times a week,' he admitted. I raised my eyebrows. Krung Thep wasn't cheap, and I couldn't imagine making it my regular *cantine*. 'It used to be a lot cheaper,' he added, as though he'd read my mind. 'The food was better, too. But like everywhere half decent in this neighbourhood, prices have doubled. It's the cost of gentrification.'

'How long have you lived around here?' I asked him, thinking how nice it was to know someone with a wealth of local knowledge.

'I was born in Paris,' Matthias replied. 'In the eleventh, near Père Lachaise, in a hospital called Les Bleuets. Which means I've always lived within a five-kilometre radius of where I am now.'

'Wow, a *real* Parisian,' I exclaimed. 'I think you may be the first one I've ever met.' It was true: so many of the French people I knew had moved to the capital to find work once they'd completed their studies. To meet a bona fide Parisian, born and raised in the city, was relatively rare. 'I considered having Lila at Les Bleuets,' I added, 'although I never visited it. Les Lilas seemed the obvious choice, with the direct métro . . .'

'Lucky for her. Lila is a much nicer first name than Bleuet,' joked Matthias. 'I have no idea how you translate either of these flowers into English.'

'Lilacs and cornflowers,' I replied, playing along, although we hadn't named Lila after her birthplace. British people always assumed I'd been influenced by Kate Moss christening her daughter Lila Grace, a couple of years before Lila arrived on the scene. But Nico had come up with the name: it was his mother Catherine's middle name.

When the bill arrived, we split it down the middle without discussion and Matthias helped me back over the banquette and into my coat. Squinting at my watch as we left, I was amazed it was already past eleven. The last three hours had gone by in the blink of an eye.

'If you fancy one last drink, we could go back down the hill to the Folies,' Matthias suggested, 'or I have some beer at home . . . I live right here.' He gestured towards a moss-green door on the opposite side of rue Lesage. 'Unless you're tired and you need to get an early night before work tomorrow . . .'

I was all too aware of the signals I might be sending if I accepted this invitation. But I didn't feel much like going back to my empty apartment just yet, nor could I face traipsing back down the hill to the Folies, where we might struggle to find a free table at this hour. 'I'd be intrigued to see your apartment,' I said cautiously. 'Isn't it funny that it turns out we live practically on each other's doorsteps? I've always wanted to make a *friend* in my own neighbourhood, but I never got very far with the other parents at Lila's school . . .'

Matthias's mouth twitched and I took this as a signal that my message — the exaggerated emphasis I'd placed on the word 'friend' — had been received, loud and clear. Tapping in his door code, he ushered me inside. A series of leafy, stone-paved courtyards led to his building, the third removed from the road. Once inside, there were four flights of stairs to climb and my breathing became increasingly laboured until, at last, we stopped in front of a narrow door.

'You'll have to excuse the mess,' Matthias cautioned me, reminding me of Jérémy for a moment, as he pushed open the front door and switched on the hall light. 'I usually clean up on Sundays, but it was my grandma's birthday today, and I had to go out for a big family gathering . . .' I followed him through the hallway and into the kitchen-cum-dining room, a rectangular room with two large windows. Matthias paused to pull two small bottles of 1664 out of the fridge, then opened a drawer and began digging around for a bottle opener. 'There used to be more walls,' he said, gesturing towards the point where the kitchen-floor tiles gave way to wood floors. 'The previous owners knocked this wall down, and then when I arrived, I took out that one over there.' Where he was pointing, opposite the dining area, the plaster had been stripped back until only a series of ancient wooden beams remained. Peering through the gaps, I could see into the living room beyond.

'If this is messy, I'd love to see what tidy looks like,' I joked as Matthias handed me an open bottle. It was true: compared to Jérémy's place, it was positively minimalist. I followed him into the living room, a sparsely furnished space with only a sofa, a coffee table, a TV and a large bookcase, its shelves filled with oversized hardback books. Running my finger along their spines, I saw they fell into three distinct categories: books about art, about architecture and *bandes dessinées*, the hardback comic books the French take so seriously that entire sections are devoted to the *neuvième art* in high-street book shops.

On the white wall opposite the sofa hung a collection of framed black and white photographs. 'Did you take these?' I asked, glancing at Matthias, who had taken a seat. 'I seem to remember you saying you were into photography, from your profile?' Matthias nodded, and I turned back to the photos, studying each one for far longer than necessary, using them as an excuse to remain standing. They were beautiful photos. Portraits, mostly, of people from the African village he'd told me about earlier, and he'd captured something of the essence of each person he'd photographed. But there was only so long I could stand and gaze appreciatively at them before I crossed the room and perched on the opposite end of the sofa. 'Did you live here with the girlfriend you mentioned earlier?' I asked, hoping he wouldn't object to the personal question.

Matthias shook his head. 'I moved in after we broke up. This place fell into my lap at the right moment, just when I needed to make a fresh start.'

'I thought as much,' I admitted. 'It's lovely, but it lacks all those little details that a woman might think of . . .'

'Don't tell me, you'd add curtains, a few plants, string some fairy lights across the beams . . .' Matthias grinned. 'A few of my female friends have said similar things,' he explained. 'You're right. I don't doubt it would stand to benefit from a woman's touch.' Setting down his drink, he surveyed the room, his expression difficult to fathom, and we shared our first embarrassed silence of the evening. 'You know, I probably should get an early night,' I said, wondering whether accepting his invitation had been a mistake. 'I enjoyed tonight a lot, but you're right, I do have to get up early for work tomorrow . . .'

'Okay,' said Matthias, his voice husky, 'but there's something I need to do first.' Leaning forward, he plucked the bottle from my hand, cupped my face in his palms and kissed me, catching me completely off my guard.

I was woken the next day by pale sunlight filtering through the flimsy fabric of a pair of unfamiliar curtains. From the kitchen, I heard the tinkle of a teaspoon landing on a saucer and, a few seconds later, the convulsive juddering of an espresso machine springing to action. For a few delicious seconds my brain indulged itself in a daydream that the person at the controls was Jérémy. But when a sleepy-looking Matthias walked into the room, his hair damp, a towel knotted around his waist, I felt guilty for entertaining such blasphemous thoughts while I lay in his bed. He deserved better. The sex the previous night had been astonishingly good, taking both of us by surprise. When it was over, he'd curled around the small of my back and we'd fallen asleep, entwined, as though sleeping together were the most natural thing in the world.

'*Je t'ai fait un petit café*,' said Matthias, stifling a yawn. 'It's quarter past seven.' I pulled myself up into a sitting position, gathering the duvet around me and trapping it under my arms – even if it was a bit late to be worrying about preserving my modesty – and accepting the cup he held out to me with a shy smile. I was sure my hair looked like a bird's nest, and I wondered how much of the previous night's make-up had found its way into the corners of my eyes, but somehow under Matthias's gaze I felt dishevelled, but sexy. It wasn't a feeling I was used to.

The progression from Matthias's sofa to his bedroom had been slow and natural, that first gentle kiss on the sofa burgeoning into something more insistent. When Matthias pulled back, got to his feet and held out his hand, his eyes never leaving mine, I took it, silently, and allowed him to lead me into the bedroom. There we eased off one another's clothes, one item at a time, in the semi-darkness and resumed our kissing on the bed, side by side, our bodies shivering with a growing need. This time there had been little alcohol in my bloodstream, and I'd been there, in the moment, my head completely clear, my nerve endings primed, delighting in the contact of our skin. When I could bear the wait no longer, it was my turn to pull back and ask him, shyly, whether he had some protection. My first climax made me cry out, amazed at its intensity, and prompted Matthias to stop moving altogether. 'What about you?' I said, once I'd scraped myself off the ceiling and was able to string a few words together. 'You didn't . . . At least I don't think you did?'

'Plenty of time for that.' I heard the sound of a condom being removed and discarded and saw Matthias's teeth glint in the dark. It wasn't long before our whispers were stifled by a second round of kisses. And this time no one was left lagging behind.

Once I'd drained the dregs of my coffee and thrown on the previous day's clothes, it was time to dash home for a shower and a costume change, before work. Matthias, wearing jeans and a crisp white shirt under a dark grey jacket, walked me to the front door of his building, pausing to remove a copy of *Libération* from his letterbox. 'I had a lovely evening, and a lovely night,' I said, touching my lips to his, conscious that his mouth smelled of toothpaste, while mine smelled of coffee. 'You took me by surprise, but in the nicest possible way . . .'

'Me too,' Matthias replied, holding the door open for me to step through and giving me a half-wave, half-salute with his free hand. Neither of us said anything about calling or seeing one another again.

On the short walk home and, later, on my way to the métro, I was conscious of how men's eyes slid inside my open coat and over my body, lingering on the swell of my breasts and the curve of my hips. It was as though they could sense something different about me this morning; as though it was plain to see I'd risen from the tousled sheets of a man's bed moments earlier. Did I radiate some kind of sexual aura? Had they caught a faint whiff of pheromones on the breeze? Or did they see something they recognized in my eyes, my posture or my gait?

Whatever the explanation, there was no doubt in my mind that I turned more heads that morning than I had in years. My journey home didn't feel like a 'walk of shame' at all. Could it be that I'd just had my first ever enjoyable one-night stand?

23

Monday morning's lessons flashed by in a bleary-eyed blur as I stifled my yawns behind cupped hands and taught on autopilot, lack of sleep leaving me strangely detached from my surroundings.

I lunched alone in a salad bar in a side street close to Delphine's office, more than a little relieved that my fortnightly lunch with Kate would fall the following Monday. I was too lost in my own thoughts today to be good company for anyone. My mind was like the needle on a scratched record: it kept jumping back to the night I'd spent with Matthias.

It was impossible to compare how I felt today – elated, self-satisfied, sated – with how I'd felt the morning after my one-night stand with Australian Rob. There was no sour aftertaste of remorse, no feeling of having been used and abused. Rob had thought only of plundering me to satisfy his own, selfish needs, but with Matthias the pleasure was shared and mutual, more about giving than taking. It had been far too long since anyone had touched me that way, exploring the contours of my body as though I were exciting, uncharted territory. What we'd had, I realized, was the kind of sex you expect to have with a long-time lover, not an *amant de passage*.

But when I'd opened my eyes that morning, my first thought had been that I wished Matthias were someone else, proof that all those kisses, all those intimate caresses, hadn't lifted the spell Jérémy had cast over me. Now, I found myself longing for Jérémy to kiss me that way, to guide me wordlessly into his bedroom, to slowly undress me. I wanted to drink a post-coital coffee by his side in the morning, with his bedclothes wound around my naked body. The night I'd spent with Matthias had given shape to these previously half-formed desires, making them more concrete, more urgent, more real.

Waiting on the cream leather sofa for Delphine to materialize half an hour later, I fiddled with my new silk scarf, which I was wearing for its inaugural outing. Kate had shown me how to tie it when she helped me get ready for my date with Jérémy the previous weekend. But I was far from sure I'd got it right and I half expected Delphine to frown, tut and re-tie it as soon as she laid eyes on me.

I was surprised to hear an unfamiliar sound – Delphine humming – as she swept along the corridor to meet me, grinning as she caught sight of her gift around my neck. Her buoyant mood seemed to suggest things were going well with the man she'd met over Christmas and, once we'd reached the sanctuary of our teaching room, I resolved to quiz her about him, reasoning that, as long as we conducted our conversation in English, I was almost within my lesson remit.

'I take it your mystery man is responsible for this cheerful humming?' I shot Delphine a knowing glance as I set my satchel on the table. She shot me a blank look, and it took me a moment to realize my choice of vocabulary was to blame. Temporarily unable to dredge up the French for 'humming' from my sluggish brain, I was forced to perform a reluctant demonstration instead.

'Ah, *je frédonnais!*' Delphine pulled out the chair opposite mine. 'I 'ad not notice' I was doing this! But you are right: I am very 'appy right now. Things are going well.'

Delphine had proved my pessimistic predictions wrong, somehow managing to find time in her busy schedule to see the man she now referred to as her 'boyfriend'. They'd been joined at the hip this past week, while her daughter spent the first half of her school holidays skiing with her father in the Alps.

'And is he keen to meet Suzanne?' I enquired, proud of myself for remembering her daughter's name but also conscious that my interest in her situation wasn't entirely unselfish. How did Delphine plan to handle the logistics of seeing her new man now that her daughter was back home? I wondered. How did one decide when the time was ripe to bring a child into the equation?

'Robert 'az no children from his marriage,' Delphine replied, relishing the sound of her lover's name as she pronounced it, 'but 'eez looking forward to meeting with Suzanne very much. I think we are going to organize a lunch . . . Maybe at ze weekend . . .'

'Ah, so Mr Eligible Divorcé is called Robert,' I said, pouncing on this new piece of information. 'And what does this Robert do for a living?'

'E works for a company who do . . .' Delphine paused, searching, in vain, for an unfamiliar English word. 'Sally, 'ow you say "*conseil en management*"?'

'He's a management consultant,' I said slowly, the tiniest whisper of a possibility suggesting itself to me as I spoke. It was a long shot: there could be any number of consultants called Robert in Paris. But wasn't the Robert I taught every Tuesday also recently divorced? And, what's more, hadn't I noticed a white band on his ring finger, back in October? 'Delphine,' I continued, 'this is going to sound odd, but I don't suppose by any chance Robert's surname is Cazenove?'

Delphine gasped and, to my surprise, her face fell. How odd. Why would she find the fact that I knew Robert upsetting? 'Sally, 'ave you seen Robert on Rendez-vous?' Delphine said after a pause, her voice trembling with anxiety. 'Did 'ee contact you?'

'No! Of course not!' I hastened to reassure her. 'It's nothing like that! I teach him English on Tuesdays, that's all, and when you mentioned his name and his occupation, it occurred to me that my pupil Robert no longer wears his wedding ring . . .'

Delphine clapped a hand over her mouth to stifle a giggle of pure relief. 'And 'ow is 'eez English?' she asked me slyly, when she had recovered her *sang froid*. 'Tell me, Sally! Eez it better than mine?'

As I rode the métro home after my final lesson, once I'd checked my phone, for the fifth time that day, for a message from Jérémy, I reflected on my exchange with Delphine. Seeing how she'd panicked when I'd unmasked Robert's identity had reminded me of how I'd felt when things were still dauntingly new with Nico. When our relationship had begun to blossom, I'd been giddy with happiness, delirious with excitement. But there had been a flipside: the paralysing, irrational fear that something or someone would snatch it all away. Both the giddy feeling and the paranoia had dissipated by the time the real wolves began circling, ten years later. The irony of this was not lost on me now.

When I embarked on a new relationship, I knew I'd be plagued by the same insecurities and, indeed, they'd probably be magnified tenfold given the way Nico had trampled all over my trust. But, like Delphine, in spite of all my baggage, I sensed I was starting to feel ready to ride the rollercoaster again. All I had to do was persuade Jérémy to ride it with me.

I'd walked halfway to Lila's school before I remembered, in a blinding flash, that today was the day Sophie had taken Lila and Lucas to Disneyland Paris. Retracing my steps to rue de Belleville to avoid taking a shortcut along Matthias's street, I quickened my pace. I'd left my apartment looking like a war zone this morning, leaving the previous day's clothes littering the floor and damp towels strewn across the sofa. I'd have to hurry if I were to have time to straighten the place up before Sophie materialized. Goodness only knew what she'd think of me otherwise.

The doorbell rang soon after six, and when I peeped through the spy hole, I was greeted by the sight of Lila and Lucas wearing matching hats with Mickey Mouse ears, and identical grins. Sophie, who was bringing up the rear, looked exhausted. After the long drive back to Paris from Marne la Vallée with the children, I was willing to bet she was itching to light up a cigarette.

'*Alors?*' I cried, throwing open the door and sweeping Lila off her feet for an enthusiastic hug. 'Did you two have fun with Auntie Sophie?'

'I did meet Mickey Mouse for real real REAL!' shrieked Lila, her high-pitched tone verging on hysteria. 'He was driving a special car. And he did wave at me while I was riding in a teacup.'

'You'll see,' said Sophie, winking at me over Lila's shoulder. 'I took many photographs . . .'

'Do you want to have a breather here before you drive home?' I set Lila down and motioned towards the sofa. 'You look worn out, Sophie. It was brave of you to take the two of them out for the day. I'm not sure I could have done it . . .'

'I suppose I've got time for a quick drink,' said Sophie gratefully, moving towards the window and reaching into her coat pocket. 'Lucas, Lila,' she said, slipping into French to address the children, 'why don't you get those coats off and Lila can show you the toys in her room?' Once they had complied, discarding their coats on the floor and scampering off to the bedroom, chattering incessantly about their favourite rides of the day, Sophie lit up a cigarette. She took a couple of long, needy drags in quick succession, leaning over the balustrade to exhale her smoke into the courtyard. 'It was hard work,' she admitted, her eyes lighting up when I produced two bottles of beer from the depths of my fridge and set them down on the kitchen counter. 'The queues, and all those kids crazy from eating too much sugar. If I never have to hear the music from that "Small World" ride with the singing puppets, I will not be sorry . . .'

'Are you going back to work tomorrow?' I twisted the metal tops off the beers, using a tea towel to protect my hand from the serrated edges. Sophie shook her head. 'It must be nice,' I said wistfully, 'working for yourself and deciding your own hours. My five weeks of annual holiday sound like a lot in theory, but they don't go far, considering Lila's off school for three times longer . . .'

'Shouldn't Nico have looked after Lila for one half of this two-week holiday?' said Sophie with a frown. 'I wanted to ask him about that this morning, but in all the excitement I completely forgot . . .'

'Strictly speaking, yes' I said with a shrug, 'but we're not religious about sticking to those rules. Sometimes Catherine takes Lila for more than half the holidays. Like when I moved in here, for example, she did me a real favour. So I don't mind cutting him some slack. And, realistically, I know how hard it would be for him to leave his office in time to fetch Lila at five-thirty.'

'I see,' said Sophie, stubbing out the end of her cigarette on the balustrade. She hesitated for a moment, as though she was unsure how to frame what she wanted to say next. 'I owe you an apology, Sally,' she said ruefully, her eyes downcast. 'Some of the things I said when we went to the park back in the autumn . . . I realize now – after going to pick Lila up this morning – that things with Albane are much more serious than I thought.'

'You don't need to apologize, Sophie,' I said with a half-smile, almost enjoying the mental image I'd conjured up of Albane opening the front door, wearing Nico's bathrobe, and Sophie's flabbergasted expression. 'I know you didn't mean any harm . . .'

'Well, I won't be interfering in future, I promise,' Sophie replied. 'But I would like to see more of you and Lila. She and Lucas play well together, and he asks about her a lot.'

'I'd like that too,' I said, handing her a beer and taking a sip of my own. 'And I know what to do if you step out of line,' I added. 'I'll start humming the tune from "It's a Small World" . . .'

I rose extra early the next morning, making up my bed with clean sheets and giving the floors a quick once-over with the vacuum cleaner. After work, Lila and I would be going to Gare du Nord to meet Mum from the Eurostar and escort her home for her first visit since we'd moved here, almost a year ago. Ever since Mum had announced her intention to come over – even if it was for a ridiculously short visit – I'd been pushing her impending stay to the back of my mind. It was the evenings I was apprehensive about. Tomorrow I'd be out at work and Mum would spend some quality time with her granddaughter. But once Lila was tucked up in bed, what then? I was dreading the inevitable questions about Nico, about my personal life, about Rendez-vous. What a shame Dad couldn't have come too, I thought to myself as I surveyed my living room, trying to imagine how it would look through Mum's critical eyes. His presence had a welcome soothing effect on me.

'We'll be going to meet Grandma at the railway station after the *Centre de Loisirs*,' I reminded Lila as I pulled a polo-necked jumper over her head, tickling her tummy while she held her arms aloft and eliciting a full-bodied giggle. 'Are you excited about seeing her? You'll be able to show her all around the neighbourhood, and help her out if she needs to speak some French . . .' Lila clapped her hands in glee. First Disneyland, now Grandma coming to stay: life as a four-year-old didn't get much more exciting than this. But a moment later, a cloud passed across her face and she paused, mid-clap, to give me a serious look.

'You're not going to shout at Grandma, are you, Mummy?' she said in a bossy voice. 'Because it's not nice when you do that.'

'Oh honey,' I said, running a hand through her hair, dismayed that not only had Lila overheard our Christmas fireworks, she'd committed them to memory. 'You don't need to worry about that! Remember, Grandma is my mummy and I'm her little girl. So sometimes we argue – just like me and you – but it doesn't mean we don't love each other . . .'

Lila's words echoed in my ears all the way from the *Centre de Loisirs* to the métro. So, when I opened my newspaper and folded it back to the classifieds page, it was a relief to see a new *Transports amoureux* entry. Translating it would help take my mind off whatever the evening held in store.

'*Film muet inachévé,*' it began, which struck me as a wonderfully poetic way of describing an emotionally charged encounter during which no actual words had been exchanged. Translated into English, the full entry read: 'Unfinished silent film. You: salt-and-pepper hair, brown eyes; me: redhead, blue eyes. Leaving métro line 5 at République at 7.11 p.m., we both tried to catch one another's eye to share one last smile. To write the next scene, call me.'

The mention of greying hair and brown eyes summoned up a fleeting memory of Matthias and, when my phone vibrated in my pocket to signal the arrival of a text message a few seconds later, I was thoroughly spooked: it was almost as though I'd summoned him forth. 'Sally.

Envie de te voir – M,' his message read, succinct as a *Transports amoureux* entry. As I stared, nonplussed, at the screen, I had a sudden flashback to Sunday evening and began to blush. My skin remembered Matthias's lips grazing my collarbone then moving lower, lower, until they reached my right breast, his tongue teasing my erect nipple. Shivering involuntarily, I closed my eyes and experimented with cutting Matthias from the sequence and pasting in Jérémy in his place instead. If only the text message had been signed with a 'J' instead of an 'M'.

I hadn't even begun thinking about formulating a response when a second message arrived, diluting the forcefulness of the first. 'Sorry. Didn't mean to sound like I was giving you orders. Would just very much like to see you again – M.'

'Not sure yet when I'll next be free, but will be in touch – S,' I replied, effectively putting the whole question of what, if anything, to do about Matthias on hold. It was untrue. I knew precisely when I'd be available, as Nico had offered to take Lila on Saturday night to compensate for the previous weekend's upheaval. But I'd earmarked Saturday evening for Jérémy, and I wasn't ready to give up on him yet. Okay, so he hadn't been in touch, but it had only been three days since I'd seen him last.

Tuesday's lessons would have been uneventful if it hadn't been for my two o'clock session with Robert Cazenove. I'd promised Delphine I wouldn't let on that I was aware of their liaison, but it was much more difficult to behave naturally than I'd anticipated, knowing what I now knew. Robert seemed to be making an extra effort with his appearance for Delphine's sake: he was preceded by a potent smell of aftershave, and there was something different about his hair too. They made a handsome couple, I decided, narrowing my eyes and grafting an image of my favourite pupil on to his arm as he crossed the room. There couldn't be many men in the city who wouldn't be dwarfed by Delphine in heels, but fortunately she'd found an unusually tall specimen.

When Robert pulled out the seat opposite mine, I suppressed the impulse to beam at him, shuffling my papers instead and looking down at the table. I was pathetically grateful when he opened his mouth and made a series of genuinely irritating mistakes a few seconds later. No one who murdered my mother tongue with such aplomb deserved any form of special treatment. I reverted to no-nonsense teacher mode in no time at all.

After lessons were over, I rushed back to Belleville to collect Lila and we made our way to Gare du Nord, arriving only seconds before Mum's train eased itself into the station.

'There she is!' I said to Lila with forced cheerfulness, as soon as I caught sight of Mum's familiar figure wheeling a compact suitcase, scouring the sea of waiting faces as she advanced towards the end of the platform. Seeing her out of her comfort zone, far from the familiarity of her own home, I was surprised by how much older she looked, all of a sudden, and how much less self-assured. Perhaps seeing each other on *my* territory for a change would do our relationship good, I reasoned. It couldn't hurt to shake things up a little.

Mum began to look a lot more like herself once she was seated on my sofa with a cup of tea in her hand. 'I'm afraid the milk's only UHT,' I apologized, returning to the kitchen and poking around in the freezer for something for Lila's dinner. Lila had done a great job of monopolizing Mum's attention from the moment she'd arrived, regaling her grandma with endless stories about her trip to Disneyland, but she'd fallen silent now, her batteries beginning to go flat.

'The new Saint Pancras terminal was lovely,' Mum remarked, ignoring my comment about the milk, although I saw her grimace when she took her first sip of tea. 'It was just a pity that, by the time I got out of the tunnel, it was dark at the other side, so I didn't get to see much of France.'

'And how do you like our new place?' I said, doing my best to make my question sound casual. Turning my back on her, I set three fish fingers under the grill.

'Well . . . Obviously it feels small, compared to what you were sharing with Nico before . . .' I could hear that Mum was choosing her words carefully, which was most unusual. 'But you've managed to get it looking cosy,' she continued, 'and you've made a lovely job of Lila's room.' Lila was sitting by her side on the sofa and poring over the pages of a new Charlie and Lola book Mum had produced from the front pocket of her suitcase, along with gifts of Cheddar cheese and Branston pickle. But at the mention of her name, she looked up at her grandma and smiled.

'My mummy did paint my room all on her own, Grandma,' she said proudly. 'I know, because she still has some splodges of purple paint on her jeans!'

Once Lila's light was out and her door positioned just so, I poured two glasses of Côtes du Rhône and popped the lasagne I'd prepared the night before into the oven. There was nothing for it now but to take a seat on the sofa by Mum's side and try to make small talk. Switching on the eight o'clock news with Claire Chazal wasn't an option: Mum wouldn't understand a single word.

'So, how's Dad?' I said, choosing the safest subject I could think of. 'Still looking forward to retirement?'

'Oh, you know. Same old, same old,' said Mum with a shrug. 'I think he was going to take himself off to the pub tonight for his dinner. You know how helpless he is in the kitchen. Can't even boil an egg . . .' She took a long sip of her wine and I braced myself, sensing she was about to say something important. 'It was your Dad that insisted I come over to see you,' she said slowly, looking me in the eye. 'He said I needed to see things here for myself if I was to have any hope of understanding what your life is like now.'

I said nothing at first, digesting this interesting new piece of information. So this visit was Dad's doing. What else had he said? I wondered. It struck me, all of a sudden, that I had little idea of how the land lay between Mum and Dad when I wasn't around.

'I can't believe it's coming up to a year since I moved out . . .' I replied when I'd pulled myself together. I was reluctant to mention Nico's name, given how our last discussion on that thorny subject had ended. 'I should warn you,' I added, 'in case Lila talks to you about it . . . Albane's living with him now. I found out – quite by accident – last weekend.'

By the time I'd finished telling Mum that story, complete with a lengthy tangent to explain why Kate and

I had spent the day together, I could smell the béchamel beginning to brown on the top of our lasagne. Mum had been uncharacteristically quiet while I talked, listening intently and giving me the occasional nod. 'I worry about you, you know, Sally,' she said now, her eyes looking suspiciously watery. 'The things I said about you and Nico, about online dating . . . I suppose I wished that things hadn't come to that, for all of your sakes. But your dad says I have to remember you're a sensible girl with her head screwed on right. He says we both know you'll do what's best for you and Lila . . .' She paused for a moment, as if unsure of what to say next.

'And,' I prompted her, 'do you think that Dad might have a point?' I could see what Mum was doing. It was easier to quote Dad than to pull her own words out of the air. And while this was a step in the right direction, I needed to hear a real apology. Something that didn't start with the words 'Your Dad says'.

Mum nodded, her cheeks colouring. 'I shouldn't have said what I did at Christmas,' she said quietly. 'It came out all wrong, as usual, and I can see why it upset you. You've got enough on your plate, without me making things even harder.'

I don't think I fully realized how much Mum's attitude these past few months had preyed on my mind until her apology hung in the air between us. Whenever I'd felt vulnerable and less than proud of my actions – after the New Year's Eve party, for example, or my disastrous one-night stand with Rob – her words had come back to haunt me with a vengeance, eating away, insidiously, at my certitudes. Now, hearing her say she was sorry, hearing her say she'd been wrong, I felt a huge weight lifting. What a relief to have Mum on my side, back where she belonged.

'I have to hand it to Dad,' I said, blinking back the tears welling up in my eyes. 'It was an inspired idea, suggesting that you come over. I can't help thinking he knows the two of us far better than we know ourselves.' The oven bell rang and I jumped to my feet, glad of the interruption, dabbing my eyes covertly with a tea towel while my back was turned.

'I tell you what,' I added, setting the lasagne dish down on the dining table and beckoning Mum over. 'When we've finished dinner, maybe I'll even show you this evil dating site of mine . . .'

24

I ran into Anna early the next morning quite by chance, catching sight of a streak of vivid blue out of the corner of my eye as the métro doors sprung open and I stepped out on to the platform of Pyramides station. I called out to her, stopping her in her tracks, and before we hurried off to begin our respective lessons – mine at a bank on avenue de l'Opéra and hers inside the glass building in the middle of place du Marché Saint Honoré – we had enough time to knock back bitter espressos, standing at the counter of a nearby bar.

When Anna let slip that she and Ryan were meeting for dinner after work, I felt a familiar twinge of jealousy. I fought valiantly to maintain a poker face, but Anna's discomfort over her slip-up was clear: she couldn't change the subject quickly enough. This seemed to confirm what I'd long suspected. I was gradually being relegated to the sidelines, while the pair of them made their own plans, assuming I'd be tied up, and no longer even bothering to extend an invitation to me.

So when I called home to check in with Mum and Lila at lunchtime, and Mum made her suggestion, it couldn't have been more perfectly timed. 'You know, Sally, I was thinking . . .' she said cautiously. 'I'm not here for long, but while I am, you might as well make use of me as a babysitter. You don't get out much. Maybe you could go on a date or something? I'm sure it would do you good . . .'

'You really wouldn't mind?' I asked, for the sake of form. 'You're here for such a short time . . .' But Mum insisted that she didn't. The official reason was that being with Lila all day was going to tire her out, but I suspected there was more to it than that. We'd managed to get through a whole evening in one another's company without even the shadow of a disagreement, which had to be some sort of record. Perhaps Mum was worried that if we tried for a repeat performance, we'd be pushing our luck.

'Mum offered to babysit tonight,' I texted Anna, 'so maybe I could gatecrash your dinner?' To take the edge off the word 'gatecrash', I added a wink, composed of a semi-colon, a dash and a closing bracket. Within a matter of seconds I'd received two replies: a 'cool' from Anna, and a 'hurrah!' from Ryan, who had no doubt been brought into the loop by Anna. A quick call home to confirm my plans, and everything was settled. I'd spend an hour or two with Mum and Lila before I met up with my friends, and Mum was more than happy to eat with her granddaughter.

I arrived at the Café Cannibale first, standing at the corner of the wood-panelled bar and checking my phone to see if I'd overlooked an incoming message from Jérémy while I sipped a glass of white wine and waited for my friends to show up. Ryan arrived ten minutes later, apologizing profusely for his tardiness. We left the bar and took a seat at the table he'd reserved, at the far end of the dimly lit dining room.

'So, Anna tells me you and Eric have been joined at the hip lately,' I teased. 'You will invite us to your PACs ceremony, won't you, Ryan? I wouldn't miss it for the world . . .'

'Oh dear God, no!' Ryan threw up his hands in mock-horror. 'The man's a banker and he earns a fortune. There's no way in the world I'd enter into a civil partnership with him and take joint responsibility for his horrendous tax bill . . .' I giggled. Ryan was on flamboyant form. But I'd known him long enough to suspect that, underneath the play-acting and camp, theatrical gestures, his feelings for Eric nonetheless ran deep. 'Things are going surprisingly well,' he acknowledged, when I prodded him for more information. 'In fact, I'd have accepted Eric's offer to move into his place by now, if it wasn't for the Clyde conundrum.'

'He asked you to move in?' This was news to me. I hadn't realized things were that serious. 'So what's the Clyde conundrum? It sounds like a Robert Ludlum novel. Does Eric have allergies? Did he give you an ultimatum? "If you want to be with me, the cat goes"?'

It was Ryan's turn to chuckle. 'Nothing quite so dramatic,' he said, shaking his head. 'Eric isn't terribly keen on having a litter tray in his apartment, that's all. But I'm sure we'll find a compromise.' He took a sip of his kir, then started, as though he'd remembered something important he had to tell me. 'Eric tells me Yves will be back in the Paris office on Friday,' he murmured. 'I don't suppose you've heard anything from Kate?'

'I knew he was due back soon, but I had no idea it was imminent . . .' I wondered whether Kate and Yves were having a huge showdown at that very moment. It had to be make or break time for those two. I hoped Kate would call me the moment there was anything to tell.

When Anna arrived, a few minutes later, her face was like thunder. 'Sorry I'm late, you guys,' she said, stowing her coat next to mine on the shelf which ran along the back wall, glancing at her harried reflection in the mirror just above it, then taking a seat on the red banquette by my side, propping up her chin with her hands. 'I got caught up on the phone with Tom,' she explained. 'We were having another shitty discussion about the divorce. God! I'll be so glad when all this crap is out of the way. I'm done spending hours in line at the American Embassy waiting for meaningless documents.'

'Someone needs a drink,' said Ryan, winking at me, and beckoning over the nearest waitress. 'And we should probably order something to eat, shouldn't we, ladies? What do you fancy? A cannibal burger? A steak? A platter of *charcuterie*?' Once these practical matters had been dispensed with and Anna had a beer in her hand, Ryan turned to me, no doubt hoping to ease the conversation into more light-hearted territory. 'How about you tell us all about how Rendez-vous has been treating you, Sally? Anything interesting to share?'

It was a relief to be able to recount at length the events of the previous weekend – not a subject I'd felt able to broach with Mum, even if I had showed her how the Rendez-vous site worked – and I found myself lapping up my friends' rapt attention as I talked, enjoying being the focal point of the conversation. Who would have guessed, a few months earlier, that my love life would ever become eventful enough to hold listeners spellbound? But when I'd finished bringing them up to speed and passed around my phone to show them Matthias's text messages from two days earlier, Anna and Ryan's reactions took me by surprise. I'd been expecting words of sympathy and encouragement, not frowns of disapproval.

'I can't believe you're telling us you're still infatuated with this Jérémy, the flaky guy who's been blowing hot and cold and didn't even kiss you on the second date,' said Anna, her expression dubious. 'He must really have something about him, to have you like putty in his hands when he hasn't even put out!'

'Hmm. And it sounds to me like you're using this poor Matthias boy,' Ryan concurred. 'This boy, who seems so lovely and, what's more, lives so very conveniently around the corner. You had a great connection, by the sounds of things, and you say you wound up having mind-blowingly good sex on your first date. But, despite all that, you're still holding out for Jérémy . . .' His expression was both pained and perplexed. 'I'm sorry, Sally, but none of this adds up.'

'I don't think I would say I *used* Matthias . . .' I countered, affronted by his accusation. 'I mean, there was nothing calculating or pre-meditated about what happened. I tried my best to make it clear I saw him as friendship material. He ended up taking me by surprise at the end of the evening, that's all. And I got caught up in the moment . . .' The waiter appeared with our orders and I clammed up, too embarrassed to go on in his presence.

'But you went back to *his* place! I don't know . . .' Ryan rolled his eyes, ignoring the platter of *charcuterie* before him. 'You complained at length about Jérémy's mixed signals, but frankly, my dear, your behaviour is no better than his.' He was wagging his finger at me now, in his best imitation of a pre-school teacher reprimanding an infant. If it was intended to be humorous, it wasn't having quite the desired effect. It felt as though my friends were ganging up on me, and I didn't like the feeling one little bit.

'If it's friendship you were after, Sally,' Anna said doubtfully, 'you've got to admit Rendez-vous wasn't the most logical place to start. Matthias obviously thought your actions spoke louder than your words . . . And judging by those text messages you showed us, he still does . . .'

'Well, like I said, I've kind of put him on hold for now,' I said, defensively, my cheeks reddening. 'I had no way of knowing he was going to want to see me again.' I hoped this would be the end of the discussion. The spotlight was beginning to feel uncomfortably warm, and I longed to tuck into my steak.

Anna frowned, unwilling to let the subject drop. 'Do you think it's fair to keep him simmering on a low heat while you explore your other options?' she said. 'Would you want someone to treat you that way?'

'Wait a minute,' I interrupted, throwing down the chip I'd been about to pop into my mouth in disgust, conscious that I was raising my voice now as my own resentment boiled over. 'If you cast your mind back to that conversation we had when we were walking the dog with Lila in the Parc de Belleville, wasn't that what *you* were doing with Alex? A host of other guys were clamouring for your attention and you were all for keeping your options open then, stalling Alex to buy yourself some extra time . . .' How could Anna have such double standards, I thought to myself, beginning to see red. How could Ryan, former king of the one-night stand, lecture me about 'using someone for sex'? It was as though they thought there was one rule for me and one rule for them. In short, it was singularly unfair.

'I did say those things,' Anna admitted, her cheeks flushed, whether in anger or embarrassment, I wasn't sure.

'And I carried on going on dates with other people behind Alex's back for a while after that. Until this one day when I was in a bar with someone else and Alex walked right past the window . . .'

'Ooh! Did he catch you?' Ryan interrupted, choking down a piece of *saucisson sec*. 'Did he storm in and make a horrible scene?' He was doing his best, I realized, to diffuse the tension which had begun to crackle between Anna and me, before things got too ugly.

Anna shook her head. 'He didn't see me, no . . . But I realized how awful I'd have felt if he had confronted me. I stopped agreeing to meet my other "possibles" and "maybes" after that.' She gave me a meaningful look. 'I decided that if I didn't have the balls to be honest with him and tell him I still wanted to date other people, then I had no business doing it. Sneaking around was dishonest. It made me no better than Tom.'

I hung my head, looking down at the Roquefort sauce which had been congealing on my steak as we talked. Deep down, I knew that much of what Anna and Ryan had said about my infatuation with Jérémy and my cavalier treatment of Matthias made perfect sense and, if I'd allowed my hackles to rise, it was partly because I was still sore about having to learn about this evening's dinner quite by accident. To my mind, Anna and Ryan were the ones who were guilty of doing all the skulking, behind *my* back.

'It's so easy for you both,' I said sullenly, sentiments I'd been keeping under wraps for months spilling forth before I could hold myself in check. 'Look at you two. You have your perfect boyfriends. You have all this freedom you take completely for granted: you can go out whenever you choose. I've been on my own for almost a year. I rarely get to go out. I've forgotten the meaning of the word "spontaneous". Instead, I get to leave parties when they start to get interesting. I get to watch my friends cosying up together behind my back without the slightest intention of inviting me along . . .'

My voice wobbled as I got to the end of my self-pitying monologue. There was a stunned silence and, raising my eyes from my dinner plate, I glanced first at Ryan, then at Anna. They wore matching dumbfounded expressions, and seemed to have lost both their tongues and their appetites. Had I alienated two of my favourite people, for good? What on earth had I done?

'Sally,' said Anna in a pained voice, 'I had no idea you were feeling this way . . . When I think that, all this time, I've been feeling jealous of you.' She shook her head. 'I guess it goes to show that people always want what they can't have.'

'You? Jealous of me?' I couldn't believe I'd heard her correctly. 'How can that be possible? I . . . I don't understand.'

'Let me spell it out for you,' said Anna evenly. 'You have an amazing daughter, this little person who loves you unconditionally, and who gives you a reason to get up every morning and who you can go home to every single night. You speak amazing French, which means you can communicate properly with everyone around you, and hold meaningful, adult conversations with your dates or the Frenchmen you meet at parties. You're a European, which gives you the absolute right to live in this wonderful city for as long as you choose. Do I need to go on?'

My throat constricted, and I didn't trust myself to speak, shaking my head mutely instead.

'Me, on the other hand,' she continued regardless, 'well . . . I'm fighting for the right to live and work in this city once my divorce is finalized, because somehow it's gotten right under my skin. I can order a baguette, but I can't have anything but the most stilted, superficial conversations with Alex, or any other French person I might meet. I hate living alone, and there are many, many nights when I dread going back to my empty apartment.'

'If you ladies would allow me to interrupt your pity party for a moment,' Ryan interrupted, his expression grave, 'then I'd like to add my two euros' worth, if I may. Now, I can see why you might feel like everything is ten times harder for you, Sally.' Ryan sighed, covering my hand with his. 'And I sympathize, honey, I do. But try and look at the situation from where I'm sitting for a moment. It's hard to know what to do for the best. If I invite you out when I'm almost certain you're not free, I worry that hearing about what you're missing will make you feel worse. If I don't, I'm accused of skulking behind your back. But, regardless of what you seem to think, Anna and I didn't make some sort of unanimous decision to exclude you tonight. We knew your Mum was staying. End of story.'

'It's funny,' I said sheepishly. 'Now that I've said some of that stuff out loud, I realize how much I've been guilty of getting things out of proportion. I'm so sorry. Lashing out at you two is the last thing on earth I should be doing.'

'Well, hopefully we've cleared the air, now that you two have said your *quatre vérités*,' said Ryan philosophically. 'You've both had a tough year, and you're dealing with it well, in your different ways. I for one think we should all take a deep breath, put this behind us, and move on.'

'We ought to tuck into this food before it gets any colder, too,' I added, gesturing at my untouched steak and Anna's 'cannibal burger', which she'd only got as far as slicing in half.

When we left the Cannibale, a couple of hours later, I hugged Ryan and Anna tightly before we parted company. I wasn't proud of the scene I'd caused but, as Ryan had said, getting it all off our chests, telling our 'four truths', as the French expression went, had done us all the power of good.

First Mum and I had surrendered our weapons and called a much-needed ceasefire, and now I'd dealt with the undercurrent of jealousy that had been threatening to sabotage my friendship with Anna for some time. And Anna's unexpected words had given me pause: she'd reminded me that there were always two ways of looking at any situation. I'd been staring, despairingly, at a half-empty glass, but from her own parched perspective, it had looked half full, all along.

Mum's flying visit came to an end on Thursday evening, when I bundled her into a taxi at six o'clock to catch the last Eurostar. She'd be staying overnight with my Aunt Sarah in London, then travelling up to Yorkshire the next day.

'I'll come for a bit longer next time,' she promised, while the taxi driver loaded her suitcase into the boot of his car. 'And maybe, by then, you'll be able to introduce me to some nice young man . . .'

Lila and I waved at the departing taxi until it had turned the corner into rue Lesage, then made our way back inside.

As we crossed the courtyard, my eyes darted across to the windows that must belong to my new neighbour Pete's apartment, but all was in darkness, the shutters closed.

I was sinking into the sofa after Lila's bath and bedtime story, my hand poised on the remote to switch on the eight o'clock news, when I heard a knock at the door. Several possibilities flickered through my mind in quick succession. Could it be Kate, reeling from a confrontation with Yves? Or Pete, back home and pretending he needed to borrow some sugar, or using some other – equally contrived – pretext to get to know me better? But, when I peered through the peephole, it was Matthias I saw. Unlocking the door, I stared at him, wide-eyed. He wore a hesitant smile and he was carrying half a dozen long-stemmed gerberas in fiery reds and oranges.

'*J'espère que je te dérange pas* . . . I happened to be in the neighbourhood,' Matthias said, his lips twitching at his own joke. 'I thought if it was difficult for you to come out, maybe I could make a house call, instead. Bring the mountain to Mohammed . . .' He held out the bunch of flowers and I took them, still too stunned to speak, to move aside or motion him inside. With my free hand I made a futile attempt to smooth down my frizzy hair. I might have complained to Anna and Ryan that my life lacked spontaneity, but this wasn't exactly what I'd had in mind.

'I should have called first, I'm sorry . . . I'm trespassing. It was a stupid idea . . .' Matthias took a step backwards and turned, as though he were about to leave.

'No. Wait! You caught me by surprise,' I replied, recovering my composure, 'but it's okay, you can come in for a while.' I drew back to let him pass. 'And actually,' I added, remembering the previous night's conversation with Ryan and Anna, 'I needed to talk to you anyway.'

Matthias walked to the centre of the living room and contemplated his surroundings with evident interest. I was suddenly conscious of the unwashed dishes in the sink, Lila's crayons littering the coffee table and the sheets I'd stripped off Mum's bed and left in an untidy pile in a corner of the room. There was an uneasy silence while I put the flowers in water and fetched two glasses and a carton of grapefruit juice from the kitchen. 'I'm afraid I don't have anything stronger,' I said, pouring a glass and handing it to Matthias. 'My Mum's been staying and, between us, we polished off every drop of alcohol I had in the house.'

'What did you want to talk to me about?' Matthias peered through the window at the courtyard beyond, but I could see his reflection in the curtainless window, and his expression was apprehensive. 'I have to admit,' he added, turning to face me again with a wry expression, 'I don't much like speeches that begin that way. They generally continue with something along the lines of "I really like you," followed by a list of reasons why things won't work out . . .'

I lowered myself into the sofa, trying to work out exactly what I wanted to say and how I was going to say it. Just as I was clearing my throat to speak, I heard the unmistakable whine of the hinges on Lila's bedroom door. Sure enough, the door was opening and, a moment later, she stood in the doorway, her face flushed with sleep, her hair standing on end. 'I need to go wee wee, Mummy,' Lila murmured, not noticing Matthias at first, blinking as her eyes adjusted to the light. She began padding across the parquet floor in the direction of the bathroom, pausing when she suddenly became aware of the male stranger standing by the window.

'Lila, honey, this is a friend of Mummy's, called Matthias,' I said, rising to my feet and instantly regretting my use of the third person 'Mummy' in his presence. 'He came over to say hello.' Lila nodded, seemingly satisfied with my explanation, then gestured towards the bunch of flowers I'd stowed inside a water jug on the kitchen countertop, for want of a vase. 'Did your friend bring you those pretty flowers, Mummy?' she asked, looking at Matthias with renewed interest when I nodded to confirm that this was so. '*Elles sont jolies*,' she said, staring at the flowers for a moment before she continued her trajectory towards the bathroom, pulling the door closed behind her.

'*Elle est adorable*,' said Matthias, his voice filled with admiration. 'And perfectly bilingual. No wonder you're so proud of her.'

'Lila's never met a male friend of mine before,' I said quietly, my eyes remaining fixed on the closed bathroom door. 'I made a decision when I joined Rendez-vous to keep my single life separate from my time with her.'

'I think that's sensible,' Matthias replied carefully. 'And of course I can see why you'd feel that was a good idea. But I'm honoured to have met her, tonight, even if I did rather force your hand.'

Lila emerged from the bathroom – leaving the toilet unflushed, as I noted with some embarrassment – and I watched in silence as she padded back to her bedroom, blew me a kiss and disappeared inside, leaving her door ajar. I was confused. Unwittingly, Matthias had ridden roughshod over my rules, showing up unannounced like this. And yet, instead of resenting him for it, I'd found the experience oddly liberating. My two worlds had collided – accidentally – and it hadn't been anything like the big deal I'd expected it to be. Lila had taken an alien male presence in our home in her stride, and I couldn't have hoped for the scene to play out in a more natural way.

'Before your daughter's charming interruption, you were about to say something,' Matthias prompted gently.

'I was,' I said reluctantly, sinking back down on to the sofa, then wishing I hadn't, as Matthias now dwarfed me with his height. 'There's this person I met on Rendez-vous a couple of weeks before you,' I continued, looking up at him through my eyelashes. 'I found myself liking him a lot. And I have no idea where things are going with him – the whole thing is far from clear, just now – but, under the circumstances, I thought it was only fair to tell you. What happened between us the other night was lovely, and I don't regret it, but I never intended for it to happen. And I'm really, really flattered that you want to see me again, but I think it would be unfair to continue seeing one another while my head is elsewhere . . .' I refrained from adding something clichéd about how I wished we could remain friends, even if I'd have loved to be able to keep Matthias within my orbit. By sleeping with him, I was pretty sure I'd burned those bridges. Matthias was staring at me, his expression difficult to read.

'I see,' he replied, finally. 'Well, I suppose I do appreci-ate your honesty . . .' He sighed, and glanced over at the door, as though he wished he were already on the other side of it. 'I had an amazing time with you that night,' he continued, 'and I thought it made sense to explore where it might lead . . . But if you like this other man as much as it seems, then you're right, I'm wasting my time . . .' He took a step towards the sofa, and for a second I found myself wishing he would pull me to my feet and kiss me. But whatever he'd been planning to do, he seemed to think better of the idea. 'Good luck with everything, Sally,' he said, turning towards the door instead. 'It was nice knowing you.'

I watched mutely as Matthias left the room. I knew Ryan would have applauded my honesty, had he been a fly on the wall. I'd done the right thing by Matthias: he didn't deserve to be messed around. There was nothing for it now but to consign the wonderful, sensual night we'd spent together to memory, filing it under 'one-night stand', and accepting that it would never be repeated.

I'd made my bed and, for now, I'd have to lie in it alone.

25

When Kate called the next morning, I was running around like the proverbial headless chicken. Lila and I were about to leave the house, with only a few minutes to spare before we were officially late for the *Centre de Loisirs*. I stared at her name on the phone's display screen for a moment, weighing up my burning desire to find out how Yves' homecoming had played out against my fear of incurring the wrath of the dragon guarding the school gates. Kate won, but only by a hair's breadth.

'Kate! I'm about to run out of the door with Lila, but I've got a couple of minutes, so please, tell me in a nutshell how it went?'

'Good news, Sal,' trilled Kate, her voice ecstatic. 'He got back last night and we had a long talk, and I really think we're going to be all right . . . I was wondering whether I could catch you for lunch today for a proper chat. I've got so much to tell you . . .'

'That's fantastic, Kate!' I shrieked. 'And I'd love to catch up!' I grimaced at my watch, frustrated that I had no time to beg her to elaborate. 'Listen, I'm going to have to sprint off now, but how about you take a look at my timetable and you can text me to tell me where and when we should meet?' Replacing the receiver, I grabbed Lila's hand and slammed the front door closed behind us. My watch read 8.40 a.m. I was thrilled to hear Kate sounding so positive, and dying to hear all the details, but the smile she'd summoned to my lips wouldn't afford me any protection against the door dragon.

As we approached Lila's school I set the door in my sights, lunging forwards as it began to swing closed in excruciating slow motion but hearing the fatal *clunk* of the locking mechanism catching while I was still a couple of paces away. Groaning, I waited outside for a moment, hoping to dart inside as another latecomer left. But no such latecomer was forthcoming, and the door remained stubbornly closed. I had no choice but to ring the intercom, draw attention to our plight and brave the icy stare of the *gardienne*.

'*Oui?*' said a stern voice, intent on prolonging my agony rather than simply opening the door.

'*C'est la maman de* Lila Canet,' I replied, casting about for a watertight – if fabricated – excuse for our lateness. 'I'm sorry to be arriving so late, but I had to deal with an urgent family matter on the phone . . .' It wasn't so far from the truth. Kate was almost family.

'The doors will open again at 1.30 p.m.,' the disembodied voice replied, devoid of compassion. 'You can come back then if you'd like to drop her off for the afternoon.'

'*Non! Ça va pas aller du tout!*' I cried, beginning to panic now. 'I'm a single mother, and I work full time. I can't afford to risk losing my job!' I couldn't believe how humiliating it was being forced to beg over an intercom, even if I knew that Kate would never fire me for something like this. Lila, seeing how close I was to tears, looked up at me in genuine alarm and tightened her grasp on my hand. Suddenly, there was a click as the lock mechanism was released and, when I gave the door a violent push, it obligingly swung open.

'*Rentrez vite!*' the *gardienne* hissed. 'Before the *directrice* gets back to her office.' Her face remained impassive, but I detected a glimmer of compassion in her eyes. Something I'd said must have struck a chord. Her heart had thawed, if only for a moment.

Once I'd signed Lila in to the *Centre de Loisirs* and she'd joined one of the groups of children drawing pictures in a corner of the *préau*, I waved her a hurried goodbye, conscious that my problems weren't yet over: there was still the small matter of getting to my first appointment on time. At the front door, I placed my hand on the doorknob and glanced at the *gardienne*, waiting for her to release the mechanism and set me free.

I couldn't be sure, but I could have sworn that, just as I was leaving, I heard a whispered '*Bon courage, Madame*'. Mumbling a bemused '*merci*', I escaped into the street and began my sprint towards the métro.

When Kate swept into the bistro she'd chosen for lunch, close by the Arc de Triomphe, the transformation in her was inspiring. Back on top of her game, groomed, perfumed and wearing her favourite carmine nail polish, she swept across the room, causing several of the lunching businessmen present to raise appreciative eyes from their *steak-frites*, just like she used to. As she drew closer, I noted that her cheekbones still protruded a little too much for my liking, but Paris wasn't built in a day. It would only be a matter of time, now, before she was back to her old self.

'You look incredible,' I exclaimed, rising to my feet and giving her an enthusiastic hug. 'I feel like I've travelled back in time for a lunch date with the old Kate!'

'You're looking pretty good yourself, Sal.' Kate took a seat, then reached across to caress Delphine's scarf. 'I don't know whether it's your experiences on Rendez-vous lately that have changed you, but you seem different somehow . . .'

I was feeling upbeat, but I didn't think it would be fair to let Rendez-vous take all the credit. Seeing how keen Matthias had been to take things further had certainly given me a confidence boost – even if I had pushed him away – but the fact remained that Jérémy still hadn't manifested himself, and it was now almost a week since our previous date. In the meantime, I suspected making my peace with Mum and clearing the air with Anna and Ryan had played a far more important role.

'*Vous voulez commander, Mesdames?*' A waitress had appeared at my elbow, wielding an order pad and paper. 'I can recommend the *steak tartare* today,' she said, pointing with her pen at the chalkboard listing the specials. 'It's one of our chef's most popular dishes.'

'I think that's a little hardcore for me,' I said to Kate in a low voice. 'Rare I can deal with, but I think it'll take me another decade in France before I graduate to raw . . .' I ordered the *provençale* cod, instead, and Kate did the same, closing her leather-bound menu with a decisive snap. She requested a half-bottle of Chablis and some sparkling water to accompany our meal, and I raised an eyebrow.

'Wine at lunchtime? I think it's about time you told me what we're celebrating.' Placing my elbows on the table, I rested my chin on my hands. 'I mean, I got the gist this morning. But I need details! What exactly happened between you and Yves when he got back?'

'Well, I confronted him,' Kate said with a half-smile, pausing for dramatic effect. 'I asked him if something had been going on while he was away, and he admitted he'd been infatuated with a colleague in New York.' I gasped. This wasn't at all what I'd expected to hear. I thought Kate had *good* news. 'Hence the makeover, you know,' Kate continued, her pace accelerating, as though she didn't wish to dwell on this part of the story, 'and the haircut, and the new suits . . . But when the opportunity to make a move on this woman presented itself, he froze. He realized he couldn't go through with it. He said all he wanted to do at that moment was get on the next plane and come home to patch things up with me.'

Kate's eyes slid downwards to her napkin for a moment, her cheeks flushed, as though she was remembering some precise detail of their reconciliation. 'Sal, the make-up sex was amaaazing,' she confessed, blushing a shade deeper. 'And afterwards, I felt like I'd been reborn. I was ravenous. Yves had to get dressed and dash out to hunt and gather me some takeaway . . .'

'So you're both going to put all this behind you? You're not curious about the other woman?' I didn't mean to rain on Kate's parade, but in her shoes, I knew I'd have been consumed with a morbid desire to know what the mystery lady looked like. I could all too easily picture myself scouring the bank's website for photographs of the women in his team, wondering who had cast a temporary spell on my husband.

'I'd rather keep my ignorance intact,' Kate replied firmly. 'In the same way that Yves will never be privy to the details of what went on between me and François, if I can help it. I mean, look how destructive it was when you found all the evidence of Nico and Mathilde's affair . . . I often think

329

you'd have been so much better off if you'd spared yourself all the gruesome details.'

'You're right, of course.' I sighed. 'I doubt I'll be able to buy Lila a Chupa Chups lollipop without thinking about those two as long as I live . . .' I was aware of how ridiculous that sounded, but it was true, nonetheless. 'And I'm sorry, Kate, I didn't mean to be negative about any of this. I'm delighted for you both. I'm so glad Yves saw sense and came back when he did. I've been worried about you, these past couple of months.'

'Nonsense,' said Kate, brushing aside my concerns. 'You've been brilliant, Sal. When I think how worried I was about telling you about the whole thing in the first place, because of Nico . . . We've come a long way since then.'

'While we're speaking of the devil, you'll be unsurprised to hear that Nico came clean about Albane moving in with him,' I added. Kate said nothing, but gave me a questioning look. 'I feel surprisingly okay about it,' I reassured her, moving my neatly folded serviette aside so that the waitress could lay my plate before me. 'I suppose it must be weird for Lila, though, getting used to seeing Albane taking my place in our old apartment.'

'I think children of that age can adjust to almost anything,' Kate said confidently. 'And Albane seems nice – from the little I saw of her – but she's so young. I bet Lila considers her as more of a friend, or a babysitter, which is a blessing, I think. This way, there's unlikely to be any confusion about her role versus yours . . .' She paused for a moment before continuing. 'I never wanted to spell this out before, but imagine how much worse it would have been if Nico had someone older and more experienced in his life or, worse still, a woman who already had kids of her own.'

I hadn't really given that subject much thought before now – after all, Albane had been on the scene ever since I moved out – but I took Kate's point. Albane's youth may have brought all my insecurities about my age and appearance to the fore, at first, but Kate was right, I'd never perceived her as a threat as far as Lila was concerned. 'And how about the Rendez-vous situation?' Kate enquired, after the Chablis had arrived and we'd toasted her new-found happiness. 'I spoke to Ryan earlier, and he hinted you had an awful lot going on . . .'

I decided to edit out the events of the previous evening, which I hadn't shared with anyone, as yet. 'Well, let me see,' I began. 'Jérémy, the one you know most about, hasn't called since the night you came to babysit Lila, but that hasn't prevented me from thinking about him far more often than I should.' Although I'd managed to keep my tone of voice flippant, my anxiety levels were rising fast, and I'd graduated from checking my phone once or twice a day to on the hour, every hour. 'Then there was this other guy, Matthias,' I continued, 'who I had a lovely date with, but decided not to meet again, on account of being too hung up on Jérémy.' I decided not to admit that Matthias and I had slept together on our first date, and was relieved when Kate didn't press me for more information. 'Oh, and there's this single dad called Pete, who recently moved into my building,' I added, noting how Kate sat up and took notice when she heard an English name. 'He's from Liverpool,' I said, 'and he seems quite nice . . . I wonder whether we might become friends. But so far we've exchanged all of a dozen words, so there's not a lot to tell . . .'

'Well, it sounds like it's becoming even more urgent for you to put Jérémy on the spot and find out where things are going,' Kate insisted. 'We can't have you turning down this Pete, or anyone else for that matter, while Jérémy's keeping you in the dark . . .'

'I suppose I could ring him?' I said, my expression doubtful. In fact, I'd resolved that if I heard nothing from him by the end of the day, I'd send him a carefully worded text message.

'Of course you can. There's no law against you calling *him*, is there?' said Kate scornfully. 'Give the man one more chance. But if he doesn't step up and say what you want to hear, for God's sake, Sal, cut him loose and move on.'

My next appointment of the day was with Kate's newest client, the human resources director of an insurance company based out at La Défense. I tended to avoid trips out west if I could help it. Not only was the business district outside the city limits at the end of *ligne* 1 – almost as far from Belleville as it was possible to travel by métro – but it was the most soulless place I'd ever had the misfortune to visit. When I climbed the steps leading on to the vast concrete *parvis* extending from the Grande Arche to the foot of the surrounding skyscrapers, the crosswind whipping across the forecourt almost took my breath away. How I pitied the people who had to commute here every single day.

I was half an hour early for my appointment so, once I'd consulted the La Défense map and established that my destination was above the Quatre Temps shopping complex, I decided to venture inside for a coffee. Quatre Temps was as depressing and claustrophobic as every other American-style mall I'd ever set foot in. There was no natural light whatsoever, and I could almost feel the weight of the tower blocks overhead bearing on to the ceilings above my head. Just inside the entrance, I spied a Paul bakery with a seating area. I was about to venture inside to get a coffee when my telephone began buzzing in my pocket. At long last, it was Jérémy.

'*Allô?*' I hadn't let the phone ring three or four times, but Ryan would have been proud of me for maintaining the illusion that I still hadn't stored Jérémy's number in my phone. Leaning against the bakery window, I stared at a display of pastel-coloured *macarons* without really seeing them. Appetizing as they might be, they were no match for the picture of Jérémy I carried inside my head.

'Sally? *C'est* Jérémy. *T'aimerais sortir boire un verre un de ces quatre?*' My heart leapt in my chest. He did want to see me again. Despite all the negative things my friends had to say about him, here was the proof that I'd been right to trust my own instincts, all along. He liked me. Enough to plan a third date. Whatever issues he needed to work through, all I had to do was be patient. We'd get there in the end, and he'd be well worth the wait.

'I could do something tomorrow night . . .' I suggested, praying Jérémy didn't have plans on my one and only night of freedom.

'That *could* work,' Jérémy replied, after a long, unnerving pause. 'I have a rehearsal earlier in the evening, but we could meet up afterwards, if ten isn't too late?'

'Ten would be fine,' I replied, dizzy with relief. 'Why don't you phone me when your rehearsal is finished and we'll take it from there?'

When I replaced my phone in my work satchel and looked around me once more, my surroundings no longer seemed quite so oppressive. Could it be that at long last – almost a year to the fateful day when I'd stayed home sick and found the evidence of Nico and Mathilde – everything was falling into place in my new life? I drifted through the rest of the afternoon's lessons on a cloud of optimism, and nothing – not even the elderly pervert on the métro home who tried to slip a hand inside my coat – could bring me back down to earth.

When I emerged from Belleville station, I was greeted, to my surprise, by grey skies and icy drizzle. Criss-crossing the city below ground level could be treacherous that way. I'd lost count of the number of times I'd left a sun-drenched Champs Elysées only to be greeted by gloomy skies at Bastille or pavements made as slippery as a skating rink by a recent downpour at Châtelet. Paris might be small in geographical terms, but it sometimes seemed as though every arrondissement had its own micro-climate.

Groping around in the depths of my satchel for my absent umbrella, I bowed my head in resignation and forced my way through the loiterers and free-newspaper distributors clogging up the street corner between the métro exit and the newspaper kiosk. At least Lila had worn her waterproof jacket that morning, I thought to myself, as the drizzle morphed into a more persistent, drumming rain.

The *préau* was in semi-darkness when I ventured inside, the children sitting with unexpected docility on rows of chairs, hypnotized by a television screen. When I spotted Lila, on the near end of the front row, I sidled up to her and dropped to my knees to whisper in her ear. 'Time for home now, sweet pea,' I said, bracing myself for a battle. To my surprise, however, she came willingly, putting her hand in mine and without further ado leading me to the peg where her coat hung.

'We were watching a film called "Les Trois Brigands" that I already seen at the *cinéma* with *Papa*,' Lila explained as I zipped her up and pulled the drawstring tight on her hood. 'We did watch it another day: me, Daddy and Albane. And we ate some popcorn *au caramel*!'

I felt a spasm of voyeuristic discomfort as my daughter offered me this fleeting glimpse into the secret life she led with Nico and Albane when I wasn't around. Maybe I found it easier to deal with the idea of them all being together when their doings remained shrouded in mystery, like her days at school, which she could seldom be prevailed upon to describe to me in detail. But this was the most vivid snapshot I'd been confronted with to date: the three of them sitting together in the dark – Lila, no doubt, in the middle – munching their toffee-covered popcorn in unison while they watched cartoon images dance across the screen.

As we trudged home – Lila doing her utmost to splash through every puddle – I was so preoccupied that at first I didn't notice Pete standing in the doorway of our building, his back braced against the open door, a little boy's hand clutched in his. Pete was wearing a hooded top in lieu of a coat, and he was shivering, in spite of the long scarf wound around his neck. He wasn't drenched like me, though: in his free hand he held a battered-looking black umbrella.

'Hi Sally, Lila. This is my son Ethan.' Ethan squinted up at us through a pair of blue-rimmed glasses. The lenses were covered in raindrops, and I doubted he could see through them, but he smiled nonetheless, proudly displaying a missing front tooth.

'Pleased to meet you, Ethan,' I said solemnly, before turning to Lila. 'Ethan is our new neighbour, sweetie,' I explained. 'He lives with his mummy sometimes, and with his daddy sometimes, like you . . .'

'Would you like to come in for a cuppa?' suggested Pete. 'Seeing as all four of us are in the same place at the same time?'

'I'll just check my post, and then, yes, why not,' I replied. 'I've got half an hour before I need to think about making Lila's dinner.' Unlocking my letterbox, I winced as I caught sight of an envelope marked *Electricité de France*. Pete didn't seem to be enchanted with the contents of his letterbox either. One letter, addressed to him in loopy French hand-writing, appeared to be so unwelcome that he dropped it – as though it had burned his fingertips – and slammed the metal door closed, leaving it trapped inside.

It never ceased to amaze me how different two apart-ments within the same building could look, and Pete's was no exception to this rule. Whereas mine and Lila's had been recently renovated by its owner, who had opted for the white walls and varnished oak floorboards so typical of Parisian rentals, Pete's home was like the apartment time forgot. 'I gather it belonged to an old dear who was living in a nursing home,' Pete explained when he caught me staring at the orange and brown patterned wallpaper in the hallway. 'I know it could do with some work, but I'm renting, so I don't really see the point of redecorating at my own expense.'

'Well,' I said, scrabbling around for something positive to say, 'I hear wallpaper with seventies motifs is making a comeback at the moment.' But stepping through into the next room, I did a double take: I hadn't realized Pete's place was a studio. The single room – which obviously served as bedroom, living room and dining room – was starved of natural light and pitifully furnished. There was a futon, a coffee table and a tiny portable TV with a radio aerial. A single mattress, wedged upright into the space between the sofa and the wall, served as a spare bed, when Ethan was staying. In front of the fireplace was a cardboard box filled with toys, but most looked as though they'd belonged to a much younger Ethan and had long since been outgrown.

'Can I have my Game Boy, Dad?' Ethan asked in a wheedling voice before we'd even had a chance to remove our damp coats. Pete retrieved the hand-held console from the mantelpiece and Ethan snatched it from him without a word of thanks, shrugging off his coat and sinking on to the futon sofa. Lila took Ethan's lead, casting aside her own wet coat and taking a seat by his side, peering over his shoulder at whatever he was playing. I was none too impressed with the boy's manners now that he was on his home turf but, on the other hand, what else was there for him to do when he came to stay here? I couldn't bear the idea of living in such cramped quarters with Lila: we'd be climbing the walls in no time. As it was, we'd only been here five minutes, and I was already hankering after the sanctuary of my own home. But I'd been invited in for tea, and it would be rude to leave before the kettle had even boiled. So, reluctantly, I left Lila to her own devices and followed Pete along the corridor.

In the kitchen, the geometric motifs gave way to brown tiles with white flecks. A low-slung, old-fashioned enamel kitchen sink took up the lion's share of the room and, other than that, there was a tiny Formica table, two folding chairs and an ancient-looking fridge topped with a free-standing, two-ring electric hob. Like many *Bellevillois*, Pete must use one of the local laundrettes. Judging by the underpopulated shelves, the room served for little other than tea-making and warming up cheap canned ravioli.

'I realize it's not exactly a palace,' Pete said, in what was surely the understatement of the year, 'but money's a bit tight . . . I came off worst from the split with Ethan's mum. I work as a techie on film shoots, but the work's intermittent, you see, and I managed to mess up my paperwork last year, so I'm having to jump through all sorts of hoops to try to get the benefits I'm meant to be entitled to between jobs . . .'

'What happened between you and Ethan's mum?' I said, watching as Pete filled a plastic kettle, its element caked with limescale. 'I mean, if it's not too personal a question. I don't mean to pry . . .'

'Oh, the bitch shacked up with her boss,' Pete retorted, the vicious emphasis he placed on the word 'bitch' causing me to recoil inwardly. 'It was all very romantic being involved with a guy like me when it was just the two of us, you know?' he continued, placing sachets of Lipton yellow tea into two chipped mugs. 'But when Ethan came along, she got this bee in her bonnet about security and responsibility and, all of a sudden, nothing about me was good enough for her any more. Now she's got her house in the suburbs and her Renault Espace, and here I am, living like a student.'

The more Pete talked, the faster my desire to get to know him better evaporated. Becoming his confidante held no attraction for me whatsoever. Regardless of what he seemed to think, I didn't consider myself a kindred spirit. I undoubtedly had baggage of my own, but I'd never speak of Lila's father with such venom in my voice. I found Pete's negativity – his determination to blame his every misfortune on his ex, as though he were a helpless victim – utterly repellent. This wasn't an attitude I wanted to be around. It was time to get myself, and Lila, out of there.

'Damn! I've just remembered a friend of mine is popping by this evening,' I said, clapping my palm to my forehead as the kettle began to boil. 'Do you mind if we do this some other time, Pete? I need to get Lila home.'

'Oh, okay. Another time, then.' Pete looked disappointed, but whether this was because we were leaving, or because he'd seen through my feeble excuse, it was impossible to tell. Tearing a rather subdued Lila away from Ethan and his Game Boy, I gathered up her damp coat and let myself out, turning to wave at Pete, who stood nursing his tea in the kitchen doorway.

So much for having a friend in the building, I thought to myself as the lift doors folded shut behind us. Instead, I was likely to have my work cut out avoiding Pete for a while, as I politely refused any further advances. What a mistake it had been to assume that our Britishness, coupled with the fact that we were both single parents, would automatically make Pete an ally, a friend, or maybe even something more.

With first Matthias out of the picture, and now Pete, I reflected, suddenly there was an awful lot riding on my date tomorrow evening. Jérémy, I thought to myself grimly, had better not disappoint me.

26

My bedside clock read 1.42 a.m. when I was awoken from a heavy, dreamless sleep by Lila's 'Muuummmy?' From the day she'd been born, it was as though I'd been reprogrammed to stir at her faintest whimper or cough, and the baby monitor Nico's parents bought for us had never left its original packaging. My built-in sensor was far superior to any electronic device.

Hurrying to my daughter's bedside, I found her sitting bolt upright and, even before I'd switched on the night light on her bedside table, I could see the tears glistening on her cheeks. 'What's the matter, my love?' I whispered, taking a seat on the bed and gathering her clammy body into my arms. 'Did you have a bad dream?'

Lila nodded, burrowing her wet face into the cavity between my cheek and my shoulder. I held her tightly until her hiccupping sobs subsided, planting tiny kisses in her hair and making soothing noises. 'I did have a *cauchemar*,' she confirmed, looking up at me through damp eyelashes. 'It was about that boy Ethan and the nasty things he did say.'

'Ethan said nasty things to you? Oh, honey, why didn't you tell me earlier? I had no idea!' I cursed myself for not having noticed something was amiss. Lila had been downcast when we'd returned home from Pete's place, but I'd chalked that up to nothing more than disappointment at having her playdate cut short.

'When you were in the kitchen,' Lila said in a small voice, 'Ethan did say that his mummy doesn't love his daddy any more. His mummy calls his daddy bad things in French, like a *paresseux* and a *connard* and a *bon à rien*.' Lila paused, and I sensed she was coming to the part which had upset her most. 'And he did say that my daddy must be the same because my mummy doesn't live with him any more.'

If I could have laid my hands on Ethan – or either of Ethan's parents for that matter – I would gladly have throttled one or all of them, just then, for putting such hateful thoughts into my daughter's head. 'Lila,' I said, tilting her chin gently upwards with my hand so that I could look deep into her eyes as I spoke. 'What Ethan said wasn't true. Your daddy isn't any of those things.'

'So why can't we go back to live with him, then?' said Lila, quick to exploit what she saw as a gaping hole in my logic.

'Honey, Albane lives with your daddy now,' I replied. 'You can visit whenever you like, but I can't go back to live there . . .'

'But what if we ask Albane to go away?' Lila said, undeterred. 'Then there'd be enough space for me *and* you. I could help you pack up my toys.'

I sighed. It was plain to see that Lila's apparent acceptance of the new status quo had been masking a multitude of misunderstandings. She had no concept of the permanence of the situation, and refused to believe it was irreversible. At risk of being labelled as the villain of the piece, my duty was to disabuse her of these fantasies; to extinguish these futile hopes. 'Lila, your daddy will always be a very good friend of mine,' I explained. 'But we're both happy not living in the same house. You need to understand that I won't be going back to live with Daddy. Not ever. Daddy lives with Albane now and, one day, I hope I'll meet somebody nice that I can be with, too.'

Lila considered what I'd said for a moment. Her mouth trembled and turned down at the corners, but she gave a tiny nod. 'Somebody nice like the man who did bring you flowers?' she said, managing a wan smile. 'Or maybe like the prince that saves the Little Mermaid from the wicked witch . . .'

'Yes, a man like that,' I said, picturing Jérémy crossing the threshold of my apartment with a huge bouquet. 'Now, how about we have a big cuddle and then we'll both go back to sleep?'

The next time I opened my eyes, it was morning and, as the purple walls came into focus, I realized I'd fallen asleep by Lila's side. She lay with her back to me now, the curve of her buttocks pressed into my tummy, the soles of her feet cool against my calves. Her breath whistled in her nose, and when I raised myself up on one elbow to look down at her sleeping face, I could see her eyes darting about behind her eyelids.

Easing myself gingerly out of bed so as not to wake her, I slipped out of Lila's room and fetched my dressing gown. Resting my elbows on the kitchen countertop next to Matthias's flowers, I debated whether to pick up the telephone and dial Nico's number. We really ought to discuss the events of the previous night while Lila was out of earshot, I decided. But when I called Nico's mobile, I was transferred straight through to voicemail. Moments later, Lila emerged from her bedroom, rubbing sleep from her eyes and clamouring for breakfast as though nothing were amiss. I'd have to wait until I took her over there at eleven. Maybe Albane could be prevailed upon to occupy Lila for a few minutes while I hijacked Nico and had a quiet word in his ear.

When I rang the doorbell a couple of hours later, however, we were greeted not by Nico or Albane, but by a deeply tanned Catherine. '*Mamie!*' cried Lila, launching herself into Catherine's arms, delighted to see her grandma. '*Je savais pas que tu étais là!*'

'This is indeed a surprise.' I smiled shyly, conscious that we hadn't laid eyes on each other since that curious afternoon in November when Catherine had confided in me about her husband's infidelity. '*Vous allez bien?* Did you and Philippe have a good holiday in Mauritius?'

'Marvellous, thank you,' Catherine replied, hugging Lila, then suggesting she might like to go and hunt for her *papy* who, she informed us with a wink, had last been sighted smoking a cigarette at the kitchen window.

'Is Nico here?' I asked, shooting a cautious look along the corridor. 'There was something I needed to speak to him about.'

'*Il est sous la douche,*' Catherine replied, rolling her eyes in exasperation. 'He was still in his pyjamas when we arrived ... But why don't you come in? I'm sure he'll only be a few minutes.'

'I don't know whether I should ...' I bit my lip, reluctant to cross the threshold. But Catherine, who'd guessed the root cause of my reticence, was quick to reassure me. Albane, she disclosed, was out at the hairdresser's. She'd be back for lunch but, for now, the coast was clear.

'I take it you've met her then.' I stepped into the front hallway and closed the door behind me. I made a supreme effort to keep my voice neutral, aware that it would be politically incorrect to allow myself to be drawn into comparing notes on Nico's new flame with my ex mother-in-law.

Catherine shook her head. 'Not yet. Which is part of the reason why we invited ourselves over today, if the truth be told,' she added, in a stage whisper. 'When Sophie told me Albane was living here, I thought it was about time Nicolas introduced us.'

As though his ears were burning – or whistling, as the French say – Nico chose that moment to emerge from the bathroom, looking suitably surprised to see me chatting to his mother in the hallway. In honour of his parents' visit, he was clean-shaven and wore a white shirt and a smart jacket and trousers. No doubt the five of them would be eating out somewhere chic, and I was secretly glad Lila had insisted on wearing a dress that morning.

'Sally tells me she needs to have a word with you in private,' Catherine said, apparently unconcerned that Nico might have heard the mention of Albane's name. 'Maybe Philippe and I could take Lila out for a walk and give the two of you some space?'

'Or we could nip downstairs for a coffee,' I suggested, realizing I'd prefer to transpose our chat on to more neutral territory. Perching on the edge of my old sofa, in my old living room, while Nico settled into his favourite leather armchair would be too uncomfortable. I hadn't set foot in that room for almost a year.

The proprietor of the café which occupied the ground floor of Nico's apartment block had begun setting his tables for lunch, covering them with blue tablecloths and yellow paper placemats and laying out cutlery and glassware. We managed to find a small table he hadn't reached yet, in a quiet corner, away from the handful of customers standing at the bar. Nico ordered a double espresso, joking that he'd need at least three more before he was ready to face lunch with Catherine and Philippe, and I ordered a *grand crème* and – out of solidarity with Catherine – refrained from making any snide comments about his parents.

'I thought you ought to know that Lila got a bit upset last night.' I launched into an abridged explanation of how the neighbour's son had said some unforgivable things to Lila while my back was turned, and how they had come back to haunt Lila once night had fallen, in the guise of a nightmare. 'For the record,' I insisted once I'd finished my account, 'I have no intention of seeing either the father or the son ever again. Meeting them both made me realize how grateful I am that we've managed to keep things civil.'

'I tried to tell you, back in November, that Lila hadn't fully understood the situation, didn't I?' Nico spoke without rancour, as though he was wary of getting my back up. 'As I recall,' he added wryly, 'you gave me a lecture about how nightmares were normal at her age and children can adapt to new situations without any outside intervention.'

'Don't get me wrong,' I replied. 'I still don't think Lila needs therapy. She asked her questions, and I answered them, and she'll understand what it all means, in time. I just wanted you to be aware of what was said yesterday. So that we can be consistent. And in case she repeated anything that horrible little boy said to her.' I smirked.

'I didn't want you thinking I'd called you a *connard* or a *bon à rien*, or anything like that . . .'

'One day,' Nico said gravely, 'when Lila's old enough, I do intend to tell her that it was my fault her mother felt she had to leave.' I was so surprised to hear him say this that I let my mouth drop open. 'I mean it,' Nico said, noting my reaction. 'I appreciate what you're doing, protecting my image, trying not to portray me in a bad light, but I don't think I deserve to be seen as blameless, and I certainly don't want Lila to blame you for walking away.'

'That's, um, awfully big of you,' I said, not quite able to believe what I was hearing. This was the closest thing to an apology or an admission of guilt I'd ever heard cross Nico's lips.

'I just don't want you to think that I learned nothing from my mistakes.' Nico swilled the dregs of his coffee around in his cup to capture any remaining grains of sugar, then poured the liquid down his throat and set his cup down on its saucer with a clink. 'I know what I did derailed me and you and, even if it's far too late to fix that, I don't intend to let history repeat itself.'

I paused for a moment, my eyes fixed on Nico's saucer. If I prodded him, it seemed likely that he was ready and willing to give me some sort of explanation for his behaviour. Maybe he'd managed to rationalize why he'd given in to the urge to take what Mathilde offered. Did I want to hear what he had to say? I wondered. Was it time to seek closure, so that I could turn the page and move on?

'Well, I suppose that's all good news as far as Albane's concerned,' I said a moment later, rejecting my brief impulse to rake over the cold embers. Whether it was indeed too late, or I was afraid I might find I hadn't healed quite as thoroughly as I'd led myself to believe, I wasn't sure. 'I'd better get going,' I added, glancing at my watch and rising from my chair. 'I've got a million things to do today . . .' Nico remained seated, signalling to the owner behind the bar with his cup to indicate he was in need of a refill.

As I turned and left, I was conscious of Nico's gaze following me across the café, all the way to the door.

My heart sank when I walked into La Patache – an unassuming bar in rue de Lancry with yellowing walls covered in a multitude of posters, a stone's throw from Chez Prune – a little after ten o'clock that evening. Jérémy stood at the bar with his back to me, a half-empty bottle of beer in his hand, hemmed in by a group of people he clearly knew well. One I even recognized: Elsa, the actress we'd seen performing on stage; the woman who had spirited him away from me the last time we'd met.

I'd imagined a cosy tête-à-tête, and had chosen my outfit and applied my make-up with seduction in mind. After I'd left Nico, I'd dashed to the nearest branch of Comptoir des Cotonniers on rue Saint Antoine and bought a grey silk tunic dress, despite a price tag that would give me palpitations every time I thought about it for months to come. Whiling away the hours once I got home, waiting for Jérémy's rehearsal to end, I'd tried on my new dress with every imaginable combination of underwear, tights and shoes, eyeing my silhouette critically in the mirror. After much vacillating, I'd worn it with a push-up bra, opaque grey tights and black knee-high boots, added a touch of smoky eye shadow and twisted my hair into a loose chignon.

Walking down rue de Belleville to catch the métro, the caress of the silk dress against my thin tights made me feel sexy: my powers of seduction were at their peak. But from the moment I caught sight of Elsa, effortlessly elegant in worn jeans and barely there make-up, my confident bubble burst. I felt overdressed now, and as painfully self-conscious as if I'd walked into the bar wearing my birthday suit. I'd misjudged the context, badly, and my efforts reeked of desperation. It was all I could do to prevent myself executing a swift volte-face and slipping back outside before anyone could recognize me.

Elsa saw me first, looked me up and down unhurriedly, then smiled a knowing smile and leaned forward to murmur something in Jérémy's ear. He whirled around to face me, beckoning me closer and grazing my cheeks with his lips. The fine lines around the outside of his eyes crinkled as he smiled, reminding me for a second of Nico. My legs turned to cotton wool, even though, on the inside, I was cursing him internally for looking as irresistible as ever. '*Viens rencontrer mes amis*,' he said gaily, oblivious to my discomfiture. '*Les amis?*' Jérémy paused to ensure he had everyone's attention. 'This is a new friend of mine: Sally. She's a *petite anglaise*, and she teaches business English, like Thomas.'

I hadn't expected Jérémy to introduce me as his girlfriend. '*My* new friend' would have sufficed. 'A new friend of mine', on the other hand, was so dismissive, so impersonal, that he might as well have slapped me in the face. His choice of words told me everything I needed to know about the coming evening: I shouldn't expect to receive any special attention or preferential treatment. For whatever reason, Jérémy was holding me at arm's length. His careful use of the indefinite article had made that excruciatingly clear.

Elsa required no re-introduction, but Jérémy reeled off the names of his other friends one by one, working around the group in an anti-clockwise direction. To his left there was Théo, an attractive – possibly gay – twentysomething who worked as a junior concierge in a well-known five-star hotel. By his side stood Kamel, a Tunisian bar owner whose recurring sniff and frequent trips to the toilet suggested an unhealthy fondness for white powder. Then there was Max, a set designer with a long ponytail and metal-rimmed glasses, and his spiky-haired girlfriend, Marina. The irony of the situation was that if I hadn't been so set on having a romantic one-on-one 'third date' with Jérémy, I would have loved meeting this eclectic crowd. They made a refreshing change from the teachers, lawyers and bankers who made up my own circle of friends and I was curious to hear how they'd all met. With the exception of Elsa, who shot me hostile sidelong glances from time to time and refused to leave Jérémy's orbit for even a moment, his friends were welcoming and friendly.

But instead of relaxing and allowing myself to enjoy the novelty of meeting new French people, I smarted from Jérémy's lack of attention. Once he'd dispensed with the obligatory introductions, he left me to fend for myself, remaining deep in conversation first with Max, then with Elsa. I refrained from shoehorning myself into their conversation – I suspected they were talking shop, in any case – and kept a dignified distance instead. If Jérémy wanted to seek me out, all well and good. But I wasn't about to make a fool of myself by fawning all over him in front of an audience.

So for the next hour or so, while I propped up the bar, I chatted to Théo, who had met Jérémy when he worked as an extra on a short film. Théo had some fascinating anecdotes about some of the rich and famous clients who patronized his hotel, and his deadpan delivery and sense of comic timing suggested he'd fine-tuned his material over many tellings and re-tellings. But even as I giggled at his descriptions of a well-known American singer and her extended entourage or feigned shock at his tales of male clients ordering in high-class escort girls for 'room service', in truth I was having problems staying focused. Every so often my eyes would dart towards where Jérémy stood to steal another glance at his profile.

Making the most of my strategic position at the bar, I sank several bottled beers in quick succession before making the ill-advised switch to vodka and tonic, my previous resolutions about alcohol on dates going out of the window. In my excitement I'd skipped dinner, and it wasn't long before the alcohol I was pouring into my empty stomach began to make its presence felt. Instead of numbing my disappointment, the drink only served to exacerbate it. Why had Jérémy even bothered to invite me here tonight if he'd intended to ignore me? said a belligerent voice inside my head. The more I drank, the more difficult I found it to keep a lid on my growing resentment. If I didn't take myself off home soon, I knew it would only be a matter of time before I started berating Jérémy in public, making an undignified scene I'd come to regret.

'I think I'm going to head home,' I said to Théo around midnight, loud enough – I hoped – for Jérémy to overhear. I grabbed my coat – which I'd made the elementary mistake of hanging from one of the pegs protruding from the side of the bar, and which now smelled of spilled beer – and bent to pick up my handbag from where I'd wedged it between the rail running around the base of the bar and the floor.

'*Tu pars déjà?*' Jérémy had broken off his conversation with Elsa, as I'd hoped he would. As I straightened up, head spinning, handbag in hand, I had his undivided attention for the first time that evening. 'But I haven't even had a chance to speak to you yet, Sally,' he said, looking genuinely bewildered. 'Why leave now? Is something the matter?'

'If you want to talk to me, you can walk me to the métro,' I said curtly. Taking my leave from Jérémy's friends with an apologetic collective wave and a vague excuse about an early start the next morning, I strode out of the bar, with Jérémy hot on my heels.

The haughty, reproachful monologue I'd been finessing in my head for the past twenty minutes or so, while listening with half an ear to Théo, had began to unravel a little by the time I came to perform it for Jérémy. My sentences tumbled out in quick succession and my tone was drunkenly petulant, reminding me of the night I'd stayed over at Manu's.

'I thought you were so special, when I first met you,' I said wistfully, fixing my eyes on the still, inky water of the canal up ahead and quickening my pace so that Jérémy had to trot to keep up with me. 'Things didn't move along the way I hoped they would, but we shared that amazing kiss and you wanted to see me again, so I thought you must be feeling something too . . . I made excuses for you. I told myself maybe you needed to take things slowly, maybe you'd had an awful experience in the past that made it hard for you to trust someone again . . .'

The road in front of us was empty, and I strode across it. We'd arrived at the cobbled towpath, and I paused for a moment, putting a hand out to steady myself on the leather saddle of a parked motorbike, which was cold to the touch. Jérémy said nothing, waiting for me to finish. The fact he'd made no move to contradict anything I'd said so far didn't bode well at all. So when I took a deep breath and continued, my voice was filled with self-loathing.

'I see now that I'm an idiot,' I said savagely. 'I've been deluding myself, and tonight I finally understood that you never saw me as girlfriend material. I think maybe you've enjoyed having me around. It must be gratifying to have an infatuated woman to wheel out whenever it suits you to show off to your friends, or to make Elsa jealous, or whatever tonight was supposed to be about . . .'

Jérémy sighed and put a hand under my chin, lifting it so that I had no choice but to make eye contact. His gesture reminded me of the way I'd forced Lila to look at me when we'd spoken about her bad dream, but there was something phoney and rehearsed about the way Jérémy did it, and I wondered whether it was a choreographed move he'd used on stage. '*Je suis désolé*, Sally,' he said earnestly, his eyes sombre. 'I never meant to upset you like this. I like you a lot — although perhaps, as you say, not in quite the way you were hoping — and I really thought we could be friends. I didn't realize it had to be a relationship or nothing . . .'

'Well, I think you ought to have considered spelling that out to me two weeks ago.' I jerked my chin out of his hand and took a wobbly step backwards. 'Instead you've been sending me mixed signals, stringing me along and wasting my time. I mean, there was no ambiguity on my side: I made it pretty obvious I was interested. I even kissed you, for God's sake!' I was past caring that my tone was now openly belligerent and accusing. What more did I have to lose? A sudden image of Matthias, smiling at my dishevelled appearance as he handed me a cup of coffee in bed, floated to the forefront of my mind. 'And to top it all off, because of you, I even turned someone down,' I cried, suddenly remorseful. 'Someone I liked; someone who liked me back. But I was too busy obsessing about you.'

'*Je suis désolé,*' said Jérémy again, shrugging his shoulders. 'I don't know what more I can say.' His apology didn't even ring true any more. It was as though he was tiring of our little scene and had decided it was unworthy of his acting talents.

'I'm going to go.' I took a step backwards, moving out of range of the light cast by the street lamp overhead, taking refuge in the shadows. I could feel angry tears welling up, threatening to spill over, and I didn't want to give Jérémy the satisfaction of seeing me cry. 'There's no need to walk me to the métro,' I added, although I suspected his offer had been tacitly withdrawn. 'And I don't think there's any point in you calling me again . . .'

It required a superhuman effort not to turn and steal one last glance at Jérémy's retreating form as I zigzagged along the towpath. It was when I veered left into rue du Faubourg du Temple and saw his name on the interphone button outside his building that the tears began to overflow. Head bent, hands balled into tight fists deep inside my pockets, I drove myself forward, trying to attract as little attention as possible. I cried without making a sound, saline tears trickling down my face and dripping from my chin.

Over the past few days I'd felt like I was on a roll: everything in my life had fallen slowly into place, with Jérémy's call as the icing on the cake, filling me with false hope. I hated the way I'd let myself get carried away. Jérémy had been nothing but a mirage. With every step I'd taken towards him, he'd receded, just a little, until tonight, he'd disappeared altogether.

I was drawing close to Belleville métro station, when my stomach began to heave. Stepping off the pavement, I paused in the gap between two parked cars, hands on knees, head drooping towards the gutter, willing the queasiness to pass. Straightening up again, I could have sworn I heard someone call my name and, for a brief moment, I entertained one last fantasy. Jérémy had returned to La Patache and realized he'd made a terrible mistake. Dashing back out into the night, he'd managed to catch me up and now stood a few metres away, poised to make a heartfelt declaration. But when I lifted my head, there was nobody in my line of vision. Aside from a couple of Chinese teenagers, their hair gelled into stiff, gravity-defying peaks, withdrawing money from the hole in the wall outside the Crédit Lyonnais, the pavement was empty. My imagination was playing evil tricks on me. I was drunk, nauseous and alone and now apparently also suffering from unusually vivid auditory hallucinations.

'Sally?' This time the voice was accompanied by a very real and very concerned clean-shaven face, which appeared, as if from nowhere, inches away from my own. A loud, strangled sob welled up from somewhere deep inside my core, and I staggered forwards, propelling myself into a pair of waiting arms which closed around me with comforting force.

'I got everything wrong,' I sobbed, pressing my face against a warm chest, with little thought for the damage my teary mascara would wreak on his crisp white shirt. 'I'm drunk and I feel like a fool and I just want to go home.'

'I'll take you home,' a voice whispered soothingly into my hair. '*T'inquiète pas*, Sally, *ça va aller . . .*'

The first thing I became aware of the next morning was the smell of freshly brewing coffee. The second was the dull pain pulsing behind my eye sockets and the unpleasant sensation of eyelids gummed together with congealed make-up and stale tears. The third was the *plink* as a large disc of soluble aspirin made contact with the bottom of a glass of water. While the tablet hissed and fizzled its way into oblivion, I felt the bed shift under the weight of someone, as he took a seat on the edge, by my side.

'Before you ask,' Matthias said hastily, 'nothing happened last night. We talked – although I doubt you remember much of what was said – and then you kind of passed out.' I suspected there was more. I seemed to be wearing a T-shirt, for one thing, which suggested I'd been helped out of my silk dress. And I had a momentary vision – not quite a memory, more like a fleeting image of myself seen from above – of a woman crumpled over the toilet bowl while hands that were not her own held her hair back from her face. 'I'm so sorry you had to see me in such a state,' I moaned, eyes still clamped closed, paralysed by humiliation.

'I was sorry to see you in that state, but I wasn't sorry to see you,' Matthias said simply. He teased a few stray hairs out of my face with his fingertips, then traced the contours of my right cheek with his thumb. 'You asked me to wake you.' I heard him swilling the water around in the glass, hurrying along the last of the remaining aspirin. 'I think your daughter is due back this morning,' he added. 'But I'm not sure exactly when.'

'*Merde!*' I wrenched my eyelids open and heaved myself upright, almost knocking the glass of opaque liquid out of Matthias's hand. 'Nico's supposed to be bringing Lila over at ten.' My voice was filled with panic. 'What time is it now?'

'*Du calme*, Sally,' said Matthias in a soothing voice. 'It's only nine-thirty. All you have to do is drink this, take a shower and get yourself dressed . . . I'm sure you'll look more presentable than me.' He gestured at the charcoal-coloured smudge on the front of his white shirt with a rueful smile. 'And there'll be a mug of extra-strong coffee waiting when you're done . . .'

'I think I could get used to this,' I said, taking the glass he held out to me and steeling myself before I knocked back its contents. I wasn't sure what was worse, my blinding headache or the bitter aftertaste of French soluble aspirin. But I was certain of one thing: facing the day hungover with a compassionate Matthias by my side wasn't nearly as depressing a prospect as facing the day alone.

'I think I'd like that,' Matthias replied. 'Now come on, be brave. Let's see you down this *cul sec*.' My eyes locked on to his, and I obeyed, knocking back my medicine in one gulp.

Looking back on that Sunday, weeks later, I knew it had marked a turning point in my post-Nico life. Physically, I was in such a mess that even the phrase 'death warmed up' didn't begin to do justice to how vile I was feeling. But despite the glancing pain in my head, despite the late-onset nausea which plagued me all afternoon, I was aware of something else too; something that had crept up on me by stealth. I'd freed up the space that Jérémy had been occupying – under false pretences – at the forefront of my misguided brain and I was beginning to see, now, what should have been staring me in the face all along.

Under the pretext that he had a couple of errands to run, Matthias left me alone nursing my coffee just before ten. I heard him taking the stairs instead of the lift, minimizing the possibility of a premature encounter with Nico and Lila. When he returned an hour later, he knocked first, before letting himself in with a borrowed key. He smelled fresh and soapy and wore a clean T-shirt. In addition to my keys, he carried a bulging bag of groceries.

Prostrate on the sofa, a fleece blanket wrapped around my shoulders, I must have cut a sorry figure. Lila, who had understood within seconds of her arrival that all was not right with Mummy, was ministering to me dutifully with her plastic doctor's kit. When the front door creaked open she paused, her hand pressing the yellow plastic chest piece of her toy stethoscope to my T-shirt, pretending to listen to the beating of my heart. But her hazel eyes were riveted on Matthias. She frowned, as though trying to locate the precise memory of where and when she'd seen him before, and then gave a tiny, almost imperceptible, smile of recognition.

'*Tu n'apportes pas de fleurs pour ma maman aujourd'hui?*' she asked him slyly, removing the stethoscope from her ears and letting it fall to the floor.

'*Pas aujourd'hui, Docteur* Lila,' Matthias replied, closing the front door behind him and glancing over at the flowers he'd brought the other evening, which had begun to wilt in their water jug. 'But you know what, I may not have brought any flowers today, but I'm going to make your *maman* some lunch instead. Perhaps you could help me find everything I'll need? If you've finished tending to your patient, that is?'

I watched with amusement as Lila, puffed up with her own self-importance, fetched a miniature wooden chair from her bedroom and carried it to the kitchen so that she could elevate herself to the level of the countertop and give orders from her new vantage point. Meanwhile, Matthias unpacked his groceries: half a dozen eggs, a packet of the round slices of the cured ham that passes for bacon in France, and a loaf of sliced bread. 'I'm going to attempt to cook you an English breakfast,' he explained, hunting around in the metal drawers under the hobs for a frying pan. 'How do you like your eggs, Sally? Fried or scrambled?'

'I'd love my eggs scrambled,' I replied. Then, pinching myself theatrically on the forearm, I asked him whether I was dreaming and about to wake up in the gutter where he'd found me the night before.

'Mummy, why would you sleep in a *caniveau*?' Lila exclaimed in a horrified voice, drawing a blank when she tried to find the English word 'gutter'. 'They are all dirty and full of germs.'

'Talking of germs, Dr Lila, I think we should both wash our hands before we touch any food,' Matthias suggested, winking at me over the top of my daughter's puzzled head.

I was so grateful to him for deflecting Lila's attention away from the disturbing image I'd called forth that, on a whim, I blew him a kiss. Laying my head on the armrest of the sofa and closing my eyes, I continued eavesdropping on their banter while Matthias cooked up a storm, marvelling at how this man I'd met only twice before seemed to know instinctively how to handle this new situation. He proceeded to take charge of our day, somehow managing to pamper me without once seeming overbearing. Lila he treated like an equal, including her in every conversation. And it worked: by the end of the afternoon, an easy camaraderie had developed between them.

'Mummy? Do you mind if I ask Matthias to read me my story tonight, instead of you?' Lila peered over the edge of the bath, eyeing me cautiously, her damp, freshly washed hair plastered to her cheeks. Cross-legged on the floor, my third aspirin of the day fizzing in the tooth mug I gripped in my right fist, I could hear Matthias phoning to order pizza through the half-open bathroom door.

'I don't mind at all,' I replied, setting down my cup and leaning over the side of the bath to give her a fierce, impulsive hug which left a wet patch on my shoulder. 'But I think you'd better ask him yourself,' I added once I'd released her. 'Let's get you washed and into your pyjamas first, and see what he says.'

Once Lila had made a great show of kissing both of us goodnight, Matthias joined me on the sofa and I rested my head on his shoulder, feeling pleasantly drowsy. 'I've been thinking about something you told me last night, Sally,' he said softly, putting up a hand to stroke my hair.

'You'll have to enlighten me,' I admitted sheepishly. 'My memory of last night is hazy at best.'

'Well, you told me about your dilemma when you joined Rendez-vous, and about that dreadful talk show you saw about single mothers and dating,' Matthias explained. 'And, to be honest, I can't get my head around why anyone who liked you could see all this' – he made a sweeping gesture with his hand – 'as a problem. I know *I* wouldn't. Lila is a lovely kid. And I happen to think your being a mother adds an extra dimension to your personality. It's just another facet of who you are; another string to your bow . . .'

Profoundly touched by his words, I lifted my head and gave him an eloquent look. 'There's something I need to do,' I said purposefully, echoing what Matthias had said to me, seated on his own sofa, a week earlier. Cupping his face in my palms I gave him a forceful, passionate kiss. 'I can't believe I almost managed to push you away,' I said when we came up for air, shaking my head as though to dislodge the unwelcome thought of what might never have been.

'I can't believe I almost let you,' Matthias replied. 'I'm so glad I ran into you when I did.'

'Sally?' said Ryan, emerging from the bathroom with a triumphant expression on his face. 'Are my eyes playing tricks on me, or did I count *three* toothbrushes in there?' I giggled, feeling the telltale heat of a blush creeping across my cheeks.

'Look who's talking,' Anna snorted. Ryan had spent the past half-hour regaling us both with tales of his search for an apartment to share with Eric. They were looking for something with a balcony and a door leading on to it which would be compatible with a cat flap, a compromise they'd devised to solve the infamous Clyde conundrum. It was Ryan's turn to blush a deep shade of crimson now. He really was in no position to mock my new-found domestic bliss.

Anna was the only one of us who'd had to deal with an emotional reversal this spring. A few days after I'd begun seeing Matthias in earnest, Alex had suggested she move in with him. Anna had hesitated: things were moving too fast for her comfort. Alex had read her dithering as a rebuttal, but Anna had been surprisingly philosophical when they'd parted company. 'He was a lovely guy,' she'd told me over lunch soon afterwards, 'but the timing wasn't right for me. I mean, my divorce wasn't even finalized, and I didn't feel ready or able to commit to living as part of a couple again . . .'

Now, two months later, with the ink drying on her divorce decree, Anna was determined to dip her toes back into the dating pool. Indeed, one of the aims of our hastily improvised weeknight get-together was for me, Ryan, Anna and Kate to put our heads together and come up with a suitable *annonce*. Anna had decided to take the plunge. Taking heart from my success story, she was ready to create her own profile on Rendez-vous.

'Come on then,' I said, motioning for Ryan to join Anna and me on the sofa, and pulling my laptop on to my knee. 'There's no time to waste here, people. We've got work to do!'

'What about Kate?' said Ryan, raising his eyebrows. 'She is joining us, isn't she? I haven't seen hide nor hair of the boss lady lately. Ever since Yves got back from New York they might as well have been away on their second honeymoon . . .'

I nodded, concentrating on maintaining an impassive expression. 'She's just running a bit late,' I said airily. 'Don't worry, I'm sure she'll be here soon.'

'Okay, well, how about we start by having a peek at your profile, Sally?' Anna suggested. 'I think I'm the only one who never laid eyes on it . . . I remember all those emails you sent out, sharing the corniest pseudonyms and the nastiest chat-up lines you'd harvested. But I need to see exactly how you went about snagging that toy boy of yours.'

'I'm afraid I can't do that,' I said ruefully. 'I would if I could. But I deleted it yesterday.'

Matthias had come over the previous night to share a takeaway meal from Krung Thep. We'd knocked together our bottles of Singha beer to celebrate two months since our first outing together to the Thai restaurant, taking special care to look one another in the eyes as we did so, mindful of the superstition which condemns anyone who toasts without doing so to seven years of bad sex. After dinner, while checking his emails on my computer, Matthias complained about the deluge of junk mail he was still receiving from Rendez-vous as the subscriptions team doubled and re-doubled their efforts to entice him back with promises of discounted membership.

'I realized the other day my profile is still up.' He shook his head in disgust. 'It's dishonest, when you think about it. That means when you surf the site, half the profiles you see may well belong to people like me who no longer log on and can't even access their messages.' After hunting around fruitlessly for quite some time, he'd finally located the button enabling him to delete his inactive profile altogether. 'Love may only be a click away,' Matthias noted, 'but they certainly make it difficult for people to cut their ties with Rendez-vous when they believe they've found it.' Matthias's elliptical reference to love melted my insides. We hadn't spoken the all-important words aloud, but it was only a matter of time.

When he passed me the computer, I entered my log-in details and took a long look at my own profile. 'Show me how to delete mine?' I said, giving him a meaningful look. My account was still in credit – and would be for several months to come – but I knew I no longer required their services. When a pop-up window cautioned me against how much credit I'd be forfeiting, and a second – annoyingly persistent – message asked me '*Vous êtes sûr?*', I ignored the warnings and clicked emphatically on '*oui*'.

'I can't believe you deleted Belleville girl!' wailed Anna. 'Didn't you save her page anywhere first, for posterity?' Before I could answer, I heard a quiet knock at the front door. Sliding the laptop sideways on to Anna's knee, I darted over to let Kate in.

'Here, take my place on the sofa.' I helped Kate out of her jacket, aware that I was fussing over her a little more than was strictly necessary. 'What would you like to drink? Juice? Perrier? Tea?' Ryan and Anna, both sipping from overfilled wine glasses, frowned up at me in unison. Anyone would think I'd offered her poison.

'I'm on this special diet,' said Kate quickly, pre-empting their questions. 'Don't know how long I'm going to manage to stick at it, but I'm off alcohol, for now.' There was more to it than that, as I well knew, but Kate had told me about her new pregnancy in the strictest of confidence and, given what had happened last time, she'd asked me to keep mum until she'd made it past her three-month scan. Of course, being Kate, she hadn't yet put on an ounce of weight aside from a little extra fullness around her breasts, so only her new teetotal lifestyle had the potential to give the game away.

Once I'd poured Kate a Perrier, I perched on the arm of the sofa. Anna had pulled up the Rendez-vous homepage, with its familiar logo of interlocking, pixellated hearts. 'Oh my, get a load of that one!' Anna exclaimed, her expression a mixture of amusement and horror. She'd taken exception to one of the random selection of profile pictures I'd always referred to as 'bait', which were scrolling merrily across the bottom of the screen. I had a sudden flash of *déjà vu*, remembering the day I'd signed up, filled with doubt and trepidation. Seven long months ago, here on this very sofa.

'Okay, I'll admit, he does look pretty slimy,' said Kate. 'But remember, it only takes one decent one to make this whole enterprise worthwhile. And put it this way, you're more likely to find someone here than, say, you might in the *Transports amoureux*.' She shot me a knowing glance over Anna's head and I flashed her a smile of complicity.

Kate was harbouring a little secret of my own, and I'd sworn her to secrecy.

Libération, Transports amoureux, 14 *avril* 2008
 '*Nos regards virtuels se sont croisés sur un site de rencontres. Elle: jolie maman anglaise cachant sa timidité derrière un brin de sarcasme. Lui: jeune voisin de* Belleville *avec photo de profil déroutant. Complicité immédiate. Et si on faisait un bout de chemin ensemble?*'

Calling all girls!

It's the invitation of the season.

Penguin books would like to invite you to become a member of Bijoux – the exclusive club for anyone who loves to curl up with the hottest reads in fiction for women.

You'll get all the inside gossip on your favourite authors – what they're doing, where and when; we'll send you early copies of the latest reads months before they're on the High Street and you'll get the chance to attend fabulous launch parties!

And, of course, we realise that even while she's reading every girl wants to look her best, so we have heaps of beauty goodies to pamper you with too.

If you'd like to become a part of the exclusive world of Bijoux, email
bijoux@penguin.co.uk

Bijoux books for Bijoux girls

Ever wish real life could be as romantic as a novel?

Want to be wooed with words?

Live your own love story at
penguindating.co.uk

He just wanted a decent book to read ...

Not too much to ask, is it? It was in 1935 when Allen Lane, Managing Director of Bodley Head Publishers, stood on a platform at Exeter railway station looking for something good to read on his journey back to London. His choice was limited to popular magazines and poor-quality paperbacks – the same choice faced every day by the vast majority of readers, few of whom could afford hardbacks. Lane's disappointment and subsequent anger at the range of books generally available led him to found a company – and change the world.

'We believed in the existence in this country of a vast reading public for intelligent books at a low price, and staked everything on it'
Sir Allen Lane, 1902–1970, founder of Penguin Books

The quality paperback had arrived – and not just in bookshops. Lane was adamant that his Penguins should appear in chain stores and tobacconists, and should cost no more than a packet of cigarettes.

Reading habits (and cigarette prices) have changed since 1935, but Penguin still believes in publishing the best books for everybody to enjoy. We still believe that good design costs no more than bad design, and we still believe that quality books published passionately and responsibly make the world a better place.

So wherever you see the little bird – whether it's on a piece of prize-winning literary fiction or a celebrity autobiography, political tour de force or historical masterpiece, a serial-killer thriller, reference book, world classic or a piece of pure escapism – you can bet that it represents the very best that the genre has to offer.

Whatever you like to read – trust Penguin.